TABLE *for* TWO

TABLE

for

TWO

FICTIONS

Amor Towles

VIKING

VIKING
An imprint of Penguin Random House LLC
penguinrandomhouse.com

The following two stories previously published in slightly different
form: "The Line" in *Granta* (2019) and "The Didomenico Fragment"
as an Audible Original (2021). The novella "Eve in Hollywood" first
published in significantly different form as an ebook original by
Penguin Books (2013) and as a print edition by the author.

Library of Congress Cataloging-in-Publication Data

Names: Towles, Amor, author.
Title: Table for two : fictions / Amor Towles.
Description: [New York] : Viking, 2024.
Identifiers: LCCN 2023049039 (print) | LCCN 2023049040 (ebook) |
ISBN 9780593296370 (hardcover) | ISBN 9780593296387 (ebook) |
ISBN 9780593831236 (international edition)
Subjects: LCGFT: Short stories. | Novellas.
Classification: LCC PS3620.O945 T33 2024 (print) |
LCC PS3620.O945 (ebook) | DDC 813/.6—dc23/eng/20231023
LC record available at https://lccn.loc.gov/2023049039
LC ebook record available at https://lccn.loc.gov/2023049040

Printed in the United States of America
1   3   5   7   9   10   8   6   4   2

Designed by Amanda Dewey

In Memory of My Father
Stokley Porter Towles

CONTENTS

NEW YORK

The Line

During the last days of the last Tsar, there lived a peasant named Push-kin in a small village one hundred miles from Moscow. Though Push-kin and his wife, Irina, had not been blessed with children, they had been blessed with a cozy two-room cottage and a few square acres that they farmed with the patience and persistence appropriate to their lot. Row by row they would till their soil, sow their seeds, and harvest their crops—moving back and forth across the land like a shuttle through a loom. And when their workday was done, they would journey home to dine on cabbage soup at their little wooden table, then succumb to the holy sleep of the countryside.

Though the peasant Pushkin did not share his namesake's facility with words, he was something of a poet in his soul—and when he witnessed the leaves sprouting on the birch trees, or the thunderstorms of summer, or the golden hues of autumn, he would feel in his heart that theirs was a satisfactory life. In fact, so satisfactory was their life, had Pushkin uncovered an old bronze lantern while tilling the fields and unleashed from it an ancient genie with three wishes to grant, Pushkin wouldn't have known what to wish for.

And we all know exactly where that sort of happiness leads.

2.

Like many of Russia's peasants, Pushkin and his wife belonged to a *mir*—a cooperative that leased the land, allocated the acres, and shared expenses at the mill. On occasion, the members of the *mir* would gather to discuss some matter of mutual concern. At one such meeting in the spring of 1916, a young man who had traveled all the way from Moscow took to the podium in order to explain the injustice of a country in which 10 percent of the people owned 90 percent of the land. In some detail, he described the means by which Capital had sweetened its own tea and feathered its own nest. In conclusion, he encouraged all assembled to wake from their slumbers and join him in the march toward the inevitable victory of the international proletariat over the forces of repression.

Pushkin was not a political man, or even a particularly educated man. So, he did not grasp the significance of everything this Muscovite had to say. But the visitor spoke with such enthusiasm and made use of so many colorful expressions that Pushkin took pleasure in watching the young man's words float past as one would the banners of an Easter Day procession.

That night, as Pushkin and his wife walked home, they were both quiet. This struck Pushkin as perfectly appropriate given the hour and the delicate breeze and the chorus of crickets singing in the grass. But if Irina was quiet, she was quiet the way a heated skillet is quiet—in the moments before you drop in the fat. For while Pushkin had enjoyed watching the young man's words float past, Irina's consciousness had closed upon them like the jaws of a trap. With an audible snap, she had taken hold and had no intention of letting go. In fact, so tight was her grip on the young man's arguments, should he ever want them back, he would have to gnaw through his own phrases the way a wolf in a trap gnaws through its ankle.

3.

The wisdom of the peasant is founded on one essential axiom: While wars may come and go, statesmen rise and fall, and popular attitudes wax and wane, when all is said and done a furrow remains a furrow. Thus, Pushkin witnessed the war years, the collapse of the monarchy, and the rise of Bolshevism with the judicious perspective of Methuselah. And once the hammer and sickle were flapping over Mother Russia, he was ready to pick up his plow and resume the work of life. So, he was utterly unprepared for the news his wife delivered in May 1918—that they were moving to Moscow.

"Moving to Moscow," said Pushkin. "But why on earth would we be moving to Moscow?"

"Why?" demanded Irina with a stamp of the foot. "Why? Because the time has come!"

In the pages of nineteenth-century novels, it was not uncommon for the lovely young ladies raised in the countryside to long for a life in the capital. After all, that is where the latest fashions could be seen, the latest dance steps learned, and the latest romantic intrigues discussed *sotto voce*. In a similar manner, Irina longed to live in Moscow because that's where the factory workers swung their hammers in unison and the songs of the proletariat could be heard from every kitchen door.

"No one pushes a monarch over a cliff to celebrate the way things were," proclaimed Irina. "Once and for all, the time has come for Russians to lay the foundations of the future—shoulder to shoulder and stone by stone!"

When Irina articulated her position to her husband, using all these words and many more, did Pushkin argue? Did he give voice to the first thoughts of hesitation that leapt into his head? He did not. Instead, he began carefully, thoughtfully formulating a rebuttal.

Interestingly, as Pushkin's position began to take shape, it drew upon the very same words that Irina had used: *The time has come.* For he was no stranger to this phrase. In fact, he was practically its closest relative. Since Pushkin was a boy, the phrase had roused him in the morning and tucked him in at night. "The time has come to sow," it would say in spring, as it raised the blinds to let in the light. "The time has come to reap," it would say in fall, as it lit the fire in the stove. The time has come to milk the cows, or bale the hay, or snuff the candles. That is, the time has come—not once and for all, but once again—to do that which one has always done in the manner of the sun, the moon, and the stars.

This was the rebuttal that Pushkin began formulating that first night when he climbed into bed. He continued formulating it the next morning when he walked with his wife through the dewy grass on their way to the fields. And he was formulating it still in the fall of that year when they loaded their wagon with all their possessions and set out for Moscow.

4.

On the eighth of October, the couple arrived in the capital after five days on the road. As they rattled their way along the thoroughfares, we need not belabor their every impression: their first sight of a streetcar, of streetlamps, of a six-story building; of bustling crowds and expansive shops; of fabled landmarks like the Bolshoi and the Kremlin. We needn't belabor any of that. It is enough to state that their impressions of these sights were diametrically opposed. For while in Irina they stirred a sense of purpose, urgency, and excitement, in Pushkin they only stirred dismay.

Having reached the city center, Irina didn't waste a minute to recover from their journey. Telling Pushkin to stay where he was, she quickly got her bearings and disappeared into the crowd. By the end of the first day, she had secured them a one-room apartment in the Arbat, where, in place of a portrait of the Tsar, she hung a photograph of Vladimir Ilyich Lenin in a brand-new frame. By the end of the second day, she had unpacked their belongings and sold their horse and wagon. And by the end of the third, she had secured them both a job at the Red Star Biscuit Collective.

Formerly owned by Crawford's & Co. of Edinburgh (bakers to the Queen since 1813), the Red Star Biscuit Collective was housed in a fifty-thousand-square-foot facility with five hundred employees. Behind its gates it boasted two silos of grain and its own flour mill. It had mixing rooms with giant mixers, baking rooms with giant ovens, and packing rooms with conveyor belts that carried the boxes of biscuits right into the backs of the idling trucks.

Irina was initially assigned as an assistant to one of the bakers. But when an oven door came loose, Irina proved herself so adept with a monkey wrench that she was immediately transferred to the in-house engineers. Within a matter of days, it was commonly said that Irina could tighten the bolts of the conveyors as they rolled along without interruption.

Meanwhile, Pushkin was assigned to the mixing room, where the biscuit batter was blended by paddles that clanged against the sides of large metal bowls. Pushkin's job was to add the vanilla to each batch of biscuits whenever a green light flashed. But having carefully dispensed the vanilla into the appropriate measuring cup, the noise of the machinery was so deafening and the motion of the paddles so hypnotic, Pushkin simply forgot to pour the flavoring in.

At four o'clock, when the official taster came to taste, he didn't even need to take a bite to know that something was amiss. He could tell from the aroma. "What good is a vanilla biscuit that has no taste of vanilla?" he inquired of Pushkin rhetorically, before sending an entire day's output to the dogs. And as for Pushkin, he was reassigned to the sweeping crew.

On his first day with the sweepers, Pushkin was sent with his broom to the cavernous warehouse where the sacks of flour were stacked in towering rows. In all his life, Pushkin had never *seen* so much flour. Of course, a peasant prays for an ample harvest with enough grain to last the winter, and maybe a bit left over to protect against a drought. But the sacks of flour in the warehouse were so large and piled so high, Pushkin felt like a character in a folktale who finds himself in the kitchen of a giant, where mortal men are dropped into the pie.

However daunting the environment, Pushkin's job was simple enough. He was to sweep up any flour that had spilled on the floor when the dollies were whisked to the mixing room.

Perhaps it was the general sense of agitation that Pushkin had been feeling since his arrival in the city; perhaps it was the memory of swinging a scythe, a motion that Pushkin had happily performed since his youth; or perhaps it was a congenital muscular disorder that had yet to be diagnosed. Who can say? But whenever Pushkin attempted to sweep the flour that had fallen to the floor, rather than push it into the pan, his motion would kick it into the air. Up it would go in a large white billow settling like a dusting of snow on his shoulders and hair.

"No, no!" his foreman would insist, as he grabbed the broom from Pushkin's hands. "Like this!" And in a few quick strokes the foreman would clear four square feet of flooring without setting a single mote of flour into flight.

A man who was eager to please, Pushkin watched his foreman's technique with the attention of a surgical apprentice. But as soon as the foreman had turned his back and Pushkin had set his broom in motion, up into the air the flour went. Such that after three days on sweeping detail, Pushkin was dismissed from the Red Star Biscuit Collective altogether.

"Dismissed!" shouted Irina that night in their little apartment. "How does one get fired from Communism!"

In the days that followed, Irina might have tried to answer this question, but there were gears to be adjusted and screws to be tightened. What's more, she had already been elected to the workers' committee at the factory—where she was known to boost the morale of her comrades by quoting from *The Communist Manifesto* at the drop of a hat. In other words, she was a Bolshevik through and through.

And Pushkin? He rolled about the city like a marble on a chessboard.

5.

With the ratification of the new Constitution in 1918, it was the dawn of the Proletarian Age. It was also a period of the rounding up of enemies, the forced procurement of agricultural output, the prohibition of private trade, and the rationing of essentials. Well, what did you expect? A frosted cake and your pillows fluffed by a housemaid?

Between her twelve-hour shift at the plant and her duties on the workers' committee, Irina hadn't a minute to spare. So, as she headed off one morning, she thrust the ration cards for bread, milk, and sugar into her idle husband's hands and told him, in no uncertain terms, to replenish the cupboards before she returned at ten o'clock that night. Then she pulled the door shut with such force that Vladimir Ilyich swung on his hook.

As Irina's shoes sounded down the stairs, our hero stood where she had left him, staring wide-eyed at the door. Without moving, he listened to her exit the building and walk to the trolley. He listened to the trolley clatter through the city and the sound of the whistle as Irina marched through the gates of the collective. Only when he heard the conveyor belts beginning to roll did it occur to Pushkin to utter the phrase "Yes, dear." Then, with the ration cards firmly in hand, he donned his cap and ventured out into the streets.

As he walked along, Pushkin anticipated his task with a certain amount of dread. In his mind's eye, he could see a crowded shop where Muscovites pointed, shouted, and shoved. He could see a wall of shelves lined with brightly colored boxes and a counterman who asked what you wanted, told you to be quick about it, then set the wrong thing down on the counter with a definitive thump before shouting: *Next!*

Imagine Pushkin's surprise when he arrived at the bakery on Battleship Potemkin Street—his first scheduled stop—and found the setting as quiet as a crèche. In place of the pointing, shouting, and shoving there was a line, an orderly line. Composed mostly of women between the ages of thirty and eighty, it stretched gracefully from the doorway and made its way politely around the bend.

"Is this the line for the bakery?" he asked an older woman.

Before she could answer, another standing nearby gestured forcibly with her thumb. "The end of the line is at the end of the line, comrade. In the back of the back."

Offering his thanks, Pushkin turned the corner and followed the line three whole blocks to the back of the back. Having dutifully taken his place, Pushkin learned from the two women in front of him that the bakery offered each customer only one product: a loaf of black bread. While the women reported this bit of news in annoyance, Pushkin was heartened by it. If there was only one loaf of black bread per customer, there wouldn't have to be any squinting or selecting or thumping down of items. Pushkin would wait in line, receive his loaf, and bring it home, just like he'd been instructed.

As Pushkin was having this thought, a young woman appeared at his side.

"Is this the end of the line?" she asked.

"It is!" exclaimed Pushkin with a smile, glad to have the chance to be of service.

———

In the next two hours, Pushkin advanced as many blocks.

For some of us, maybe most of us, the ticking of these minutes would have sounded like the drip from a faucet in the middle of the night. But not for Pushkin. His time in the line made him no more anxious than would the wait for a seedling to sprout or the hay to change hue. Besides, while he waited he could engage the women around him in one of his favorite conversations.

"Isn't it a beautiful day?" he said to the four of them. "The sun could not be shining more brightly, nor the sky a bluer shade of blue. Although, in the afternoon, I suspect we may be in for a bit of rain. . . ."

The weather! I hear you exclaim with a roll of the eyes. *This is one of his favorite conversations!?*

Yes, yes, I know. When God the Father is smiling on a nation, when average incomes are on the rise, food is plentiful, and soldiers are biding their time with card games in their barracks, nothing seems worthier of condescension than a discussion of the weather. At dinner parties and afternoon teas, those who routinely turn to the topic are deemed boring, even insufferable. The possibility of precipitation seems worthy as a topic only to those without the imagination or intelligence to speak of the latest literature, the cinema, and the international situation—or, in short, the times. But when a society is in turmoil, a discussion of the weather doesn't seem quite so unwelcome. . . .

"Why, yes," agreed one of the women with a smile. "It is a beautiful day."

"Though," observed another, "it does seem from the clouds behind the cathedral that you might be right about the rain."

And just like that, the time seemed to pass a little more quickly.

At 1:00 that afternoon (with his loaf of bread tucked under his coat), Pushkin made his way to Maxim Gorky Street, where he had been instructed to obtain the sugar. Once again, he felt a flash of anxiety as he neared the shop, though this time the anxiety was countered by the slightest hint of hope. And what did he find when he arrived at his destination? By the grace of God, another line!

Naturally, as it was later in the day, the line at the grocer was longer than the one at the bakery had been. But the brief rain, which, in fact, had fallen on Moscow from 12:15 to 12:45, had cooled the streets and freshened the air. And as Pushkin approached, two women he had met in the bread line gave him a friendly wave. So, he took his place with a general sense of well-being.

Across the street from where Pushkin was standing happened to be the Tchaikovsky Conservatory, as fine an example of neoclassical architecture as existed in all of Russia.

"Isn't that building delightful," Pushkin said to an old woman who had joined him at the end of the line. "Just look at those scrolly things at the top of the columns, and the little statues tucked beneath the eaves." And she, who had lived in the neighborhood for over forty years and who had passed the building a thousand times without giving it a second thought, had to admit, upon closer consideration, that it was, indeed, nothing short of delightful.

Thus, time in the grocery line also began to pass a little more quickly. In fact, it passed so quickly that Pushkin hardly noticed the afternoon slipping away. . . .

That night when Irina returned home, Pushkin was standing by the door in such a state of trepidation that the second she saw him she let out an anticipatory sigh.

"What has happened now?" she demanded.

Having the good sense not to mention the fine weather, or the architecture of the conservatory, or the friendly women whom he'd met, Pushkin explained to his wife that the lines for bread and sugar had been so long there hadn't been time to wait in the line for milk.

When Pushkin held out the bread and sugar as evidence of his best intentions, he could see his wife clench her jaw, lower her eyebrows, and close her fists. But even as Pushkin prepared for the worst, he saw his wife's eyeballs begin to shift. Suddenly, she found herself wrestling with her husband's failure to complete three simple tasks on the one hand, and the implied shortcomings of Communism on the other. Were she to express her anger at Pushkin, wouldn't that in some way suggest her acknowledgment of the unacceptability of having to wait in line for one's bread and sugar and milk? Were she to cuff him on the head, wouldn't she to some degree be cuffing the Revolution? Sometimes, one plus one does not so easily sum to two.

"Very good, husband," she said at last. "You can get the milk to-morrow."

And in that moment, Pushkin felt a great sense of joy. For to serve the ones we love and receive their approval in return, need life be any more complicated than that?

6.

It didn't take long for the citizens of Moscow to realize that if you had no choice but to stand in line, then Pushkin was the man to stand next to. Graced with a gentle disposition, he was never boorish or conde-scending, neither full of opinions nor full of himself. Once he had com-mented on the fineness of the weather or the beauty of a building, he was most likely to ask about your children. And so sincere was his inter-est that his eyes would brighten with satisfaction at the first suggestion of a success, and cloud with tears at any hint of a setback.

While for his part, Pushkin had settled into city life with a grow-ing sense of contentment. Waking in the mornings, he would take a glance at the calendar and think, *Ah, it is Tuesday. The time has come to wait in line for bread.* Or *Is it already the twenty-eighth? Once again, the time has come to go to Yakusky Street to wait in line for tea.* And thus, the months would have run into years and the years into decades without cause for remark, but for an unanticipated occurrence in the winter of 1921.

On the afternoon in question, after waiting three hours for a head of cabbage, Pushkin was about to proceed to a small department store on Tverskaya Street to wait for two spools of thread, when an acquaintance hailed him from the back of the cabbage line. A thirty-year-old mother of four, she was clearly in a state of distress.

"Nadezhda!" our hero proclaimed. "What is it?"

"It is my youngest," she replied. "He has a fever of one hundred and two. And while I need to pick up a head of cabbage for my family's soup, I fear that where I should be standing is in the line at the pharmacy." Pushkin's expression reflected all the anxiety in this poor woman's heart. He looked to the sky and noted from the position of the sun—which was dipping behind the rooftops—that while Nadezhda would have time for one line or the other, she would never have time for both. Without a second thought, Pushkin looked to the eight women behind Nadezhda (who had all been leaning forward to hear the exchange).

"Perhaps these fine ladies wouldn't mind if I were to hold your place while you visited the pharmacy. As it is Tuesday, the line there shouldn't be too long. And once you've obtained Sasha's medicine, you could hurry back and resume your spot."

Now, were you or I to have had made this simple suggestion, it would almost certainly have been met with looks of disdain and a reminder that a line is a line, not a carousel that you can hop on and off to your heart's content! But at one time or another, all these women had waited with Pushkin and experienced his gentleness of spirit. So, without objection, they made room for him as the young mother hurried away.

Just as Pushkin had anticipated, the line at the pharmacy was only thirty people long. So, when Nadezhda reached the cash register with the medication in hand, feeling a burst of goodwill she splurged on a bag of brightly colored candy sticks. And when she resumed her place in the cabbage line, she overcame Pushkin's objections and insisted that he take a handful of the confections as a token of her gratitude.

7.

Times of upheaval throw off orphans like sparks. Wherever the grinder meets the metal, they shoot in the air in dazzling arcs, then either bounce once on the pavement and disappear, or settle in the hay and smolder. On a morning in 1923, one such castoff—a boy named Petya— sat on the cold stone steps of a decommissioned church with his elbows on his knees and his chin in his palms as he aimlessly watched the bread line across the street.

To the uninitiated, a bread line might seem a promising spot for an urchin. After all, most of those waiting were women who had cared for offspring of their own—an experience that was almost certain to trigger feelings of compassion toward a motherless child. Well, maybe so. But as Petya could tell you from experience, young lads who approached the women in the bread line with their hands outstretched received a twist of the ear.

On this particular morning, while Petya eyed the progress of the women with the watchful resignation of a well-trained dog, something extraordinary caught his attention. As a man near the front of the line was chatting amiably with the women at his side, a young wife in a yellow kerchief appeared from around the corner with a bag in her arms. When she approached, the man doffed his cap, greeted her warmly, and stepped out of the line in order to give her his place.

Now, if the mothers in the bread line were prone to twist the ear of an orphan, they were sure to give a line-cutter a dressing-down she'd not soon forget. But the women didn't shout or shake their fists. They made room for the newcomer. Then, as the man in the cap bid them all goodbye, the young wife reached into her bag and offered him a link of dried sausage. Upon seeing it, the man assured her that this gesture was unnecessary. But when the young wife insisted (insisted, mind you!), he accepted the sausage with his humble thanks and another doff of the cap.

Petya, who was now sitting upright, watched the man in the cap get summoned by a woman farther back in the line. As she pointed this way and that, the man listened with apparent sympathy. Then, when he nodded his head, she darted off, and he assumed her place without incident.

Petya ended up spending the rest of the day on the church's steps, and during those hours he saw the man in the cap go through the line three separate times on behalf of three separate women, receiving the link of sausage, a can of beans, and two cups of sugar!

When at last the baker latched his door and the man headed home, Petya followed in hot pursuit.

"Hey, doffer," he called.

Turning in some surprise, Pushkin looked down at the boy.

"Are you calling to me, young man?"

"You and nobody else. Listen. I've been around this town all my life. And I've seen my share of smooth-talking schemes. But what sort of racket is this?"

"Racket?" asked Pushkin.

With the narrowed eyes of the worldly, Petya was about to press his point, when a fifty-year-old apparatchik approached, out of breath. From the manner in which this fellow's belly strained against his vest, you could tell that his bread came buttered on both sides. Yet, he addressed the doffer with an unmistakable air of respect.

"Pushkin! Thank goodness! I was worried I might have missed you!"

Noticing Petya, Mr. Bread-and-Butter put an arm over Pushkin's shoulders, turned him ninety degrees, and continued in a lowered voice.

"I have it on good authority, my friend, that a shipment of electric lamps will be arriving in the illumination department of GUM tomorrow afternoon. Needless to say, I am in meetings most of the day. Do you think you might have time to hold a place for me until I can get there?"

Standing on his toes and leaning to his right, Petya could see that this Pushkin, who was listening with the utmost attention, was suddenly overcome with regret.

"Comrade Krakovitz, I am afraid that I have already promised Marya Borevna that I will stand in line for her at the butcher's while she is at Gastronome Number Four getting figs in honor of her husband's name day."

Krakovitz dropped his shoulders with such disappointment he nearly burst his buttons. But when he turned to go, Petya piped up.

"Comrade Pushkin," he said. "Surely, we cannot afford to have the gentleman preparing for his meetings without the benefit of electric light! As your assistant, perhaps I could stand in line at the butcher's, while you stand in line at GUM."

"Why, of course!" said Krakovitz, his face lighting up like the lamp he was hoping to procure. "How about it, Pushkin?"

So, the very next day, while Pushkin waited at GUM, Petya waited at the butcher shop. And when Marya Borevna came to assume her spot, as a token of her gratitude, she handed Petya a fistful of figs.

"How nice of Marya to share with you some of her fruit," said Pushkin, when Petya came to GUM to deliver his report. "You have certainly earned them, my boy." But Petya would have none of that. He insisted the two of them split the figs fifty-fifty, on the grounds that while he had performed the labor, the business plan was Pushkin's.

Thus, it began. Within a week, Petya was standing in two or three lines a day, so that Pushkin could stand in two or three more. A professionally minded lad, Petya took pains to behave exactly as Pushkin would. That is, he never expressed the slightest impatience; rather, he remarked on the weather and the buildings across the street; he asked about progeny, either nodding his head in approval or shaking his head in sympathy as the circumstances demanded; and in parting, he always doffed his cap. In this manner, Petya was quickly accepted as Pushkin's proxy, and he was welcomed just as warmly by all the women who waited.

8.

If there is a terrain conducive to apple trees, within a few generations there will be all manner of apple trees growing branch to branch. If there is a neighborhood conducive to poetry, all manner of poets will soon be scribbling side by side. And so it was with the lines of Soviet Moscow. At any given moment, across the city could now be found lines for staples and lines for sundries. There were lines to board buses and lines to buy books. There were lines to obtain apartments, school placements, and union memberships. In those years, if there was something worth having, it was worth standing in line for. But of all the various lines, the ones that Petya kept his eye closest on were the lines that served the elites.

Before meeting Pushkin, Petya had assumed there was no such thing. After all, wasn't that the whole point of climbing over the shoulders of your fellow men? To be free of the lines once and for all? But if the elites didn't need to stand in line to get what everyone else was waiting for, they had their *own* reasons to stand in line. They wanted bigger apartments. They wanted a car and driver. They wanted a fur coat for their mistress and a dacha on the outskirts of town.

One didn't have to read an annotated copy of *Das Kapital* to understand that those who wanted things of greater value were likely to express a greater sense of gratitude whenever their wishes came true. And since you can't break off a chunk of a dacha or divvy up a cashmere coat, the elites tended to show their gratitude in the form of cash.

But whatever their compositions—long or short, shy or shifty, fish or fowl—Moscow had more lines to stand in than Pushkin and Petya had feet. So Petya recruited a few of his fellows, and then a few more. Such that by 1925, Pushkin had ten boys waiting in thirty lines, each of them handing tokens of gratitude up the chain of command.

9.

The human race is famously adaptive, but there is nothing that a human will adapt to more quickly than an improved standard of living. Thus, while Irina had arrived in Moscow dedicated heart and soul to the upending of the social order—that is, to the defeat of the privileged and the victory of the proletariat—as the years unfolded, her understanding of how this might best be achieved evolved. . . .

The evolution began, naturally enough, back in 1921 with that handful of candy sticks. When Pushkin had returned home with the cabbage in one hand and confections in the other, Irina was prepared to berate him from top to bottom for wasting hard-earned money on the fancies of a child. But when Pushkin explained how he had come by the candies, she was stymied. Her husband's willingness to wait in line for a mother in need seemed comradely to the core; and since he hadn't anticipated receiving the candies, one could hardly brand him a speculator. So, Irina decided to save her top-to-bottom for another day. And when Pushkin came home later that week with a sausage, after a moment's hesitation Irina nodded that this too was perfectly correct. After all, hadn't Lenin himself predicted that the successful transition to Communism would result in a little more sausage for us all?

As sausages evolved into cloaks and cloaks into cash, Irina began to recognize another achievement of Communism—through the transformation of her husband. For when they had lived in the country, Irina had always considered her husband to be a man without energy, intention, or sense. But it had become increasingly clear that Pushkin had merely *seemed* that way. Once her husband had been freed by Bolshevism from the quasi-serfdom of the old regime, he had been revealed as a man of considerable talents; and not only did he help wives and widows obtain their necessities, he had virtually adopted a whole generation of orphans and turned them into productive citizens! With a touch of moral satisfaction, Irina allocated the sausages to the pantry, the cloaks to the closet, and the cash to the bureau's bottom drawer.

Then one day in 1926, Comrade Krakovitz, who happened to be an undersecretary in the Department of Residential Accommodations, asked if Pushkin would wait in line for a case of French champagne. When Pushkin succeeded, Comrade Krakovitz was loath to show his appreciation by giving up a bottle; instead, with the stroke of a pen he reassigned Pushkin to a generous apartment in the Nikitsky Towers—a brand-new complex on the banks of the Moskva River.

Later that night, when Pushkin got home and explained to Irina what had happened, Irina soberly considered the turn of events. It was a common misconception—or so her thought process unfolded—that Communism guaranteed an identical life for all. What Communism actually guaranteed is that in place of lineage and luck, the State would determine who should get what after taking careful account of the greater good. From this simple principle, it followed that a comrade who plays a greater role in attaining the greater good for the greater number of people should have greater resources at his own disposal. Just ask Nikolai Bukharin, editor of *Pravda* and champion of the peasant, who lived in a four-room suite at the Metropole Hotel!

Through this indisputable logic, Irina came to see their improved situation as the natural course of events; and she now often referred to Pushkin as *Comrade Husband*.

10.

Just as the poet in Pushkin's soul had once written odes to sprouting shoots and summer rain, he now turned his verses to pigeons that perched on pediments, and trolleys that rattled in the lane. Which is to say, once again Pushkin's life with Irina was so satisfactory, he wouldn't know what to wish for. That is, until the second of May 1929.

Earlier that week, the NKVD had swept up five intellectuals and quickly convicted them of counterrevolutionary activities under Article 58 of the Criminal Code. Once these traitors were safely on their way to Siberia, a team was sent to their apartments with orders to gather up their pamphlets, journals, and books, and deliver them to the municipal furnace. Now, it just so happens that as this disposal truck laden with printed matter was taking the left onto Tverskaya Street at full speed, the centrifugal force from the turn sent a magazine flying through the air at the very moment our hero was about to step from the curb, such that it spun twice and landed at his feet.

As Pushkin wasn't much of a reader, he was about to step over the magazine and continue on his way, but something about the article it had flopped open to caught his eye. Bending over, he picked the magazine off the ground. Then having looked once to his left and once to his right, he tore out the page and tucked it in his coat.

Fifteen minutes later, when Pushkin arrived home, he called out to Irina. Hearing no reply, he went to their bedroom and closed the door. But realizing he wouldn't hear his wife arrive if the bedroom door were closed, he opened it again. Then he sat on the bed and removed the page from his coat.

The article appeared to be in English, a language Pushkin neither spoke nor read—so he was not intrigued by the prose. What had caught Pushkin's eye was the large black-and-white photograph that served as an illustration to the piece. It was a picture of a young woman lying on a chaise longue in a long white dress with a double strand of beads draped around her neck. Her hair was blond, her eyebrows thin, her lips delicate and dark. Simply put, she was the most beautiful woman that Pushkin had ever seen.

But she was not alone.

With an arm behind her head and a smile on her face, she was look-ing at a man who was seated with his back to the camera—a man in a tuxedo with a drink in his hand and a cigarette in reach.

For the first time in his life, Pushkin felt a pang of envy. It was not for the young couple's wealth that he felt envious, nor for the glamorous serenity they seemed to be sharing on this elegant terrace that must have been in the fabled city of New York. No. What made him envious was the smile the beautiful young woman was directing toward her com-panion. In all Pushkin's life, he had never imagined being smiled upon in such a way by such a woman.

In the weeks that followed, when Pushkin got home he would sit on his bed with the door ajar, take the picture from his wallet, and look at it anew. Often, he would notice something he hadn't noticed before—like the white roses that grew along the terrace, or the sparkling bracelet on the woman's wrist, or the high-heeled shoes on her slender feet. And late at night when he couldn't sleep, Pushkin found himself imagining that *he* was the man in the chair; that he was the man with a drink in his hand and a cigarette within reach being smiled upon by this beauti-ful young woman in a dress of white.

II.

Some months later, while Pushkin was waiting in line to buy a soup bone, he happened to be next to a gentleman in his late fifties by the name of Sergei Litvinov. After they had shared their views about the approach of autumn, the gentleman happened to remark that he worked at a local el-ementary school, where he was responsible for sweeping the floors.

"Bless my soul," exclaimed Pushkin. "I too was once a sweeper of floors!"

"Were you, now?" said Litvinov with reciprocal enthusiasm. And as the two men discussed the differing aerodynamics of paper scraps and flour motes, the minutes went jogging along. But when Pushkin asked if the gentleman had always been a sweeper, Litvinov grew solemn and shook his head. It seems that in the decades before the war, Litvinov had been a portrait painter of some renown. In fact, two of his portraits had hung in the Tretyakov Gallery. But as he had primarily painted members of the aristocracy, in 1920 the Moscow Union of Artists had deemed him aesthetically unreliable and revoked his license to paint. Thus, to make ends meet, he had taken the job as a sweeper.

"After all," said Litvinov with a smile, "isn't a broom just a very large paintbrush?"

Pushkin had never been to the Tretyakov Gallery, or any museum for that matter. But he had knelt before many an icon in his day, and he had always marveled at an artist's ability to render the human face in such convincing detail. To possess such a gift and no longer be allowed to put it to use struck Pushkin as heartbreaking, and he could not help but ask if Litvinov felt some resentment.

Litvinov responded with another smile.

"I have lived under these circumstances for nine years, my friend. That is a long time to give one's life over to resentment."

Then after a moment of reflection, Litvinov continued.

"My grandmother was fond of saying that whatever one chooses to do with one's life, one still must do one's part. And though the life of a painter may seem frivolous to some, whenever I would unveil a finished work before my subject and see their expression, I knew that I had fulfilled my grandmother's maxim. But you see, my friend, I was only half kidding when I compared my broom to a paintbrush. For—perhaps to my own surprise—whenever I see the children running down the freshly swept hallways of the schoolhouse, I feel that once again I am doing my part."

Though Pushkin was not familiar with the word *magnanimity*, he knew well enough that he was in its presence when he spoke to this painter-sweeper, such that upon parting, he shook Litvinov's hand with feelings of the deepest admiration.

But when Pushkin ran into Litvinov thirty days later, the gentleman looked like he had aged as many years. A parent, it seems, had filed a complaint with the District Educational Committee—that a painter of Tsarist cronies should be working in a schoolhouse filled with children. The next day, Litvinov's little apartment had been searched by the police, then he'd been taken to the Lubyanka, where he was held for three days of questioning. Though no charges were brought, upon Litvinov's return to the schoolhouse he was reprimanded by the headmaster for his absenteeism; the teachers who were in the habit of chatting with him as he emptied their wastebaskets now remained silent; and worst of all, the students who had once returned his wave in the hallways now averted their eyes.

"Back in seventeen, when my fellows folded their easels and fled to Paris, I shook my head. 'Our calling is to paint the faces of our countrymen,' I said, 'with all of their whims and worries, all of their virtues and vices. What matters it to us, whether they wear grand mustaches or a pointed goatee?' So I said at the time, but now . . ."

Litvinov was quiet for a moment. Then with a heavy heart, he acknowledged that while sweeping the schoolhouse floors, he had begun to daydream of standing in a railway station with an overnight bag in one hand and a bright yellow card in the other—a bright yellow card marked by a crimson stamp.

Pushkin's eyes grew wide.

"A stamp in the shape of St. Basil's?"

"Yes," admitted Litvinov with a hint of shame. "From the Agency of Expatriate Affairs."

———————

Now, of all the lines in Moscow, the line that was the most elusive, the most daunting, the most insurmountable was the one that led to the Agency of Expatriate Affairs—that department in which one applied for an exit visa from Russia. Just finding the line was a significant challenge. For the agency's office was located deep within the Kremlin, up two and down three sets of stairs, at the end of a long series of lefts and rights, on a narrow corridor with forty doors that each looked alike.

Should you be lucky enough to navigate this maze and locate the office, once inside you were handed a pencil, a twenty-page form, and directed to the back of the line. Naturally, the form requested your name, address, occupation, and date of birth, along with your educational history, religious upbringing, and social origin. But in addition, it required you to list the names, patronymics, diminutives, and other endearments for all family members, alongside their ages, sexes, and professions; it required your history of ailments, infirmities, and treatments; your involvements with the judicial system whether as a plaintiff, defendant, or witness; the sources of your income and the sum of your savings; etc. At the conclusion of this exhaustive survey came the essay questions: *What is the country to which you want to travel? Have you ever traveled there before and why? For what purpose do you wish to travel there now? And more to the point, why would you want to leave Russia in the first place!*

After waiting several days (which was just as well, since it took several days to fill out the form), you would reach the little window where you could submit your application. The clerk, in turn, would carefully grade it, taking into consideration your thoroughness, clarity, and penmanship. Should the clerk award you a D or F then, congratulations, your application was torn to shreds and you were sent to the back of the line. Should you be given a grade of B or C, you would be handed a new pencil along with instructions on how to correct your submission— while everyone waited behind you. But were you one of the fortunate few who completed his application flawlessly on the very first go, you were ushered to an interior office where a caseworker sat behind a little metal desk with your application in hand.

Starting at the top, the caseworker would ask you every single question anew, presumably in search of discrepancies. At any point in the interview, the raise of an eyebrow or a truncated cough could signal that you were on your way back to the end of the line. But should you survive the interview, you would be asked to wait as your file was sent upstairs for consideration by an untold number of scrutineers. Only if every single one of them initialed the application to indicate they found no cause for concern would it circle its way back to the caseworker's desk, where it would receive that crimson stamp which opened, for a moment, the gates of the Soviet Union.

Though, naturally enough, most applications were refused, there were well-known stories of whole families making their way to Paris or London with the implicit blessing of the Politburo. But on what grounds these lucky few were allowed to leave remained a mystery. One citizen seemed to be granted passage on account of his spotless record as a Communist and his extended family in Berlin; while another was refused his visa *because* he was a spotless Communist with relatives in Berlin. Your visa could be stamped or rejected on the grounds that you were or were not a scientist, were or were not hardworking, were or were not a Jew. So unpredictable was the decision making of the department that rumors circulated of a locked room in a subbasement where ten colorful wheels like those in a carnival would be spun every morning to determine the ten criteria that on that day would result in the awarding of a visa!

"Yes," admitted Litvinov with a hint of shame. "From the Agency of Expatriate Affairs."

Pushkin studied his new friend. "If one cannot sweep in Moscow," he said after a moment, "then one should paint in Paris."

Litvinov smiled in appreciation of Pushkin's support, but sadly shook his head.

"They say that waiting in that line can take weeks, and Headmaster Spitsky has made it perfectly clear that any further instances of 'absenteeism' on my part will result in immediate dismissal."

"I could stand in line for you."

"Ah, my friend, you are too kind. But no one even knows where the line is."

"I know exactly where it is. And besides," Pushkin concluded with the utmost satisfaction, "we all must do our part!"

12.

The line at the Agency of Expatriate Affairs was quieter than any line in which Pushkin had ever waited. So anxious were those assembled that any effort at friendly conversation was immediately cut short by a frown. Thus, after three days of silence, Pushkin decided to fill out one of the agency's notorious forms simply to pass the time.

But what a delightful process it proved to be!

Without any desire to leave Russia, Pushkin felt no anxiety as to the political implications of his answers. Rather, he saw each question as an invitation to recall some heartwarming aspect of his past. Like his childhood in the village of Gogolitsky, where his older brother had taught him how to trap rabbits and where his mother would sing as she hung the laundry out to dry. But best of all was when it asked about his work experience. Here, Pushkin described how he and Irina had tilled their acres and harvested their harvest; and how in the lilac light they had journeyed home to their little table where the cabbage soup awaited. What wonderful years those had been! In fact, Pushkin had so many memories worth sharing that they spilled into the margins and wrapped around the page. And when he read the final question—*Why do you want to leave Russia?*—without hesitation, he answered: *I don't.*

———

After eighteen days of waiting in line, Pushkin called on Litvinov with the good news that he would reach the clerk's window on the following day by noon.

"Then I will be there at eight!" assured a grateful Litvinov.

But on the following day, Litvinov was not there at 8:00. He was not there at 9:00 or 10:00 or 11:00; and he was not there at 11:35 when the clerk at the window rang his little bell and called, *Next!*

Unsure of what to do, Pushkin looked back at the door, but the citizen who was standing behind him gave him a shove and sent him stumbling toward the window.

"Come on, come on," said the clerk. "We haven't got all day. Give us your form."

At that moment, Pushkin would have given the clerk Litvinov's form if he'd had it; but the painter-sweeper had kept it overnight in order to double-check his answers. So, with no other choice, Pushkin produced the form he had filled out to pass the time.

When the clerk saw that Pushkin had folded the form down the middle to fit in his pocket, he scowled. Laying it on the counter, he made a great show of smoothing it open to indicate to all the applicants that the folding of forms was well out of bounds. Once the form was flat, he picked up his pencil and began reviewing Pushkin's answers, ready to pounce on the slightest error. But as he read, he found himself nodding in spite of himself; and when he reached the answer that wrapped around the page—a breach of protocol that would normally have guaranteed a shredding—the clerk let out a sigh. Not a sigh of exasperation, you understand, but a sigh of such sentimental satisfaction he marked the passage with a star. But when the clerk reached the penultimate page, he looked up at Pushkin in surprise.

"You have not completed question one hundred and ten."

Pushkin looked down at the document as surprised as the clerk.

"Question one hundred and ten?"

"Yes," said the clerk. "Where one indicates the place to which one wishes to go."

Pushkin, who must have skipped over the question, didn't know what to say, for he had never given it a moment's thought. With the clerk staring at him expectantly, Pushkin racked his brain. Irina, he seemed to remember, had always wanted to visit the Black Sea, but that was in Russia. . . . The man who was next in line began audibly tapping his foot, which only made Pushkin's task more difficult. Then, suddenly, he thought of the lovely young woman in his wallet.

"New York City?" he suggested tentatively.

Not only did the clerk offer no rebuke to Pushkin, he wrote the answer in the allotted space himself, then waved Pushkin into an adjacent room. An hour or so later, a door opened and Pushkin was led not to the office of a caseworker, but to the director of the whole department. The director, who was a heavyset fellow with bags under his eyes, signaled that Pushkin should sit. In accordance with normal procedure, he was supposed to review Pushkin's form from the very beginning in search of oversights and discrepancies. Instead, he turned to the fourteenth page.

"Repeat for me, if you would, your history of work experience."

Pushkin had not bothered to memorize the words he'd used in his answers, but he hadn't needed to—for he had memorized them with his life. So, he recounted to the director how he and Irina had tilled the soil row by row. He told of the crickets at twilight and the golden hues of harvest. And the director, who was raised among the wheat fields of Ukraine, wiped a tear from his eye with as unsentimental a knuckle as had ever been fashioned by God. Then flipping back a few pages to where Pushkin had described his youth in Gogolitsky, the director spun the form around and tapped at a question.

"Here," he said. "Read this one."

Then he leaned back in his chair and closed his eyes so he could listen with greater care as Pushkin related his memories one by one.

Who knows what criteria the ten colorful wheels in the subbasement of the Kremlin landed upon that morning after spinning round and round? But when Pushkin rose from his chair, he received a shake of the hand, a kiss on both cheeks, and the stamp in the shape of St. Basil's.

13.

Not since that first day when he had succeeded in getting bread and sugar but failed in getting milk had Pushkin felt such trepidation at the sound of Irina's footsteps on the stair.

When she came through the door, she could tell at once that something was amiss. She could tell from the expression on her husband's face, from the shuffling of his feet, and from the manner in which he asked about her day, which is to say, in triplicate.

"As I've told you twice already," Irina replied, "my day was productive. What about yours? And why are your hands behind your back?"

"Behind my back?" asked Pushkin. "Well, yes, you see, earlier today, up two flights of stairs and down another three, at the end of a long series of lefts and rights, it just so happened, through no fault of my own . . ."

"Yes, yes?"

Then out spilled Pushkin's tale: of his friendship with Litvinov, the painter-sweeper, and the importance of doing one's part; of the unusual silence at the Agency of Expatriate Affairs and the filling of forms to pass the time with reference to crickets in the knee-high grass.

Irina was staring at her husband in confusion. Who was this Litvinov and what was a painter-sweeper? Which office was up and down, left and right? And what did crickets have to do with it?

Here, at a loss of what to add, Pushkin simply brought his hands from behind his back and held out the bright yellow card, which Irina snapped from his fingers. If Pushkin had feared the card would fill his wife with fury, he was not mistaken. When she saw typed across its top in capital letters the words *REQUEST FOR A VISA,* her cheeks grew red. When she saw her own name listed as one of the applicants, her ears grew red. And when she saw the requested destination identified as "New York City," the blood that was boiling in her heart reached every single extremity. But even as the boiling blood raced through her veins, a series of thoughts raced through her head, holding her instinct to bludgeon her husband in check.

First, there was the reassessment of her husband's qualities. Once an aimless, unimaginative idler, he had proven to be the very personification of the Bolshevik ideal: tireless, single-minded, and effective. So, like all good Bolsheviks, he deserved the benefit of the doubt. Then there was her deep-seated respect for the Kremlin's stamps. These were not tossed about like apples in an orchard. Whatever evidence to the contrary, the very appearance of such a stamp should confirm that a piece of paper had been carefully reviewed and deemed in perfect alignment with the Bolshevik cause. But to even consider leaving the Soviet Union so near its moment of triumph—and for New York City, no less—was this nothing more than the act of a turncoat?

Rather than look to her husband for an answer, Irina looked to the portrait that was hanging on the wall. Returning her gaze with sober affection, the Father of the Revolution reminded her that the victory of the proletariat would come only when every worker of the world was united in the brotherhood of socialism. From the beginning, the Bolsheviks' intention had been to establish a *foothold* in Russia and then expand the movement across the globe. And as to New York City, when a blacksmith hopes to shape a piece of iron, where better to thrust it than the center of the furnace?

"Very good," Irina said as the blood withdrew from her fists. "Very good, Comrade Husband."

But having come to this conclusion through the soundest of reasoning, Irina suggested that they pack their clothes into one suitcase, their cash into another, and leave without further delay. After all, Irina may have been a Bolshevik through and through, but she was no fool. And as if Fate itself wished to acknowledge the aptness of Irina's instinct, when she and Pushkin emerged from their building with their suitcases in hand, they found a limousine idling at the curb.

14.

In the years before the war, while working as a truck driver in Moscow, Maximilian Shaposhnikov had looked down upon the city's chauffeurs—finding their servile manners and silly black caps reason enough for derision. But under Communism, he quickly discovered the life of a chauffeur had its advantages. Specifically, if one was lucky enough to serve a vigilant member of the Party (the sort who routinely worked from dawn till dusk and sometimes through the night), then one had much of the day in which to use the boss's car as one saw fit. And in the new Russia, there was no shortage of black marketeers, prostitutes, and other people of consequence who needed to get from point A to point B, who deserved to do so in style, and who were willing to pay for the privilege. Shaposhnikov had just dropped off one such client at the Nikitsky Towers when Pushkin and Irina came through the door.

Upon seeing the couple, Shaposhnikov didn't think twice. He donned his silly black cap and stepped from the car.

"Hey there, comrades," he called. "You look like you're off on a journey. Need a lift?"

Irina turned to her husband.

"Hire this fellow to take us to the station. I've forgotten something upstairs."

While Irina went to retrieve the picture of Lenin she'd left hanging on the wall, Pushkin explained to Shaposhnikov that they were, in fact, headed to the train station to catch a train.

"The overnight to Leningrad?"

"Why, yes."

"For an extended visit?"

"No. We are actually going to Leningrad to catch the boat to Bremen and from there the steamer to New York."

Maximilian Shaposhnikov may have been a man of Moscow, but he was also a man of the world. A couple living in the Nikitsky Towers heading to Bremen to catch a steamer for the States with two stuffed suitcases could only mean one thing—that the time had come to shear the sheep.

"Ah, the life at sea," said Shaposhnikov with a nostalgic smile, though he'd never laid eyes upon it. "Do you already have your tickets for the crossing . . . ?"

"I'm afraid we don't even have our tickets for the train."

The chauffeur puffed out his chest and straightened his cap.

"Providence is smiling on you today, good sir. For I happen to know just the man to secure you a suitable carriage for the train ride to Leningrad and another to secure you a suitable cabin for your crossing." Which was largely true! For from his days as a truck driver, Shaposhnikov had come to know a slew of fellows who now manned the docks and depots of Russia.

At the station, Shaposhnikov proved the perfect majordomo. He found Irina a comfortable seat and a cup of tea. He found a porter to take care of the bags. He introduced Pushkin to the ticket master (who would ensure they had a first-rate berth in the sleeping car) and to the head conductor (who would ensure they had a first-rate table in the dining car). What's more, he contacted his friends in Leningrad to ensure that for their crossing to America they would be ticketed, portered, and cabined in the first-rate manner by first-rate men. And at each juncture, Shaposhnikov gave Pushkin a little guidance on how best to show his gratitude to those who'd been of service.

Thus, with every step made smoother than the last, on the twenty-fourth of October 1929, Pushkin and Irina arrived in Bremen and climbed the gangplank. A horn was given three great blasts, confetti was showered over the docks, hats were waved at the rail, and the steamship set out to sea—at the very moment that the stock market in the city of New York began its precipitous plunge.

15.

Irina knew herself well. Not only did she know what she was capable of, she knew what she needed to do and when she needed to do it. What she did not know was that she was prone to seasickness. With the first swell of the ocean, it seemed as if a serpent had slithered into her stomach and now spun round and round. So, most of her Atlantic crossing was spent measuring the distance between the pillows on her bed and the porcelain in the water closet.

Pushkin offered to remain at Irina's bedside with a cold, wet cloth. But knowing full well that her husband's constant attention would make the journey interminable, she pushed him out of their berth, insisting he enjoy the freedoms of the ship from stem to stern. And despite his initial hesitations, that's exactly what Pushkin did.

Naturally, he enjoyed the endless vistas, and the four-course meals, and the jazz band in the bar. But what he enjoyed most of all was the ocean liner's staff. It seemed to Pushkin that for every passenger on board there were two members of the crew eager to ensure one's comfort. On the lower decks were chambermaids, cabin boys, and valets. In the dining room were maître d's, waitresses, and a fellow with a high white hat who carved the beef. While on the upper decks were fine young men who would arrange your chair and fine young women who would bring your tea. And to his utter delight, Pushkin found he had ample opportunity to show his appreciation to each and every one of them. Such that when Pushkin and his wife disembarked in New York five days later at seven in the morning, they had no need of a porter because one of their suitcases was empty.

16.

"Empty!" exclaimed Irina, as she stood with her husband in the passenger terminal on the West Side piers. "Empty!"

As Pushkin began to enumerate the many kind people who had shown their willingness to be of assistance over the course of the journey from Moscow to New York, she stared at him in amazement. In bewilderment. In disbelief. Who in his right mind would dole out a small fortune in hard-earned currency to a pack of gracious wolves on the doorsteps of a foreign country? Who?

But in a flash, Irina knew the answer: *The man she married. That's who!*

Oh, how sweet had been the notion that her husband had been transformed; that after decades of aimlessness, he had proved to be a man of purpose and imagination; and that her judgment in marrying him had not been so misguided, after all. A delicious notion, indeed. A sugar-dusted, chocolate-frosted, custard-filled pastry puff of a notion.

But surely such transformations are not unheard of, ventured a sympathetic little voice in the back of Irina's head. *Doesn't a man have the capacity to change?* By way of answer, Irina shouted at her husband: "Does a fish grow feathers?" Then without another word she walked out the terminal door.

"Does a tortoise grow tusks?" she could be heard calling out as she marched along the quay at her epiphanous pace. "Does a butterfly grow a beard?" And so engaged was she in this menagerie of common sense, she barely paid heed to her surroundings as she passed under the tracks of an elevated train and entered the rough-hewn streets of the lower West Side.

"What am I to do now?" she demanded of no one.

But when she reached the corner of Tenth Avenue and Sixteenth Street, she came to a stop. A few strides ahead, a lone woman in shirtsleeves was leaning against a wall smoking a cigarette, while across the street a crowd milled in front of a loading dock door. In a single glance, Irina recognized the people in the crowd. She recognized them from the ruggedness of their clothes and the determination on their faces. The only difference between this assembly and the factory workers in Moscow was that they appeared to come from every corner of the globe. In their number were Africans and Asians, Germans and Italians, Irishmen and Poles. Wondering what she had happened upon, Irina looked up and saw a billboard on the building's roof displaying a golden disc the size of the sun.

Suddenly, the loading door rolled up with a clatter to reveal a man in suspenders in the company of two armed guards. In unison, every member of the crowd began to shout and wave their hands. For a moment, the foreman looked them over, then he began to point.

"Him, her. Her, him . . ."

Those whom he singled out were waved inside by the guards—having been bestowed the privilege of doing a hard day's work—while the rest were left to swallow their disappointment just as they had swallowed their pride.

When the loading door came down with a bang, the woman in shirtsleeves was no longer leaning idly against the wall. Having tossed her cigarette into the street, she began thrusting a piece of paper in the hands of every member of the proletariat who passed, while rattling off a few urgent sentences. Some of the workers glanced at the leaflet as they walked away, others stuffed it in a pocket, but many let it fall to the ground. When a gust of wind raced down the street, one of the leaflets was swept in the air and dropped at Irina's feet.

Irina couldn't read a word on the leaflet, but embedded in the middle of the text, staring back at her with an expression at once determined and wise, was none other than Vladimir Ilyich Lenin, the very man who, not a week before, had reminded her that the revolution in Russia was meant to be a foothold.

Irina scanned the departing sample of the world's citizens, and sure enough, there among them she spied two young women wearing the headscarves of home. Rushing across the street, Irina called to them.

"Hey there! Sisters! Do you speak Russian?"

The two women stopped.

"We speak Russian."

"I have just arrived in America. What is this place?"

"It is the National Biscuit Company," replied the one while the other simply pointed to the roof.

Gripping the leaflet in both hands, Irina watched the two women follow their fellows into the heart of the city. Then she looked up again at the giant sun of a biscuit that towered over the building, and suddenly, even though she was an unflinching atheist, she knew exactly why God had brought her here.

17.

But what of our old friend Pushkin?

When Irina walked out of the terminal, he assumed that having quickly gotten her bearings, she would head into the city, secure a new apartment, and then come back for him, just as she had on their first day in Moscow. So, he waited. Given all the people moving about, Pushkin understood the important thing was to stay in the spot where Irina had left him, so she could find him upon her return.

In the hours that followed, his fellow passengers gathered their luggage and greeted their families, the taxis came and went, the porters dispersed and the terminal emptied, but there was no sign of Irina. At one point, Pushkin thought he saw her on the quay looking about, as if unsure of where she was. "Irina!" he called as he ran outside. "Irina, Irina!" But when he took her by the shoulder, she turned out to be a stranger who just happened to dress like his wife. Disappointed, Push-kin returned to his waiting spot only to discover that where once there had been two suitcases, only one remained—the empty one, of course.

Assuming that some weary traveler had picked up the wrong bag in error, Pushkin went back outside onto the quay, where, in fact, he saw a man in a fedora walking away with what looked like his case.

"Excuse me," shouted Pushkin, as the hatted man crossed a busy street. "Excuse me!"

Since the man didn't seem to hear, Pushkin waited for the traffic to subside, then scrambled after him. When he reached the first two inter-sections, Pushkin could still see the hatted man with his case walking ahead; but when he reached the third, the man was gone. Coming to a stop, Pushkin looked left and right, just in time to see the hatted man cross an intersecting avenue and cut through an alley. So, as quick as he could, Pushkin crossed and cut—only to find himself suddenly in the middle of Times Square, where the street signs flashed, the subway rumbled, the automobiles blared, and a thousand men raced north and south, every last one of them sporting a fedora. Dashing up the boule-vard in a state of panic, Pushkin was suddenly plagued by second thoughts and doubled back. But now, not only could Pushkin see no sign of his case, he could see no sign of the alley he'd emerged from. In other words, he was lost.

Feeling the threat of a tear, Pushkin tried to mimic the stoicism that his friend Litvinov would have shown. Then saying something about two flights down and three flights up, he fell in step with the movement of the crowd.

Though in every single line of Moscow, Pushkin was known as a man of the finest architectural sensibilities, as he proceeded down Broadway he barely took note of a pediment. At Herald Square, he took no notice of the skybridge that connected Gimbels department store to its annex. At Madison Square, he took no notice of the Flatiron Build-ing with its whimsical shape. And when he entered City Hall Park, at five o'clock in the evening, he took no notice of the Woolworth Building, despite the fact that until quite recently it had been tallest building in the world!

What Pushkin did take note of, as he collapsed onto a bench, was how cold and hungry he had become. While he had had the foresight to bring a winter coat and scarf to America, both were still in his suitcase; and while he had eaten a hearty breakfast on the ship, that must have been twelve hours ago. As if in confirmation, a nearby clock tower began to chime the hour of six.

Rubbing his hands together and pounding his feet on the flagstones in a halfhearted attempt to make himself warmer, Pushkin suddenly noticed that an old man in a threadbare coat on the bench across the way was trying to get his attention. Pointing in the direction of the clock tower, the man said something to Pushkin, then he pointed in the other direction.

"I'm afraid I don't understand," said Pushkin with a mournful shake of the head. "I don't speak a word of English."

Seeming to grasp the spirit of Pushkin's reply, the man nodded with a sympathetic smile. Then rising from his bench, he pointed again in the opposite direction of the clock and signaled to Pushkin in a manner that clearly meant: *This way, my friend. Come along.*

Persuaded by the old man's smile, Pushkin began to follow him down Broadway. After they had walked a block, the old man pointed ahead to a steeple. Pushkin assumed they were headed to the church to get out of the cold by attending an evening service. But when they arrived, rather than enter the great carved doors, the old man led Pushkin around to the back. And there, they came upon twenty ragged men waiting patiently by the vestry door, as the aroma of chicken soup began to drift through the air.

Without hesitation, Pushkin took his place at the end of the line. But even as he did so, he noticed that another man in a threadbare coat was emerging from a nearby alley. Catching the gentleman's eye, Pushkin gave him a friendly wave as if to say, *It's over here. This way, my friend,* and then he smiled. For while Pushkin was standing at the end of the line, he knew that when the new fellow arrived, it would no longer be the end of the line. In fact, it would no longer be the end of anything at all.

The Ballad of Timothy Touchett

1.

A few years before the end of the millennium, one Timothy Touchett sat in the Main Reading Room of the New York Public Library's Fifth Avenue branch with a copy of Maxwell Perkins's *Collected Letters* before him. What had brought this young man from the suburbs of Boston to such a majestic spot on a sunlit afternoon? Better yet, what had brought him to New York in the first place? Quite simply, his determination since childhood to become a celebrated novelist. With his bachelor's degree from a well-regarded liberal arts college firmly in hand, he had set out for that city where countless luminaries had pounded the pavement and burned the midnight oil. He moved in with Dan, an aspiring actor from NYU who needed a new roommate in his East Village sublet. He got a job as a waiter in an Italian restaurant. He bought composition books, pens, and paper for his typewriter, despite the fact that this story takes place more than a decade after the rise of the personal computer!

Many young authors finding themselves so satisfactorily situated would have waded into the choppy seas of their ambitions without a moment's delay, using their free hours to spin sentences into paragraphs and paragraphs into pages, melding memories and fancies with immediate impressions until their first novel was ready for its miraculous debut. But having spent a few weeks tapping his pencil on the top of his desk, Timothy decided that before he began this endeavor in earnest it behooved him to study the *practices* of his heroes. How did they approach their craft? Did they write in the morning or at night? Sober or intoxicated? Did they outline with care or allow their prose to unfurl before them like a red carpet before the procession of a king?

"All the finest composers and architects have studied the craftsmanship of the masters before setting out in search of their own inimitable style. . . ." Or so Timothy opined to Susie, the abstract expressionist from Oberlin who lived down the hall.

But in sharing this sensible view, Timothy was not being completely honest with his neighbor. He was not being completely honest with himself. For what had caused Timothy to delay the start of his novel was not a desire to investigate methodologies, but a fear so dark and disturbing it could barely be acknowledged—the fear that he had no story to tell.

Consider for a moment the lives of Timothy's heroes. Faulkner had come of age in the Jim Crow South, a time and place with its own idiosyncratic language and an abundance of majestic themes, including Family, Race, and the Land. Hemingway had been a journalist and driven an ambulance in the First World War before hunting lions on the African savanna. And what about Dostoevsky? He had been sent to Siberia for his views. Not metaphorically, you understand. He had been put on a train and shipped to the *actual* Siberia. The one with the steppes and the snow! At one point, he had even been called before a firing squad, only to receive a last-minute reprieve from the Tsar. How could one expect to craft a novel of grace and significance when one's greatest inconveniences had included the mowing of lawns in spring, the raking of leaves in autumn, and the shoveling of snow in winter? Why,

Timothy's parents hadn't even bothered to succumb to alcoholism or file for divorce.

Oh, what crueler irony could there be than for the gods to infuse a young man with dreams of literary fame and then provide him with no experiences? But as I've noted, this was a secret that Timothy kept from everyone, including himself. So, every morning at 10:00, it was off to the library, where he postponed the writing of novels through the study of practices.

Now, reading a collection of letters is not like reading a novel. There are no settings to speak of, no pithy exchanges, no plot devices ingeniously designed to prompt the turning of a page. Reading one letter after another requires both patience and attentiveness, two qualities that Timothy simply did not possess.

As he sat in the library staring down at a facsimile of a letter from F. Scott Fitzgerald, rather than taking notes on elements of craft or branching off on some promising ideas of his own, Timothy found himself copying Fitzgerald's signature over and over, even as the minute hand on the Reading Room's clock advanced irreversibly toward eternity.

"I see you are a fellow admirer of Mr. Perkins."

Startled, Timothy looked up to find a little old man in an ill-fitting suit standing to his left. The old man gestured toward Timothy's composition book.

"A dissertation, perhaps?"

"No," said Timothy, while clearing his throat and casually obscuring his handiwork with an elbow. "I am a novelist."

"Ahhh," said the old man in appreciation. "How fine. May I?"

Without waiting for an answer, the old man took a seat and in a voice that was suitably hushed, asked Timothy his opinion of the famed editor. As it turned out, not only did the old man take an interest in Timothy's views, he shared many of them. What's more, he related an anecdote that Timothy had never heard about an encounter between Hemingway and Fitzgerald in the lobby of the Plaza Hotel. Then he recalled his own encounter with the young Philip Roth at the reference desk in this very room! When at last the old man stood to go, having thanked Timothy for a delightful exchange, he seemed to hesitate.

"It so happens," he said after a moment, as if confessing to a weakness, "I am in the field myself."

Here, he produced his card:

Peter Pennybrook

Purveyor of Used and Rare Editions

800 Lafayette Street

New York, New York

"Should you ever be looking for a little work, I hope you'll stop in. I could almost certainly use a man of your talents."

As Mr. Pennybrook shuffled from the Reading Room, Timothy looked down at the card in his hand. It was a little soiled and bent at the corners, as if it had lingered in its master's wallet a few months too many. To a seasoned New Yorker, this might have triggered a moment of doubt. But Timothy, who had never been handed a business card in his life, felt only the warm winds of good fortune, and he decided right then and there to visit Mr. Pennybrook's shop first thing Monday morning.

Or maybe Tuesday afternoon, so as not to appear too eager . . .

2.

Come Tuesday, as Timothy walked up Lafayette Street, his visit to Mr. Pennybrook filled him with excitement. Though new to the world of commerce, Timothy understood perfectly well that a position at a bookstore wasn't likely to make him rich; but the notion of having such a job appealed to him on *artistic* grounds. You see, Dan the actor was earning his keep as an usher at the Public Theater; and Susie the abstract expressionist was a receptionist at the Leo Castelli Gallery. Which is to say, Dan and Susie had each immersed themselves in the *milieu* of their art. Five days a week they were proving their fealty to their calling through the unwavering completion of menial tasks for menial pay— while at the same time enriching their creative sensibilities through strategic osmosis. When Timothy's loose circle of friends gathered on Saturday nights at a local bar, what wonderful anecdotes Dan and Susie had to relate from the front lines of their fields, making references not only to the latest artistic trends, but to some of the leading practitioners— whom they had seen with their own eyes! Whereas, whenever Timothy happened to be asked about his job at the restaurant, his cheeks burned with shame.

But what if he were to work in a bookstore?

Not for nothing have writers been called wordsmiths for centuries. The craft of writing demands all the specialized training and physical stamina of the blacksmith. The serious writer sweats at the forge of his imagination while hammering out sentences on the anvil of language, and so on. Where better for an aspiring writer to earn his daily bread than right in the blacksmith's shop? With this heightened sense of purpose, Timothy arrived at Mr. Pennybrook's; and when he went inside, he found it to be everything he had hoped for and more. Which is to say, less.

In terms of square footage, the shop was not much bigger than Timothy's East Village sublet. The bookshelves, which had been fashioned from pine planks during the Vietnam War, were as yellowed and warped as the books they supported. At the front of the shop, there was a small station at which an associate could ring the cash register, while at the very back was Mr. Pennybrook's old oak desk and a glassed-in cabinet housing first editions and other rarities.

"Ah, Timothy!" said Mr. Pennybrook, looking up from a tome. "You have found me in my domain. Is it possible that you have been tempted by my proposal? I'm afraid I cannot offer you much in the way of wages, but what I can offer is a delightful harbor for one who hopes to sail the seas of literature."

And since Timothy could not have put it better himself, he took the job on the spot.

3.

On Timothy's first day, Mr. Pennybrook gave him an official tour, taking care to indicate where in the small labyrinth of shelves the biographies gave way to histories, the histories to mysteries, and the mysteries to the golden age of science fiction. He introduced him to the workings of the cash register and, with a touch of ceremony, gave him his own set of keys so he could open the store should Mr. Pennybrook ever run late. In essence, he let Timothy know he had "the run of the place." He even encouraged Timothy to bring in his composition book so he could apply himself to his calling whenever the shop was quiet.

Taking Mr. Pennybrook at his word, Timothy brought in his composition book a few days later, and he was setting down some preliminary thoughts on a potential short story, when Mr. Pennybrook happened by his desk.

"I was a little worried, Timothy, that the demands of the job might stand in the way of your artistic ambitions. It does my heart good to see your pen at work!" For emphasis, Mr. Pennybrook lightly touched the page on which Timothy had been writing, then he paused.

"Why, isn't this the very notebook you were using the day we met?"

When Timothy confirmed it was, Mr. Pennybrook hesitated.

"I hate to be intrusive, but at the library, I couldn't help noting you seemed to be inscribing Mr. Fitzgerald's name. . . ."

Timothy blushed in silent confirmation.

"May I see?"

Timothy turned back to the page with the author's signatures, but as it turned out, he had no cause for embarrassment. For Mr. Pennybrook exhaled audibly in an expression of unmitigated appreciation.

"Oh, that's very good, Timothy. Very impressive. You really have it, my boy." Mr. Pennybrook pointed to the loop-de-loop of the *S*. "You can just see the excitement of Fitzgerald's early successes. And here, in the flourishes at the top of the two *F*'s, is reflected the lavish lifestyle he enjoyed in his heyday. And here, in the downward slope of the terminal *d*, a foretelling of all the sorrows to come. . . ."

Mr. Pennybrook shook his head in acknowledgment of either Fitzgerald's destiny or Timothy's art.

"This particular signature," explained Timothy, "was in a letter to Perkins while Fitzgerald was scrambling in Hollywood and Zelda was in an institution in Asheville, North Carolina."

"Of course, of course," said Mr. Pennybrook. "It's all there. It's all there."

After these encouraging remarks, Timothy couldn't help himself. He turned back a few pages to where he had done a similar study of Hemingway's signature, circa 1925.

"Oh, Timothy!" Mr. Pennybrook's face lit up with a smile of pleasant surprise. "Look at that *y*! You have perfectly captured the casting of the fly in 'Big Two-Hearted River Part II.' And your slanted *i* is no less than the lance of the picador projecting from the back of a bull."

Mr. Pennybrook smiled with another shake of the head, then tapped the desk twice to conclude the conversation. But when he turned away, rather than walk back to his desk he stopped and stared at the passing cars. Then, as if in reply to some unspoken question, he sadly shook his head and said, "I couldn't."

"What is it, Mr. Pennybrook?" Timothy asked with a touch of concern. "Is there something I can do for you?"

The purveyor of books turned back and looked his employee in the eye.

"I don't know, Timothy. Perhaps there is. Perhaps there is."

With that, Mr. Pennybrook went to the glassed-in cabinet at the back of the store and returned a moment later. Delicately, he placed a blue-hued volume on Timothy's desk. It was a first edition of *The 42nd Parallel* by John Dos Passos, a little worse for wear but with the original dust jacket mostly intact. Laying his hand on the cover of the book, Mr. Pennybrook explained that he had an old friend who was quite ill. On his deathbed, in fact. Since his youth, this friend had been devoted to Dos Passos and, over the years, had collected a signed first edition of every single work by the author.

"Every single work, that is, except *The Forty-Second Parallel*."

Mr. Pennybrook sighed.

"I wonder, Timothy, if you might be willing to sign this edition on Mr. Dos Passos's behalf. . . ."

Timothy looked up in surprise.

"You mean sign his name?"

"I know, I know," Mr. Pennybrook said, nodding sadly. "Normally, such a thought wouldn't cross my mind. But to have a signed first edition of this work would make such a difference to Edward; and it would make *no* difference to Dos Passos. . . ."

Sensing Timothy's hesitation, Mr. Pennybrook went back to his cabinet and returned this time with a copy of *The Fourteenth Chronicle*, a collection of the author's letters and journal entries. "John Dos Passos was the conscience of a nation, a portrayer of America's inequities. And through his *U.S.A. Trilogy*, he provided us with a radical new sense of what the novel could be. Despite these irrefutable facts, at the time that Dos Passos was writing these profound and weighty works, his signature expressed an almost youthful whimsy. . . ." Placing the book on Timothy's desk, Mr. Pennybrook turned to a facsimile of a letter from the early 1930s.

In an instant, Timothy could see it was just as Mr. Pennybrook had observed. Belying the social and artistic import of the author's work, the capitalized *J*, *D*, and *P* were each finished with a loop that drifted high above the other letters, such that his signature gave the impression of a line of children walking in single file, three of whom were holding a helium balloon on a string.

"To pay a fitting homage to such a signature," Mr. Pennybrook observed, "one would need to render that sense of youthful playfulness through the movement of one's own hand. . . ."

Which is exactly what Timothy did—on Mr. Dos Passos's behalf.

The next morning, when Mr. Pennybrook arrived at 11:30, he stopped at Timothy's desk.

"Last night, I paid a visit to Edward at the hospital—in the ICU. If you could only have been there to see the expression on his face when he turned to the title page and saw Mr. Dos Passos's signature. What surprise. What joy. What consolation in an hour of distress." Here, Mr. Pennybrook adopted an unusually serious expression. "Now, Timothy, my boy, I know you will be predisposed to object. But in fulfilling this man's wish, you have given not only of your time and attention, you have given of your talent. And for that reason, I insist that you accept this . . . honorarium." Mr. Pennybrook took an envelope from his jacket and laid it on Timothy's desk.

In point of fact, Timothy *did* object. The execution of the signature had taken only a few minutes and, under the circumstances, it was the least he could do. But Mr. Pennybrook held up a hand to indicate that any quibbling would offend his honor. So, Mr. Pennybrook's envelope was stowed away in Timothy's drawer.

Later that night, when Mr. Pennybrook had gone home and Timothy was about to lock up for the night, he took the envelope from his desk and opened it. Inside, he found a $50 bill so crisp and clean it must have come straight from the bank. The tactile impression of withdrawing the bill from the envelope immediately recalled for Timothy how in his youth his grandmother from St. Louis would send him a birthday card with a $10 bill just as fresh.

Presumably, this sentimental association, or perhaps the word *honorarium*, diminished any qualms Timothy had felt. For when he left the shop, rather than meeting his friends at their favorite Mexican restaurant on Sixth Avenue (where a burrito and two frozen margaritas could be had for $8.99), Timothy stopped instead at a French bistro in SoHo that he had passed a hundred times before. Seated alone at a little square table covered in bright white paper and illuminated by a votive, Timothy surveyed the evening's specials, which were written on a chalkboard in a gay European cursive. He ordered steak frites and a glass of Côte du Rhône. And before he broke bread, in lieu of grace, he raised his glass to John Dos Passos and to socially conscious fiction from the thirties and beyond.

Did Timothy have any suspicions, you might rightfully wonder, when Mr. Pennybrook asked him to sign the Dos Passos for an ailing friend? Did he question the veracity of the story or wonder if, morally speaking, he was about to dip his toes into murky waters? In a word, no. Flattered by Mr. Pennybrook's compliments, intrigued by the artistic challenge, and sympathetic to the wishes of a dying man, Timothy had signed the book without pausing to consider such ambiguities.

Well, if he was not suspicious on that occasion, then surely he had his doubts when ten days later, Mr. Pennybrook appeared at his desk with a shaking head, a first edition of T. S. Eliot's *Poems 1909–1925*, and word of a bookish friend—a schoolteacher, no less—who had been scouring the city in search of a signed Eliot collection to give to her husband on the occasion of their fortieth anniversary in order to commemorate the fact that he had read to her from "Prufrock" during their courtship. No again, I'm afraid. Never mind that the poem in question paints such a sad view of marriage that no young man in his right mind would read it to a young woman whom he was trying to seduce.

But then, in a steeplechase, does the thoroughbred that has cleared the first hurdle suddenly slow down to consider the second? Of course not. Taking confidence from the success of his first leap, losing himself in the thrill of the contest and the sound of his own thundering hooves, he takes the second hurdle without a second thought. Just so, when Timothy executed this second signature, he easily cleared the moral obstacles and raced around the track while perfectly capturing the Nobel Prize winner's thick-rimmed spectacles, the off-center part in his hair, and his well-known predilection for tweeds.

And on the following day, Timothy was paid another visit at his desk by Mr. Pennybrook, with another envelope and another report of another satisfied soul.

4.

The road along which a young man discovers what he is capable of is no midwestern interstate. It has no uninterrupted views to the horizon, no painted white lines, no brightly lit signs indicating the distance to one's destination. Rather, it is a narrow and winding byway crowded with undergrowth and overhung with branches. Along his journey, the young man is presented with sudden intersections, divergent footpaths, and fateful detours, each of which, if taken, will lead him to other byways with their own intersections, footpaths, and detours. So intricate are the paths and so wooded the way, at any given point it is almost impossible for a young man to see from whence he's come, never mind to where he's headed.

At each crossing, faced with the decision of whether to go left, right, or straight ahead, the young man may rely upon the advice he has been given as a child, or the sum of his experiences, or the flip of a coin. But of all the forces that are likely to influence him as he proceeds from one fork to the next, there are few more powerful than the moderate increase in income.

Long gone are the days when the world was divided into manors and huts. In their place, we have an era in which the necessities of food, clothing, and shelter are experienced in a thousand gradations. Thus, while once we needed to marry an heiress or found a railroad in order to change our lot, today an extra fifty dollars a week will allow us to take one more step up the ladder of well-being to a tier where the soups are a little more tasty, the shirts a little more stylish, and the living rooms a little more exposed to natural light.

"*But,*" you may very well ask, "*is this incremental improvement in daily life really enough to make a difference? Is it enough to enhance a young man's happiness, boost his ego, and silence the nagging voice of envy, if only for a minute?*" Suffice it to say that at the fork in the road, offer a young man an extra fifty dollars a week in exchange for a modest adjustment to his dreams, and you will have him by the throat.

5.

Perhaps this assessment is too cynical.

In all likelihood, it is influenced by the author's own experiences with compromise and his unselfconscious desire to make his choices seem inevitable—the sort of choices that anyone else would have made under similar circumstances. But it may not be fair to our protagonist, who, after all, is the reputed subject of the tale. Like parents, authors have no business attempting to relive their glories or redeem their sins through the lives of their creations. Authors must learn to stuff these burdens in their kit bags and lug them up the trail themselves. So, in all likelihood, Timothy deserves a more measured assessment.

Besides, since the days of antiquity, those sitting in judgment of the gravest crimes have required evidence of a man's intent and sought to classify his awareness of the moral implications of his actions. Even when one man *kills* another, we separate the accidental from the spontaneous and the spontaneous from the carefully planned—despite the fact that such distinctions provide no comfort to the dead. So, how would Timothy stand up under such judicious scrutiny?

First, let us acknowledge that Timothy was not a reflective soul. He was not one to ponder or mull. When bringing a book to bed, he generally drifted off after a sentence or two and then slept soundly through the night. And you certainly could not accuse him of pursuing an elaborate plan that was carefully engineered and coldly executed. Rather, it would be more appropriate to observe that, in his actions, Timothy was following the "path of least resistance," which is the very path that rivers follow as they make their way from the mountains to the sea—a phenomenon that has been celebrated by Romantic poets, American transcendentalists, and a long line of mystics ranging from Heraclitus to Lao Tzu. And what's good for the goose, as they say, should be good for the gander.

6.

In the weeks that followed, Mr. Pennybrook took care to describe for Timothy the particular individual who was seeking a particular volume along with his or her ailment, handicap, or history of charitable acts—because Timothy had seemed so interested in the whos, whys, and wherefores. But come autumn, Mr. Pennybrook no longer needed to go to this trouble. Timothy's interests had turned almost exclusively toward the artistry of his craft.

And what a rich and varied craft it was.

For signatures do not span a simple spectrum like the hues of a rainbow. Rather, each signature is a color unto itself. So fundamentally idiosyncratic is a man's signature that it is as binding in the eyes of the law as his fingerprints or a trace of his DNA. In the rare books and manuscripts room of the New York Public Library, Timothy familiarized himself with all the little nuances that collectively defined this manifold array. He studied those signatures that sloped and those that spiked; those that dashed ahead and those that dragged their feet; those that recalled the staccato of a machine gun and those the lilt of a lullaby.

But as two bottles of wine harvested from the same vineyard in different years are at once similar and distinct, just so two signatures by the same person scrawled at different times are both recognizable as coming from the same hand and yet expressive of the different circumstances under which they were penned. Thus, the perfect rendition of a signature requires not simply a mastery of the signatory's underlying calligraphic style, but an understanding of his or her state of mind at a given moment in time.

To that end, Timothy spent hours bent over histories, biographies, and memoirs. Not only did he introduce himself to the friends of the authors, metaphorically speaking, he ingratiated himself with their acquaintances and invited himself for dinner. He listened at keyholes and peeked over transoms. In this manner, he mastered the signature of Dashiell Hammett at the height of his romance with Lillian Hellman; the signature of John O'Hara at the height of his struggles with alcoholism; and the signature of Ernest Hemingway at the height of his struggles with himself. Hammett, O'Hara, Hemingway, he signed on behalf of them all. And on behalf of many more.

Which is not to say that Timothy would sign *anything*. He was not a young man without a code. For instance, while he was perfectly willing to sign on behalf of some of our finest authors who have come and gone, he drew a line when it came to the living. As Mr. Pennybrook himself had once observed, signing a book on Dos Passos's behalf

made no difference to Dos Passos. What's more, with Dos Passos in the grave there was no opportunity for ardent admirers—the carriers of his torch, as it were—to obtain his signature under their own initiative. But this was hardly the case with Toni Morrison or John Updike. These luminaries were still living, still writing, and still appearing, upon occasion, in public. So there was still an opportunity for a devotee to track them down with a pen in one hand and a favorite volume in the other. Although Timothy may not have articulated this argument as clearly as I have just now (on his behalf), Mr. Pennybrook intuited the young man's scruples, respected his ethics, and planned accordingly.

The exception that proved the rule was Paul Auster. Mr. Pennybrook, it seems, knew a mother superior in Garrison, New York, who was a lover of Auster's work, but who rarely passed beyond the walls of her nunnery. With a touch of Catholic guilt, she had confessed to Mr. Pennybrook that as the happy owner of a signed copy of the first volume in the so-called *New York Trilogy,* upon occasion she had prayed to God for a complete set.

Acknowledging that Timothy normally signed books on behalf of those who could no longer sign for themselves, Mr. Pennybrook wondered whether he might consider making an exception in Mr. Auster's case given the nature of the author's narratives. After all, weren't his books filled with conundrums and rebuses? With doppelgängers and ghosts? Within the bounds of his oeuvre, was there not Auster the author, Auster the character, and Auster the impostor?

At Mr. Pennybrook's encouragement, Timothy reread *The New York Trilogy* (or rather, finally read *The New York Trilogy*) and, upon conclusion, had to agree that given the nature of Auster's work, the author would probably have no problem with his books being signed on his behalf. In fact, he might even take some artistic satisfaction from the idea. After reading the three books in as many days, Timothy had such a strong sense of Auster's point of view that he rattled off the two

additional signatures for the mother superior in the course of an after-noon.

7.

As all this unfolded, did Timothy notice that the authors on whose be-half he was signing were becoming more revered? The editions more rare and, by extension, more valuable? Not really. That Hammetts should evolve into Hemingways, an envelope with a fifty into an enve-lope with a few hundreds, and an East Village sublet into a one-bedroom apartment on lower Fifth Avenue all seemed to Timothy as natural to the course of events as autumn evolving into winter and winter into spring. In this spirit, Timothy gave almost no thought to the arcane eco-nomics of Mr. Pennybrook's business. He gave them almost no thought, that is, until a Friday night in May when he was dining alone at the bar of the somewhat swanky Gotham Bar & Grill. . . .

Having placed his order with the bartender, Timothy idly surveyed the lead stories in *The New York Times*. But when he shifted his atten-tion to below the fold, he came upon a piece describing a Bay Area com-pany that, as a leading member of the "New Economy," had just introduced a "profit-sharing program" for its "entire workforce." Timo-thy had to read the opening paragraph a second time just to make sure he understood it. For while the words *work* and *force* struck him as a perfectly natural pairing, he had been educated to assume the words *profit* and *share* were incompatible.

Turning to the page indicated by the jump, Timothy suddenly found himself for the first time in his life in the paper's Business section. The story regarding the "profit-sharing plan," which continued on page B4, was illustrated with a large photograph of the company's employees. As our hero studied the smiling faces of the executives, programmers, sec-retaries, and custodians (yes, even custodians!), he had such an epiphany

that he hardly noticed the twenty-two-dollar hamburger being set down on the bar in front of him.

If Timothy understood the gist of the article, then here, at last, was a chance to combine the virtues of sharing he had learned about in kindergarten with the virtues of capitalism he had learned about in Econ 101. All he need do was raise the topic with Mr. Pennybrook, explain the particulars, and the two of them could cross over into the New Economy hand in hand. But first, Timothy thought it wise to gather a little more information.

So, on the following day, Timothy went to his usual table at the New York Public Library, and rather than bending over literary memoirs, he bent over ten issues of *Forbes* magazine, which were literally (well, not literally literally, but figuratively literally) brimming with exciting new words and concepts.

From the library, Timothy proceeded to Madison Avenue, where Bauman's, the revered rare bookseller, had long maintained its place of business. Stepping inside, Timothy was stunned by what he found. The interior looked less like a shop than J. P. Morgan's personal library. It had couches upholstered in leather; bookcases lined from floor to ceiling with first editions; and in the center of the room—under a chandelier— a glass case displaying Newton's *Principia Mathematica*, Darwin's *Descent of Man*, and a Folio of Shakespeare!

As Timothy stared in amazement, a woman not five years his senior wearing a white blouse and horn-rimmed glasses asked if she could be of assistance. Timothy replied that she could be of assistance. And she was of assistance. Very much of assistance.

Within the hour, Timothy had learned three things from the accommodating Miss Chambers. First, he learned just how valuable a first edition could be. While Timothy was responsible for ringing the cash register whenever a customer purchased a secondhand book from the open shelves, Mr. Pennybrook personally handled all the sales from the glassed-in cabinet. So, while, in principle, Timothy understood that the first edition of a famous novel should be more valuable than its paperback, not in his wildest dreams had he imagined that someone would be willing to pay fifty thousand dollars for a copy of *Tender Is the Night* in its original dust jacket!

Second, Timothy learned that an author's signature could increase the value of a first edition by as much as 50 percent. For a moment, this fact astounded Timothy—that someone would be willing to pay 50 percent more for the pleasure of having a quickly drawn inscription on an interior page of a book he rarely opened.

But wasn't that the genius of capitalism? Wasn't it a system in which the forces of supply and demand establish a perfect state of equilibrium such that a price in a transaction reflects *exactly* what an object is worth to its buyer? If customers were willing to pay a 50 percent premium for signed editions, it must be because the signed editions made them 50 percent more satisfied. In fact, the knowledge that this coveted volume was safely in their bookcase probably made their whiskey taste 50 percent better and allowed them to sleep 50 percent more soundly. Happiness, Timothy understood triumphantly, is not a "zero-sum game." For the purchaser of a signed edition to become 50 percent happier did not require the happiness of others to be diminished one iota.

The next day, when the store was closing, Timothy asked Mr. Pennybrook if he had a moment. Sitting down, he brightly explained the case for profit sharing, drawing on all the terminology he had absorbed from his reading of *Forbes*. He began by referencing the influence of *scarcity* on the desirability of goods. He followed with the *added value* that was created by the signing of a book on an author's behalf, and the well-established merits of an *alignment of interests*, concluding with a proposal that henceforth he and Mr. Pennybrook share equally in the profits of their endeavor.

Throughout Timothy's argument, Mr. Pennybrook listened with utmost attention—not unimpressed by the facility with which his assistant was making use of his newfound lingo. A seasoned capitalist in his own right, one who had been bargaining with vendors and customers for over thirty years, Mr. Pennybrook could probably have called Timothy's bluff. With a sorry shake of the head, he could have expressed his disappointment that Timothy should be broaching such a subject after Mr. Pennybrook had shown him such confidence and trust—and left it at that. But the reality was that while Timothy did not have complete command of the notions he was bandying about, he was more on point than he knew.

For the sudden availability of rare signed editions in Mr. Pennybrook's little shop had materially changed his standing in the field. Having long operated on the dusty periphery of the used-book business, where sleepy purveyors trafficked in dog-eared seventh printings of murder mysteries from the 1970s, he suddenly found himself in the inner sanctum of the inner circle. His name was now whispered among collectors and competitors alike. Not a day went by without someone calling to ask if he didn't have some rare and desirable book. "No," Mr. Pennybrook would say, "I do not have a signed copy of that edition. But I may know where I can get my hands on one. . . ."

As a result, he too had climbed a few rungs on the ladder of well-being. He was now dining in finer restaurants and shopping in fancier stores, and he had recently let the manager of his building know that should a larger apartment become available on an upper floor he might be interested—developments that not only pleased his wife but impressed his son, an insurance broker in Connecticut who had not been impressed with his father since the age of fourteen. And while profit sharing was not only anathema to the bookseller's upbringing but to his sense of patriotism, the threat of stepping down the rungs of the ladder he had so recently ascended seemed equally un-American.

So, in the spirit of the hour, Mr. Pennybrook unleashed a little business lingo of his own. He said that he was open to the notion of *profit sharing*. But as *sole proprietor*, not only was he responsible for all the *sales* and *marketing* of their little enterprise, he had put up the *capital* to secure their *inventory* as well as their *long-term lease*, and he was entitled to a certain *return on investment*. Ergo, an even splitting of profits could hardly be viewed as fair.

In the end, they settled on an arrangement in which Timothy would receive 25 percent of the premium that the signed editions commanded in the marketplace relative to their unsigned alternatives. As such, when the next three volumes (a Henry James, a Henry Miller, and a Henry David Thoreau) were delivered to their satisfied customers for an aggregate price of fifty thousand dollars at a 25 percent premium to their unsigned alternatives, Timothy received an envelope containing twenty-five brand-new hundred dollar bills.

8.

That Friday, Timothy made his weekly visit to the bank to deposit his weekly pay. A young man of old-world sensibilities, Timothy passed the automated teller machines without so much as a glance, preferring to do his business with a human being. But when he had filled out his slip and passed the twenty-five hundred dollars through the gap in the bulletproof window, the teller asked Timothy to wait a moment, then disappeared behind a door. When a few minutes later a middle-aged man in a dark gray suit suddenly appeared, Timothy felt a flash of anxiety. In the movies, a request to wait a moment followed by the sudden appearance of a man in a suit almost always presaged bad news. It was often followed by a stern request of "Could you please come this way?" as a bank guard stood by with his hand on the butt of his firearm. But having identified himself as the bank's branch manager, Mr. Robertson wanted simply to thank Timothy for his business, and to point out that as interest rates on savings accounts were historically low, it might be in Timothy's best interests to explore some alternatives, such as a CD (which, as Mr. Robertson explained, was short not for *compact disc* but for *certificate of deposit*). To that end, perhaps Timothy would be interested in meeting with one of the bank's financial planners . . . ? Timothy thanked Mr. Robertson for the suggestion, said he would certainly consider doing so, and left the bank with a warm and fuzzy feeling.

That night when Timothy went to the Gotham Bar & Grill, rather than sit at the bar as was his habit, he asked for a table. Instead of his normal hamburger, he ordered the twelve-ounce dry-aged New York strip (medium rare). And when the waiter asked if he would like a glass of wine to accompany his steak, Timothy, who knew next to nothing about wine, replied:

"Perhaps a Bordeaux?"

"Of course," said the waiter. Then he asked Timothy to wait a moment.

Less than a minute later, a middle-aged man in a dark gray suit suddenly appeared at Timothy's side. It was the sommelier with the wine list. Leaning at the waist with one hand behind his back, Mr. Metier pointed to various vintages of Bordeaux at various price points, any one of which would prove a perfect accompaniment to his meal.

It did not escape Timothy that this was the second time in a day that he had entered a familiar place of business and been asked to wait, only to have a middle-aged man in a suit—whom he had never seen before—suddenly appear at his side. It dawned on Timothy there must be men just like Mr. Robertson and Mr. Metier in places of business all across Manhattan. Dressed in tailored clothing, educated in comportment, they waited behind closed doors ready to offer specialized advice to customers of a certain class. A class to which, apparently, Timothy now belonged! This realization had as much effect on Timothy's head as the bottle of Château Margaux that he enjoyed with his steak.

9.

One afternoon six weeks later, as spring was skipping toward the threshold of summer, Mr. Pennybrook called Timothy to the back of the store. With an expression of utmost reverence, he set a weathered nineteenth-century book on top of his desk. The particular book? The first volume of a first edition of Leo Tolstoy's *Anna Karenina* in the original Russian. When Mr. Pennybrook spoke, his voice quavered with emotion.

"This afternoon, my boy, I present to you a challenge like none you've faced before—one that may outstrip even your prodigious talents." The challenge at hand was not simply to sign this indisputable masterpiece, but to add an endearment, a message of paternal affection to Alexandra Lvovna Tolstoya, the author's youngest and most beloved daughter, on the occasion of her fourteenth birthday.

"You see the problem . . ."

Here, Mr. Pennybrook did not elaborate, for he didn't need to. Timothy could see the problem in an instant. Though *Anna Karenina* was published in 1878, when Tolstoy was fifty years old, he was making a gift of the book to his daughter twenty years later. By that point, Tolstoy had fully embraced those tenets of mystical Christianity that led him to an ascetic mania entailing vegetarianism, sexual abstinence, and an opposition to private property. The penmanship of the inscription would have to suggest all of this. What's more, it would have to be executed with a fountain pen—and in nineteenth-century Cyrillic, no less.

Faced with the enormity of this task, like any true artist Timothy retreated from public life. He was no longer seen passing time with his friends in the East Village or dining at the Gotham Bar & Grill. He spent hours in the rare manuscripts rooms of the Public Library and the Morgan. He read biographies and letters. He took an extension class at NYU in rudimentary Russian. He went through two reams of paper and three bottles of ink. And, as if in sympathy with Tolstoy, he began to grow a beard.

No stranger to the delicate sensibilities of the artist, Mr. Pennybrook didn't pester or prod. He didn't hover or even casually inquire. From his desk, he watched Timothy out of the corner of his eye, trying to gauge from the boy's posture whether he was feeling demoralized or elated. As days went by, then weeks, Mr. Pennybrook was the very personification of monastic patience; and his patience was rewarded. For on the fifteenth of July, Timothy arrived in the store with a single sheet of paper.

Without a word, he laid it on the desk of his employer (or, perhaps more aptly put, his partner).

Mr. Pennybrook did not rush. He set the book he was reading aside and cleared his throat. He delicately touched the page with his fingers, so as not to stain it with the natural oils of the skin—as if *it* were the 110-year-old manuscript. Then he carefully took it in.

"Oh, Timothy."

Mr. Pennybrook took off his spectacles in order to dab at an eye with a handkerchief because he had shed a tear—a genuine tear!

"Your preparations have not been in vain, my boy. You have sought for and discovered it. Every bit of it. But, do you feel you are ready . . . ?"

"I do."

"Then, here. Please."

From a bottom drawer, Mr. Pennybrook retrieved the first edition and set it on the desk. Then he rose and surrendered his chair. Suspecting that Timothy might need an hour or more to complete his task, Mr. Pennybrook took a few steps away. But with the assurance of a surgeon and the flair of a magician, Timothy executed the inscription in less than a minute.

When Timothy rose, Mr. Pennybrook gripped the young man's right hand in both of his and looked him in the eye.

"I have spent my career—nay, my life—peeking through the windows of art. I can only imagine the satisfaction you must feel, the sense of accomplishment, the aesthetic bliss from having brought such a work of genius into the world. The rest of the day is yours. Treat yourself to a fine dinner and a good night's sleep. My boy, you have earned them."

For all his limitations, it could not be said of Timothy Touchett that he was vain. He was not prone to brag among friends any more than he was prone to stare in the mirror when alone. If anything, Timothy was one who was shadowed by the persistence of self-doubts. But on that day, when he left the shop—just as Mr. Pennybrook suspected—Timothy felt the elation of the artist in his moment of triumph.

Having invested his talent, time, and effort into an outward expression of the human heart, Timothy felt like the pianist who, having just struck the last chord of the concerto, waits for the audience to erupt in applause. Why, Timothy felt almost as Tolstoy himself must have felt when he completed the last page of his novel, knowing that he had surpassed not only his previous efforts but those of his peers and perhaps even those of his heroes.

Just as Mr. Pennybrook suggested, Timothy went home, showered, donned the three-piece suit he'd recently had made, then headed uptown to the Pool Room of the Four Seasons. Housed in a midtown tower and designed by Philip Johnson in the midcentury style, the Pool Room was a gathering spot of movers and shakers, where *every* member of the staff wore a dark gray suit. Seated in a Mies van der Rohe chair, Timothy dined on foie gras for the first time in his life, then on a Dover sole, which, earlier that day, had been flown in from Dover. For dessert, he ordered the bananas Foster, having discovered that the dish was wheeled to your table and set on fire before your very eyes. In fact, the whole experience at the Four Seasons was so divine, Timothy resolved to return as soon as possible—with the accommodating Miss Chambers as his guest!

When Timothy stepped back onto Fifty-Second Street, he wondered for a moment whether he should take the subway or a cab. But before he could finish his wondering, a shiny black Town Car pulled to the curb and offered its services. Timothy knew that Town Cars were not supposed to pick up passengers at the curb in Manhattan. He also knew that the ride would be twice as expensive as a taxi and four times as expensive as the subway. But in recognition of the genius of capitalism, Timothy climbed in the back seat knowing that the ride would be worth exactly what he paid for it.

When Timothy arrived home shortly after nine, he collapsed into a chair. Feeling the lingering pleasures of a job well done and a meal well eaten, he listened with satisfaction to the sounds rising from the street eight stories below: the honking of horns, the shouting of drunkards, the barking of dogs, even the siren of a police car. Together, they all combined to form the symphony that is the city of Manhattan on a warm summer night.

10.

When Mr. Pennybrook sent Timothy off to celebrate, he did so in recognition of the boy's achievement, but also because he had planned a little celebration of his own. Retrieving from his desk the bottle of Dom Pérignon that he had bought the week before, he buried it in a small metal trash can loaded with ice. Then, being careful to dry his hands, he took up the Tolstoy and opened to the title page. For the moment, he fended off any thoughts of the remuneration he would receive, any thoughts of the envy his colleagues would feel when they learned of his coup—knowing that he would be able to explore both the remuneration and the envy to his heart's content later that night while lying in bed, once his wife had begun to snore. Instead, he took the opportunity to admire Timothy's handiwork solely on artistic grounds. Like the cursive *L* that looped so completely it seemed to be a figure eight leaning into the wind. And the top of the capital *T*, which extended with such authority, it was sure to shelter the lowercase *o* in the event of rain. What intelligence, what intensity, what human grandeur the penmanship expressed. Why, if Mr. Pennybrook had not personally commissioned the signature, there would have been no doubt in his mind that it had been inscribed by Tolstoy himself while sitting at his desk at Yasnaya Polyana, the family estate a hundred miles from Moscow.

At six o'clock, Mr. Pennybrook closed the volume with a sigh and sealed it in the manila envelope he had already addressed to a wealthy collector in Connecticut. Then he spun the Dom Pérignon (to ensure it would evenly chill), assembled the plastic flute (he'd had the foresight to purchase when he'd bought the champagne), and shuffled to the front of the store to throw the bolt. But just as he did so, two men in suits appeared at the door.

Now, normally, Mr. Pennybrook would have thought it odd or even ominous for two suited men to appear at his shop at that hour of day—which would have been all the more reason for him to wave them off while mouthing the word *closed*. But feeling in high spirits and thus unusually gracious toward his fellow men, Mr. Pennybrook unlocked the door and opened it just enough to inform them in a more personable fashion that while the store was currently closed, they would be welcomed back on the following morning, anytime after ten.

But having delivered this message, as Mr. Pennybrook began to shut the door, one of the men deftly inserted the toe of his shoe in front of the jamb. Before Mr. Pennybrook could express his consternation at this breach of commercial decorum, the suited stranger reached into his pocket and produced a single piece of paper that, in compliance with the Fourth Amendment to the United States Constitution and in accordance with the laws of the State of New York, allowed him and his colleague to enter Mr. Pennybrook's establishment—despite the hour—and search it from top to bottom.

What had brought about this visit from the local authorities at such an inconvenient hour? A simple twist of fate . . .

One week to the day before Timothy had signed *Anna Karenina* on Mr. Tolstoy's behalf, Paul Auster—the author, not the character—had spoken at a seminar in the English Department at NYU. Later that evening, Auster was scheduled to dine with his editor. So, when class was dismissed, rather than returning to Brooklyn where he lived, Auster took advantage of the fine weather to wander toward midtown at an unhurried pace. At Astor Place, he eyed the post-punk regalia of the local youth with an inward smile. At Tenth Street, he had a cappuccino at a café he had frequented in his thirties. And when he reached the corner of Twelfth Street, he crossed the threshold of Mr. Pennybrook's shop, it being contrary to his nature to pass a secondhand bookstore without stopping in.

Nodding politely to the young man at the front desk who was bent over a biography, Auster stepped farther into the shop and idly browsed the shelves. When he got to the end of the middle aisle, he found himself before an empty desk on the top of which was a copy of his second novel, *Ghosts*, with a label indicating the volume was a signed first edition. With an almost sentimental smile, Auster picked up the book and opened the cover.

But when he reached the title page what struck Auster like a punch to the gut was how pompous his signature appeared. How grandiose. How sure of itself. Despite the fact that he was alone, the author blushed at this irrefutable evidence of his own youthful arrogance. That he was only thirty-seven when the book was published, and still basking in the public praise for *City of Glass*, seemed to Auster no excuse. But even as he leveled this reprobation upon his younger self, he noted the rather impressionist execution of the *P*. Surely, at that point in his career he was articulating the capital letters with a little more precision.

Funny, he thought.

And he would probably have left it at that, had he not realized that a copy of *The Locked Room* had been underneath *Ghosts*. Setting down the first volume, he picked up the second. Here too the signature was and wasn't his own. Once again, it suggested an author aware of his success, but by the publication of *The Locked Room*, his wife was already pregnant with their daughter. Where were the senses of joy and humility that had sprung so profoundly from that happy news?

Shaking his head, Auster set the second volume down on top of the first and retreated back into the summer night. Walking eastward, he looked about with a vague sense of unease—like one who finds himself in an unfamiliar city, or who suddenly realizes that he has an important meeting later that day but can't remember where, when, or with whom.

As he turned up Third Avenue, this sense of unease transitioned into a sense of suspicion, which in turn transitioned into a sense of conviction: He had *not* signed those books! He was certain of it. To stumble across one book with a signature that was and wasn't his own was one thing. But to stumble across two on the same desk? One on top of the other? This suggested something far more dubious. Even nefarious! (At least, in the context of literature.)

As it turned out, despite his love of conundrums and rebuses, doppelgängers and ghosts, Paul Auster did not find any artistic satisfaction in the notion that someone had signed these editions on his behalf. In fact, having begun to feel indignant at Sixteenth Street, by the time he reached Twenty-First Street he was practically in a lather.

For Mr. Pennybrook and Timothy, the timing of Auster's outrage could not have been worse—since Twenty-First Street happened to be the home of the 13th Precinct.

Just as when one enters a hospital and must explain one's ailment four times in succession—first to the receptionist, then the admitting nurse, then the intern, and at long last the physician, just so, Auster, with a growing sense of exasperation, had to explain his suspicions first to a uniformed officer, then the desk sergeant, then a detective, before finally reaching the lieutenant in charge of the bunco squad. Lieutenant McCusker had never heard of Paul Auster—the author or the character. And in his considered opinion, an investigation into the autographs on the title pages of two novels from the 1980s was hardly the best use of the bunco squad's time. Yes, this story takes place during the well-reported drop in crime in American urban centers, so there were fewer murders and armed robberies occurring on a daily basis. But that didn't mean there weren't serious instances of malfeasance to be investigated! At that very moment, there was a crew of fast-talking operators selling promises of citizenship to newly arriving immigrants in Chinatown, and another that had been opening up lines of consumer credit under borrowed identities. Never mind that the boys with the MBAs had begun building Sistine Chapels of larceny right there on Wall Street.

Nevertheless, having sworn to serve and protect the citizens of New York, Lieutenant McCusker assured Mr. Auster that the matter would be investigated, and it was promptly handed over to Detective Dawson, an officer with more than twenty years on the force.

Given his experience, Detective Dawson knew better than to start his investigation with an interview of the suspect. Con men were notoriously skittish, ready to clean out their closets at the first sign of trouble. Instead, he started by getting a lay of the land. He spoke to a number of well-regarded book dealers uptown in order to get a feel for the business and a sense of Pennybrook's reputation. From these conversations Dawson learned that the sums of money involved were not to be laughed at; that while Pennybrook had been shuffling around for decades, only in the last year had he become known as "a man who could get his hands on something"; and that Pennybrook had recently suggested to a competitor with a wink that he was on the verge of the greatest transaction of his career. With this information in hand, a warrant was issued and a visit was paid to the little shop on Lafayette Street.

———————

Having gained admittance, Detective Dawson and his partner, Schwartzy, carefully went through the bookshop looking for the fraudulent Austers, to no avail. Next, they took every single volume from the glassed-in cabinet and turned to the title page in search of dubious signatures. But as a practice, Mr. Pennybrook generally asked Timothy to inscribe a book once he had a paying customer in hand. So, the search for signatures also proved fruitless. Next, Dawson turned his attention to Pennybrook's desk.

As Pennybrook stood aside, Dawson noted the bookseller wasn't even sweating, which reinforced a growing suspicion that this whole investigation had been one big waste of time. But like the professional he was, Dawson went through the desk drawer by drawer. There he found Post-it Notes, pens, a stapler, one letter in French, another in Russian, and various bills of sale—all for transactions under two hundred dollars.

When Dawson finally closed the drawers, contrary to NYPD policy he leaned back in Mr. Pennybrook's chair and let out an audible sigh. And that's when he noticed that even if Pennybrook wasn't sweating, the bottom half of his trash can was. Leaning to his right, Dawson tilted the can and discovered an unopened bottle of champagne in a pool of icy water. As a detective, Dawson knew full well that most everyday objects can signify very different things when discovered under different circumstances; but no matter where you find an unopened bottle of chilled champagne, it can only signify one thing: an intent to celebrate.

Dawson leaned back again, though this time without a sigh. For almost two minutes he sat motionless in Mr. Pennybrook's chair. Then he reached across the desk and took the thick manila envelope from the stack of outgoing mail.

"That's the property of a client," interjected Pennybrook politely.

"Not until it's been mailed, it isn't," replied Dawson. Then he opened the envelope and withdrew an old brown book.

"Please be careful, Detective Dawson. That is a first edition of *Anna Karenina.*"

Detective Dawson turned the book once in his hands, then opened to the title page. There, in a faded blue ink, were a few sentences in Cyrillic followed by a signature.

"It's an inscription from the author to his daughter," explained Pennybrook. "On the occasion of her fourteenth birthday."

"You don't say . . ."

Detective Dawson opened the middle desk drawer, took out the "letter" in Russian that he had seen earlier, and laid it beside the inscription, which it happened to match stroke for stroke.

"Well, what do you know," said Detective Dawson.

The draft of the inscription and the old brown book were carefully placed in Ziploc bags while Mr. Pennybrook was carefully placed in the back of Detective Dawson's car. They all traveled together to the 13th Precinct, where, in a room without windows, the little old bookseller sang like the proverbial canary.

For thirty years, Mr. Pennybrook explained (with his arthritic hands resting prominently on the table), he had been an honest purveyor of used and rare editions. He had supported a wife, raised a son, attended church. But on the fifteenth of the previous September—oh, that fateful day—a young man named Timothy Touchett (that's with two *t*'s on the end) had entered his shop claiming to be a lover of literature and asking for a job. Shortly after entering Mr. Pennybrook's employ, the young man had come into work with a book from his own collection, a signed edition of *The 42nd Parallel* by John Dos Passos that he wished to sell. So—acting on the young man's behalf—Mr. Pennybrook had sold the book to a collector. A week later, when Timothy appeared with another signed first edition, was Mr. Pennybrook suspicious? Of course he was. But did he confront the boy?

Here, Mr. Pennybrook hung his head.

No. He did not confront him. Instead, he sold that volume and many more—a lapse in moral fortitude, for which he expected no sympathy.

"For I have no doubt, Detective," Pennybrook concluded with a sob, "that the boy is a forger through and through. And I suspect that in his apartment (at Ninety-Six Fifth Avenue), on the pages of his composition books, you will find conclusive evidence to that effect."

As he revealed all of this, Mr. Pennybrook displayed the slight befuddlement, the readiness to trust, and the susceptibility to intimidation that made the elderly such frequent targets of con men and manipulators. And when he signed his statement, he did so with a signature that expressed all the regret of an honest man who, late in a hardworking life, has veered from the straight and narrow. Why, there in the droop of the capital *P*, you could almost see the old man's head hanging in shame.

At 8:30 that night, even as Timothy was enjoying his bananas Foster at the Four Seasons, Detective Dawson was standing in the office of Lieutenant McCusker providing a detailed report on the case of the Lafayette Street forgeries.

Having delivered such a report a thousand times before, Detective Dawson was pretty sure of what to expect from his superior. Given that this was a single storefront, two-man book-collecting scam (which would rank it one notch below the sale of faux Gucci bags on Canal Street), and given it was dinnertime in the McCusker household, in all likelihood the lieutenant would receive Dawson's report with a seasoned indifference and a touch of impatience.

But what Dawson did not anticipate was that, like so many children of the Five Boroughs, Lieutenant McCusker was a product of the melting pot. For while his father was as Scottish as a bottle of Glenlivet, his mother was the only daughter of a Muscovite who, at the onset of the October Revolution, had fled his homeland with what little he could carry. So, having initially listened to the detective's summary with the anticipated indifference and impatience, when Detective Dawson plopped the volume of *Anna Karenina* on the desk, Lieutenant McCusker went cold.

Noticing the change of expression on his superior's face, Dawson ventured a little tentatively, "Apparently, this is a copy of—," but Mc-Cusker cut him off.

"I know what it is, Detective."

The two men were silent for a moment, then Lieutenant McCusker picked up the book. Removing it from the Ziploc bag, he opened the cover as gently as Mr. Pennybrook had. But when he read the inscription, rather than shed a tear, he felt every tendon in his body tighten with a moral indignation of the highest order—that is, one simultaneously informed by a pride of heritage and a sense of professional duty.

"I gather you've got the old man in hand. Where is this . . . Touchett?"

Detective Dawson was mystified by the controlled fury that now expressed itself quite clearly in his superior's manner. But you didn't become a detective first grade by investigating the psychological foundations of your superiors' emotions. You got there by responding to them accordingly.

Dawson stood at attention.

"He lives on lower Fifth Avenue, sir. Number Ninety-Six. I'm picking him up first thing in the morning for questioning."

McCusker looked up from the novel.

"Is Riker's closed for business, Detective?"

"No, sir."

"Is it fully booked?"

"At Riker's Island there is always room for one more."

"Then why on earth would you wait until tomorrow morning?"

"I'm on my way to get him right now, Lieutenant."

McCusker gave a nod of commendation and Dawson turned to go. But then McCusker held up a hand.

"Wait a second."

Leaving the one hand in the air, McCusker telephoned his wife with the other to let her know that he would not be coming home for dinner. Then, for the first time in seven years, he rode along in the unmarked car in order to participate in the arrest. And though Timothy's apartment was in the neighborhood, and no one was in danger, Lieutenant McCusker instructed Detective Dawson to sound the siren, which in turn blared with such a sense of purpose that even from five blocks away it could be heard in an eighth-floor apartment.

Oh, Timothy.

At long last, here comes your experience.

Hasta Luego

I HAD NOTICED SMITTY thirty minutes before we met. You couldn't help but notice him. We were both standing in the customer service line at LaGuardia Airport on a Friday at five in late December. At 4:30, the monitor at my gate had shown four flights delayed. Fifteen minutes later, it showed fifteen—including my 5:35 to National. According to the agent at the desk, the delays were due to weather. You wouldn't know it from looking out the window, but she assured me an unexpected shift in the prevailing winds was sending a Great Lakes snowstorm directly toward Manhattan at the speed of forty miles an hour.

Whatever the cause, I had learned long ago that when the delay count on an airport monitor increases from four to fifteen flights in as many minutes, you're at the beginning of an escalating disaster. Additional delays were sure to be announced, followed by cancellations. Lines at the gates would start to grow, all populated by disappointed travelers seeking to rebook themselves on the next available flights; and as the next available flights moved further and further into the future, often entailing onerous connections, the customers would become increasingly testy, the agents increasingly exhausted, and one's options increasingly unappealing.

So, as soon as the delays began to light up, I abandoned the gate. I jogged back through the terminal to the customer service center, where the airline was sure to be staffing up with their best approximation of a crisis management team. By the time I got there, I was seventh in line, with two customer service agents manning eight available spaces. Ten minutes later, with a touch of grim satisfaction, I noted that the line behind me was as long as it was in front of me. The race to the bottom had begun.

EMOTIONAL CONTAGION IS A term coined by behavioral scientists for a fairly universal aspect of human nature—that we tend to mirror the mood signals of others. Thus, when someone smiles at us, we are likely to smile in response, which in turn makes us feel a little more positively about them and our circumstances in general. In this manner, laughter will tend to prompt laughter, anger will prompt anger, and tears will prompt tears. From an evolutionary standpoint, the emotional contagion is an important trait. It's what allows a mother to comfort a child so effectively. It's also what allows us to immediately adjust our demeanor when suddenly encountering friend or foe in the wild.

Well, with an incoming snowstorm on a Friday night just six days before Christmas, you can imagine how the emotional contagion was working its magic at LaGuardia. The professional commuting class were just trying to get home for the weekend as usual, but many travelers, laden with gifts, were on their way to spend the holidays with their families. Many more were headed to warmer climates for a vacation that would cost five hundred dollars a day whether they showed up or not. People were variously tired, frustrated, or furious, and all the related indicators—the audible sighs, the eye rolling, the muttered profanities— were being picked up and mirrored back by everyone.

That is, nearly everyone.

In the midst of all this madness, all this perfectly understandable ill temper, the man standing five people in front of me emanated an unmistakable sense of goodwill. Six foot four and two hundred and fifty pounds, dressed in a loose tan suit two seasons out of season, he wore the smile of someone who was about to see his favorite Broadway musical from the best seats in the house. He seemed to have a gentleness that belied his size. As I watched, he turned and lowered his head in order to say something to the older couple behind him, who were each holding long rectangular boxes wrapped in the spirit of the season. When the couple began to laugh, he adopted a look of surprise, as if he hadn't realized that what he'd said would be funny; but then he started laughing, which prompted the woman in front of him to start laughing too.

Immediately in front of me were two young Wall Street types holding matching Nokias to their ears. As they both repeated instructions to their personal assistants in tones of belabored patience, a third came up saying he'd gotten through to Carey Limousine. The way things were going, he figured they could get to Boston faster by car than plane. Carey had a driver who could be there in fifteen minutes. Were they in or were they out?

They were in. And I found myself two slots closer to the service desk.

As my curiosity had been piqued by the gentle giant, I was a little disappointed when one of the agents waved at him and called "Next." But true to form, he turned to the older couple between us and encouraged them to go ahead.

"I'm in no rush," he said. As the old couple walked to the counter, he smiled and leaned his head toward me. "Fire trucks."

"Fire trucks?"

He pointed to the long rectangular packages. "For their grandsons in Des Moines. They're identical twins!" He began to shake his head in appreciation, then stopped as if struck by a sudden thought. "Do you think they're identical fire trucks?"

In spite of myself, I smiled.

"That *would* give them less reason to fight."

"Exactly," he agreed. "On Christmas morning, there's such a thin line between elation and disappointment. Do you have kids?"

"No."

"Ah," he said, as if a little let down.

"But we're trying."

"Then you have something to look forward to!" He stuck out his hand. "I'm Smitty."

"Jerry."

"Nice to meet you, Jerry."

From a distance, I had observed that Smitty had a gentleness that belied his size. But standing next to him I realized the gentleness was probably *because of* his size. Towering over others in his bearlike way, he had learned to modify his posture, soften his voice, and add a bit of fumbling to his gestures in order to put others at ease. A panda in the body of a polar bear.

"Are you headed out or headed home?" he asked.

"Home. To Washington."

"D.C.?"

"Yes."

"Oh," he said a little wistfully, "that must be grand. What with the White House and the Jefferson Memorial and the Air and Space Museum."

"The Bureau of Engraving," I added.

"Right! Where they make all the money."

"Or most of it."

"Most of it?"

"The Federal Reserve opened a second printing facility in Texas."

"Making the same bills?"

"Except for the mark of origin."

Smitty seemed so intrigued by this little fact I found myself taking a $10 bill from my wallet to show him the little FW that indicated the bill had been engraved in Fort Worth.

"Fascinating!" Looking up from the bill, Smitty made eye contact with the man behind me. "Did you see this?" And he was about to show him the mark when the two agents called "Next" simultaneously. "It must be our lucky day," he said to me with a smile.

If only one agent had called out, I suspect Smitty would have let me go first, just as he had the older couple. In fact, he probably would have stood there all night long letting one weary traveler after another go past him.

By the time I finished rebooking my flight for the following morning (a middle seat in the thirtieth row, thank you very much), Smitty was gone. Noting the line now snaked out of the customer service bay and past the newsstand, I congratulated myself on my traveling savvy, only to realize a few minutes later that I had made a classic rookie mistake. For when I called the St. Regis on my Motorola and explained to the woman in reservations that having just spent three nights at the hotel, I needed a room for one more night, she explained to me that the hotel was fully booked. So was the Peninsula. And the Carlyle. While I had been fascinating myself with my analysis of human behavior, every hotel room in the city had been getting snatched up.

Snapping my phone shut, I was about to sigh, roll my eyes, and swear all at once, when the gentle giant appeared before me with his own Motorola to his ear. Pointing at the phone, he said, "I'm booking a room at the Grand Hyatt. Do you want one?"

The Grand Hyatt, I thought with a wince. Under normal circumstances, the answer would most certainly have been no. But these were far from normal circumstances.

"That would be great," I said.

He held up a finger. "Yes, Janice. That's Smith. S-M-I-T-H. But before you go, can I trouble you to book a second room? That's right, a second room. Fantastic. It's under Jerry. Jerry . . ." He looked to me.

"Brooks," I said, resisting the temptation to spell it.

"Brooks. Terrific. See you soon!" Putting away his phone, Smitty gave me a smile of satisfaction. "Now we can share a cab!"

And so we did, as the snowflakes began to fall. Only when we were exiting the Midtown Tunnel did it occur to me that Smitty didn't have a bag.

"You're traveling light," I observed.

"What's that? Oh. Yes. I flew in from Chicago this morning just for the day. I didn't think I was going to need anything."

He didn't say why he had come to New York for the day. I guessed it was to see the Empire State Building and the Statue of Liberty and the Brooklyn Bridge. I considered mentioning that the Federal Reserve had a facility near Wall Street.

Taking out his phone, Smitty called his wife and left a message that his flight had been canceled, that he'd be home the next day, and that he missed her already.

Right! I thought to myself, taking out my phone to leave a similar message with a similar sentiment.

"Here we are," exclaimed Smitty, as we pulled up to the front of the hotel. "One of my favorite spots in the city. And don't worry. Berenice— the customer service agent at Delta—assured me the Grand Hyatt would accept their voucher."

"Voucher?"

"You didn't get a voucher?" he asked with a mix of surprise and concern.

"No," I said, "but that's all right. My firm will pick up the tab."

Which was true. Although I couldn't help feeling a little gypped. I would have cursed my customer service agent under my breath, if I had bothered to learn his name.

AFTER SMITTY AND I HAD checked in and taken the elevator to the fifth floor, I let myself into my room and, despite its shortcomings, issued a sigh of relief.

If open-ended delays in a crowded airport represent a circle of Hell even Dante couldn't have imagined, having your flight home canceled at a reasonable hour can be something of a gift. After spending three days in the city, rushing from meeting to meeting, attending interminable dinners with interminable clients, what you're probably heading home to are the compromises of marriage. These will govern when, what, and how you eat. They'll govern when, what, and how you watch. So, the canceled flight can create something of a temporal oasis—a twenty-four-hour period in which no concessions need be made to anyone.

My plan was to shower, then head downstairs for a rye Manhattan and a burger with the works. After dinner, I'd order a glass of the most expensive Cabernet on offer, take it back to my room, and watch two episodes of *Law & Order*. Maybe three.

Dropping my bag on the bed, I went through my normal arrival routine.

First, I checked the digital clock on the bedside table to make sure the alarm hadn't been left on by the previous occupant. There is nothing worse when traveling than being woken at 4:00 a.m. by someone else's alarm. And trust me, if the alarm goes off, it will be at something like 4:00 a.m., because it was inevitably set by some poor bastard heading home to Wichita by way of Atlanta.

Next, I gathered up the pamphlets, brochures, and local magazines scattered about the room and dumped them in a drawer. Because even in a nice hotel, all that printed matter can make you feel like you've taken up residence in the waiting room of your dentist's office.

The one piece of printed matter I don't stash is the narrow card on which you can order your breakfast for a specified hour by hanging it on your doorknob before going to bed. For while I refuse to order room service for dinner (since it tends to arrive cold and congealed), I always order it for breakfast. The knock on the door by a man bearing coffee is a much better way to wake up than the bleating of a digital alarm. Besides, when you walk into a hotel restaurant at eight in the morning and take your seat under the deplorable lighting, you're likely to realize that everyone in the room—regardless of gender—looks exactly like you. Dressed in dark suits, you're all off to the same sort of meeting where you'll say the same sort of things to the same sort of people for the same sort of reasons. It's a realization that is likely to ruin your day. Better to celebrate the illusion of your individuality over an egg sandwich in your room.

After hanging my suit in the closet, I took my Dopp kit from my bag and placed it on the bathroom counter with a touch of pride.

Yes, pride.

For the seasoned business traveler, every little example of efficiency is cause for self-satisfaction; and the well-packed Dopp kit is near the top of the list. Whenever I zip it open, I take pleasure in knowing that within its compact dimensions is everything I'll need. In addition to a collapsible toothbrush and two disposable razors are a travel-size shaving cream, travel-size toothpaste, travel-size deodorant, and travel-size bottle of Advil. There's also a styptic pencil, a Band-Aid, and two safety pins. When I get home, I restock the kit as needed and return it to the upper shelf of my closet, where it sits ready for action like the backpack of a Navy SEAL.

Twenty minutes later, showered, dressed, and ready for my Manhattan, I went to the elevator bank—and there was Smitty.

"Jerry!" he exclaimed, as if we were old friends who hadn't seen each other in years.

"Smitty," I replied.

"I was just heading downstairs for a burger. Want to join me?"

"Why not."

When we stepped onto the elevator we both reached for the keypad.

"Go ahead," I said.

He pushed the *L* and down we went.

I noticed he suddenly had a big smile on his face. I figured it was thanks to the Muzak Christmas carol playing overhead. But it wasn't. It was due to a sentimental memory.

"I grew up in a small town in western Massachusetts," he explained, "where the tallest building was three stories high. But once or twice a year, we'd drive to Boston to visit our grandmother, who lived in a ten-story apartment building. One of the most exciting aspects of the trip was the elevator ride. My brother and I would fight over who got to press the button.

"Elevators," he concluded with a smile.

"There wouldn't be a Manhattan without them," I observed.

He looked at me as if startled. Then quite seriously, he said: "They don't get the credit they deserve."

UNSURPRISINGLY, THE GRAND HYATT'S restaurant looked tired, as did the décor, the diners, and the food.

"How about we eat at the bar?" I suggested.

Smitty, who was already on a first-name basis with the hostess, gave me a look of disappointment.

"Come on," I prodded. "We're just having a burger. Where better to burger than at a bar. Besides: You got to push the button on the elevator."

As it was 7:30, the bar was already busy, but we lucked out and got the last two stools. When we sat, Smitty took his phone from his pocket and set it on the bar.

"I don't want to miss my wife, if she calls," he explained.

"Me neither," I said, following suit.

When the bartender finally got to us, we ordered two burgers (with the works).

"Anything to drink?"

"A rye Manhattan straight up," I said.

Smitty, whose gaze was moving back and forth across the wall of backlit bottles, indicated he wasn't ready to choose.

It struck me as we waited that he was a little out of sorts, but it was probably just hypoglycemia, because once our burgers were in front of us, his spirits revived. I could tell because he was back to asking questions.

"What do you do, Jerry? In Washington, I mean."

"Sell shovels," I answered wryly.

"Really?!"

"No. I'm a strategy consultant."

"For the military?"

"For political candidates. We advise them on demographics, registration drives, message tailoring. In essence we help build their campaigns."

"Campaigns for what?"

"The House. The Senate. The presidency."

"No kidding?"

"No kidding."

"For Democrats or Republicans?"

"Both. That's what I meant about selling shovels."

Smitty looked perplexed for a moment, then gave a smile of comprehension. "Like selling shovels in a snowstorm."

"We usually say in a gold rush, but snowstorm works. What about you, Smitty? What do you do?"

"I work for my father-in-law," he said, smiling a little apologetically. "He has a manufacturing company. I was in town today for a meeting of the regional sales reps. You know, to discuss our game plan for the coming year."

"What does the company manufacture?"

"Gidgets."

"What's a gidget?"

"Something between a gadget and a widget."

"Ah," I said with a smile. "Something small but necessary."

"Oh, yes. *Very* necessary. Practically essential."

We both took a bite of our burgers.

"Have you always been in gidgets?" I asked.

"No. I used to be in national accounts at NBC. Selling ad time for

ers, per se, but who, upon occasion, in the spirit of the season, could be convinced to have a glass of sherry. Or two.

Smitty was certainly a winning sort, and as I watched him, I began to understand why. He had this endearing rhythm of interaction whenever he met someone new. It began with a question, followed by an expression of surprise, a wistful admission, then a vow—all capped off by a toast.

"Where are you from?" he would ask, or "Where are you headed?"

"You don't say!"

"I wish I could go there one day . . ."

"I *will* go there one day!"

"To X—!"

That sequence of conversation isn't so uncommon, you might protest. Maybe not.

But what made Smitty's approach so unusual was that he took each step in the sequence so sincerely. He was genuinely curious about where you were from or where you were headed. He was genuinely surprised by some aspect of your answer. He was genuinely wistful, wishing that he too had been where you'd been. And when he vowed to go there, everyone seemed to share in his excitement. It was such a beautiful thing to observe, I found myself resolving for New Year's to practice the very same genuineness in all my dealings with others. Never mind that practicing genuineness is something of a contradiction in terms.

By nine o'clock, thanks to Smitty, we all knew where we were coming from and headed to. We all knew our vacations and vocations, and at least two branches of our family tree. Which was no small achievement, given that there were now more than fifty people around the bar.

At some point, Smitty got hold of the remote control for the television that was mounted on the wall. When he switched away from the Rangers game, I thought the two loyal fans (with the jerseys to prove it) were going to carry him outside and throw him in a snowbank. Before they got the chance, Smitty stopped advancing the channels with a shout of "Linus!"

Sure enough, there on the screen was Linus van Pelt in the company of a clearly dispirited Charlie Brown. After Charlie throws up his hands in exasperation, Linus says something reassuring, then advances to center stage, dragging his blanket behind him.

"Quiet everybody!" shouted Smitty. "Quiet!"

Pointing the remote at the screen, Smitty turned up the volume to the maximum just in time for us to hear Linus reciting. "Fear not: for, behold, I bring you tidings of great joy, which shall be to all people. For unto you is born this day in the city of David a Savior, which is Christ the Lord. And this shall be a sign unto you: Ye shall find the babe wrapped in swaddling clothes, lying in a manger. And suddenly there was with the angel a multitude of the heavenly host praising God, and saying, Glory to God in the highest, and on earth peace, good will toward men."

When the music of the Vince Guaraldi Trio resumed and everyone began patting each other on the back, as if patting on the back was still the sort of thing that people did, in the warm haze of my two Manhattans and three tequila shots, it struck me that Smitty was *our* Linus van Pelt, entering center stage, reciting chapter and verse so that we would remember the true meaning of the season, and so on.

As the shared celebration subsided, Albert and Alice made their way to where we were standing. They had an early flight and were packing it in, but they wanted to tell Smitty what a pleasure it had been to meet him, a message that Smitty echoed twofold.

Then Albert tipped his hat and said: "*Hasta luego.*"

"What does that mean?" asked Smitty, with wide-open eyes and a slight slur to his speech.

"Until next time."

"Until Mex time?"

When we all laughed, Smitty looked surprised.

"Until *then*," I explained to him. "As in, *until we meet again*."

Smitty nodded his head in appreciation of the sentiment, and you could tell his appreciation was sincere. For while such commonly used phrases don't always align with a person's innermost feelings, this one was tailor made for him.

AT AROUND ELEVEN, I told Smitty I was packing it in too. He said he wanted to stay for one more drink, so we agreed to meet in the lobby at 7:30 and I weaved my way into an elevator. After pushing the button for the fifth floor, I lit up every button from six to sixteen with a great sense of satisfaction, only to feel a little sheepish when an old woman—who happened to look a lot like my first-grade teacher, Mrs. Peterson— stepped on the elevator, extended a finger toward the button for the fifteenth floor, then frowned.

We rode to the fifth floor in an uncomfortable silence.

"Happy Holidays?" I asked, when I was stepping off the elevator. She responded by pushing the button that promises to close the doors more quickly.

Once in my room, I collapsed on the bed. For the first time since college, I was tempted to sleep in my clothes. If only I'd had the foresight to turn off the overhead light.

Outside, the snow continued to fall, but five stories below I could hear the metallic scrape of the city's plows beginning to clear the pavement. *Selling shovels in a snowstorm*, I thought. It was an apt revision. Because the milieu I operated in was definitely more like a blizzard than a gold rush, complete with plummeting temperatures, limited visibility, and dangerous driving conditions. The only difference was that the shovels we sold weren't for clearing the snow, they were for piling it on.

With that sorry admission, I sat up, gave my head a rub, and readied myself for the trip to the bathroom, when my telephone buzzed, no doubt with a good-night call from my wife.

Putting the phone to my ear, I answered: "1-800-Dial-a-Date. How may I help you?"

But there was silence.

"Who is this?" asked a woman—who wasn't my wife—in a tone more accusatory than confused.

"Who is *this*?" I asked back.

"This is Jennifer. Where's Creighton?"

Jennifer had one of those insistent voices that tends to accompany women with petite frames. It was their way of ensuring they weren't too readily dismissed on account of their size, and they rarely were. I didn't know this Creighton from Adam, but I was already feeling sorry for the guy.

"Lady," I said, "you've got the wrong number."

"I do not have the wrong number."

To make my point, I rattled off mine, concluding smugly, "*That's* what you've dialed."

"But I didn't dial," she said. "I used the number saved on my phone."

For a few seconds, I stared out the window at the snowfall. Then I put my free hand over my eyes.

"Your husband's last name wouldn't happen to be Smith . . . ?"

"Of course it would."

"I'm sorry," I said, sitting a little more upright. "Your husband and I were at the airport together. We shared a cab to the hotel. I must have picked up his phone by mistake."

"That's fine. Just let me speak to him."

"I'm in my room and he's still at the bar, but I'll bring him the phone right now."

As I rose from the bed there was a moment of silence on the other end of the line.

"He's in the bar . . . ?"

"I left him there just a few minutes ago."

"The bar of the hotel."

"That's right."

. . .

"What did you say your name was?"

I hadn't said what my name was.

"It's Jerry."

"Okay. Listen to me, Jerry. I need you to go downstairs, find Creighton, and bring him back to his room. Do you understand?"

I did not understand and said so.

"My husband is an alcoholic, Jerry. You've got to go downstairs and get him out of that bar."

A little taken aback, and mindful of Smitty's size, I said I wasn't so sure I could get him out of the bar.

She was silent for a moment. When she spoke again, it was with a sense of growing realization.

"Were you drinking with him, Jerry?"

I didn't answer.

"Of course you were. I can hear it in your voice. How many drinks did you have together?"

I didn't answer that either.

"Oh, fuck. You've got to be kidding me. You have got to be fucking kidding me. He's been sober for more than a year, Jerry. Sober for more than a year. Do you have even the slightest idea what that means?"

"Look," I said, feeling a little defensive, "for the record, I don't even know your husband. I just met him a few hours ago."

"Oh, please. Don't give me any of that this-isn't-my-problem bullshit! Because *for the record*, Jerry, this is definitely your problem."

I could feel my face growing flush with anger. Or embarrassment. Or guilt. Either way, I was through talking to this woman.

"I'm going to bring your husband his phone," I said, "and I'll tell him that he needs to call you. But I'm hanging up now."

"What's that?" she demanded. "Don't you hang up on me, Jerry. Don't you dare hang up on me!"

"I'm hanging up now," I said again and began taking the phone away from my ear. But on the other end of the line I could hear a choking sound, as if she suddenly couldn't breathe. It took me a moment to realize she had begun to cry.

"Don't hang up on me," she finally said through her tears, but this time in supplication. "Don't hang up on me, Jerry. For the love of God."

. . .

"I'm not hanging up on you."

I could hear her trying to regain her composure, then raw with emotion she continued: "I'm sorry I raised my voice at you, Jerry. I know it's not your problem. But what do you expect me to do? I'm a thousand miles away. Our girls are asleep in their beds. What do you expect me to do?"

"All right," I said. "I'll get him. Okay? I'll go and get him right now."

"Okay," she said, her voice softening with some mixture of gratitude and relief. Then ever so slightly, it hardened again when she added: "Here's what you need to do."

BY THE TIME I got downstairs, the crowd at the bar had shrunk to thirty people. Smitty was talking to two glassy-eyed young women in skirt suits.

"Jerry!" he said with a smile. "You're back."

"Yeah. Can I talk to you a second?"

"Sure."

As Smitty followed me away from the bar, I tried to figure out what I was going to say. I knew I didn't want to get into a discussion about his drinking or his wife. One thing I had going for me was his insistence earlier that we share a cab to the airport. I opted for an appeal to his common sense.

"Listen," I began, "it occurred to me upstairs that it's going to be a madhouse at the airport tomorrow. There's bound to be unusually long lines at security. And bad traffic because of the road conditions. It's probably a good idea if we get an earlier start. Like around six thirty."

As Smitty was listening to me, he nodded his head amiably.

"Sounds like a plan, Jerry."

"So, maybe we should call it a night."

"Terrific. Let me just finish my conversation with these young ladies. I'll be right behind you."

All told, I hadn't been upstairs for more than twenty minutes, but I could hear from Smitty's voice that he'd grown drunker in the interim. Or maybe I was sobering up.

"The thing is, Smitty, I picked up your phone by mistake, and while I was upstairs . . . your wife called."

As he took in this piece of information, I could see the various aspects of his demeanor—his childlike curiosity, his affable smile, his pandalike posture—undergo the slightest transformation.

"I'll give her a call," he assured me after a moment, then began to turn away.

Grabbing him by the arm, I turned him back.

"Smitty—" I said.

But suddenly there were two men at our side. It was the Rangers fans, only now they looked like they were going to throw me in a snowbank.

"Is he bothering you?" one asked Smitty while the other kept a watchful eye on me.

For a moment, I was afraid Smitty was going to say yes. He certainly looked like he was considering it. Instead, he confirmed I wasn't bothering him and made the necessary introductions. "Sean, Kevin, this is Jerry. Jerry, Sean and Kevin."

As Sean and Kevin nodded at me with a slightly reduced hostility, Smitty seemed to be weighing his next move.

"You know what, gentlemen?" he said to the two of them. "Jerry and I have an early start, so we're going to call it a night. It was a pleasure meeting you both!"

He shook hands with them, then accompanied me to the elevator, not bothering to bid anyone else good night. When we reached his room, I told him I'd meet him in the lobby at 6:30. As he was about to disappear behind the door, I remembered to switch back our phones.

"Jerry," he said, "you're the salt of the earth."

When I got back to my room, I sat on the bed and breathed a sigh of relief. Then the telephone rang.

It was an out-of-state number. I answered, a little wary.

"Hello . . . ?"

"Are you with him?"

It was Smitty's wife.

"How did you get this number?"

"You gave it to me, Jerry."

Thinking back, I remembered rattling off my number to make a point. But that had been in a matter of seconds. How could she possibly have remembered it?

She must have been reading my mind, because she said, "It took me four tries to get it right."

I could just imagine the four strangers answering their phones at this inconvenient hour only to find insistent Jennifer on the other end of the line. They wouldn't have been any more polite than I had been, and she wouldn't have been any more deterred.

"Everything's all right," I assured her. "He's back in his room."

"Then why isn't he answering his phone?"

"I don't know. Maybe he's taking a shower. But we're meeting first thing in the morning and heading to the airport together."

"Okay. But you got his shoes, right?"

. . .

"Jerry. I told you to take his shoes."

I shook my head for no one's benefit. Not even my own.

"I'm not going to take another man's shoes," I said.

She was quiet for a moment.

"You need to go back to his room, Jerry. You need to go back and make sure he's there. But don't hang up. Just walk to his room right now and knock on the door while I'm still on the line."

I hadn't known Smitty's wife for very long, but I already understood that to argue with her was going to take more energy than to do what she asked. So I went down the hall and knocked on the door with my phone to my ear.

"Smitty?" I called. "Smitty?"

"What's happening?" she said. "Did he answer?"

"I think he's asleep."

She let out a sigh.

"He's not asleep, Jerry. He's in the bar. You need to go back to the bar."

"I'm not going back to the bar."

"You've come this far, Jerry. Don't fold on me now."

"I'm not folding," I said in exasperation. "Look. I understand your husband has some kind of history. But I've been with him for most of the night, and all I can tell you is that he has been delightful. There's just no other word for it."

"Not all drunks become mean, Jerry. They don't all become violent. Some become quiet. Others become the life of the party. But when they're drinking, there's one thing they all become. And that's liars. Every last one of them."

Jennifer took a deep breath. I could tell she was readying herself for some final plea, some final line of argument. I readied myself for it too. When she spoke it was in a tone of shared acceptance, a recognition that she and I couldn't change what had happened, but nor could we avoid what must be done.

"Look, I get it. You got stuck at an airport and met a big friendly guy and ended up at a bar. You didn't know there was anything wrong. How could you? But you've let the genie out of the bottle, Jerry. Not the wish-giving genie. The lying genie. And now, you've got to go downstairs, grab him by the tail, and stuff him back in the bottle."

SMITTY WAS IN THE BAR. There were only ten people now, and thanks be to God, the Rangers fans weren't among them. Smitty was talking to one of the glassy-eyed young women from before.

Dressed in a navy skirt suit she looked like she was two years out of law school, working in a large firm with every expectation of making junior partner in three years. That may seem like a lot to surmise from fifty feet, but when you work in D.C., spotting ambitious young lawyers is like spotting aspiring actresses in Hollywood.

When Smitty saw me, he turned a little to the side, as if an oblique angle would somehow disguise his bearlike frame. Even he seemed to recognize the futility of the gesture, because a moment later he turned back in my direction, acted pleasantly surprised, and waved me over.

"Jerry! Come over here. I want you to meet somebody."

On the bar were two empty shot glasses. I crossed my fingers that they were someone else's. They weren't.

"You've got to hear this shtory, Jerry. Am I telling you!"

"Some other time, Smitty. Right now, we've got to go."

"We will be going. For certainly. But first—"

I held up my phone.

"If you don't come with me, I'm calling your wife."

Now it was the young woman who was turning her back to me. Then she was quietly sliding down the bar. She suddenly seemed to have realized that for a young attorney with her heart set on making partner, nothing good could come from getting drunk with a married man in a hotel lobby in midtown. It was a valuable lesson learned cheaply.

"Jerry, Jerry," he said with a smile, "you don't have to do that." It was a nice big Smitty smile, but it lacked the sincerity displayed earlier in the evening. It was a smile that would have been more at home on the face of a political candidate. Or a campaign strategist.

I flipped open my phone.

"All right, all right. I'm coming, I'm coming."

He turned to the young woman to explain, no doubt, that we were getting an early start, and was startled to find her gone. We made our second trip across the lobby and up in the elevator, our second trip to his room. But this time, when he opened the door, I followed him in.

"Why don't you give me your extra key card," I said, as he sat on his bed. "In case you oversleep."

When I held out my hand, he pointed to the credenza. I slipped the card in my pocket.

"Now give me your shoes."

At such a demand, a normal person would have looked outraged, indignant, angry. I certainly would have. He pouted. But he pulled off his shoes and tossed them on the floor in my general direction. I picked them up.

"Six thirty," I reminded him.

He fell back on his bed and stared at the ceiling, just like I had an hour before. As I let myself out, I wondered if he would be weighing the moral ambiguities of trafficking in gidgets.

I FORGOT TO PUT the breakfast card on the doorknob.

When I woke and saw it was 6:15, I had one blissful moment of forgetting, then sat bolt upright, feeling the unpleasant surge of adrenaline that comes when one is late and can't afford to be. Throwing back the covers, I went to the bathroom and jumped in and out of the shower. With my back still wet, I dressed in yesterday's clothes, zipped up my bag, and headed out the door.

By 6:28 I was standing in Smitty's room.

He wasn't far from where I'd left him—curled up on the bottom of the bed in his boxer shorts. Impressively, he had put his suit pants and jacket on a hanger, but they'd still wound up on the floor, as if he'd aimed for the hanging rod and missed.

I shook him awake. "Come on. We've got to go."

He sat up and rubbed his eyes, looking around the room. "I need a shower."

He was right that he needed a shower. The whole room needed a shower.

"We haven't got time. Douse your head and put on your clothes."

"All right, all right," he said. But then he gestured to his near nudity. "At least you could give me a little privacy."

"You've got two minutes," I said, as I went into the hall.

It took him four. However bad I looked, he looked worse, his hair uncombed, his shirt untucked, his face a pale shade of green. In the confines of the elevator I could smell the vapors of tequila that were still seeping through his pores, mixing with the odor of his stale breath.

Which made me think of my own unbrushed teeth. . . .

"Shit!"

"What?"

In my rush, I'd left my Dopp kit in the bathroom.

"It's nothing," I said, obviously not meaning it.

He didn't press me. From experience, he knew that whatever had gone wrong would be blamed on him, and he would probably deserve it.

As we stepped off the elevator, he said, "Listen, Jerry, I think I'd better rebook my flight for a little later in the day. I just don't feel up to it right now."

"Don't give me any of that you're-not-up-to-it bullshit, Smitty."

Even as I said this, I realized I was using his wife's phrasing. He must have recognized it too, because it shut him up. Taking him by the elbow, I steered him halfway across the lobby, then stopped and looked back at the elevators.

"Did you forget something?" he asked.

I pointed to a chair.

"Sit here. I'll be right back."

"Sure thing," he said accommodatingly.

A little too accommodatingly.

"Give me your shoes," I said.

"What?"

"You heard me."

I snapped my fingers at him.

This time Smitty summoned up a look of indignation, but only for a moment. Then his shoulders drooped. When he leaned forward to remove his shoes, I saw he wasn't wearing socks.

All the better, I thought, as I headed back to the elevator bank.

When the elevator door opened, there was a woman with a roller bag waiting to get off. It was Mrs. Peterson's doppelgänger. We both registered a look of surprise, then she punched every button on the panel.

When I finally got to the fifth floor, I ran down the hall and slipped my key card in the slot. Instead of making a satisfying whirr, the electronic lock blinked red. I rubbed the card on my pants and tried again with the same result. "Shit," I said. Then I realized it must be Smitty's card. Patting all my pockets, I found mine and let myself in.

I was in the bathroom reaching for the Dopp kit when my telephone buzzed.

DOWNSTAIRS, I WAS RELIEVED to find Smitty where I'd left him.

"Here," I said, handing him his shoes. As I did so, I practically had to hold my breath because of the boozy aroma emanating from his person. Only this time, it had a hint of . . . whiskey?

Looking over my shoulder, I confirmed the lobby bar was closed—as well it should be in accordance with local blue laws, Judeo-Christian morality, and common sense.

Turning back to Smitty, I said, "Empty your pockets."

He gave me his perplexed look.

After we stared at each other for a second, I lunged forward. He tried to fend me off, but was too late. I already had my hands in the pockets of his suit coat. Stuffed into them, I found his socks and two little plastic bottles—taken, no doubt, from the minibar while I was giving Smitty his moment of "privacy." Dropping the socks in his lap, I held up the unopened bottle of Absolut in one hand and the empty bottle of Jack Daniel's in the other.

"You should have drunk the vodka first," I sneered. "It doesn't smell so much."

"That wasn't a very nice thing to say."

"I'm not feeling very nice. Put on your shoes."

In the time it had taken for me to go upstairs, a line of four customers had formed for the two available stations at the checkout desk. Worse, a glance across the lobby revealed a line of six people waiting for taxis outside.

I led the freshly shod Smitty to the end of the checkout line, told him to stay put, then went outside. Approaching the doorman, I slipped him ten bucks and told him there was another ten behind it, if a cab was waiting for me once I'd paid my bill.

Inside, some junior executive had taken his place at the end of the line. He scowled when I stepped in front of him to join Smitty.

"We're together," I said.

While we waited, Smitty didn't ask the two women in front of us where they were headed or where they were from. He wasn't asking anybody anything, which suited me just fine. When the two women finished paying their bills, the two desk clerks said "Next" simultaneously.

"Another lucky day," I said.

As I pushed Smitty toward one clerk and headed for the other, the junior executive shouted, "I thought you were together."

We had been at the hotel for one night, so I figured the checkout process would only take a minute or two, then we'd be on our way. But once I'd paid my bill and collected the receipt for the boys in accounting, Smitty was still at the desk; only now he and his clerk had been joined by a man whose age, posture, and expression all suggested management. The manager began explaining something to Smitty, who in turn explained something back. Then all three men looked at me.

Next thing I knew, the clerk was helping a new customer, Smitty was standing off to the side scuffing the carpet with his shoe, and I was at a corner of the desk speaking to the manager, who was giving off a distinctly European vibe, despite hailing from somewhere closer to Akron, Ohio.

"I gather you are traveling with Mr. Smith," he said.

"Not really."

"Oh? But I understood that your reservations were made at the same time."

"Yes," I conceded. "That's true."

"Ah."

"Look, what's the problem?"

"It seems that Mr. Smith's bill exceeds the limit on his credit card."

I think I gaped. The room rate was only two hundred bucks a night. How could Smitty's credit card have maxed out at two hundred bucks? But in a flash, I knew. Jennifer had set a low limit on his card, just in case. Another feature of Smitty 3.0.

"All right," I said. "I'll cover his room."

"Actually, Mr. Smith's room is already covered. By his hotel voucher. It's the bill for the incidentals that needs to be satisfied."

"Then I'll satisfy that."

"Excellent."

I took my personal card out from behind my corporate card and handed it to the manager as he slid the bill across the counter.

"Wait!" I exclaimed, pointing at the tally. "A thousand dollars of incidentals!"

"So it seems."

"How is that possible?"

"I gather you and Mr. Smith hosted last night's festivities."

It was my turn to look perplexed.

Dropping his European demeanor, the manager said flatly: "You bought drinks at the bar."

"For whom?"

"For everybody."

I glanced at Smitty. He glanced at his shoes.

"It could have been worse," observed the manager, pointing to the fifty-dollar credit at the bottom of the bill.

"What's that?"

"Mr. Smith's food and beverage voucher."

In the early hours of the morning, the blizzard had moved on to New England, leaving the New York City skies unusually brisk and blue: a perfect day for flying. When I made eye contact with the doorman, he tilted his head to his left and we followed him past the waiting guests to a cab that was just pulling up.

"There's a line," said Smitty.

"No kidding," I replied.

Shoving Smitty in the cab, I gave the doorman his promised bonus, and told the driver we were headed for LaGuardia. As he pulled forward, everyone in the line gave me a withering look, except for Mrs. Peterson. She gave me the finger.

ONCE AT LAGUARDIA, WE picked up our boarding passes (Smitty had been given a seat in first class, naturally) and went through security without incident. When we came to the fork in the terminal that led one way to my gate and the other way to his, he stuck out his hand. I shook my head.

"I'll see you all the way."

"That's not necessary."

"It's very necessary. Practically essential."

Earlier that morning, when my phone had buzzed in the bathroom, I nearly hadn't answered it. But when I had reached for my Dopp kit, I'd found my unshaven face staring back at me from the mirror, daring me to let the call go to voice mail. I took the phone from my pocket and flipped it open.

Yes, Smitty was up, I'd said. Yes, we were ready to go. Yes, I would ride with him to the airport, and yes, I'd see him to his gate.

"Not to his gate, Jerry. Onto the plane. You've got to get him onto the plane. I'm going to be waiting right there for him when he disembarks."

They won't let her through security without a boarding pass, I thought to myself. Reading my mind again, she said: "I've bought a ticket so they'll let me through security."

I shook my head. Smitty's flight was scheduled to leave at 9:00 and mine at 9:15. That gave me barely enough time to put Smitty on his plane and still get back to my gate. Barely enough, but enough.

"Okay," I said. "I'll see him on the plane."

"Promise me."

. . .

"I promise."

But when we reached Smitty's gate, the screen above the check-in desk said that Smitty's flight was delayed by forty minutes. Dragging Smitty behind me, I went back into the hallway to get a look at the big monitor, fearing that the last twenty-four hours was about to repeat itself. But other than Smitty's flight to Chicago, every single flight on the screen showed an on-time departure—including the 9:15 to National. Which meant if I saw Smitty onto his plane, I was going to miss mine.

Every day, there are plenty of flights between New York and D.C. So many, I had often changed from one flight to another at the very last minute. But given yesterday's cancellations, it wasn't going to be so easy to switch. All the morning's flights were sure to be full and most of the afternoon's. If I gave up my seat on the 9:15, who knew when I would finally get out of LaGuardia?

I led Smitty back into the gate area and sat down beside him. As we waited, I watched the clock over the check-in desk and he watched the carpet. At quarter to nine, I turned to him and said, "I've got to go to my gate. . . ."

He looked up with a new alertness.

"But here's the thing, Smitty. I promised Jennifer I would see you onto your plane. So, I need you to promise me you're going to get on it."

"I promise," said Smitty, after a moment.

We looked each other in the eye. Then I got up and left. I left him in his chair without shaking his hand or saying goodbye. I jogged through the terminal back to the fork where I turned the acute angle and headed toward my gate with my shoulder bag banging against my hip. I arrived just in time to hear the last section of coach being called. Then my phone dinged to indicate a message had been received.

With a touch of dread, I took the phone from my pocket and opened it.

"I'm counting on you, Jerry," it read.

Then it dinged again with an addendum: "We're counting on you."

I didn't need italics to know where the emphasis was placed.

The desk agent announced the last call.

"Fuck," I said.

Then I jogged back toward Smitty's gate. When I turned the acute angle a second time, I began to run, glancing at all the restaurants, looking with a heightened sense of fatality for a bearish figure at the bar.

But Smitty was just where I'd left him.

Panting, I walked the final fifteen feet and dumped my bag on the floor before reclaiming the empty chair at his side. As I did so, he looked up in surprise, and I could see that in my absence, he'd been crying. The tears were still working their way down his cheeks.

"Jerry," he said with a mix of relief and anxiety, his voice and body trembling. "I want to go home."

"I know, Smitty."

Then he reached over and took my hand. Not simply to give it a squeeze, but to grip it. And he continued to grip it when the agent announced they were about to board and when she welcomed those with special needs and travelers with children. He continued to grip it until they called first class.

Again, we parted without saying goodbye. But before entering the gangway, Smitty turned. With his apologetic smile, he held up a hand and said, "*Hasta luego*, Jerry."

I held up my hand in return and said, "*Hasta luego*." Though what I was thinking to myself was: "*Hasta nunca*."

And yet, when Smitty disappeared down the gangway, I stayed at the gate and watched each successive group board. I watched the desk agent run whatever report it is they run on their dot-matrix printers. I watched her shut the door to the gangway. I watched the plane pull back from the gate and taxi out toward the runways under the unusually brisk and blue sky. Only when the plane had rolled out of sight did I get up and make my way to customer service.

You might imagine that as I walked through the terminal passing the flights to Boston and Dallas and Nashville I was thinking about Smitty. Thinking about what would happen to him when he arrived in Chicago, or in the years ahead. But I wasn't thinking about Smitty. What I was thinking about was his wife.

We all have our flaws. Some large and some small. Some that come and go, others that persist. I, for one, don't remember birthdays. I'm not always welcoming to perfectly nice people whom I'm meeting for the first time. When inconvenienced, even slightly, I can't resist the temptation to let the person who's inconvenienced me know that I've been inconvenienced. And I tend to allow my priorities to overshadow the priorities of others, even of those I love. Perhaps, especially of those I love.

As I stood there in the customer service line thinking of all that had just transpired, what I found myself hoping, what I found myself almost praying for, was that despite all my flaws, when the time came, as it surely would, my wife would be willing to fight for me as hard as Jennifer had fought for her husband.

My wife, her name is Ellen.

I Will Survive

I t was a lovely Saturday afternoon in early May. Nell and I were just about to go to the farmers market with our canvas bags in hand when her mother, Peggy, called from the Upper East Side. I handed Nell the phone.

"Hey, Mom. What's up?"

"Can you come uptown?"

"When?"

"Now."

"*Right* now?"

"There's something I need to discuss with you."

Nell rolled her eyes for my benefit. The last time her mother had summoned her uptown because she had something she needed to discuss, it was to express her dissatisfaction with what Nell had worn to Ellie Houghton's engagement party at the Colony Club. (Too black, too short, too zippery.) A few months before that, it was to remind Nell of the importance of sending thank-you notes to aunts, even the ones who give you socks for your birthday.

Nell could have asked what was on her mother's mind, but there would have been no point. If Peggy had decided to tell you something in person, you weren't going to hear what it was until you were sitting face-to-face. And in the meantime, she'd be dwelling on it, becoming more dissatisfied, more convinced that some essential lesson of your upbringing had been carelessly disregarded. So, Nell and her sister had learned long ago that when Peggy had something to discuss, the sooner you discussed it the better.

"All right," said Nell, handing me her empty bag. "I'm on my way."

NELL'S MOTHER AND STEPFATHER, John, lived on Eighty-Third and Park in a grand building with two elevator banks and four doormen. The various rooms of their apartment were painted in colors so dark and rich they immediately suggested a sense of moral confidence—a sense of moral confidence that Nell and I apparently lacked, given that all the walls of our one-bedroom apartment were painted in eggshell or ivory.

Peggy received Nell at the door and led her into the kitchen, where she offered Nell a cup of tea. Nell should have known right then that something was out of the ordinary. Peggy generally shared her opinions about your life in her living room, and never over tea.

While on the subway, Nell had tried to anticipate what her mother was going to complain about. Number one on her list was the importance of having children while you were young. Peggy had been circling this topic for a year, by admiring young mothers with strollers whom she happened to pass on the street, or mentioning in an offhand way that the older sister of one of Nell's schoolmates was spending a small fortune at the fertility lab. Like any good attorney, Nell was tempted to prepare some rebuttals, but rebuttals never carried much weight with Peggy. So, once they were seated at the little table in the kitchen with their cups of tea in front of them, Nell simply braced herself.

"Is Jeremy well?" her mother began.

"He is."

"I'm glad to hear it. And he's still fact-making at that magazine?"

"It's fact-checking, Mom. At *Harper's*."

"Yes, of course."

Peggy was taking longer than usual to get to the point. She even poured herself a second cup of tea.

"Do you want some more?" she asked Nell.

"No thanks. I'm really more of a coffee person."

"Would you like me to make you some coffee?"

"That's not necessary."

"It wouldn't take me more than a moment."

"Mom, I'm fine! Now, what's this all about?"

Peggy set her cup down and straightened her posture.

"I think your stepfather is having an affair."

Nell let out a little laugh.

Peggy tightened her lips.

"I don't appreciate being laughed at."

"I'm sorry, Mom. I wasn't laughing at you. You just caught me by surprise. I mean, John isn't really the type. And what is he? Sixty-eight?"

"I don't see why that has anything to do with it."

"Okay. Why don't you tell me why you think he's having an affair."

Peggy took in a breath.

"For as long as I can remember, your stepfather has played squash on Saturday afternoons at the Union Club."

"Right."

"Well, two weeks ago, I opened the club's monthly mailing to check when the spring bridge tournament is going to be held. While reading through the calendar, I noticed the squash courts are scheduled to be reopened on the first of July—after a six-month renovation."

Nell sat back in her chair, a little unnerved.

"And he's been playing this spring?"

"Every Saturday. That's where he is now."

Nell said nothing for a moment, then shook her head.

"I'm sure there's a perfectly reasonable explanation, Mom. There must be a hundred squash courts in Manhattan. He's probably just been playing somewhere else."

"He's never mentioned he's been playing somewhere else."

"That doesn't mean he hasn't been."

"Or, it's one of those things when someone conveniently leaves something out."

"A lie of omission."

"Exactly."

"Have you approached him about it? Have you asked him where he's been going?"

"You can't ask your husband a question like that," Peggy said dismissively. Then she shifted in her chair. "That's why I called you."

"You want *me* to ask him?"

"Of course not. I want you to follow him."

"Follow him!"

"Yes. Follow him."

Peggy began talking with a little more urgency.

"I want you to find out what he's been doing all these Saturday afternoons. Where he's been going. Who he's been meeting. As you say, there may be a perfectly reasonable explanation. Or . . ."

From a pocket, Peggy produced a folded piece of paper. As Nell opened it, she could see it had been torn from the monthly mailing of some other private club. It was one of those pages that showcase the attendees of a recent event. In the center was a photograph of three women in brightly colored dresses with similarly coiffed hair. Peggy pointed to the sixty-year-old woman in the middle.

". . . He could be with her."

Nell took the page in hand.

"Who is she?"

Peggy turned away from her daughter to look at the stove. Having gathered herself, she turned back and laid a finger on the caption below the photograph. It indicated the woman in question was Lydia Spencer, chair of the garden committee.

"I think she's from Cleveland," said Peggy, as if it were a slur. "Or somewhere else in Ohio. I really couldn't say. But she's always had an eye for your stepfather, I can assure you of that. I suggest you be on the lookout for her."

Nell slowly put the page back on the table.

"Mom, I'm not going to be on the lookout for anyone, but if you want me to *talk* to John, I'll—"

"You are not to say a word to your stepfather about this! Not a single word. Do you understand me?"

Peggy's voice was shaking.

"Okay," said Nell, putting up her hands. "I won't say a word."

Peggy stared at Nell for a moment to make sure she was understood. Then she looked at the stove again. But this time, when she turned back, she had not collected herself. She had begun to cry.

"I don't understand why you can't help me, Nell. I never ask you for anything. And all I'm asking now is for an hour of your time. An hour of your time to find out where my husband has been going."

When Peggy had first expressed her suspicion and Nell had let out her little laugh, this was in part because her mother had a long and well-established history of getting worked up over nothing. Worked up over the fact that the Nickersons had not attended her Christmas party; that Mario, the doorman, insisted upon calling her *Ma'am*; that Nell's sister, Susie, had been married out of doors! But mostly, Nell had dismissed her mother's suspicion because the notion of her stepfather philandering was so profoundly out of keeping with his character. He was a man who personified the straight and narrow, in the best possible ways.

Which could not so easily be said of Nell's father. . . .

In many respects, Harry Foster had been a perfect match for Peggy. Like her, he had been born and bred on the isle of Manhattan. He had come from a good family, gone to good schools, and landed a good job at a good Wall Street firm. But for all of Harry's breeding—or more likely because of it—one understood that he was not above skirting a rule. In high humor, he liked to tell a boarding school anecdote about the sharing of answers to a test on *The Age of Innocence* that went horribly awry. He told another about the time he answered a colleague's phone and ended up with a large new client. Mulligan, he liked to joke, was his closest friend at the golf club. It could have been more accurately observed that Mulligan had been his closest friend in life.

When Nell was twelve and her sister fourteen, Harry got in the habit of bringing flowers home to Peggy once a week. A dozen tulips, a dozen lilies, a dozen roses. Peggy couldn't have been more pleased by the gesture. It appealed to her sense of romance, her sense of ritual, and her sense of décor. After snipping the stems, she liked to arrange the flowers in vases and place them in prominent spots like the foyer or on the dining-room table as a centerpiece. And whenever a dinner guest commented on the arrangement, she took great pleasure in explaining, rather casually, how her husband brought home a different bouquet every Thursday night.

But in time, it would be revealed that Harry had begun bringing flowers home to Peggy because he had noticed the attractive young woman working at the flower shop across the street from his office. Every Thursday afternoon, he would stop in to buy a dozen of whatever was on hand, just so he could chat her up. When July rolled around and Peggy and the kids decamped to his family's old summerhouse in Maine, Harry began buying the flowers for the young woman; and it was in her one-bedroom apartment in Queens that they were being trimmed, arranged, and displayed.

As usual, Harry joined the family in Maine for the last week of August. But when Labor Day arrived, once the refrigerator had been emptied and the station wagon packed, Harry announced to Peggy that he would not be going back. Not to New York. Not to his job. Not to the marriage. He was in love with someone else and they were going to live in the summerhouse for the winter. Or at least until the baby arrived.

If this summary strikes you as rather cold and abrupt, imagine how it sounded to Peggy.

The airing of well-seasoned complaints, unspoken animosities, suspicions and recriminations; feelings of shame and indignation; the retaining of attorneys and the dividing of spoils; the endless explaining of developments to family and friends; to which might be added all the grim and unanticipated practicalities like disposing of one's wedding album and waiting in line to get one's maiden name restored to one's driver's license: There are so many painful facets to divorce, too many to enumerate here. Most of them are probably familiar to you anyway, whether through first- or secondhand experience. So, there may be some virtue in trying to distill the entire emotional outcome into a phrase. If one were to do so for Peggy, it would be: She felt cheated.

Oh, Peggy felt cheated, all right.

And not simply in terms of her husband's infidelity. She felt cheated by the implicit promises of her youth. Cheated by institutions like Smith College, the Episcopal Church, and Jane Austen, each of which openly celebrated the sacrament of marriage. Cheated by old friends who either sided with Harry or diplomatically expressed their neutrality. Cheated by members of her social circle who were less likely to invite her for dinner because she made for an odd number at the table. Ultimately, cheated by Life, which had forced her to endure the scandal, the loneliness, the indignities of marital collapse—even as less-deserving women all around her exuded a sense of moral superiority secured by an untarnished union.

This overarching sense of having been cheated left Peggy bitter and angry. It left her bitter and angry long after Nell and Susie had made some sort of peace with their situation, long after New York society had stopped wondering or caring what had happened to Harry Foster. In fact, Peggy was bitter and angry for so many years, Nell and Susie began to assume she would be bitter and angry for the rest of her life.

Enter John Wells.

A sixty-four-year-old widower who had lost his wife to cancer ten years before, John was everything that Harry had never had the interest or energy to become: hardworking, trustworthy, and respected. So much so, he was not only the personal lawyer to a slew of successful executives, he had been named executor of their estates and trustee of their children's inheritances. John never mentioned the Ivy League school he attended, the exclusive clubs to which he belonged, or the eminent men to whom he gave counsel. He never talked out of school or through the side of his mouth or behind people's backs. And he never took Mulligans.

That's why Nell had given her little laugh. Because it tickled the feet of reason to imagine that John was meeting the chairwoman of the garden committee in some local hotel room for an hour or two on the occasional Saturday afternoon.

So, while Peggy did have a history of getting worked up over nothing, when she began to cry in the kitchen, Nell understood that what her mother had been living with ever since she'd read the Union Club calendar was the fear that she was about to have her life turned inside out all over again.

"All right," said Nell. "I'll follow John."

IF, IN THE KITCHEN, Nell had been initially dismissive of her mother's concerns, in the cab on the way downtown she was beginning to recalibrate.

For three years, she reminded herself, she had been a lawyer on the staff at the national headquarters of Planned Parenthood. While in a narrow sense her work was the defense of a woman's right to choose, more generally she had been a woman's advocate. She had been an advocate for a woman's health, dignity, and liberty. She had been an advocate for Hispanic women in the barrios of Los Angeles, for Black women in the post–Jim Crow South, for teenage girls being raised by Evangelical parents in the Midwest. Maybe, after all these years, it was time to become an advocate for her own mother.

By the time she came through our door, she was committed.

"Where's that camera we used in Jamaica?"

"The camera?" I asked, lowering the paper.

"That little digital one."

"The Canon?"

She began opening the drawers in the kitchen where we kept chargers and batteries and tools.

"Are we going on a trip?" I asked.

She looked up with an expression of annoyance.

"Would you stop kidding around and help me find it."

I went to the drawer in the desk where we kept the camera.

"Here," I said. "But can you tell me what's going on?"

And so she did. She told me about tea in the kitchen and the squash game that wasn't a squash game, about her mother's suspicions and, more importantly, her fears. She even showed me the photograph of the three women, which Peggy had insisted she take.

"You're going to spy on your stepfather?" I asked.

"I'm not going to spy on him," she said, while trying to locate the camera's on-off button. "I'm just going to wait outside their building next week, and when he comes out with his squash racket, I'm going to see where he goes."

I laughed a little nervously.

She looked at me with narrowed eyes. "What?"

"Honey, I'm not sure this is such a good idea. . . ."

"Because?"

"Because . . . I don't think you've thought things through to their conclusion. I mean, what if you follow John and discover he isn't playing squash somewhere else? What if he is meeting Miss Garden Club? Then what are you going to do?"

"Tell my mother."

I shook my head, more in disbelief than disagreement.

"What?" she demanded again.

I took the breath of one about to wade into waters of uncertain depth.

"You and your sister both like to joke about what a mess your lives would be if it weren't for John. You say how lucky your mother was to find him, and what a gentleman he has been at every turn. Maybe how he spends his Saturday afternoons is better left . . . unexamined."

"Let me get this straight. What you're saying is that a man should be able to do what he wants as long as he's discreet about it."

"Not exactly. But in Europe that sort of thing happens all the time."

"Oh! You're going to give me the Europe argument! It's okay if a husband cheats on his wife because François Mitterrand did!"

"Honey . . ."

"If you call me honey again, I'm going to pop you in the nose."

"You call me honey."

"Okay. But there's a time and a place for saying honey. And this isn't it."

We were silent for a moment.

When Nell spoke again she had altered her tone, lowering her voice and allowing a bit more of her own uncertainty to show through.

"Look, I understand what you're saying, Jeremy. But if my mother wants to know where her husband has been going on Saturday afternoons, I think she has the right to—not in spite of what she went through with my father, but because of it. And in my entire life, how many times has she asked for my help? Once? Twice?"

Appreciative that Nell had tried to change the tenor of the conversation, I tried to reciprocate by chipping in.

"What are you going to wear? I mean, if you're going to follow John, you should probably change your appearance."

"I was thinking of borrowing one of your baseball caps."

"Okay," I said, "that's a start. You can borrow one of my jackets too. But don't take the Mets hat. John is a Mets fan. And when one Mets fan sees another, he's bound to come over and commiserate."

———

The following Saturday, Nell was ready. She had spent the week planning and preparing. She intended to set out from our apartment by one o'clock in order to make sure she was in place by two. She borrowed my dark blue bomber jacket and the dark blue *Jeopardy!* baseball cap I'd received from my brother for my birthday. With the jacket, the hat, and her Ray-Bans, she looked like one of those pictures in the tabloids of a movie star going to Starbucks. She had me "reacquaint" her with how the Canon worked. Then she asked me how to tail somebody.

"How should I know?"

"You're the detective story fan!"

She gave me a look of disappointment, and she had a point. For all my literary aspirations, I had not found the time to read Marcel Proust or Thomas Mann. But I had somehow found the time to read mystery novels. A lot of them. I'd read the entire published works of Raymond Chandler and Dashiell Hammett twice; I'd read Rex Stout and Ross Macdonald and Georges Simenon. I'd seen a lifetime's worth of film noir, to boot.

"All right," I said, channeling my inner Sam Spade, "if you're going to tail someone, you've got to keep an eye on them without letting them see you. Ideally, you should follow them from half a block back—on the opposite side of the street."

Nell nodded.

"Pedestrians can provide you natural camouflage, but they can also obscure your line of sight. The good news is that John is six foot two and silver haired. You should be able to spot him from a good distance, even on a busy sidewalk."

"Right," she said, getting into it.

"When two people have arranged to meet," I continued, thinking out loud, "they're going to show up separately. But they're likely to leave together. If you follow John to a restaurant or hotel, you may have to wait outside for an hour or more to see who he's with. So, you might want to bring a snack."

"And a bottle of water."

"Don't do that," I cautioned. "You don't want to have to take a bathroom break in the middle of your surveillance."

"See?" she said with a smile. "I knew you could be helpful."

Having prepared herself, tactically speaking, Nell had also prepared herself mentally, by fully embracing her role as her mother's advocate. She would be the person who, in defense of her mother's dignity and right to know, would doggedly pursue the truth. Which made it all the more difficult when, at the very moment that Nell was slipping on my jacket, the telephone rang.

"It's your mother," I said, putting my hand over the mouthpiece.

"Tell her I'll call later."

"It sounds urgent."

Nell rolled her eyes and came to the phone.

"What's up, Mom? I've got to get going."

"I'm glad I caught you!" Peggy was whispering, presumably because John was in a neighboring room. "I don't want you to go."

"What's happened?"

"Nothing's happened. I just don't want you to go."

"Mom," said Nell, a little exasperated, "a week ago, you were insistent."

"Well, I've had time to think about it and I've realized he is probably playing squash somewhere else."

"Exactly. Which is all the more reason for me to go. So you can put your suspicions to rest."

"I don't have any suspicions."

"What about Lydia Spencer?"

"I never should have told you."

"Mom, there's nothing wrong with wanting to know the truth."

"Nelly. I am telling you right now that I do not want you to go. Do you understand me?"

. . .

"I understand you."

"Then promise."

"Promise what?"

"That you're not going to go."

Nell closed her eyes for a moment. "I promise,"

Peggy hung up without saying goodbye.

Nell shook her head and returned the phone to

I shrugged.

Then Nell stuffed the camera and a granola bar i

"What are you doing?" I asked.

"Going uptown."

My mouth may have opened in shock. I pointed to

"Don't start with me, Jeremy."

"Start with you? Nell! You just promised your i
weren't going to follow John."

"She made it perfectly clear last week that she want
truth."

"Then she changed her mind."

"And she might change it back."

"What if she doesn't?"

"Then I won't tell her what I learn. But I intend to fi
John's been going."

"Nell," I said, shaking my head, "where John has been
of your business."

"He's *my* stepfather. So, it may or may not be my busii
certainly none of yours."

Then she walked out the door with what, I think, objecti
ing, you would have to describe as a slam.

In the aftermath of a heated conversation, bad ideas travel at
of light. Here are just a few I had in the seconds after the s
should call Peggy and tell her that Nell is on her way uptown. 2)

hn and tell him not to go to his squash game. 3) I should go after
and try to talk some sense into her—right across the street from
other's apartment. Like I said, bad ideas.

stead of doing any of the above, I cleaned up our brunch.

e'll turn back, I thought as I washed and dried the dishes.

o, she won't, I thought, as I put them away.

ell was in action mode now. She was going to see it through.

o be perfectly honest, by that point, I had grown a little curious my-
I was curious about where John was going. I was curious about
ther he was having an affair. I was curious to see how the pictures
e out.

But for all my curiosity, I knew I wasn't going to sit around and wait
Nell to come home. Instead, I was going to call my buddy, Dave, and
if he wanted to go to a movie. Maybe a double feature. Because Nell's
uptown was already beginning to feel like something we would
ver want to talk about again, and it hadn't even happened yet.

IE AFTERNOON WAS WARM and sunny—more beginning of summer
an end of spring. By 1:40, Nell was standing behind an elm tree about
n car lengths from the Eighty-Third Street entrance to her mother's
uilding. John came through the doors at precisely 2:00, just as Peggy had
redicted. He was wearing tan pants, a white oxford shirt, and a blue
lazer in accordance with the Union Club's written and unwritten dress
odes. In his hand he held a sports bag, out of which the handle of a
squash racket jutted conspicuously. Having exited the building, he walked
to Park Avenue and headed south. Nell waited a few seconds befor
emerging from behind her tree, then she went in hot pursuit, ready to f
low her subject from half a block back on the opposite side of the str
just as I'd so shrewdly advised. But as soon as she turned the corner
was cursing me. Park Avenue was six lanes wide with a median!
could she possibly follow him from the opposite side? And as it wa
Avenue on a Saturday, there were no pedestrians to provide cam

As she followed her stepfather, she couldn't help recognize that of the two of them, she was the one acting suspiciously—pausing occasionally behind lampposts with the bill of her baseball cap lowered to the tip of her nose. While John, on the other hand, walked along in his typical manner, taking long easy strides and looking straight ahead. On the corner of Seventy-Ninth, he even stopped for a moment to pet the dog of an acquaintance, then continued on in his breezy way. If he had been a whistler, he would have been whistling.

He wasn't going to the Union Club, Nell was sure of that. But the Racquet Club was also on Park Avenue in the midfifties. And didn't the Yale Club have squash courts? John had received both his undergraduate and law degrees from Harvard, but he had no shortage of friends and acquaintances who went to Yale. True, the Yale Club was forty blocks away and most men in their sixties wouldn't walk that far, but John would. Especially on a day like this.

"This is ridiculous," Nell was saying to herself, on the verge of abandoning the whole endeavor—when John suddenly crossed Park and headed west on Seventy-Eighth. There are no squash courts on Fifth Avenue, thought Nell. But there are plenty of hotels: The Sherry Netherland. The Plaza. The Peninsula. The St. Regis. Nell felt the stirring of conflicting emotions—of excitement and anxiety, righteousness and dread. But as John was walking at a rapid pace, there was no time to sort through nuances. With the traffic light about to change, Nell skipped to the corner and dashed across Park Avenue's six lanes, prompting two taxis to honk their horns. She jogged past Madison and turned the corner onto Fifth just in time to see her stepfather disappearing into Central Park.

If Park Avenue had been relatively quiet, Central Park was the opposite. It was teeming with people. There were joggers and bikers, dog-walkers and tourists, mothers with prams, fathers with little boys in Little League uniforms, pigeon feeders and newspaper readers all enjoying the unseasonably warm weather, the last of the cherry blossoms, and the first of the azaleas.

At least I had been right on one account: John's height and silver hair made him easy to track in the crowd.

As Nell followed him from a distance of twenty yards, the indignation and dread that she had been feeling were gone. In their place was a pervading sense of perplexity. So bewildered was she by their presence in the park, she barely noted passing those landmarks of her youth that she never failed to remark upon when we found ourselves in their vicinity: the statue of Alice in Wonderland that she climbed upon as a child; the Boat Pond where Caleb, her annoying cousin, would sail perfectly rigged yachts of his own construction; the Bethesda Fountain, where she and Betsy Madison smoked cigarettes in seventh grade and marijuana in tenth.

Famously, the streets of Manhattan are laid out in a grid. But if you were to study an overhead view of Central Park, it would look like a map of a cardiovascular system with streets and paths of varying widths bending and intersecting in every which way. As a result, it was incredibly easy to get disoriented in the park, even for seasoned New Yorkers, prompting the inevitable pauses and the occasional backtracking. But as John made his way, he did so without hesitation, taking each left and right without a second thought, as if he had made this trip a thousand times before. The only time he broke stride was when he stopped in the small building that housed the public restrooms just south of Bethesda Fountain.

Nell took up a position behind an oak, sending two squirrels scurrying in opposite directions. A little ways ahead was a large crowd that suddenly let out a cheer. With a glance, Nell could see what all the "excitement" was about. The crowd was gathered around one of those street performers whose secondary skill was that he could leap over a line of people bending over at the waist. Secondary, Nell observed, because their primary skill had nothing to do with gymnastics. It was that of the raconteur. Once the line of people was assembled, the entire stunt, from takeoff to landing, lasted all of three seconds. As impressive as it was, the feat didn't provide the time to gather a suitable crowd and stir up the necessary sense of anticipation to result in a reasonable payday.

So, what each of these performers excelled at was the run-up. He excelled at describing in colorful detail the feat he was about to attempt and the dangers it posed to his life and limb. He excelled at slowly selecting the people for the line, making good-natured jokes about their hometown, their appearance, or their hesitation to take part. The performer enhanced the drama by shifting the arrangement of the four volunteers and, at the last minute, adding a fifth. Every now and then, he would seek encouragement from the audience by asking them to give a loud cheer, thus attracting more onlookers to whom he could eventually pass the hat.

When John had gone into the restrooms, the performer was wrapping up his preamble by asking for one final cheer of support. Despite the distraction, Nell showed the professional discipline to keep her eyes on the bathroom door. That is, until, at the performer's insistence, the crowd began counting down from ten. Then it was just too much to bear. Nell turned her head and watched as the performer, who had assumed the stance of a sprinter in the starting blocks at the sound of *three*, dashed forward at the sound of *one*, leapt into the air, and soared over the backs of the ragtag group of volunteers, landing safely on the other side.

He probably makes a pretty good living, thought Nell, as she turned her attention back to the bathroom and waited for John to reappear.

And waited.

And waited.

After ten minutes, a middle-aged tourist went into the bathroom. When he came out, Nell approached.

"Excuse me. I'm looking for my father. Did you happen to see anyone else inside?"

"There wasn't anyone in there."

"Are you sure?"

"Trust me," he said. "You wouldn't spend any more time in there than you had to."

When he walked away, Nell stared at the bathroom door for a moment, then went inside. Just as the tourist had said, it was uninhabitable and empty.

As Nell came out, she was cursing herself. Why did she have to watch that stupid stunt? In her days at NYU, she had seen it at least ten times!

Spinning around in place, she couldn't see John in any direction. But since entering the park, he had definitely been heading south. So, that's the way she went, jogging toward Poets Alley. When she reached the tree-lined walkway, she had an unimpeded view for fifty yards, yet there was no sign of her stepfather. With a shake of the head, she turned and went back the way she'd come, figuring she would exit the park at Seventy-Second Street and head from there to the subway. But before she'd walked a hundred feet, the opening riff of the Bee Gees' "Stayin' Alive" suddenly started playing from a boom box to Nell's left, and that's when she saw him.

If it weren't for his silver hair, she would have missed him altogether. For in the minutes that her stepfather had been out of her sight, he had experienced something of a transformation. Gone were the tan pants, white oxford, and blue blazer. In their place, John now wore silky red jogging shorts, a blue T-shirt emblazoned with the figure of Mr. Met, a white headband à la Björn Borg circa 1975, and on his feet a pair of roller skates. Not Rollerblades, roller skates. Ankle-high, white-leather roller skates with long white laces.

He was in a loose assembly of skaters, all of them moving in a circle to the beat of the music. Round and round went John, weaving smoothly among the others at a velocity that belied the circle's narrow circumference.

"Ho lee shit," whispered Nell with a smile of amazement on her face.

At the moment, there were maybe ten skaters and as many onlookers. Most of the skaters were dressed in brightly colored clothes, including one woman in sequins. John was the oldest skater by far, but no one seemed the least put out by his presence. In fact, a wiry young Black man dressed in hot pants and a tank top would occasionally skate beside John and they would nod their heads to the rhythm, moving together in time.

After watching for a moment, Nell reached in her pocket for the camera. Because *no one* was going to believe this! She even took the chance of moving a little closer, drawing confidence from the fact that among the onlookers were two tourists also taking pictures.

When the song ended, the wiry Black man skated to a bench, plopped down, and lit a joint that had been resting on one of the bench's posts. Nell went over and took a seat beside him, casually.

He looked at her askance.

"You here to bust me?"

"Excuse me?" asked Nell in surprise.

He waved his joint at her outfit.

"You look like an extra from *Law and Order*, sister."

"Oh, sorry."

With a sheepish smile, she took off her sunglasses.

When he offered her his joint, she declined.

"Suit yourself."

He took a second toke while watching the other skaters.

"Can I ask you something?" said Nell after a moment.

"Asking's for free. That's the way God made it. But answers, on the other hand . . ."

When Nell looked surprised, he smiled.

"I'm just jerking your chain. What's your question?"

"I was admiring the skating of the older man in the circle. Does he come here often?"

"Who? You mean Gloria? Sure. He's here most Saturdays."

Gloria . . . ?

Nell suddenly wished she had accepted the toke.

But taking a fresh look at John, she thought, "Of course! How could I have been so stupid?" The refined gentleman who rode out of the mist in a light-gray suit to marry a middle-aged divorcée. A man with a love of nineteenth-century paintings and midcentury antiques. A man who sneaks out of the house under the guise of a squash game, enters a public men's room, and reemerges as Gloria.

Nell's neighbor was also watching John—who was now skating backward in a crossover style to the tune of "Back Stabbers".

"I'm not surprised that Gloria caught your eye," he said with a smile. "I've been coming here a long time and I can tell you with some assurance that he's the best old-style skater in all of Central Park. Maybe all of New York."

He took another puff and leaned back on the bench.

"Does he have a . . . friend?" asked Nell.

"A friend?"

"I mean a boyfriend."

He turned and studied Nell for a moment. "Who says he's gay?"

"I just thought . . ."

"You just thought," he echoed with a shake of the head. "You just thought because he dances on roller skates in bright red shorts to the sounds of disco that he must be a queen."

Nell could feel her face growing red.

"You said his name was Gloria," she pointed out in her own defense.

"If I told you his name was Luke, would you assume he had the Force?"

After delicately snuffing out his joint with his fingertips and returning it to its perch, he stood and turned away, ready to skate back to the circle. But after letting out something of a sigh, he turned back. He spoke to Nell in the manner of one who's going to explain something even though he has no responsibility to do so.

"We call him Gloria because his number is 'I Will Survive'. By Gloria Gaynor. We've all got our number. Our favorite song to skate to. The song when we pull out all the stops and show each other what we've got. We all know each other's number, so when yours comes up, everybody'll spread out to the edge of the circle. To give you a little more room and watch the magic happen."

With a big smile he pointed his thumb to his chest.

"They call me Car Wash."

Nell looked back blankly.

"You know: 'Car Wash.' The theme song from the movie? By Rose Royce?" He clapped his hands in a rhythm that was vaguely familiar to Nell. "Jesus," he said, shaking his head. "It's like my momma says: the more channels they've got on TV, the less people know."

Suddenly, Car Wash held a finger in the air, as the sound of a piano chord emanated from the boom box, followed by a tinkling up and down the keyboard.

"You say you were admiring how Gloria skates? Well, now you're really going to see something to remember."

ONE HOUR LATER, NELL was sitting at her mother's kitchen table in a state of eager excitement. Her mother, on the other hand, had received her daughter's surprise visit with a wary posture and no offer of tea.

"What are you wearing that hat for?"

Nell smiled.

"I forgot I had it on!"

Taking it off, Nell set it on the table. When Peggy frowned, Nell moved it to an empty chair.

"So," said Peggy, sitting up. "What brings you uptown?"

Nell nodded, adopting a more serious expression.

"Right. What brings me uptown. Well, before you get mad at me . . ."

Peggy went stone-faced.

"You did it. You followed him. Even though I explicitly asked you not to."

"I know but—"

"And you gave me your *word*! Is that what your word is worth?"

"Mom. Please. Can you let me talk for just a moment?"

Peggy looked off at a forty-five-degree angle, somewhere between

Nell and the refrigerator. Nell leaned to her left in order to reestablish eye contact.

"Can you look at me?"

Peggy returned her gaze, but she put her hands in her lap as a gesture of protest.

Nell let out a sigh.

"I did follow John, even though you asked me not to. But I think you're going to be glad I did. No marriage benefits from an aura of doubt. It's almost always better to clear the air than let a suspicion linger. And that's especially so when the suspicion is unwarranted."

Peggy shifted in her seat, not quite ready to forgive her daughter's transgression, but interested to learn what she'd discovered.

Noting her mother's curiosity, Nell allowed herself a small smile of triumph.

"John is not playing squash. But he is not seeing Lydia Spencer either. He's not seeing anybody!"

"Then what on earth is he doing?"

Nell paused for dramatic effect.

"Roller-skating."

"What?"

Peggy's confusion was so profound, it was as if she didn't understand the term.

"Roller-skating," repeated Nell. "Like in the fifties. Here, look!"

Nell shifted around the table so she was sitting adjacent to her mother and produced the camera.

"On Saturdays, instead of going to play squash, he goes to Central Park to roller-skate. To disco!"

Turning on the camera, she pointed to the first image. She could tell from her mother's expression that she was still confused. She was confused as to why her daughter was showing her an assembly of strangely clad young people taken somewhere in the park.

"There," said Nell, pointing to the man left of center. "In the headband."

"I don't understand," she said.

"Here."

Nell scrolled past the various photographs she had taken until she arrived at the film and pressed play.

As the scene unfolded, Peggy stared at the little screen intently. Taking it in. Taking in the music and the motion. The brightly colored clothes of the skaters, the cheers of the onlookers, and the tall, silver-haired man who was suddenly spinning in the center of the circle.

"Can you believe it?" Nell said with a laugh.

And that's when John entered the room. Dressed once again in his Union Club uniform with his exercise bag in his hand.

Normally, when someone comes home and walks into their kitchen, they move at the speed of a stroll—the natural pace by which we get from one spot to another when there's no need to rush. But when John came into the kitchen, he entered at a fraction of that speed. He walked at the pace of someone who has stopped just outside the door, who has listened to the faint sound of a familiar song, listened to his stepdaughter's laughter and his wife's silence, before finally deciding to go in, because where else was one to go?

When Nell looked up at the sound of John's muted entrance, having realized that he must have been standing outside the door, she expected to see an expression of indignation or disappointment on his face. Instead, what she saw was embarrassment, perhaps even shame. Because, of course, his expression wasn't meant for Nell. It was meant for the woman to whom he was married; the woman to whom he had been lying; the woman who stood up from the table, took two steps forward, and slapped him across the face.

IN THE WEEKS THAT FOLLOWED, a quiet sense of distance established itself between Peggy and John. Like pieces on a chessboard, their mobility suddenly seemed to be governed by different rules, one moving forever diagonally, the other moving forward and back, or side to side. Due to an apparent uptick in his workload, John began heading to the office a little earlier, such that he and Peggy had their morning coffee in the kitchen at different hours. The various boards on which they served and the charities with which they were affiliated started having their annual spring events, such that the husband and wife were often dining in different places, making the normal apologies for each other's absence. When Memorial Day rolled around, Peggy went to Boston to celebrate her college roommate's sixtieth birthday while John went to California to see his new grandchild, naturally enough. Then in June, Peggy decamped to their house in Southampton, as was her habit. The fact that the two rarely landed on the same square at the same time seemed so perfectly reasonable, so predictable, so in keeping with the rules of the game, it hardly bore notice, much less comment.

That is until the Friday before July Fourth, when Nell and I drove out to the Hamptons to spend the long weekend with Peggy and John. Given a late start and plenty of traffic, by the time we arrived Peggy was already standing at the island in the kitchen making the final preparations for dinner.

"How was the drive?" she asked.

"Predictably unbearable," said Nell.

Peggy turned to me.

"I got the gin you like, Jeremy. There are some limes on the cutting board and tonic in the fridge."

"Thanks, Peggy. Dinner smells delicious."

"Chicken cacciatore. It's just about ready."

"Should I get John?" Nell asked as I handed her a drink.

"That won't be necessary," answered Peggy.

Nell looked at me with a puzzled expression. I tilted my head toward the dinner table, where three places had been set. Nell put down her glass.

"Is John here, Mom?"

"It's just the three of us tonight," said Peggy, as she tossed the salad.

"Is he coming tomorrow?"

"He won't be here this weekend."

"Where is he?"

"I really couldn't say." Peggy turned her back on Nell in order to take a roasting pan from the oven. Then she carried it to the table and set it down on a pair of pot holders. "Now. What would you like to drink with dinner? White wine or red?"

"Mom! What do you mean you don't know where John is?"

"He's a grown man, Nelly. He doesn't need to report on his movements. Now, let's eat while it's hot. Jeremy, why don't you sit at the head."

I hesitated, not certain I wanted to sit at the head of the table.

"Sit, sit," insisted Peggy.

So we sat. Then Peggy served the chicken onto our respective plates with a large serving spoon.

Nell, who was directly across from her mother, hadn't taken her eyes off her since setting her drink on the island.

"Mom, what the hell is going on?"

"You needn't use that language at the table, Nell."

"Forget the language. Can't you answer a simple—"

Peggy, who was still holding the serving spoon, slammed it down, sending a small explosion of tomato sauce and capers across the felt runner that adorned the center of the table.

"Enough!" she shouted.

The three of us were silent.

After correcting her posture, Peggy began to cut her chicken. Then stopping, she quietly set her silverware down, stood, and left the room.

We both watched her go.

When Nell pushed back her chair, exhibiting a sort of coiled energy, I reached out and put my hand over hers.

As soon as I did it, I felt I had made a mistake, that Nell would snap back her hand and offer me a spousal rebuke. Instead, the urgency seemed to drain out of her. She seemed to accept the reasonable finality of her mother's command. For whatever had happened, whatever had been said, for the time being, it was almost certainly enough.

OVER THE COURSE OF JULY, as the estrangement between Peggy and John continued, so did Peggy's silence. Whatever was going on between them, she clearly had no intention of talking about it. This was a fact she signaled by a pursed smile, a curt demeanor, and a general insistence upon acting as if nothing out of the ordinary was happening.

To that end, she continued to play bridge on Tuesday afternoons. She continued to closely oversee the weeding of her flower beds and the pruning of her bushes. She continued to shop at the IGA rather than at that overpriced place in town where they sell heirloom tomatoes at eight dollars a pound. And when we drove out on Friday nights, Peggy continued to greet us in her apron with limes on the cutting board, tonic in the fridge, and dinner served for three with a choice of white or red.

Whatever confusion Nell felt about her mother's silence was compounded by John's. The few times Nell had called the apartment on Eighty-Third Street, she got the answering machine. When she finally sent an email asking how he was doing, he replied in a manner so brief and polite, it gave the inescapable impression that she needn't reach out again.

When she showed me John's email, she shook her head to express her bewilderment—with her mother. "What on earth is she thinking? She's acting like she's been betrayed all over again!" After another shake of the head, she turned from the computer screen to me and asked, "What do you think we should do?"

What can one ever do when two adults are working through a private crisis?

"Cross our fingers."

THE AUGUST AFTER NELL and I moved in together and before she started working at Planned Parenthood, she took the opportunity to go hiking with some girlfriends out West. As Peggy always spent the summer in Southampton and John commuted back and forth, he reached out, suggesting we have a bachelors' dinner. John and I didn't know each other very well then, but I accepted, figuring he'd pick up the tab at a restaurant above my means and I'd still get home early enough to watch a movie. But we ended up having a grand old time, drinking martinis and working our way through two seafood towers. In fact, we had such a grand old time, it became something of a tradition: an annual fandango at Balthazar on the second Wednesday in August, just the two of us.

Nonetheless, I was a little surprised when he emailed me a few weeks after the slamming of the spoon, expressing his hope that we would meet as usual.

The invitation opened an array of questions. For instance: If, for the time being, Peggy wasn't speaking to John, was I supposed to maintain my distance from him out of loyalty to Nell? Or at this stage, didn't John and I have a relationship of our own? Didn't we have the right to maintain some sort of qualified friendship? And wasn't it potentially in everyone's interests for me to keep channels open with him—like a diplomat in a time of escalating tensions—in the hopes of securing a détente? Most importantly, if I accepted the offer, should I tell Nell?

After a moment's hesitation, I replied to John's email with an acceptance. It was a tradition, after all. And it just so happened that Nell was scheduled to be out of town that week, so circumstance seemed to be providing its own form of discretion.

When the night rolled around, I dutifully hung up my blue jeans, donned one of my two blazers, and headed for Balthazar. Once we were seated, as usual we ordered martinis. As usual he asked me how my work was going, and as usual he offered me a bit of advice disguised as friendly encouragement. But as we were finishing our drinks, when the waiter approached the table asking if we were ready to order, after a full beat John turned to me and wondered if we should have another round.

A second round before we ordered dinner was decidedly not usual. But I could tell that John had something he wanted to talk about before we had the distraction of the shellfish in front of us.

"Why not," I said.

Sure enough, once we had clinked our glasses and taken our first swig of the second round, John changed the topic. Earlier that summer, he said, when Nell had left messages on their answering machine, he hadn't called back; and when she had reached out by email, he had replied rather tersely.

I acknowledged as much with a nod.

Well, he wanted to apologize for that. Or rather, he wanted me to relay an apology to Nell on his behalf. Or something like an apology.

John was being unusually inarticulate, and it wasn't the second martini. He took a breath.

"It wasn't my preference," he said. "It was for Peggy."

"For Peggy?"

"Before she left for the Hamptons, she asked me not to communicate with Nell."

"Seriously?"

"Quite seriously," said John, with an expression to match. "But you shouldn't judge her harshly for that, Jeremy. If she and I are going through a difficult time, she has every right to be the one who decides when and what to say to her own children. In my profession, I've occasionally seen husbands or wives step around each other in order to make their cases to friends and family, but it never helps. Ultimately, a problem in a marriage is something that must be worked out between the principals, if you'll excuse the term. So, I want you to relay to Nell my contrition for not returning her calls and for the tone of my email; more importantly, I want you to affirm my love and admiration for her.

The only catch is that in doing so, you can't tell her about Peggy's dictum."

"Okay."

"Perhaps you can tell her the decision to maintain a bit of distance was mine."

"I'll figure something out, John."

As he expressed his thanks, the waiter, who had just served a neighboring table, took the opportunity to make eye contact with us, to see if we were ready to order now. But John didn't give him the nod. Instead, he looked down into his drink. There was something else on his mind. When he looked up, I could tell from his expression it was something harder to talk about.

"You probably think me a fool," he said, after a moment.

"A fool?"

"A grown man spending his Saturday afternoons on roller skates . . ."

"I'm a grown man who plays video games in his pajamas! Believe me, John. You're the last person I think of as a fool."

John smiled and said, "Thank you," acknowledging the politeness of my assurance without committing to believe it. Either way, he wasn't done with what he had to say. He was just getting started.

"I was raised in St. Paul, Minnesota," he began. "Have you ever been?"

"I haven't."

"It's a lovely city. A simple city, in many ways. A few hundred thousand people living on the banks of the Mississippi. To the south there's hundreds of miles of farmland, to the west the lights of Minneapolis, and to the north the ten thousand lakes . . ."

He allowed his voice to drift off with a touch of sentimentality.

"Anyway. It's a hockey town. I had three brothers and we all skated. In fact, as soon as the temperature fell below freezing—which could happen before Thanksgiving—my father would build a makeshift rink in the backyard. The outdoor spigots were all drained for winter, so we would run five lengths of hose from our kitchen sink in order to fill the rink. Although it was only six inches of water, it could take a few days for it to freeze all the way. For the four of us, it was like waiting for Christmas. On the morning the ice was finally solid, we would rush out after breakfast, put on our skates, and it seemed like we didn't take them off again until spring."

We both smiled at the thought.

"Occasionally, the neighbors would join us, and we'd have real hockey games. Four on four, or six on six. Sometimes even eight on eight. But for hours at a time, it was just the four of us, skating. Racing one another around the rink. Doing sprints from goal to goal to test not only our speed but our ability to stop and reverse direction. We invented jumps and spins without helmets on our heads or pads on our knees. Of course, we all played hockey for our high school team; and then I played at Harvard."

"You played hockey at Harvard!"

John smiled.

"This was over forty years ago, Jeremy. Hockey at Harvard in the 1950s wasn't quite like it is today. But yes, I played. And, initially, I loved it. I enjoyed the camaraderie and the precision of a well-executed assist. I enjoyed the excitement when the momentum of a game would suddenly shift. But in my junior year, being on the team began to feel a bit like a chore—what with getting up at dawn for the early practices and taking the long bus rides to other schools.

"Then one afternoon, when we took to the ice in order to warm up before a game, I suddenly realized that this was the moment in which I was happiest as a hockey player—when we were circling the rink without a puck on the ice. Because it was the skating I loved. Not the game. Later that night, I resigned from the team.

"When I announced my decision, everyone seemed disappointed in me. My coach, my teammates, my brothers. Certainly my father. When I called to tell him, all he said was: *I never thought of you as a quitter.*"

John looked back down into his drink as if, after all these years, he could still feel the sting of that rebuke.

In the decades that followed, John finished Harvard and went to Harvard Law; he moved to New York, married, and had children; he became a partner at his firm; he lost his wife to cancer; then just as he had reconciled himself to the life of a widower, he had met Peggy. And during all that time, he never skated once.

"Then one summer night a few years ago—a night not unlike this one—after a late meeting with a client on the Upper West Side, I decided to walk across the park, something I rarely did. I remember marveling at the improbable beauty of it all. This idyll of trees and flowers in the middle of Manhattan. When suddenly, there I was at the edge of the Circle. That's what they call the skating area—what *we* call it—and I found myself watching in amazement. It was an odd group, much as it is now, all dressed up for show. And the music wasn't my style. But they were skating, Jeremy. They were *really* skating.

"The next week, I bought a pair of roller skates and brought them to the park. I must have been a little over sixty at the time, and I was worried I was going to embarrass myself with a spectacular collapse. Or worse, I'd break a hip and be explaining myself to Peggy and my partners for the rest of the summer. But as soon as I had the skates on, I knew I had nothing to fear. I could have been right back on that little rink in the backyard with my brothers.

"When I was lacing up, there was a moment when the others must have thought: 'Who is this crazy old white man in the khaki pants and button-down shirt?' But once I took a few laps around the Circle, they accepted me as one of their own. I quickly understood that my outfit wasn't particularly practical, and I suppose I took some cues from the group—buying clothes that were brighter than I might otherwise have bought. I even came to like the music, the disco I mean. I know it's outdated, even a little tacky, but there's something about it that is so . . . uninhibiting."

We ended up having a bottle of white wine as we ate our clams and oysters and crab claws. So, when I clambered up the stairs, I was a little drunk. Our apartment was a one-bedroom with a kitchen and living room, small enough that it tended to either look very clean or a total wreck. Right now, given Nell's absence, it leaned toward the latter. Kicking aside the console of my PlayStation, I collapsed into the leather chair that I had turned toward the TV.

For a few minutes, I sat there thinking about John. Then I got up and went to our desk. The fallout from Nell's surveillance the previous spring had been so quick and severe, I had never seen the pictures she took in the park. When she'd come home that afternoon, she certainly hadn't offered to show them to me, and I hadn't the courage to ask. Opening the drawer, I rifled through the notepads and scissors and pens. I found the charging unit for the camera's battery and the cable that allowed you to connect it to your computer, but the camera wasn't there.

Closing the drawer, I suddenly remembered how Nell had looked for the camera in the kitchen that day. Maybe that's where she had dumped it when she'd returned in a mild state of shock after witnessing the slap. But it wasn't there either.

I moved on to our bedroom. In the top drawer of my bureau, in addition to socks and boxer shorts, there was a random array of masculine accessories like old watches, wallets, and cuff links. Maybe Nell had her own assortment of stuff in her top drawer. But it was only panties and bras, albeit in an impressive state of order.

Disappointed, I walked down the narrow hall that connected our bedroom to the living room, and suddenly stopped. On the wall was our collection of jackets and coats hanging from three Shaker pegboards that were mounted end to end. I found my bomber jacket under a raincoat. As soon as I lifted it off the peg, I could tell from the weight that what I was looking for was still in the pocket.

Settled back in my chair, I turned on the camera. When the little screen lit up, it automatically displayed the last image that had been viewed—the movie that Nell and Peggy had watched together. I pushed the little triangle that indicated play.

The initial images were a blur of pavement and legs, as Nell, having fumbled for the record button, left her place on the bench and moved into a better shooting position. Once she had the skaters in the frame, she used the telephoto function to zoom in on the skater in the red shorts and blue T-shirt. By that point, Nell had missed some of the song, but not much. Gaynor had just finished her semispoken *Once I was afraid* intro, and the drum and guitar were shifting to the main body of the anthem.

Initially, there had been about ten people circling the ring. But as the song gained momentum, the majority of skaters moved to the periphery and spun to a stop, giving John a little more room, and the undeniable attention he was due. He was skating backward now, at the tempo of the song, crossing one leg over the other, his arms out stretched, his gaze turned only slightly to the side, having no need to look back, knowing from experience how tight an arc he would have to turn.

Both the image and the sound were fractions of themselves, the six-foot-two figure of John shrunk to an inch, and the disco beat thinned to a filament by the camera's tiny speaker. But these shortcomings didn't obscure for one second the implications of what I was watching.

In the previous two months, Nell, her sister, and I had all felt a little blindsided by the severity of Peggy's response. Nell gave voice to our shared bewilderment when she had observed: "She's acting like she's been betrayed all over again!"

But as I watched John, this genteel old man surrounded by a small fraternity of admirers, with his hands crossed on his chest and his head tilted back, turning in circles to the point at which he almost blurred, I understood that Peggy had every reason to feel betrayed. Because when she looked down into the little screen of Nell's camera at the figure of her husband on his secret outing, what she saw was an image of unadulterated joy. A joy that not only existed in her absence, but seemed to require it.

IN THE SPRING of the following year, three Southern states would pass laws that narrowed access to abortion in three new ways. These would turn out to be the first salvos in a twenty-year war against reproductive rights that spread from one conservative state to the next. But at the time, they seemed like thinly argued workarounds, the actions of a few desperate players that best be stopped in their tracks. To that end, a handful of agencies that fought for the reproductive rights of women or for civil liberties in general banded together to bring the fight to the courts. At the head of this alliance was Planned Parenthood, and at the head of Planned Parenthood's attack was a small group of in-house attorneys including Nell. Though Nell would never be so callous as to put it this way, the fight couldn't have come at a better time.

For in the preceding months, her thoughts had been consumed by the developments between her mother and John. After the July Fourth weekend, Nell had assured herself that the couple would find their way through the crisis, and her mother would forgive John for whatever it was she thought he had done. But no rapprochement was forthcoming. No forgiveness. Her mother's position only solidified. And by Thanksgiving, it became clear that the mismatched moves on the chessboard we had largely ignored the previous spring had been the first steps in the dissolution of the marriage. As a gentleman, John seemed prepared to make any concession that would minimize the risk of rancor. While for Peggy's part, I suppose she took some unspoken comfort that if the marriage was going to end, at least this time she was the one ending it.

The ease with which the couple advanced toward divorce left Nell on edge. She couldn't stop raising the topic. Raising it with me. Raising it with her sister and her closest friends. In trying to make sense of what had happened, she would talk about her mother's stubbornness, or John's ready acquiescence, or their generation's collective distrust of counseling. Sometimes she would make that tried-and-true observation that no one ever really knows what's going on inside a marriage. As I say, she would return to the topic in different ways at different times with different people, but her intent was always the same. By rehashing the particulars with her inner circle, she was hoping that she would receive some confirmation, some assurance that whatever had happened, it hadn't been her fault. And as those who loved her best, we lied. Each and every one of us.

The Bootlegger

W E HADN'T BEEN IN OUR seats for more than two minutes when Tommy began to fidget. He kept looking over his shoulder toward the entrance of the concert hall with a knitted brow.

"Maybe he won't come," he said.

"Maybe he won't," I agreed. After all, it was nearly eight and the ushers were prodding the idlers into their seats.

Tommy nodded and turned his attention back to his program. "Steven Isserlis performing Bach's Gamba Sonatas," he read. Then he turned to me with his first real smile of the evening. "It says here that Mr. Isserlis will be playing a Guadagnini cello made in 1745!"

I returned the smile.

The batting average of baseball players, the horsepower of cars, the latest movements of the stock exchange. Sometimes it seems that for a man nothing is more exciting than a number. It's the boy in them, I suppose.

Suddenly, the chatter in the audience began to die down, transitioning from hushed exchanges to whispered remarks. There was a moment of collective silence set in relief by a few coughs, then a round of applause as Mr. Isserlis took the stage, accompanied by his accompanist.

Setting his program aside, Tommy joined in the applause whole-heartedly, though I suspect he was applauding the empty seat to his left more than the artist in front of him.

After giving a bow to acknowledge the warm welcome, Mr. Isserlis sat in the chair at center stage, adjusted his posture, laid his bow across the cello's strings, and closed his eyes. Then just as he was about to play the first note of the first sonata, from off to our right came the words "Excuse me."

Tommy and I both turned our heads.

Sure enough, it was the old man in his raincoat.

"Excuse me," he said again, edging his way down the row. "Excuse me."

Tommy and I rose to let him pass.

As the old man took his seat, Tommy gave me a look of exasperation, then turned his attention back toward the stage, his jaw visibly clenched. At that moment, if Bach himself had descended from heaven in order to accompany the cellist, it wouldn't have made any difference to my husband. As far as he was concerned, the night was already ruined.

BETWEEN YOU, ME, AND the fencepost, a night at Carnegie Hall was never my idea of a good time. It was Tommy who had floated the notion, as part of our 1996 Evenings Out campaign.

When our first child was born, Tommy and I stayed pretty close to home, but when our second child was born, we stayed closer. In a household with a three-year-old and an infant, there's hardly a waking moment that doesn't involve breastfeeding, back-patting, diaper-changing, or the reading of a picture book for the ten-thousandth time. With two children under four, if chance should conspire to give you an empty hour, you'd happily spend it soaking in a tub or staring at the tube—the city's nightlife be damned.

But now that Thomas, Jr., and Izzy were both taking themselves to the bathroom and sleeping through the night, Tommy and I made a New Year's resolution to go on a date at least once a week. For Tommy, an investment banker at Goldman Sachs, this allowed for one of his favorite activities: the making of a list, since—and I quote—anything worth doing is worth doing systematically. Within seconds of making our resolution, Tommy took out a piece of paper so we could catalogue the restaurants we wanted to try, the exhibits we wanted to attend, and the friends we wanted to see.

A few days after Tommy had taped the list to our refrigerator door, he read in *The New York Times* that Evgeny Kissin, the world-renowned Russian pianist we'd never heard of, was coming to play in America for the second time. Tommy suggested we go to the concert and have an early dinner at the Russian Tea Room, which, as it happened, was right next door to Carnegie Hall!

(His exclamation point, not mine.)

"I'll get the tickets and the dinner reservation. What do you say?"

When Tommy and I first began dating, like everyone else in their midtwenties in New York, we made the most of the city's low-cost splendors: its coffee shops, blues bars, and pizza parlors, God bless 'em. At the time, there was a little Cuban place on the corner of First and First just a few blocks from the walk-up where I lived. They accepted no reservations, crowded you around little Formica-topped tables, and buried every entrée under a pile of rice and beans. But shortly after 11:00, they'd start pushing tables aside, a salsa band would assemble near the bar, and everyone in the place would get off their keisters and dance, whether they knew how to salsa or not. Now, that was a night out!

In Tommy's defense, we were a little older now; and a night at Carnegie Hall was a box to be checked; but mostly, I appreciated his initiative. So, sure, I said, why not. And the world-renowned pianist was added to the list.

But nothing is ever quite as simple as it seems. At least not if you're over-educated, overpaid, and living in New York.

When Tommy called the Carnegie Hall box office, he discovered that the tickets for the Russian's performance wouldn't be on sale for a month. However, if you made a tax-deductible donation of two thousand dollars to Carnegie Hall, as a "Patron" you could purchase advance tickets for the upcoming season starting on the following Monday, and through a dedicated phone line, no less.

They probably had Tommy at tax deductible, but the promise of advance tickets sales and a dedicated phone line sealed the deal. So, a check was written and on the following Monday morning Tommy was dialing the Patron's desk the moment it opened at 10:00 a.m.

Alas, from the helpful young man who answered the phone Tommy learned there had been a slight misunderstanding. At this early date, advance tickets were only made available to Patrons who were subscribing to the hall's various *series*. If you wanted to secure tickets right now to see Evgeny Kissin, you had to purchase one of the series in which he appeared, such as *Piano Concertos* or *Virtuosos*.

"Virtuosos?" asked Tommy, predictably intrigued.

"Yes. That's the series in which four musicians at the top of their field—a pianist, a violinist, an oboist, and a cellist—each perform either alone or with an accompanist on a Saturday night in April."

Four famed musicians on four instruments in four weeks, and tickets weren't even available to the public yet? Who could say no to that? And since Tommy'd had the foresight to call the dedicated line the very minute the season went on sale, he must be able to get any seat in the house. Right?

Right?

Well, not exactly . . .

You see, as the young man explained, when someone subscribes to a series at Carnegie Hall and chooses a particular seat, he is guaranteed that seat not only for the four performances of the season, but for as many years as he subscribes to the series in the future. And as this particular series was *very* popular, there were some concertgoers who had held on to their seats for over a decade.

"All right," said Tommy. "Then what seats *are* available?"

"Let's see."

Tommy heard the young man's fingers on a keyboard. He heard silence as the young man scanned a computer screen. Then he heard the young man exclaim: "Oh!"

Tommy shifted the phone from one ear to the other.

"What is it?" he said. "How does it look?"

"It seems that seats one-oh-seven and one-oh-eight have become available in row E. . . ."

"Is that good?"

"For the performance of a symphony, the front rows of the first balcony are often favored, because that's where you can savor the fullness of the orchestra. But for solo performances, many aficionados prefer being closer to the stage, where they can see all the hand movements and facial expressions of the musician. Since seats one-oh-seven and one-oh-eight E are the center of the fifth row, for the *Virtuosos* series many would consider them the best seats in the house."

Well, you can imagine how that phone call ended.

Our nice little box-checking date to Carnegie Hall had suddenly been upgraded to four Saturday nights in April. And that wasn't the half of it.

Three traits that had made Tommy such a natural in his profession were his competitiveness, his shrewdness, and his appreciation for the benefits of ownership. But these traits also influenced nearly every other facet of his life. When we honeymooned in the Bahamas, for instance, Tommy started getting up at the break of dawn—when the hotel's employees were still raking the seaweed—so he could drop a pile of magazines and a bottle of suntan lotion on the two best lounge chairs on the beach. Then he would head straight over to the breakfast terrace to secure the sunniest table and one of the five available copies of the *International Herald Tribune*. Now that we controlled two seats in the center of the fifth row of this *very* popular series, there was the clear possibility that we would be sitting in Carnegie Hall on every Saturday night in April for the rest of our lives.

ON THE NIGHT OF the first virtuoso, the early dinner at the Russian Tea Room was delightful. We were given a banquette beside a display of samovars across from a wall of brightly colored nineteenth-century paintings. I had the beef Stroganoff, Tommy had the chicken Kiev, and, in the spirit of the hour, we each had a shot of vodka. In other words, we were off to a good start.

Arriving at Carnegie Hall thirty minutes before the performance, we visited the Patrons' Lounge, where we were given complimentary glasses of champagne, then we proceeded to our new beachfront property at the center of row E, where we dutifully read up on the first performer in the series.

He was an oboist from Switzerland named Hans. Or maybe Hanz. (Either way, it's pronounced the same.) I had no idea there were such things as oboe soloists. I'd always assumed that an oboe needs an orchestra, like a tuba needs a marching band. So, my curiosity was pleasantly piqued.

About five minutes before the concert began, a little old man in a raincoat edged his way politely past us and took the seat beside Tommy. After a brief exchange of friendly greetings, the old man sat quietly with his arms on the armrests. But once the oboist had taken the stage, Tommy elbowed me in the ribs and gestured with his head toward the old man's right arm. I assumed he was calling attention to some sort of armrest encroachment, so I made a sympathetic face and turned my attention back to the performer. But Tommy elbowed me again with a little more urgency.

"Mary!" he whispered.

"What!" I whispered back.

"Look at his wrist."

Leaning forward, I saw now that protruding from the sleeve of the old man's raincoat were two little black rods extending in a Y, like the antennae of an insect.

"What is it?"

"A microphone!"

Imagine that, I thought with a smile, classifying the moment as one of those colorful little instances of eccentric behavior the city occasionally provides as consolation for all the noise and traffic. Like when you're on the Upper East Side and you happen upon a woman in furs walking a cat on a leash. Or when in the middle of the day in the middle of the week in the middle of your very own block, you almost stumble over a cabbie who's kneeling on a piece of cardboard, in order to pray in the direction of Mecca. How can you not respect a faith that requires you to carry a compass?

But Tommy did not find the old man's behavior colorful or eccentric. Over the course of the concert, he must have looked down at that little microphone at least fifty times with an expression of unwavering disbelief.

A week later, after another early dinner at the Russian Tea Room and two more shots of vodka, we returned to Carnegie Hall to see the violinist Christian Tetzlaff. As Tommy was reading to me that Mr. Tetzlaff was a veritable master of the crescendo, the old man reappeared with his raincoat and his little black antennae. Again, Tommy spent the entire concert looking at the apparatus, though this time with an expression of unwavering disapproval.

I'll be hearing about this later, I thought to myself, picturing an airing of grievances at our kitchen counter after we had sent the babysitter home—preferably over a glass of wine. But the airing began as soon as the door of the taxicab closed.

"Can you believe that?"

"Believe what, sweetie?"

"The nerve of that guy! Recording concerts at Carnegie Hall."

I shrugged.

Tommy turned in his seat in order to face me in shock. (Tommy is very easy to shock.)

"Did you just shrug?"

Now, I sighed.

"He's probably just some lonely old man, Tommy, who loves pianos and oboes and violins. It's not like he's doing any harm."

To me, this seemed reason enough to let the matter drop, so that the old man, Tommy, Mr. Tetzlaff, and I could all go on about our business in this golden era of peace and prosperity.

I should have known better.

Before we go further, perhaps I should mention that I love Tommy. I loved him the first night we went out; I loved him when he got down on one knee to propose in his pajamas; I loved him when he almost missed the birth of our daughter because he was getting a milkshake at a diner a few blocks from the hospital; and I love him right now at this very minute. But when a man is paid to provide his opinions and he's had some success in doing so, he is bound to become a little insufferable.

A member of the Exeter debating team, a philosophy major at Yale, one of the youngest managing directors in Goldman Sachs history, Tommy rarely stumbles upon his point of view, and he never blurts it out. Having grabbed hold of some thorny issue, Tommy mulls it over for days in silence, considering it from every possible angle in every possible light. By the time he shares his opinion, not only has he carefully chosen his vocabulary, he has crafted complex sentences and persuasive analogies. He has even considered likely rebuttals and fashioned counterarguments. So detailed and well articulated is his position once he decides to air it that you feel a little helpless to argue against it—even when it never made any sense in the first place.

So, what began in the back of the cab with a shift in his seat, continued in the bathroom with a wave of the toothbrush, and concluded under our covers—despite the open book in my hands.

To paraphrase:

Contrary to common opinion, copyright infringement is *not* a victimless crime. The illicit recording of a concert implicitly steals from the composer, the performer, and the venue by subverting their opportunity to record and distribute the performance for a fee at a time of their choosing. Copyright laws were created because a world in which artists cannot secure fair compensation for their endeavors is a world less likely to contain art!

While taping a concert is unambiguously a violation of the law, can we give the old man the benefit of the doubt and assume he is making his recordings without an awareness of the moral implications? Definitely not. The old man's bad faith is clearly indicated by his subterfuge. Hiding that spy-like apparatus up the sleeve of his raincoat is as much evidence as we need to confirm his awareness of his own culpability.

"But if we set all that aside—the copyright infringement, the violation of the law, and the instance of bad faith—at the very minimum the old man's behavior is contrary to a universally accepted concert hall decorum." (That was the term Tommy used: *a universally accepted concert hall decorum.* He probably coined it while on the treadmill at the gym.) "We and the other members of the audience have come together from different walks of life and paid some portion of our hard-earned savings in order to share in the pleasure of a performance. But in order to share in this pleasure"—here Tommy raised his voice and a finger at the very same time, proving that he was a master of the crescendo in his own right—"we enter into an implicit understanding, an understanding that during the performance we will not chatter or eat potato chips; we will not get up to go to the bathroom; we will not interfere with one anoth-er's opportunity to enjoy the experience to its fullest. And the old man's little microphones, no matter how hard he has tried to hide them, are as much a violation of concert hall decorum as if he spent the whole night talking on his cell phone!"

Like I said: insufferable.

MEANWHILE, BACK ON THE third Saturday in April, I was having a gay old time. Mr. Isserlis, who had the long wavy hair of an aging rock star, struck me as perfectly delightful. While he played, he would sway back and forth in his chair, now smiling, now frowning, now nearly shedding a tear, as if he were discovering all the moods of the music for the very first time.

Say what you will about classical music, one thing it has going for it is that it lets your mind wander. Rock bands, blues bands—and yes, salsa bands too—they're all intent on securing your undivided atten-tion. That's what the drums and amplifiers are there for. But classical musicians seem more willing to let you settle down, settle in, and follow your thoughts wheresoever they might lead you.

It's a little like the wardrobe in that children's book, the one where the plucky girl passes through the coats and finds herself in a whole new world. One moment you're in Carnegie Hall listening to a sonata, and the next thing you know you're wandering in a forest where the snow's beginning to fall, and there in a little clearing surrounded by pines you come upon a lamppost.

Now, on the one hand you're thinking: *What the heck is a lamppost doing in the middle of a snowy wood?* But on the other hand, it seems per-fectly natural to find it there. There's something so friendly and inviting about a lamppost that it's a welcome addition wherever it happens to appear.

Like on the cover of that Frank Sinatra record, the one where he's leaning against a lamppost, getting ready to sing some love songs to the strangers walking by.

Or in *Singin' in the Rain*, when Gene Kelly, having kissed Debbie Reynolds at her doorstep, suddenly finds himself in a downpour and leaps onto a lamppost to sing that he's laughing at clouds and ready for love, or something to that effect.

And then there's *Harvey*. You know, that Jimmy Stewart movie in which he plays Elwood P. Dowd, a grown man whose best friend is a six-foot-tall wish-granting rabbit. The first time that Elwood met Harvey, as he explains to the young doctor from the sanitarium, was early one evening several years ago. He was just walking down the street minding his own business when he suddenly heard someone say in a deep, rich voice: "Good evening, Mr. Dowd." And there was Harvey, leaning against a lamppost.

Can you imagine? Can you imagine if somewhere out there was a magical rabbit just leaning against a lamppost waiting for you to pass by so that he could introduce himself? At least, that's what I was thinking as Mr. Isserlis played his sonata.

Was this particular sonata the one in G Minor (vivace) or the one in D Major (allegro)? I couldn't tell you. What I can tell you is that Tommy wasn't enjoying it in any key. For Tommy's mind was not wandering. As soon as Mr. Isserlis had begun to play, his attention had been focused on the little black antennae poking out of the old man's sleeve.

Under the sway of moral indignation, Tommy initially tried to shame the old man by looking down at the apparatus with a scowl. But the old man, whose eyes were trained on the performer, didn't seem to notice. So, Tommy tried making his point with an exasperated release of air, a sort of manly version of a *tsk-tsk*. But the old man didn't notice that either. Gritting his teeth, Tommy shifted in his chair and made a show of staring intently at the cellist to signal to all in attendance that he had no intention of letting the moral failings of a single scofflaw interfere with his appreciation of the virtuosity on display, a strategy that seemed to work—at least for a minute or two. Then he was whispering in my ear.

"Can you believe it?"

After discarding the first reply that popped into my head, I opted for silence.

Tommy opted for a louder whisper.

"It's outrageous!"

This elicited a shush from a woman seated behind us.

Tommy's mouth opened in shock. He looked back at the woman and then at me. That he should be shushed when he was the one defending the laws of the United States, the decorum of Carnegie Hall, and the intellectual property rights of creative artists everywhere! Apparently, it was too much to bear. Because he began to get up from his seat.

"What are you doing?"

"I'm getting an usher."

"In the middle of the performance!?"

Another shush came from the woman behind us, this one with an edge.

Tommy rose with his shoulders hunched and began shuffling down the row. Now it was he who was saying "Excuse me, excuse me, excuse me" as music lovers in the surrounding seats communicated their own versions of exasperation, indignation, and shock.

When Tommy reached the end of the row, he stood to his full height and walked up the aisle with the pace and posture of the righteous. At the top was an usher—a Black woman in her forties—standing in front of the closed doors. She looked none too pleased by Tommy's midperformance approach. Tommy ignored her disapproval and indicated he needed to speak to her outside. So, the two quietly slipped into the lobby where the usher looked at Tommy with a furrowed brow.

What follows is a transcription of events based on the direct testimony of my husband and additional intelligence gathered over nine years of marriage.

"I want to report a bootlegger," he said.

"A bootlegger?" the usher asked in surprise. "You mean a maker of moonshine?"

"No! A *musical* bootlegger." Tommy pointed at the door. "The man sitting next to me is recording the concert. And it's not the first time I've seen him do it. In fact, I suspect he's a *serial offender.*"

The usher rolled her eyes.

"Did you just roll your eyes at me?" said Tommy in shock. "I thought it was against Carnegie Hall's policy for members of the audience to record the performances."

"Of course it is."

"Well then."

"It's the middle of the concert, sir. You might have waited until intermission to lodge your complaint."

"Complaint? This isn't a complaint!"

"Isn't it?"

"Is there a problem here, LaToya?"

Tommy and the usher looked up from their somewhat heated exchange to find they had been joined by a fifty-year-old man in a light gray suit. The usher turned to the man with deference.

"Excuse me, Mr. Cornell. But this gentleman believes the man sitting next to him is recording the concert."

"I don't believe it," interjected Tommy. "I *know* it. And as a member of the audience—as a *Patron*—I insist that something be done about it."

"Sir," said Mr. Cornell, "you don't need to raise your voice, and you certainly don't need to insist. The recording of concerts is strictly forbidden in Carnegie Hall."

"Exactly," said Tommy. He couldn't resist delivering a *so-there* glance in LaToya's direction, a gesture that did not go unnoticed and was not well received by either LaToya or Mr. Cornell.

Mr. Cornell cleared his throat, as if to start again.

"My name is Lionel Cornell. I'm the manager here. And you are . . . ?"

"Thomas Harkness."

"And where exactly are you seated, Mr. Harkness?"

"In row E, seat one-oh-seven. You can't miss him. He's an eighty-year-old man in a raincoat."

"An eighty-year-old man . . . ," said Mr. Cornell.

LaToya rolled her eyes again.

"Something like that," said Tommy. "But what difference does it make whether he's eighty or eighteen? An act of bootlegging is an act of bootlegging regardless of the bootlegger's age."

"Naturally," said Mr. Cornell, though clearly not being of that opinion. "LaToya," he said, turning to his employee, "at the intermission, please ask the gentleman in question to join us in the lobby."

"Of course, Mr. Cornell."

LaToya turned and slipped back through the door into the concert hall. When Tommy made a move to do the same, Mr. Cornell cleared his throat for a second time.

"I'm afraid, Mr. Harkness, that when an audience member leaves the concert hall in the middle of a performance, it is our policy not to allow him to reenter until intermission. . . ."

As Mr. Cornell finished making his point, a security guard approached, eyeing Tommy with suspicion.

"Everything all right, Mr. Cornell?"

"Yes, Miles. It seems we may have a member of the audience recording the concert."

Miles looked from Mr. Cornell to Tommy and back again.

"This guy?"

"No. Someone else. This gentleman brought it to our attention."

Finding the guard's assumption a little insulting, Tommy intended to give him a bit of a scowl. But when Tommy caught his eye, the guard gave him two thumbs-up before returning to his post.

As Tommy and the manager waited for LaToya's return, they couldn't hear the music playing behind the closed doors. But a few minutes later, they could hear the hearty applause indicating the end of the performance's first half. . . .

As MEMBERS OF THE audience made their way to the lobby, LaToya made her way to the fifth row, where she found the old man in the raincoat in a conversation with me.

"Excuse me, sir," she said. "Can you come to the lobby for a moment?"

At the usher's request, the old man registered a slight expression of surprise, but he didn't object. Giving me an apologetic smile for having to interrupt our little chat, he rose and followed LaToya up the aisle, limping a little, in the manner of one who needs a hip replacement. Once in the lobby, LaToya led him to where Mr. Cornell was waiting patiently with Tommy.

As a wife, there are times when no matter how you feel, you need to stand at your husband's side to lend him moral support. This wasn't one of them. I took up a position about five yards away. If I'd thought to bring my program, I would have been peeking over it.

Mr. Cornell received the old man in an impeccable manner.

"My name is Lionel Cornell, the manager here at Carnegie Hall. Could I ask your name?"

"It's Fein. Arthur Fein."

"Thank you, Mr. Fein. I'm sorry to bother you, but it has been brought to our attention that you may be recording the concert."

As the manager spoke, Mr. Fein leaned a little forward with a perplexed look on his face.

"Recording the concert?" he said after a moment. "I don't understand. . . ."

Before the manager could elaborate, Miles the security guard reappeared, but this time in the company of one of New York City's finest. Upon seeing the police officer, everyone looked a little stunned, including Mr. Cornell. Everyone that is but Miles, who, with his thumbs in his belt, was already taking credit for his sense of initiative.

"What seems to be the trouble?" asked the officer.

A little reluctantly, Mr. Cornell gestured toward my husband.

"Mr. Harkness, here, has suggested that Mr. Fein may have been re-cording the concert."

The cop gave Tommy a once-over that seemed to communicate his perfect familiarity with Wall Street types who made suggestions. When he turned to Mr. Fein, his expression softened a bit.

"Is this true, Mr. Fein? Were you recording the concert?"

"Absolutely not," responded Mr. Fein in a tone more bewildered than outraged.

"He absolutely was," interjected Tommy.

The officer turned to my husband.

"He just said he wasn't."

In a state of disbelief, Tommy looked from the manager to the usher for moral support. He even looked to Mr. Fein. Of the three, Mr. Fein seemed the only one inclined to give it to him. My husband turned back to the officer.

"So that's it?"

"What do you want me to do?"

"Frisk him!"

If the collective sentiment had been leaning away from the indignant thirty-six-year-old banker in a tailored suit toward the bewildered eighty-year-old man in a raincoat, Tommy's suggestion toppled it over. Quite understandably, the officer felt that civilians had no place telling members of the New York City Police Department whom they should or shouldn't frisk. For Mr. Cornell, the notion of a lobby frisking was in violation of *his* version of concert hall decorum. And LaToya? She clearly felt that someone from Tommy's walk of life had no business ut-tering the word *frisk* in the first place.

Frankly, I had to agree with her.

"You know," added Tommy to the officer, "he never takes off his trench coat during the performances. Why don't you ask him about that!"

I couldn't help but notice that Tommy had switched from saying "raincoat" to "trench coat," presumably to better capture the sinister aspects of the goings-on.

In response, the officer held up both of his hands in the calming gesture of a horse trainer.

"All right now," he said. "Why don't we all take it down a notch. In fact, maybe everyone should just go back to their seats and enjoy the rest of the show."

Though Mr. Cornell visibly winced at the characterization of the concert as a "show," he seemed to agree with the gist of the officer's suggestion, especially when the lights of the lobby began to flicker, signaling the end of intermission.

The small gathering observed a brief, uncomfortable silence, then it began to disperse with LaToya and Miles being the first to turn away. Even Tommy seemed ready to go back to his seat. But having turned toward the concert hall door, he suddenly wheeled around and lunged at Mr. Fein in order to grab him by the sleeve.

The officer lunged too, but at my husband in order to grab him by the lapels. And he probably would have arrested him on the spot—were it not for the Sony Walkman that tumbled out of Mr. Fein's jacket and landed on the floor with a clatter.

No one moved. Then, ever so slowly, the officer got down on his haunches and picked up the Walkman. LaToya looked crestfallen. Mr. Cornell aghast. Tommy looked like he was trying not to look too victorious and failing in the effort. And Mr. Fein, he wore an expression of boundless shame.

"The gentleman was right," he said after a moment. "I was recording the concert." Mr. Fein shook his head as if he couldn't quite believe his own admission. Then he continued in the voice of the forlorn. "For thirteen years, I attended this series in the company of my wife. And in all that time it never occurred to me to record a performance. But when she became too ill to come, I began recording the concerts so she could listen to them from the comfort of her bed."

Here he turned to the manager.

"It was wrong, Mr. Cornell; and I knew it was wrong. What else can I say?"

Everyone looked miserable now. The old man out of his shame, Mr. Cornell, LaToya, and the officer out of pity, and my husband for being the cause of it all.

The officer turned to Mr. Cornell.

"Is it your intention to press charges?"

"I don't think so, Officer."

The officer nodded in support of the manager's instinct. He popped open the Walkman and removed the cassette, putting it in his pocket. Then he handed the device to the manager and went back outside, but not before giving my husband another once-over and a shake of the head.

"Mr. Fein," said Mr. Cornell, "if you would come with me."

The manager led Mr. Fein away, with Miles trailing a few feet behind. LaToya went into the hall where the audience was already applauding to welcome Mr. Isserlis back onstage. And Tommy, he was standing by himself, looking around the lobby as if unsure of what to do.

In a situation like this, there are so few things to say that are right and so many that are wrong. Since I was never very good at telling the difference, I opted for the most compassionate suggestion I could think of: "Let's go home, sweetie."

After a moment, Tommy nodded and followed me toward the exit. But even as I was reaching for the door handle, he stopped and looked back in the direction that Mr. Cornell and Mr. Fein had disappeared. I closed my eyes.

"I think I should wait for him," he said.

"For whom?"

"For Mr. Fein."

I gave a little laugh. "Really?"

"I want to apologize to him," Tommy said, looking back again. "I

want to explain how disruptive a recording device can be for the experience of—"

"So, wait a second," I said, my voice rising a little. "Are you going to
apologize or explain?"

He looked at me.

"Both."

"Sweetie, if you want to wait here so you can *explain-ogize*, that's fine.
But I'm going home."

I gave him two seconds to respond, then walked out the door.

I may have been shaking a little. Because rather than head home, I
asked a complete stranger for a cigarette, something I hadn't done in
years. After she lit it for me, I just stood at the curb of Fifty-Seventh
Street smoking as it began to rain. About twenty feet to my left was the
police cruiser with its interior light on. In the driver seat I could see the
officer dutifully completing whatever paperwork my husband's complaint had generated. Twenty feet to my right was a well-fed party under
the canopy of the Russian Tea Room trying to decide where to go next.
In front of me, the Saturday night traffic was heading in both directions. But nowhere I looked was there a lamppost that seemed worth
leaping on.

As I was weighing whether to take the subway or hail a cab, I sensed
that someone had approached and was quietly waiting. Flicking the unfinished cigarette into the street, I turned, ready to express a measure of
compassion. But it wasn't Tommy. It was the cop.

"Mrs. Harkness?" he asked.

"Yes, that's right."

After giving me a sympathetic nod, he extended his hand, saying,
"Here's a little memento for your husband."

If you'd met Tommy's parents the year after their divorce, you'd find it
incomprehensible they'd ever been married. After spending twenty years
tugging themselves to some imagined middle ground, the divorce sent

them shooting off in the opposing directions they had wanted to travel all along.

One of the biggest differences between them was that Tommy's dad cared deeply about how he was remembered by his fellow men. When he happened to give an inadvertent offense or cause a moment of conflict, the incident stayed with him for days, sometimes weeks. But Tommy's mom? When it came to the opinions of others, she couldn't have cared less. She could fight the Battle of the Bulge with you over dinner on a Tuesday night, then invite herself to breakfast the following morning without a second thought. In this regard, Tommy's sister ended up taking after her mom. You can guess who took after his dad.

Despite all his talents and accomplishments, Tommy just couldn't shake the need to fret over the opinions of others, even strangers. Come to think of it, especially strangers. A discordant conversation with a restaurant hostess, hot words exchanged at a traffic light, when these sorts of instances occurred, they sank their claws into Tommy's sense of well-being. You could see it in his expression as he went over the encounter in his mind. His whole physique was suddenly that of a man about to turn the car around and drive back ten miles to "explain" himself. Why? Who knows. But however petty or brief had been the exchange, Tommy needed an explicit affirmation from his counterpart that no ill will would linger.

So, when my husband finally returned from Carnegie Hall and entered our bedroom wearing a hangdog expression, I could tell that things had not gone according to plan.

"Hi, sweetie," I said, looking over my reading glasses, as he plopped down on the ottoman looking like he'd walked all the way home.

"I waited half an hour," he said, taking off a shoe and tossing it aside. "When he didn't come out, I went and found the manager. He said that Mr. Fein had left by way of a staff exit."

I suppose you couldn't blame him.

Tommy took off the other shoe and tossed it in the opposite

direction. After a moment, he asked: "Do you think it's spelled *F-I-N-E* or *F-E-I-N*?"

I looked up from my book again.

"Does it make a difference?"

"I don't know. But I think *F-E-I-N* is a Jewish name . . ."

He said this with an added layer of guilt. I didn't say anything.

Tommy hung up his suit, brushed his teeth, and climbed into bed. After pretending to read for a minute, he turned off his light and closed his eyes. Then he got up to put away his shoes. Once he was back with his head on his pillow, I leaned over and kissed him on the brow. Sometimes, that's what we need—a little smooch on the noggin that assures us, however improbably, that everything is going to be all right. I figured it was the least I could do. Because, in ten minutes I'd be sound asleep, while for Tommy, it was going to be a long, long night.

FOR THE NEXT WEEK, Tommy came home every night with the same hangdog expression and the same look of having walked all the way home. At dinner, he picked at his food, and at bedtime, he didn't even bother pretending to read.

When Saturday rolled around, we skipped the shots at the Russian Tea Room and the champagne in the Patrons' Lounge. When we took our seats, Tommy looked back toward the concert hall's entrance, this time hoping that Mr. Fein would come down the aisle, excuse himself into the row, and take the seat at my husband's side. But the old man never showed.

On this, the final night of the *Virtuosos* series, it was Evgeny Kissin who took the stage—the very man who'd prompted us to come to Carnegie Hall. According to the program, he was playing twenty-four preludes by Chopin. To me, it sounded more like eight preludes played three different times, but maybe that was the point. Anyway, I had a lovely time, remembering the old out-of-tune piano that was in the dining hall at Camp Pamunkey, which led me to wonder if I could name all the residents of Cabin Five. And I could! (Setting aside that girl with pigtails who was always chewing Fruit Stripe gum. For the life of me, I couldn't remember if she was Eustace, Eunice, or Eugenia.)

For his part, Kissin must have lived up to his world renownedness because when he struck the final chord, the audience erupted into thunderous applause and shouts of *Bravo!* There was even a stomping of feet after the second encore, an expression of approval I would have thought distinctly un-Carnegiesque.

Yes, sirree. By all appearances, Evgeny Kissin's return to America was a triumph. Though, you wouldn't have known it from Tommy. I don't think he heard a note.

But three nights later, my husband came home looking every bit himself. In the kitchen, as I seared the steak and he tossed the salad, he was chattering away. He must have put it behind him, I thought with a sigh of relief as he carried the plates to the table. But once he'd poured the wine . . .

"You know that old man at Carnegie Hall?" Tommy asked, as if the old man at Carnegie Hall hadn't been at the center of our thoughts for over a week.

"Mm-hm," I said noncommittally, while taking a sip of wine.

"I think I can find him."

Tommy began chewing a piece of steak with a smile. I put my glass back on the table.

"What do you mean *find him*?"

Here Tommy smiled again, eager to share the thought process he'd carefully completed earlier that day while he should have been building a spreadsheet or something.

"Remember that night, how I went to the manager's office to find Mr. Fein and they told me he'd gone out the staff exit?"

"I remember."

"Well, on the way home today, I stopped in at Carnegie Hall and found the guard who stands near that very door. And he remembered the old man. Because of the incident. And he remembered that when he opened the door onto Seventh Avenue, it was raining. So he had offered to flag down a cab. But the old man had said he didn't need a cab. . . . Because he lived in the neighborhood!"

Never mind that Carnegie Hall wasn't even close to being "on the way home." As Tommy talked, I was nodding my head to express my general amazement—my amazement at the doggedness of character, at the death-defying acrobatics of the male ego, and at a wife's unflagging ability to be surprised by what should no longer be surprising.

"So," he continued, after taking another bite, "with that piece of information in hand, do you know what the *key* question is?"

"I can't wait."

"For a seasoned New Yorker—and I think we can assume Mr. Fein is a seasoned New Yorker—how big is a neighborhood?" Tommy raised his eyebrows and smiled, which, I suppose, was his version of taking a bow. "I figure the old man was about eighty; and it was raining, right? If we take those two factors into account, I think it's safe to assume that Mr. Fein lives within the immediate vicinity of Carnegie Hall. Now, assuming you can walk a north-south block in about a minute and an east-west block in three, we can draw a likely perimeter that extends from Fifth Avenue to Tenth Avenue and from Forty-Ninth to Sixty-Fifth Street."

More amazement. Unfiltered amazement.

"I know what you're thinking," continued my husband. "That sounds like a lot of ground to cover."

That wasn't at all what I was thinking. Not even in the "neighborhood" of what I was thinking. But Tommy was gaining speed, and I didn't want to slow him down.

"But here's the thing: In the quadrant to the southeast of Carnegie

Hall, many of the blocks are dominated by office buildings, and the majority of the northeast quadrant is taken up by Central Park, leaving just two of the four quadrants to reconnoiter. I figure I could complete the search within a week, if I simply walked the neighborhood for half an hour every day."

"On your way home from work," I suggested.

"Exactly."

Having witnessed the difficulty with which Mr. Fein walked up the aisle, I probably could have saved my husband some footwork by narrowing the likely perimeter. But under the circumstances, I figured the longer it took Tommy to find Mr. Fein, the better.

Tommy took an unusually big bite of his steak and chewed it with relish. However crazy his train of thought, it was nice to see his appetite was back.

"When I was up there today," he continued, "after talking to the guard, I stopped in at the apartment building next door to Carnegie Hall, as a sort of practice run. And I'm glad I did! Because when I asked the doorman if a Mr. Fein lived in the building, he clammed up like a member of the NSA. *We don't disclose the names of our residents*, he said. So, at the next building, I went in with a manila envelope in my hand saying, *I have a delivery for Mr. Fein*, and without skipping a beat, the doorman said they didn't have a Mr. Fein at that address."

Tommy raised his eyebrows again.

I raised my glass.

Then emptied it.

Later that night, when I went to lock the front door and turn out the lights, I saw Tommy's briefcase lying on the table in the foyer as usual.

By the time we got married, Tommy and I were already living together and sharing a bank account. At our wedding, we committed to have and to hold for richer or poorer in sickness and health, till death do us part. And I had given birth to both of his children—without an epidural. So, when I saw his briefcase on the table, did I hesitate before opening it? Not for a second.

Inside there was a stack of research that was surprisingly thick given how rarely Tommy's briefcase ventured beyond the foyer. But right there on top of the pile was what I was looking for: a carefully drawn map of the Carnegie Hall vicinity. There was even a little scale in the right-hand corner indicating that an inch was an eighth of a mile, and little red check marks by the two buildings he had already visited. Looking at the map, you could understand why Tommy won the Greenwich Country Day School science fair when he was in second grade.

Under the map, I found the manila envelope. In the interests of verisimilitude, Tommy had stuffed it with sheets of blank paper to give it the thickness of a legal document. On the outside of the envelope, all that Tommy had written was the old man's name. In a bit of wishful thinking that was almost endearing, he had spelled it: *Fine.*

IT TOOK TOMMY THREE days to find the building—a twelve-story co-op on Sixty-Second Street between Broadway and Amsterdam. By the time he found it, Tommy had entered over seventy-five buildings and been told by seventy-five doormen that there was no Mr. Fein at that address. So, he was totally unprepared when the seventy-sixth doorman stuck out his hand and said: "I'll give it to him." In fact, Tommy was so stunned, the doorman had to repeat himself.

But my husband is no slouch on his feet.

"Actually," he said, "I need Mr. Fein to *sign* for it. Do you know when he'll be back?"

"He was just going to the pharmacy."

"Then maybe I'll wait."

"Suit yourself."

Tommy nodded and sat on the lobby bench as the doorman resumed his place behind the reception counter.

"Nice building," Tommy said. "Prewar?"

"You got me."

Tommy tapped his feet as the doorman turned through some paperwork.

"How long has Mr. Fein lived here?"

"I wouldn't know. I've only been here six months myself."

Tommy tapped his feet some more.

"Did he go to the pharmacy for his wife?"

The doorman looked up from his paperwork.

"What's that?"

"I was just wondering if Mr. Fein went to the pharmacy to pick up some medicine for his wife."

"No. He lives alone."

Tommy stood up.

"He lives alone?!"

The doorman was a little surprised by Tommy coming to his feet so abruptly, and by the change in his tone. "Hey, what's this all about?" he had started to say when Mr. Fein walked through the door carrying a little bag from CVS. Mr. Fein gave the doorman a smile. He gave one to my husband too, assuming he was someone who lived in the building. But then he gave my husband a second look.

"Mr. Harkness . . . ?"

In the last three days, as Tommy had walked from building to building, he had imagined this moment in every detail. In his head he had gone over exactly what he would say, a speech that expressed regret and contrition, and that at one point even included the phrase "No, let me finish." But now that the moment had come, Tommy found himself pointing a finger at the old man and saying with unmistakable outrage: "You live alone!"

"Now, hold on there," said the doorman, coming around the reception desk with the clear intention of throwing Tommy out.

But Mr. Fein intervened. "It's okay, Martin," he said. Then he turned to Tommy with an expression of confusion. "But I'm afraid I don't understand what you're saying, Mr. Harkness."

"You told us you were making recordings for your wife," replied Tommy, "because she was too sick to leave her room. But your doorman here tells me you live alone!"

"I do live alone," said Mr. Fein. "I've lived alone ever since she died."

In the next ten minutes, Tommy apologized to Mr. Fein at least five times. He started in the lobby with a couple of quick *I'm sorrys*. When Mr. Fein insisted he come upstairs for a cup of coffee, Tommy took the opportunity in the elevator to apologize in greater detail. And when they were finally in Mr. Fein's little kitchen, he did it one more time, for good measure.

"Please," said Mr. Fein, as he set two mugs on the table and took the seat across from Tommy. "You don't have to apologize anymore."

"All right. But, honestly, you must think me a terrible person."

"Not at all! I understand exactly why you were upset. Attending a performance at Carnegie Hall with the woman you love has all the makings of a wonderful evening. And my actions—my *inexcusable* actions—were ruining the experience for you. In your place, I would have done the same thing."

They were both quiet for a moment, then Mr. Fein admitted with a smile: "When I was your age, I didn't particularly care for classical music. I was more interested in Frank Sinatra and Tony Bennett. It was my wife, Barbara, who was the lover of Mahler and Mozart. As a girl, she attended the Third Street Music School Settlement in the East Village. Do you know it?"

"No."

"Oh, it's a fine school. It was started in the nineteenth century to teach music to immigrant children, and eventually became a general elementary school. It's still there in the old neighborhood. Though now it's on Seventh Street, I believe. Anyway, as a young student, Barbara learned to play the classical repertoire. She went on to study music at Vassar and even taught piano for a few years when we were first married. So, once the children were grown, you can imagine which of us wanted to go to Carnegie Hall."

"To hear the *Virtuosos?*" asked Tommy.

"To hear everything! We went to hear the symphony orchestras and chamber orchestras. The quintets, quartets, and trios." Mr. Fein shook his head to think of all the concerts he'd attended. "Of course, I could never understand the music in the way Barbara could—not in the technical sense. But over the years, I think I came to appreciate the music as much as she did. And to look forward to it too. It became part of our life. In fact, that's one of the reasons we live in this building. When I retired, we moved here so we could walk to the hall."

Mr. Fein held out a box.

"Cookie?"

"No, thank you."

"I have a sweet tooth," he confessed, helping himself. Then he continued.

"When Barbara became ill and could no longer go to the concerts, I assumed that was the end of Carnegie Hall for both of us. But she wouldn't have it. She didn't want me to stay at home like a nurse. At her insistence, I began attending the concerts by myself. When I got home, she would be waiting up to hear all about it. And I do mean *all* about it. Was Perlman as good as Bell? Did he play Bach as well as he plays Beethoven? And how did he interpret the first partita? Half the time, I hadn't the slightest idea how to answer her questions. So . . ."

Mr. Fein opened his two hands.

"I began recording the concerts. As soon as I got home, she would have me put the cassette in the player, and we would listen to the performance together from beginning to end."

Hearing Mr. Fein's story, Tommy was deeply moved. But he also felt a pang of shame. For despite all the fuss he'd made over concert hall decorum and the rights of creative artists everywhere, he knew when all was said and done, he was an impostor. He had sat in the fifth row at Carnegie Hall for every Saturday night in April because, as a Manhattanite in his midthirties with a six-figure salary and an Ivy League education, that's what he thought he *should* be doing. Just as he should be buying custom suits from boutique tailors and French wines at fine restaurants. But in a humbling manner, fate had brought him face-to-face with the devoted, the committed, the impassioned.

"That's beautiful, Mr. Fein."

In saying this, Tommy must have revealed some of the shame he was feeling, because with a sympathetic smile, Mr. Fein reached across the table to pat the back of Tommy's hand—a little like the way I would kiss him on the brow.

"Please," said Mr. Fein. "Call me Arthur."

"I'm Thomas."

"It's nice to meet you, Thomas. But tell me, why *did* you come here today?"

"Because I felt terrible about what I had done. I was hoping to tell you so on Saturday night, but when you didn't show . . ."

"Ah," said Mr. Fein.

"If you were avoiding seeing me again, I wouldn't blame you."

"Oh no, it wasn't that," said Mr. Fein with a smile. "It was at Mr. Cornell's request."

"He didn't want you to come back to the series?"

"He didn't want me to come back to Carnegie Hall."

Tommy turned red with embarrassment.

"I am *so* sorry!"

"There you go again," said Mr. Fein with a laugh. "No more apologies. You promised."

They were both silent for a moment, then a thought occurred to Mr. Fein.

"You know what? There's something I'd like to show you."

Mr. Fein led Tommy out of the kitchen into a small sitting room with a wall of bookshelves, a matching sofa and chair, and a twenty-year-old television on a wheeled cart. Mr. Fein paused in the middle of the room.

"You were right to express outrage when you learned I was living alone. I certainly wasn't very honest with Mr. Cornell when I invoked my wife's illness as an excuse. When she died a year ago, I should have stopped recording the concerts. But I couldn't. I continued tucking my recorder in my coat and committing my little acts of piracy. Only, now it wasn't for Barbara, it was for me. So that when I came home, I could listen to the concert from beginning to end. As if she were still here."

"Oh, Arthur . . ."

"No, let me finish."

As Mr. Fein had been explaining himself, he had become increasingly excited. Now he took Tommy by the sleeve and pulled him to the end of the room, where on one of the bookshelves was a row of six black plastic cassette racks—all of them empty.

"That night when we had our little confrontation in the lobby and Mr. Cornell sent me packing, I came home, here, to this room, and gathered up all the years of recordings I'd so carefully labeled and alphabetized—and threw them away!"

Having delivered this pronouncement with great satisfaction, Mr. Fein noticed that Tommy was crestfallen.

"Thomas!" he exclaimed. "I didn't show you this to make you feel remorse."

Before Tommy could even think how to respond, there was the sound of a door closing, then a woman's voice.

"Dad?"

"Oh!" said Mr. Fein, in the tone of the pleasantly surprised. "It's my daughter, Meredith!"

Mr. Fein and Tommy turned away from the empty cassette racks as a woman in her midforties came into the room carrying a grocery bag.

"Meredith!"

"I was in the neighborhood, Papa, and thought I'd pick you up a few things."

"You didn't have to do that," said Mr. Fein, though he was obviously pleased by the gesture.

Not used to finding strangers in her father's apartment, Meredith looked at Tommy with curiosity.

"This is Thomas," said Mr. Fein with a smile. "He and his wife attend Carnegie Hall with me."

"Oh," she said with some surprise. "You met at a concert?"

"Yes," said Tommy. "We actually sit next to each other."

For a moment, Meredith stared at Tommy. Then she shifted the grocery bag from one arm to the other and looked at her father.

"Is this *him*? Is this the guy?"

Mr. Fein didn't answer. But given the change in his expression, he didn't need to. Meredith turned back to my husband.

"You heartless bastard!"

"Meredith, please," said Mr. Fein.

She shifted the bag again.

"For thirteen years my mother and father went to Carnegie Hall together. For thirteen years, rain or shine. And in the course of a single intermission, he is expelled for life. Because of what? Because an old man wants to listen to some music in memory of his wife, and this offends the delicate sensibilities . . . the superior sense of justice of a . . . *stockbroker*?!"

"I'm an investment banker," said Tommy, taking a step back.

"Is that supposed to mean something to me?" said Meredith, taking a step forward.

"It wasn't my intention . . ."

"*Wasn't my intention . . . wasn't my intention . . .*," said Meredith in a singsong voice. "It's *never* your type's intention!"

"Meredith, please," said Mr. Fein again. "That's enough."

"No," said Meredith, "it isn't!" Because she too had imagined this moment in detail. She too had gone over what she intended to say word for word. "Your type!" she continued. "You're so focused on whatever it is you do, and you're so well paid to do it, that you stop paying any attention to anything beyond yourselves. Like the world of consequences. I mean, what did you *think* was going to happen when you accused an old man of recording in Carnegie Hall? That he'd receive a round of applause?"

Despite the rage in Meredith's voice, tears were falling freely down her face.

"And all the while," she concluded, "all the while, you're sitting in the very seat my mother sat in!"

Tommy may have prided himself on anticipating arguments from every possible angle, but he never saw that one coming. It hit him like a punch to the diaphragm. After the blow, he didn't even have the oxygen to apologize.

Meredith might have taken some pleasure from the expression on his face, but she had her hands over her eyes.

"Mery . . . Mery," said Mr. Fein, stepping toward his daughter. "Come now, my little one. Let me take those groceries." He took the bag from his daughter and put it on a side table, then he took her in his arms. "There, there."

Crying into her father's shoulder, Meredith said, "There's ice cream in the bag. I brought your favorite. Rocky Road."

"That's okay," he said. "The ice cream can wait." Letting go of his daughter, he took a step back. "Now sit, Mery. You too, Thomas. There's something *I* want to say. To both of you."

Mr. Fein steered his daughter to the couch. Then he gestured for Tommy to take a seat beside her. With some effort Mr. Fein turned his armchair so it was facing them instead of the television. Then he sat, leaning a little toward his daughter.

"I was just about to explain something to Thomas, Mery, but I want you to hear it too. When your mother died, I continued going to the concerts for one reason: the music helped me grieve. At times it filled me with anger, and at times with sorrow. In either case, it was speaking to my grief. But some months ago, I knew the time for grieving had passed, and the time for forgiveness had begun. The time had come for me to forgive God for taking your mother from me and to forgive myself for outliving her. But I didn't have the strength to do it. So, week after week, I returned to my seat at Carnegie Hall and walked home with my little cassette so I could sit in this chair and listen in grief. That is, until Thomas appeared. In the lobby that night, I felt such shame. But it wasn't Carnegie Hall I had let down, Mery. It was your mother. She was not a morbid or angry person. She loved the music because she loved life. And it was time for me to love life again, as she always had."

Mr. Fein turned to my husband.

"So, you see, Thomas, this is why I never wanted your apology. Because what I feel toward you is not anger, but a great sense of gratitude."

Tommy and Meredith rode down to the lobby in the elevator together. Meredith had wanted to stay behind, if for no other reason than to avoid the ride with Tommy, but Mr. Fein insisted they go together, just as he had insisted they sit side by side on the couch.

Predictably, they made the ten-floor journey in silence.

There was a mirror on one of the walls of the elevator, so Tommy had a chance to study Meredith without looking at her directly. She seemed exhausted. Did she have children? he wondered. Given her age, they would probably be in their teens, handfuls in their own right. But on her way home from work, she had gone to the store for her father and stopped in to make sure he was all right, all the while shouldering her own grief for the loss of her mother.

As they reached the lobby, he wondered if he should hold open the elevator door, or if she would be offended by the gesture. At the last instant he reached out an arm, and she said thank you.

When they stepped outside, it was already seven. Since it was the first week of May, there was still another hour of light, but a chill remained in the air. Walking a pace ahead of Tommy, Meredith didn't turn left or right, or step from the curb to hail a cab. She paused to button her coat.

Taking heart from this, Tommy paused beside her, ostensibly to button his. Making eye contact, he offered an awkward smile and she returned it in kind.

"I'm sorry about the ice cream," he said.

She looked at him with an expression of surprise, and he feared he had struck the wrong note. But then she smiled more genuinely.

"Figures," she said. "The one time they have Rocky Road, and it melts."

He smiled more genuinely too and stuck out his hand.

"I know it wasn't the best of circumstances, but it was nice to meet you."

She took his hand and they shook. But then she didn't let go.

"What did you say your name was? I mean your full name."

"Thomas Harkness."

"That's right. Thomas Harkness."

She nodded her head, but still didn't release his hand.

"The night that you complained to the usher, do you remember what they were playing?"

Tommy hesitated, unsure of where the conversation was going.

"Surely you remember," she prompted.

"It was the cellist, Steven Isserlis. He was playing Bach."

"Ah," she said with a smile. "Well, listen here, Thomas Harkness. My father has come to some sort of peace about all of this—because he's a kindhearted old man who wouldn't cast a stone at a mountain. But just because he's willing to forgive you, doesn't mean I am. In fact, I will never forgive you for what you did that night. Never . . . ever . . . ever."

Reflexively, Tommy began to withdraw his hand, but she tightened her grip.

"I hope you keep going to Carnegie Hall for the rest of your life, Thomas Harkness. And I hope that every time you're sitting there in my mother's seat, and every time you hear the music of Bach, and every time you hear a cello, I hope you'll remember me standing on Sixty-Second Street telling you what a self-righteous, insensitive son of a bitch you are."

I NEVER MET THIS Meredith. I don't know if she lives uptown or down. If she's single, married, or divorced. If she's happy or sad. But on the off chance she reads this, I want her to know that her wish came true.

For in the years that followed, when we were taking a cab to the Upper West Side and the driver happened to turn left on Fifty-Seventh Street such that we drove past Carnegie Hall, for the briefest instant I could see a pained expression cross my husband's face. I'd see the same expression at high school recitals whenever some adolescent came on-stage with a cello, and I'd see it at weddings, whenever we heard the first chords of a composition by Bach.

Some might find this ironic. But there's nothing particularly ironic about a curse. In fact, a curse is the opposite of irony. Because it intends to mean exactly what it sounds like it means, word for word, note for note, in every possible respect.

Here's the ironic part:

That third Saturday in April, when Tommy opted to excuse me, excuse me, excuse me right in the middle of the performance, I was aghast. In fact, I was so aghast, the only way I could think to stave off my embarrassment and retain the goodwill of those around me was to give 100 percent of my attention to the performance, for a change. No snowy night by a lamppost; no Gene Kelly or Jimmy Stewart; no girls in pigtails chewing Fruit Stripe gum. Just the cello, the cellist, and me.

As Tommy exited the hall, Mr. Isserlis finished the piece he was playing. Then after drawing a watch from his pocket, he joked that his accompanist must have been feeling unusually upbeat, because they had finished the first half of the program two and a half minutes early. Once the audience's laughter had died down, Mr. Isserlis said that to ensure we didn't feel shortchanged, he would now play something not on the program—the prelude to the first of Bach's Suites for Cello (in G Major).

Before beginning, the cellist gave a brief history of the suites, noting that for hundreds of years they were all but forgotten until they were rediscovered in the late nineteenth century by a thirteen-year-old prodigy named Pablo Casals. Apparently, Casals had happened into an old music shop near the harbor in Barcelona and found the suites buried under a stack of musical scores, crumpled and discolored with age. Years later, as a world-famous cellist, Casals championed the suites at every opportunity, bringing them the attention they so rightly deserved. Or, so concluded Isserlis.

Once again, there were whispered remarks in the audience, then a collective silence set off by a few coughs. Once again, the cellist laid his bow across his cello, closed his eyes, and began to play.

How to describe it?

I never studied music or played an instrument. I rarely sang along in church. So, I don't know the proper terminology. But once Isserlis was playing, within a matter of seconds, you could tell you were in the presence of some form of perfection. For not only was the music uplifting, each individual phrase seemed to follow so naturally, so inevitably upon the last that a slumbering spirit deep within you, suddenly awakened, was saying: *Of course, of course, of course* . . .

And as the music washed over the audience, Isserlis somehow conveyed the improbability of it all through his playing. For surely, it was all so improbable. To begin with you have the fact that some crumpled old sheet of music, which could have been torn or tossed or set on fire a thousand times over, had survived long enough to be discovered by a boy in an old music shop—in a harbor in Barcelona, no less. The very cello Isserlis was playing had survived two and a half centuries despite the fact that its entire essence seemed to depend upon the fragility of its construction. But the greatest improbability, the near impossibility, was that somewhere in Germany back in seventeen something something Bach had taken his deep and personal appreciation of beauty and translated it so effectively into music that here in New York, hundreds of years later and thousands of miles away, thanks to the uncanny skill of this cellist, that appreciation of beauty could be felt by every one of us.

About a minute and a half into the piece, after a series of low and almost somber notes, there was a slight pause, a near cessation, as if Bach having made an initial point was taking a breath before attempting to tell us what he had really come to say. Then from that low point, the music began to climb.

But the word *climb* isn't quite right. For it wasn't a matter of reaching one hand over the other and pulling oneself up with the occasional anxious glance at the ground. Rather than climbing, it was . . . it was . . . it was the opposite of cascading—a fluid and effortless tumbling upward. An ascension.

Yes, the music was ascending and we were ascending with it. First slowly, almost patiently, but then with greater speed and urgency, imagining now for one instant, and now for another, that we have reached the plateau, only for the music to take us higher still, beyond the realm in which climbing can occur, beyond the realm in which one looks down at the ground, beyond hope and aspiration into the realm of joy where all that is possible lies open before us.

And then, it was over.

Oh, how we applauded. First in our chairs, and then on our feet. For we were not simply applauding this virtuoso, or the composition, or Bach. We were applauding one another. Applauding the joy which we had shared and which had become the fuller through the sharing.

As we applauded, everyone in every aisle was looking to their left and right such that suddenly I and the old man were nodding at each other with smiles on our faces in acknowledgment of what we had just witnessed, what we had been a part of.

———

How I would have loved to describe that moment to Tommy. To describe for him the sense of improbability, of ascension, of joy that I had been lucky enough to partake in thanks largely to him. But, of course, for Tommy any description of that night represented another cut of the knife.

So, we never spoke of it.

And in the years that followed, only when he was away on business, and the children were sound asleep, and the city was hushed unexpectedly, like with a newly fallen snow, would I take the cassette tape the police officer had given me from the back of my drawer and listen to Mr. Fein's recording.

The DiDomenico Fragment

LUNCH AT LA MAISON

The only advantage to growing old is that one loses one's appetites. After the age of sixty-five one wishes to travel less, eat less, own less. At that point, there is no better way to end one's day than with a few sips of an old Scotch, a few pages of an old novel, and a king-size bed without distractions.

Certainly, some of this decline stems from the inevitable degeneration of the physical form. As we age, our senses grow less acute. And since it is through the senses we satisfy our appetites, it is only natural that when our eyes, ears, and fingers falter that we should begin to desire with a diminished intensity. Then there is the matter of seasoned familiarity. By the time our hair goes gray, not only have we sampled most of life's pleasures, we have sampled them in different locations at different times of day. But in the final accounting, I suspect the cessation of appetites is mostly a matter of maturity. Traipsing after a beautiful young thing late into the night, going from one trendy spot to the next and trying rather desperately to think of something witty to say while pouring a well-aged Bordeaux at our own expense . . . Really. At this stage, who can be bothered?

―――――

But if a decline in the appetites brings some sense of relief to most who age, it is particularly welcome to those in their sixties who can no longer afford the lifestyle of their forties.

On the isle of Manhattan, this population is more sizable than you might expect. Well-meaning husbands, who have put off their financial planning for one decade too many, routinely strand their widows with insufficient funds. Others, who proved capable in commerce as younger men, become careless or even foolish in retirement, wasting badly needed resources on real estate speculations, mistresses, and charity. Then there are those sensible fellows—like me—who, having carefully calculated the necessary capital to support their retirement and pru-dently set aside savings from year to year, turn a blind eye to the frothi-ness of a bull market and smugly quit their job, only to be brought up short six months later by the ensuing collapse. Whatever the excuses, many who reach their golden years on the Upper East Side find them-selves suddenly forced to live below their prior means. So, it's just as well they no longer want what they can't afford.

"Are you finished, Mr. Skinner?"

"Yes. Thank you, Luis."

"Will there be anything else?"

"Just the check."

Clearing what is left of my *salade Niçoise*, Luis winds his way to La Maison's kitchen through a maze of mostly empty tables.

There was a time when you could track the evolution of power in Man-hattan by dining at La Maison. Located at Sixty-Third and Madison, offering a serviceable execution of Continental cuisine, the restaurant welcomed real estate developers, advertising executives, financiers, and the ladies who lunched. Over the years, the décor grew a little tired, the food a little outmoded, and those "in the know" moved on to brighter venues serving brighter fare. But if La Maison was no longer the most sought-after table in town, it was not entirely déclassé. There were still a few veterans of commerce and society who, out of habit or lack of imagination, returned for the prix fixe lunch.

There in the corner, for instance, is Lawrence Lightman. A stately six foot two, Lawrence hasn't led a publishing house in over a decade, but he continues to wear a coat and tie; and he apparently made enough of a name for himself that aspirants in the field still make the occasional pilgrimage to his table.

Closer to the bar is Bobby Daniels. A former partner at Morgan Stanley, Bobby was once considered a prodigy in the field of acquisitions and divestments. In fact, this skill came so naturally to him, he acquired and divested four different wives. He now has an office at some mahogany-paneled trust company where his primary responsibility is the hanging of his hat in sight of the clients.

And over there at the table by the door sits Madeline Davis. Seventy, if a day, Madeline has been a widow for at least four presidential elections, and it shows. The dress she's wearing has gone in and out of style twice since she bought it in 1962, and she applies her makeup with all the misplaced generosity of a Rockette. She also happens to be a particularly divine example of the Park Avenue pauper.

Though she hasn't given a dime to charity, purchased a work of art, or read a book in over twenty years, when her husband was still alive the Davis name was indelibly etched onto the mailing lists of the city's museums, galleries, and publishers. This proved fortuitous, since as her income shrank, Madeline could dine at least twice a week on cold canapés and warm white wine at the latest opening or reception. In fact, at some point in the late 1990s, as these quasi-affairs were getting more extravagant, she began carrying Ziploc bags in her purse so that when no one was looking she could pilfer enough food from the buffet to last her the week.

This delightful practice went on for some time. Then one night at the Museum of Natural History—at a benefit for something or other—she came face-to-face with a pyramid of Swedish meatballs. The dish must have been her weak spot, for bypassing the crudités and cheese platters, Madeline opted to fill all three of her baggies with the delectable little spheres, spooning in some extra gravy for good measure.

At the end of the party, Madeline exited the museum with the rest of us, gripping her purse tightly to her chest. But at the very moment she was descending the steps, an enterprising Buckley boy who walked his neighbors' dogs for a fee was passing by with a motley crew of canines on intertwined leashes. Well, perhaps Madeline had been gripping her purse a little too tightly and one of the baggies had burst, because suddenly all eight dogs were tugging on their restraints. Four of them began to bark. The urgency of the pack proved too much for the lad, and breaking free, they bounded up the steps in her direction. Faced with certain death, Madeline did what any sensible woman would do: She reached into her purse and began flinging the meatballs at the oncoming dogs as her fellow Manhattanites looked on in horror. Which just goes to show that while thrift may be a virtue, every virtue has its limits.

"Here you are, Mr. Skinner."

"Thank you, Luis."

After reviewing the bill, I paid in cash, leaving Luis the requisite 15 percent, donned my coat, saluted Lawrence, waved to Bobby, and was almost out the door.

"Percival!"

"Ah. Madeline. I didn't see you there."

A wiser man would have approached with his hands in his pockets. Before I realized my error, she had grabbed my left with an arthritic claw.

"It's been ages," she said.

"I was just thinking something along those lines myself."

"We should have dinner some time."

"That would be lovely," I replied and headed for the door. Though needless to say, I'd sooner hang.

AN INQUIRY

One reason I still dine at La Maison is that it is located just a few blocks from my apartment building, a twenty-story prewar on Park Avenue. At one time, I commanded six rooms on the eighteenth floor with a sizable balcony. In preparation for retirement, I sold the place to a hedge fund manager half my age and purchased a two-bedroom on the fourth floor. I might have ended up with a little more space and a little more light had I been willing to move, but I'm too old to learn the names of a new slate of doormen.

"Hello, Max."

"Welcome back, Mr. Skinner. How was lunch?"

"Same as usual."

"And how is that?"

"At my age, a cause for celebration."

Max smiled. But when I made a move to enter, he gave a tilt of the head and lowered his voice.

"There's a gentleman waiting for you."

"For me?"

"In the lobby. He showed up around twelve thirty. I told him you'd be a while, but he insisted on waiting."

Sure enough, sitting on the bench under the framed etching of Roman ruins was a little man in a secondhand raincoat. Seeing me, he virtually leapt to his feet.

"Mr. Skinner?"

"Yes."

"Percival Skinner?"

"That's right."

The little man looked relieved.

"My name is Sarkis."

"Like the tuna?"

"What's that? Oh, I see." He let out a little laugh. "No, not Starkist. Sarkis. It's a Greek name."

"Is it, now."

"Yes. Well. I was wondering if you had a few minutes."

"To what end?"

"It is on a matter that I think will be of interest to you; and may be of profit. . . ."

"I'm listening."

Mr. Sarkis glanced around the lobby.

"Isn't there somewhere we could speak in private?"

If the gentleman's raincoat was Salvation Army, the suit underneath was decidedly Savile Row; and the shrewdness of his countenance suggested that of a buyer, rather than seller.

"Come on up," I said.

And up we went.

"Can I offer you something to drink?" I asked, as I hung my visitor's coat in the closet by the door. "A glass of whiskey? A cup of tea?"

"I would love a cup of tea, if it wouldn't be too much trouble."

"No trouble at all." I led Mr. Sarkis into the living room. "Why don't you have a seat while I put on the kettle."

He opted for the couch, sitting at the edge of the cushions with his elbows on his knees.

In the kitchen I turned on the kettle, took the teacups from the cabinet and the tea from its tin. Then, as the water warmed, I peeked into the living room. Mr. Sarkis had left his place on the couch to study the porcelains on display in the corner cupboard. After a moment, he picked up the Cantonese bowl and turned it gently in his hands. Though small, it was the most valuable piece in the room. The little Greek obviously knew his business. I made some racket while putting the tea service on its tray, and when I returned to the living room I found him back on the edge of the cushions with his elbows on his knees.

Pouring the tea, I asked Mr. Sarkis what I could do for him.

"I happen to operate a small gallery in Paris dealing in antiquities," he began, "but I also represent a certain collector who is a lover of Renaissance art."

He pronounced it *re-NAY-sance.*

"Renaissance art was one of my specialties," I said.

"Your reputation precedes you. In fact, that's what has brought me to your door."

"Is your client looking for an appraisal?"

"Not quite. The reason I'm here is that I gather you may be in possession of a work by Giuseppe DiDomenico. Or rather, a fragment . . ."

I put my teacup down.

"I am afraid you are slightly misinformed, Mr. Sarkis. You see, I did own a DiDomenico fragment, but I sold it some years ago."

"Ah," he said with a look of disappointment. "Would you be willing to tell me whom you sold it to?"

"He was a Texan."

Sarkis leaned a little forward.

"An oilman?"

"No. I believe he was a defense contractor."

"From Houston?"

"Dallas."

Mr. Sarkis nodded thoughtfully.

"That is helpful."

I didn't know if it was or wasn't, but our meeting seemed to have suddenly run its course. I rose from my chair. "I'm sorry if you've wasted your time."

Mr. Sarkis rose as well. "Every setback brings the collector one step closer to his goal," he said, sagely.

Ushering him to the door, I retrieved his coat, called for the elevator, and stuck out my hand to wish him well. But rather than take my hand, he seemed to be pursuing a new line of thought.

"I gather you spent most of your tenure at Sotheby's," he said, after a moment.

"That's right."

"More than twenty years."

"Almost thirty."

"Then perhaps you know of someone *else* in possession of a DiDomenico."

"Someone else . . ."

Mr. Sarkis took the ensuing silence as an encouragement.

"My client is a man of fine sensibilities, Mr. Skinner, but he is also a pragmatist. As such, he would be more than happy to compensate a professional whose mediation led to the successful acquisition of a DiDomenico."

"To what extent?"

"To what extent would the professional have to mediate?"

"To what extent would he be compensated."

"Ah, yes. Well, naturally, that would depend upon the size and quality of the work. But I should think an introduction that led to a purchase might be worth a finder's fee of say . . . fifteen percent?"

The elevator arrived.

"Let me think on it," I said.

"Take your time. I will be in town until the first of the year. You can reach me at the Carlyle in room four-oh-one."

He boarded the waiting elevator. I closed the door to my apartment, carried the tea service back into the kitchen, and stood at the sink thinking: *Well, well, well.*

THE FIRST OF SEVEN JOYS

Family traits are passed down from generation to generation out of the impenetrable past with no discernible point of origin, but family wealth must begin somewhere. For my family, it began with Ezekiel Hollingsworth Skinner in Milton, Massachusetts, in 1855. In that year, the thirty-five-year-old Ezekiel opened a small mill where he manufactured paper for local pamphleteers. During the Civil War, when wood pulp grew scarce, he refined the technique for turning rags into paper, such that during the postwar years with his patented process in hand,

Ezekiel turned one paper mill into ten and ten thousand dollars into a million.

In spite of Ezekiel's industry, or perhaps because of it, he and his wife produced only one child over their thirty years together, a son named Valentine. Valentine, who was raised in a house not two hundred yards from his father's first mill, joined the family business after attending Harvard and then took the helm when Ezekiel died of influenza in 1880. In the manner of his time, Valentine put a little distance between himself and the source of his wealth by moving his wife and four sons from the mill in Milton to a brownstone in Manhattan. There, with almost as strong a work ethic as his father but with a much less flinty mindset, Valentine doubled the size of the company, sold it to a competitor, and turned his attention to poetry, opera, and art.

A New England Protestant by upbringing and conviction, Valentine showed a healthy disinterest for all that was in vogue. As such, he was the last man in his circle to wear a top hat and waxed mustaches, and he furnished his townhouse with Roman statuary, medieval furniture, and Renaissance paintings. But his most prized possession, without question, was an Annunciation by the Florentine Giuseppe DiDomenico.

DiDomenico was something of a bridge between the early and late Renaissance in Tuscany. Having studied with Fra Angelico, DiDomenico opened an atelier in 1460 where, in the decades that followed, he influenced two generations of Florentine painters. (According to Vasari, Raphael's mastery of contrapposto sprang from the hours he spent at DiDomenico's knee.) But as DiDomenico dedicated more of his life to the education of artists than the completion of commissions, only a handful of his paintings survived; and the most important of these was the Annunciation that he painted for Lorenzo de' Medici in 1475. While on a grand European tour in 1888, my great-grandfather bought the painting from a dealer in Paris. He brought it home to New York and hung it in a place of honor—high on the wall behind his dining-room chair—where he could not see it, but where for all others it became fused with the image of his person.

In the mold of the founding fathers, Great-grandpa was as suspicious of primogeniture as he was of popes and kings. In his eyes, to leave all of one's wealth in the hands of one's eldest child was contrary to Christian teaching, common sense, and the American Way. Thus, having given major bequests to Harvard and the Metropolitan Opera, in his last will and testament he instructed that his house and everything in it be sold so that the proceeds could be combined with the remainder of his fortune and divided among his four sons. But the possession he could neither bear to sell nor give away was that one which had come to exemplify his devotion to Christianity, his love of art, and his place at the head of the table—the Annunciation. So, he had the painting cut into four equal parts, and at the reading of his will each of his sons was presented with his own quadrant framed and ready for hanging.

At this point, nothing would make me happier than to confirm for you, gentle reader, that a painting is just a painting—and thus, whenever the Annunciation is mentioned hereafter, you can simply insert whatever grandiose work of art you vaguely remember from your last visit to a museum or church. But I'm afraid the subject matter and format of the Annunciation have direct bearing on the events of this tale, and possibly its themes. So, with apologies to the more erudite and devout, at this juncture I offer a brief history of the Annunciation as a painting.

Bear with me. For once, I promise to be brief.

As every schoolboy knows, European art from the Middle Ages through the Renaissance was dominated by Christian imagery. At the time, the art world was virtually a *division* of the Roman Catholic Church, and the Continent was littered with scenes from the Old and New Testaments, portraits of saints and apostles, and portrayals of Jesus Christ at every juncture of his life. Within this vast almost fetishistic catalogue of holy subject matter, one popular subset was the Seven Joys of the Virgin—that is, the seven most exultant moments in the life of Mary. Generally speaking, these referred to the Annunciation, the Nativity, the Adoration of the Magi, the Resurrection, the Ascension, the Pentecost, and the Assumption. You may not be familiar with the precise nomenclature of the Seven Joys, but rest assured you have seen them all—over altars, in textbooks, on note cards, and on those brightly colored candles before which Mexicans reportedly pray.

Of the Seven Joys, the scene that most interested the painters of the Italian Renaissance was the Annunciation: the moment in which the Archangel Gabriel *announces* to the Virgin Mary that she is, miraculously, with child. All of the era's masters tackled this subject, and exquisitely so. Fra Angelico (ca. 1440), Filippo Lippi (ca. 1455), Piero della Francesca (ca. 1455), Leonardo da Vinci (ca. 1473), Botticelli (1489), Raphael (1503), etc.

But what is most interesting, and perhaps most revealing, about the masters' interest in the Annunciation, is that they all chose to paint it with the same composition. While, in theory, the scene could be imagined in a thousand different ways, for the Italian masters Mary was always on the right side of the painting and the Archangel always on the left; Mary was generally seated with a book at hand, and the winged Gabriel kneeling with a lily; Mary was always in a quasi-interior (such as under a portico or in a room that opened on a garden) while Gabriel was either outside the interior space or in front of a window—such that the countryside could be seen in the distance over his shoulder.

If we look at depictions of Abraham sacrificing Isaac, or the Wedding at Cana, or the Sermon on the Mount, there is far more variability in how Renaissance painters imagined the scenes. So why this strict adherence to form in the case of the Annunciation? I would argue (and *have* argued; see *Renaissance Quarterly* volume XX, issue 3) that for the

Renaissance masters the Annunciation was the equivalent of the sonnet for the Elizabethan poets: an artistic endeavor with strict rules that tested the ingenuity of the craftsman and allowed him to showcase his talents to his peers. The Annunciation was the perfect subject matter for such a game because it simultaneously required the rendition of a landscape in the distance and an architectural space up close, interior and exterior light, the human and divine forms, and the varied textures of fabric, feathers, and a flower. In other words, if one could paint an Annunciation, one could paint anything.

Needless to say, in tackling *his* Annunciation, DiDomenico followed form. Thus, when Great-grandpa had his painting quartered, one son ended up—more or less—with an Italian landscape, one with a detailed interior, one with the archangel on his knee, and one with the Virgin in repose.

None of Valentine's sons proved as prudent with money or as devoted to art as their father, but they loved the old man dearly. So when they died, they each followed his example and divvied up their DiDomenico into as many pieces as they had progeny. This tradition was repeated by the next generation, such that when my father died in 1982, I received a fragment measuring three inches square. And what had once held pride of place at the head of a patriarch's dining room was now a curiosity sitting on a living-room table between a jade tortoise and a snuffbox.

Over the years, all of my siblings and most of my cousins had dispensed with their fragment. Schuyler sold his to a member of the House of Saud who fancied building a museum of European art in the desert. Joel donated his to the basement of the Wadsworth Atheneum. My fragment ended up in the hands of the aforementioned Texan in 2001. But I was fairly certain that one cousin who had never parted with his painting was Billy, because just a few years prior, I had seen it myself in the guest suite of his weekend home in Litchfield, Connecticut— hanging over the toilet.

———

At four o'clock the next day, I set out from my apartment. I walked down Park Avenue, cut through the MetLife Building, passed under the great painted ceiling of Grand Central Terminal, and exited onto Vanderbilt, where lies the Yale Club.

For a man in his sixties who is no longer a man of means, the university clubs of Manhattan provide an oasis. The finer clubs in the city like the Union and the Knickerbocker are rather sticklers when it comes to matters of membership; and their doormen—like the doormen in the best apartment buildings—generally hold their positions for decades and pride themselves on knowing the names of everyone who passes through their door. "Good evening, Mr. Stuart. When's the wife returning from Palm Beach?" and so forth. But the doormen at the university clubs are in no position to know their constituents by name. The membership rolls at these clubs are relatively large and include alumni from across the country. So, if you are wearing a jacket and the old school tie, and are prepared to make the usual excuses, you can expect to be admitted without incident to a university club to which you do not pay the dues. Once inside, you can read the newspapers in the library, nibble the complimentary crackers in the bar, or even take a sauna, should you be so inclined; and, if your timing is good, you might run into an old acquaintance who offers to buy you a drink as a matter of course. Admittedly, I have spent more than my share of pleasant afternoons in the Yale Club; and that's how I knew that on most Wednesdays after four, my cousin could be found at the backgammon table near the bar.

Cousin Billy

No one is born pompous. To attain that state requires a certain amount of planning and effort. Presumably you could achieve it by a variety of means, but one sure way is to attend an old prep school that's a little past its prime; while there, exhibit some facility in a field sport that you will never have cause to play again; room with a fellow whose name is over the library door; and along the way, gain familiarity with a pastime that requires travel and specialized apparel—such as duck hunting or downhill skiing. Follow these simple steps and you are sure to gain the necessary self-assurance to expound authoritatively on wine, politics, and the lives of the less fortunate—and to generally go on and on about anything else. Case in point: Billy Skinner.

After attending both of his father's alma maters, Billy had one of those Manhattan careers that was proper and well paid, if a little hard to pin down. Over the years, he shifted from one financial behemoth to the next without ever quite being fired or poached, and though the term *vice president* was consistently bandied about, he never seemed to have authority over anyone other than a secretary. I don't know if his grandfather was more successful than my grandfather or simply more tightfisted, but the members of Billy's branch were generally better off than the members of mine. He also married well, which doesn't hurt. Having bounced around Wall Street for a socially sufficient stretch, he retired at the age of fifty-five and quickly settled into unhurried mornings and idle afternoons.

"Hello, Billy."

"Skinny!"

(Having already gone on at some length about the traits of white Anglo-Saxon Protestants, I shall leave an exposition on their horrendous use of nicknames to another day.)

"Are you stopping in for a drink?" he asked.

"No. I was just headed out."

"Ah. Too bad. I was hoping you might join me for a bit of backgammon."

I glanced at my watch.

"Well, I might have time for a game or two . . ."

"Bully," he said, God help us.

As we set up the board, he suggested we play for stakes—to make the game more interesting.

"Why not."

With a touch of bravado, he proposed five dollars a point, as if putting a few twenties at risk might elevate the game to a matter of valor. I accepted.

One benefit of speaking to the pompous is that their presumption of superiority is so strong, they are rarely guarded in what they have to say. If you set the mood and give them a little shove, they will pontificate accordingly. I let Billy win the first game and offered to set up the board while he ordered a round of drinks. Early in the second game, I left a man open so he could put me on the post. When I rolled and couldn't get in, I mentioned I was writing a little piece on DiDomenico.

"Is that so," he said without interest, rolling his dice.

"Do you still have yours?" I asked in an offhand manner.

"What's that?"

He looked up from the board.

"Your fragment from old Valentine. Do you still have it out in the country?"

"Oh. No. I donated that to St. George's years ago. I think it's hanging in the headmaster's house."

He made his move, then leaned a little forward to speak in confidence. "I give them all of the art I don't like. It's one of the great gambits. There's a lot of leeway in setting the value of an item like that. You can get a sizable tax write-off for cleaning out your attic while fending off the development boys for a year or two!"

As he concluded, I think he actually gave me a wink.

To make matters worse, when I rolled again I couldn't get in—despite the fact he'd only made three points. He doubled me, rolled a five and three, formed a fourth point, and I spent another turn on the post. When all was said and done, I was backgammoned and down forty dollars. I had no choice but to keep on playing. It took me an hour, but I won back my forty dollars and took an additional sixty from his estate. As he counted out the money, I couldn't help feeling he somehow deserved it.

I guess it was a matter of valor, after all.

When we exited the building at six o'clock, the temperature had dropped into the low fifties, so we paused on the curb to button our coats.

"It's funny you should ask about the old DiDomenico," he said.

"Oh? Why is that?"

"It's the second time it's come up this week."

"That is funny. What was the context?"

"A little Mediterranean fellow paid me a visit hoping to buy it, God knows why. Well, cheerio, Skinny." Then he walked off in the direction of Grand Central.

So, the canny Mr. Sarkis was one step ahead of me. I wouldn't be surprised if he had already paid ill-fated visits to Schuyler and Joel. But there was one member of the family he might not have been able to track down. Because Peter Skinner, Jr., had changed his name. . . .

NÉ SKINNER

Peter's father and his grandfather married relatively late in life. As a result, while he and I were both great-grandsons of Valentine, he was only half my age.

Certainly, we are all shaped by that first decade of our youth, but the first decade of our youth is shaped by the decade that preceded our arrival. Thus, while I was born in 1940, my upbringing was heavily influenced by the Depression; and while Peter was born in 1971, his upbringing was heavily influenced by the Summer of Love, Woodstock, and the landing on the moon—which is to say, the era of fairy tales. The end result was that Peter was a warmhearted young man who generally saw the best in people and hoped, by his own efforts as an elementary school teacher, to make the world a better place.

At the age of twenty-five, Peter married Sharon Mendelson, a classmate he'd met in a women's studies seminar at Middlebury. Naturally, it was a secular ceremony taking place in a meadow in Vermont. The young couple not only wrote their own vows, they walked down the aisle arm in arm and gave each other away under a pergola as a bearded friend played the Wedding March on a mandolin. Since Sharon was an only child, when she became pregnant a year later, Peter took her name to ensure the Mendelson line would carry on. (Such was the state of chivalry exemplified by the fine young men who attended liberal arts colleges in the early 1990s.)

Some years later, Peter's father died of a heart attack, leaving Peter enough money to buy a brownstone in Brooklyn, but not enough to expel the ground-floor tenant. In the interests of time, I was tempted to simply call Peter and tell him I had a buyer for his painting. But all things of importance, particularly those grounded in family tradition, should be approached with a sense of delicacy. So, having consulted my address book, I dialed the 718 area code for the first time in my life.

"Peter. It's Uncle Percy. Yes, yes, it's been far too long. That's just what I had been thinking. Why don't you and the family come for tea . . ."

A date was set for the following Saturday. As it turned out, Sharon needed to take Lucas to a music lesson, so Peter came with his second born, the three-year-old Emma, who was named, I kid you not, for Emma Goldman. With uncombed hair, a runny nose, and no respect for other people's property, Emma would have made her namesake proud.

Given our difference in age, I had always had a somewhat avuncular relationship to Peter. So despite having to follow Emma around the living room with a box of Kleenex, Peter and I had a delightful time catching up in the grand old family manner, and they were out of my hair by five o'clock.

As I had not had the foresight to cover the furniture in plastic, I had to spend half an hour cleaning the sofa cushions, but the sacrifice proved worth it. For sure enough, Peter called the following afternoon to express his gratitude and suggest I come to Brooklyn for Sunday supper.

Somewhere in Brooklyn

When I rang the bell on Sunday, I thought I was at the wrong address—for answering the door was a ten-year-old boy dressed like T. S. Eliot.

"Lucas? Is that you?"

"Hello, Uncle Percival."

I extended my hand and he shook it with a fine little grip.

"Mummy's upstairs with Emma, and Daddy's in the kitchen. Can I hang up your coat?"

"Why yes, thank you."

As he took my coat in hand, he said, "I like your vest."

"I like *yours*!"

"It's a Harris tweed."

"So I see."

"Why don't you make yourself comfortable in the sitting room. I'll let Daddy know you're here."

Lucas carried away my coat with both arms held high over his head so that it wouldn't drag on the floor. I showed myself into the sitting room.

Typical of the nineteenth-century brownstone in the Italianate style, the front room had high ceilings with elaborate plaster moldings and an intricately carved marble fireplace. The furniture was rather run-of-the-mill—a mix of hand-me-downs and Pottery Barn—and there were brightly colored plastic toys scattered here and there, but hanging over the fireplace was Peter's DiDomenico. Having not seen it in years, I believe I let out an audible gasp.

As I've mentioned, Peter and I were of the same generation: great-grandsons of Valentine. But where I was one of four children descended from four children, he was one of two descended from two. As a result, his fragment was four times the size of mine. More importantly, the luck of the sequential bisections was such that his fragment showed the face of the Virgin Mary inviolate, as if from the very beginning the painting had been intended as a portrait.

So many aspects of the Annunciation were prescribed by tradition, but DiDomenico and his peers were presented with one decision that could profoundly alter the tenor of their rendition. That is, were they depicting the moment just before the archangel informs Mary of her condition, or just after? Most opted for the latter. In these depictions, Mary has good reason to express a sense of serenity, for she has just been told she will bear a boy who will be called the Son of the Most High and will sit on the throne of David and reign over the house of Jacob forever.

But DiDomenico chose the moment just *before* the angel delivered his happy news. Rather than the self-assured beatitude of the elect, his Mary expresses a childlike awe combined with that courage before the wondrous that is reserved for the pure of heart. It is an exquisitely humane depiction; a portrayal of a woman who seems as deserving of God's grace as of our adulation.

"It's really something, isn't it?"

Lucas was at my side.

"Yes, it is," I agreed, in open admiration—having forgotten for the moment the purpose of my visit.

"There used to be more of it."

"Much more of it."

"Did you ever see the whole painting?"

"No," I said with a laugh. "That was long before my time, Lucas. But there are several excellent examples of Annunciations hanging at the Met."

Lucas blushed a little in embarrassment.

"I have never been to the Metropolitan Museum."

"Never been to the Metropolitan Museum!"

"I've been to the Brooklyn Museum on school trips," he clarified, "and to MoMA with my mom. But not yet to the Met."

"Well, my boy. We shall have to remedy *that*."

"Uncle Percy!"

Lucas and I both turned to discover Peter marching in from the kitchen, his arms extended with oven mitts on both hands.

"Dad . . . ," said Lucas.

"What? Oh!" Peter let out a laugh and removed the mitts so he could give me a hug. "I just took the roast from the oven."

"Roast beef is Emma's favorite," explained Lucas.

"While it rests, I was going to have a beer. Do you want one, Uncle Percy?"

"Or perhaps a glass of sherry . . . ?" suggested Lucas.

"A glass of sherry would be nice. Thank you."

"I'll get your beer too, Dad."

"Thanks, Lukie!"

As Lucas exited, the slight thumping of a rock-and-roll song sounded from beneath our feet.

"You still have your tenant, I gather."

Peter nodded a little apologetically, though what he was apologizing for was not exactly clear. "With just the four of us, we don't really need the extra floor." Then, perhaps to change the subject, he gestured at the painting. "I take it you two were admiring the old DiDomenico."

"We were."

Peter looked at it and smiled. "To be honest, it's a little Old World for Sharon's and my tastes, but Lucas has really taken to it. In fact, he wrote a terrific little essay about it for his English class. You know: A 'Describe a favorite object in your home' sort of thing."

Lucas returned with my sherry and Peter's beer.

"I was just telling your uncle about your essay," said Peter.

Lucas blushed again, this time out of humility. One got the sense that his father had brought up the essay in company before.

"What was your essay about, Lucas?" I asked. "The imagery? The artistry?"

"No," said Lucas. "I wrote about how an object that has been handed down can connect you to the past."

"Did you, now," I said with an outward smile and an inward frown.

In anticipating this visit, I hadn't imagined that my ten-year-old nephew would prove the sticking point to my plans. But he clearly felt a sentimental attachment to the painting, and to make matters worse, Peter and Sharon were of that generation which had set itself apart from thousands of years of human behavior by showing an interest in the opinions of their children. I began to wonder if my trip to Brooklyn was going to prove a waste. Then Sharon stepped into the room . . .

"Paying homage?" she observed drily.

Peter laughed, a little uncomfortably, then half confided: "It's not her favorite."

Sharon didn't bother to elaborate. It was plain from the expression on her face she would be happy to be rid of the painting.

But then, of course she would!

Never mind that she was Jewish. As a women's studies major with a soft spot for Marxism, Sharon must have been annoyed by the painting on multiple levels. Among other things, it represented the hegemony of Western culture, the privileges of patrimony, and the objectification of women. Why, her husband's DiDomenico stood for just about everything she had ever stood against.

"But she *is* beautiful, isn't she, Mom?" asked Lucas.

"Yes, my dear, she's beautiful," Sharon conceded while affectionately placing a hand on her son's head. Then she added, "But weren't they all," as if somehow that was the whole problem.

Peter and Sharon had maintained the formal dining room between the front room and kitchen, albeit with a bicycle in the corner.

At a fine colonial table that Peter had presumably inherited from his father, we dined on a grass-fed roast, heirloom carrots, and organic Brussels sprouts—which is to say, the beef was tough, the carrots purple, and the Brussels sprouts exactly the same as Brussels sprouts in every respect other than price. In my day, Brussels sprouts were the bane of every child's existence, but Lucas not only ate all of his, he then ate all of his sister's. (Although, to be fair, he may have eaten hers to stop her from rolling them across the table.)

After we reviewed Lucas's upcoming project on the Atlantic Ocean for his environmental science class, the conversation turned, naturally enough, to Windward, the rambling house on the coast of Maine where the Skinners had gathered every summer for generations—until the place was sold off in 1995, for all the normal reasons. Lucas, who had spent *his* summers visiting his maternal grandparents in Wellfleet, wanted to know what it was like.

"The first thing you have to understand about Windward," explained Peter to his son, "is that the water in Maine is much colder than the water on the Cape."

"Because the Gulf Stream passes it by," explained Lucas to his father.

"That's right! Anyway, every morning a cannon would go off at seven thirty to signal the raising of the flag. But then a second cannon would go off at eight, and it was generally understood that before the second cannon went off, you were supposed to be in the water."

"A delightful tradition," I recalled.

Peter laughed.

Lucas thought about it for a moment. "So, *everyone* had to go swimming before the second cannon?"

"Even the guests," replied his father.

"What if a guest didn't want to swim and stayed in bed?"

"Then they weren't invited back," chimed in Sharon.

Lucas's eyes opened wide. Then he looked to me for confirmation.

"All true," I said. "In the Skinner opinion, if you weren't willing to get in the water by eight, then you didn't have the stuff."

"Did you ever go to Windward, Mom?"

"Many times."

"And did you go swimming?"

"I'm here, aren't I?"

Lucas was impressed.

Peter leaned a little toward Lucas.

"It was at Windward—when I was just a few years older than you—that your Uncle Percival here taught me how to put a garbage can on top of the flagpole."

I believe I gasped for the second time that day. The garbage can on the flagpole! I hadn't thought of it in twenty years.

"We were at Scilla's rehearsal dinner—at the yacht club. Do you remember, Uncle Percy?"

"I do now."

Lucas may not have had the makings of a rogue, but he had the exacting curiosity of an engineer.

"A garbage can on top of a flagpole . . . But how?"

Smiling, Peter deferred to me with a gesture of the hand.

"With a broom handle," I said.

Lucas looked appropriately bewildered.

"Bring me a piece of paper, my boy."

With a notepad and Crayola crayon, I illustrated. "Here's the flagpole, and here's the halyard that you use to raise and lower the flag. What you do is tie the halyard twice around the broomstick, once at the bottom and once at the midpoint, like so." To the side, I drew the broomstick and where the two knots would be tied. "Now when you raise the broomstick, it will extend a few feet over the top of the flagpole. All you need do is plop the overturned garbage can on top of the broomstick, hoist it up the pole, shift it into position, then bring the broomstick back down, leaving the garbage can behind."

I slid the drawing toward Lucas for his files.

"Your uncle made that exact same drawing for me and my cousin Nate on the back of a cocktail napkin," said Peter. "It was just as the rehearsal dinner was breaking up. Instead of heading home, we grabbed a broom handle and a garbage can and headed for the flagpole. It took us until two in the morning, but we did it."

"How did they get the garbage can back down?"

I pointed at Lucas. "Good question."

"They had to call the fire department," said Peter. "The ladder truck rolled up right in the middle of church. Nate and I got grounded for a week."

"What about Uncle Percival? Did he get in trouble too?"

"No, Lucas," I said. "Your father never ratted me out."

After we loaded the dishwasher and set it running, Peter and Lucas took Emma upstairs to read her a book, and Sharon put Emma's bedtime bottle in the microwave. But after counting down from 1:00 to 0:55, the microwave went black, the dishwasher went silent, and the lights in the kitchen went out. Sharon released an exasperated sigh.

"It's the fuse," she said, taking a flashlight from a drawer. "Will you give me a hand? It's easier if someone holds the light."

"Of course."

Across the hall from the kitchen was a narrow pantry. On the shelves were boxes of cereal, cans of soup, and rolls of toilet paper, while on the floor were a stack of newspapers and a bag of empty bottles—a room where the survivalist and ecologist met. Navigating the clutter, we made our way to the back wall, where there was a fuse box that must have dated from before the Second World War.

"Is that to code?" I asked as I steadied the beam.

"If we all die in a fire, you'll know why."

Sharon unscrewed the blown fuse and replaced it with a new one. The lights came on. From across the hall, I could hear the dishwasher whirring again.

"Perhaps it's time for a little renovation . . . ," I suggested.

"That'll be the day."

Feeling a heightened sense of confidence, I followed Sharon back into the kitchen. For while Sharon's distaste for the painting might be classified as ideological, her appreciation for any proceeds from its sale would be entirely pragmatic.

Yes, Sharon and I were set apart by our age, gender, religion, and general worldview. But history has shown that the best alliances are often forged by the most unlikely of allies.

When I got home that night, I poured myself an extra finger of Scotch and settled in my reading chair with a book in my lap. But it was Uncle Neddie who commandeered my thoughts. What a dashing figure he had cut. A bachelor until he was forty, a capable fisherman and scratch golfer, Uncle Neddie smoked heavily, drank heavily, and swore in front of the children. When I was ten, it seemed like every weekend he would show up at Windward in the company of a different woman with a different European accent. He eventually got around to marrying the finest of the lot, fathered two delightful children, then died of lung cancer at the age of fifty-two. He's the one who taught *me* how to put a garbage can on top of a flagpole—by means of a drawing on the back of another napkin at another rehearsal dinner on another summer night even further in the past. And just as I had communicated the trick to Peter and his cousin Nathan, Uncle Neddie had communicated it to me and my cousin, my sidekick, my partner in crime, one Billy Skinner.

These sudden thoughts of my cousin and our shared shenanigans all those summers ago almost made me regret having taken the sixty dollars off him.

Almost.

The next morning, I dialed the Carlyle Hotel and asked for room 401.

"This is Sarkis."

"This is Skinner. I think I may be able to help you, after all."

"That's splendid news, Mr. Skinner! Can you tell me something about the work?"

"It's a fragment. But I think you will be pleasantly surprised by its size, its condition, and its subject matter."

"You certainly have me intrigued. If you don't mind my asking, what *is* the subject matter?"

"The Mother of God."

I heard Mr. Sarkis let out a breath of satisfaction.

"Well done, Mr. Skinner."

"But there is one small complication."

Now I heard his breathing stop—as the gears in his savvy little head began to spin.

"What complication is that . . . ?"

"While the owner has decided to part with the fragment, he is inclined to bring it to auction."

"I see."

"I think I can convince him to pursue a direct sale instead, but it might take a little effort."

"Yes, of course."

"And then there's the matter of authentication. As a professional with a reputation to consider, I would never facilitate the purchase of a painting without personally confirming its provenance and authenticity. That too will take some effort."

"Which is to say . . . ?"

"Which is to say, given the quality of the work and the demands on my time, I should think a higher finder's fee would be appropriate."

"What did you have in mind?"

"Something along the lines of twenty-five percent."

"Twenty-five percent? Naturally, I will have to raise your proposal with my client."

"Naturally."

"But tell me, Mr. Skinner. Should my client agree to this higher fee, how can he be sure that a week from now you won't reassess the value of your involvement once again?"

"He can't, Mr. Sarkis. I'm afraid that he can't."

Within the hour, Mr. Sarkis confirmed that his client was willing to proceed under the revised terms, provided I could broker a sale before the end of the year.

Hanging up, I immediately placed a call to Peter in order to set phase one of my two-part plan in motion.

"Peter? It's Percy. I'm calling to see if Lucas might like to join me on a visit to the Metropolitan Museum."

"What a wonderful offer, Uncle Percy. When would you like to go?"

"When would it be convenient for him?"

"Hold on a second." In the background I could hear Peter conferring with his son, then he returned to the phone. "He says the sooner the better."

"My thoughts exactly."

PHASE ONE

There is some measure of anxiety to be expected when one is on the verge of attaining a long-held dream. One cannot help but worry that the physical reality will fail to live up to the splendors of the imagination. To wit, as Lucas and I walked from the subway toward the Met, I noticed he was becoming less and less talkative. His footsteps were almost tentative as we crossed Park Avenue, and at Madison he actually took my hand. But when we emerged onto Fifth and the museum loomed before us, my nephew uttered a little sigh. The scale of the building, the neoclassical architecture, the wide welcoming steps, even the brightly colored banners announcing an exhibition on Monet suggested to the boy that the museum might live up to his expectations.

"Are you ready?" I asked.

"I am."

Together, we mounted the steps, passed through the doors, and entered that lobby with its vaulted ceilings and towering flower arrangements. After giving Lucas a moment to take in the room's majesty, we proceeded to the ticket desk.

One of the indisputable charms of the Metropolitan Museum is that the admission of twenty dollars is "recommended." The very notion of a recommended fee is so perfectly aristocratic. For to set a definitive price on access to the riches of the world's cultures after the robber barons had gone to such trouble to pillage them on our behalf would simply have been tacky.

"Two, please," I said to the middle-aged volunteer wearing a Chanel jacket and a string of pearls. But as I was about to put a $1 bill on the counter, I recalled the ever-attentive idealist at my side and grudgingly paid the suggested fare, taking some comfort that it had been financed by cousin Billy's losses.

Once I had collected our admission badges, I found that Lucas already had his nose in the museum's elaborate map.

"Shall we start with the mummies?" he suggested, while pointing with impressive accuracy to the north wing.

"No, my boy. I have a different plan in store for us today."

Lucas could not hide a sense of disappointment.

The young man who had been standing in line behind us—a wrangler visiting from Montana, I assumed, given his predilection for denim—looked up from his own map in apparent sympathy with the boy. *Who wouldn't want to start with the mummies?* his expression seemed to ask.

One who knows better, my expression seemed to reply.

"The first thing you must understand about the Metropolitan Museum," I explained to my nephew, "is that it is not, in fact, a museum. It is twenty museums. Here are some of the world's greatest collections of Egyptian artifacts—as you have noted—but also of Greek and Roman sculptures, early American furniture, eighteenth- and nineteenth-century period rooms, musical instruments, Asian art, Islamic art. So, one must not arrive at the Met with the hope of traveling it from corner to corner. Rather, one should choose a particular area of excellence and render unto it its due."

Lucas listened to my argument attentively, then with an expression of committed enthusiasm asked, "Which of the twenty museums are we going to visit today, Uncle Percival?"

The plucky lad.

"Today," I replied, "we are going to pay a long overdue visit to the Renaissance. . . ."

Now, the Met's collection of European paintings from the Middle Ages through the Renaissance is one of the finest in the world—a dizzying array of masterpieces spanning over forty rooms. To lead a young boy, even a game enthusiast like Lucas, into that labyrinth on his very first visit was almost sure to overwhelm. Instead, I took him to the Robert Lehman Collection at the back of the first floor.

Born at the end of the nineteenth century, Robert Lehman made a fortune on Wall Street at the helm of his eponymous investment bank. In the grand old tradition, as Lehman aged he applied his wealth to wives, thoroughbreds, and art—but especially the latter, building a collection of nearly three thousand works with a focus on the Italian Renaissance. So extraordinary was the scale and quality of his collection that when he donated it to the Met, the museum built a little wing of six galleries to exclusively showcase the bounty.

There were several advantages to bringing Lucas to the Lehman Collection. First, given that it was tucked away at the back of the first floor, it was not as heavily trafficked as the museum's other areas. Second, given the focus of the collection, one can trace the evolution of art from the Middle Ages to the Renaissance in the course of an hour. In fact, in one room a divine little Annunciation by Botticelli hangs directly above a Nativity by Lorenzo Monaco. Though the two works were painted just eighty years apart, to look from one to the other with care is to witness the invention of perspective, the effect of chiaroscuro, and that celebration of the human form that launched the rebirth of civilization in the West. But a third advantage was that the Lehman Collection provided the perfect context in which to reveal to Lucas the essential role of the serious collector in the preservation of cultural heritage.

"Isn't it extraordinary," I said (as we concluded our tour in front of the Botticelli), "that the little painting we are admiring is five hundred years old. Consider for a moment the life it has led. Over the centuries, it has hung on the walls of castles, churches, and private residences, where it has routinely been exposed to too much light or too much moisture, to the ashes of fireplaces and the greasy smoke of candles. Occasionally, it even bided its time in a cellar or an attic in the company of vermin, mildew, and dust."

(Here, an artful pause followed by a sweeping gesture.)

"If we have the opportunity to admire this Botticelli—or any of the other masterpieces in the museum, for that matter—we inevitably have a Robert Lehman to thank. The serious collector dedicates his life to the hunt for works of beauty, especially those that have been forgotten or forsaken. Having discovered one, at no little expense the serious collector engages a seasoned conservator to painstakingly reverse the impacts of time. And having gone to this trouble, does he carry the painting to his grave? Hardly. More often than not, he gives it away. He donates the painting to a museum where it will hang in a carefully controlled environment so that it can be appreciated by lovers of art for generations to come!"

When I concluded my little speech, I was not particularly surprised that the middle-aged Japanese couple standing nearby applauded. And I was pleased to see that the skeptical wrangler in denim from the ticket line, who had followed my lead and come to this hidden corner, now smiled in deferential appreciation of the collector's beneficence. But my nephew, he looked uncharacteristically glassy-eyed.

"Uncle Percival . . ."

"Yes, Lucas?"

"Can we have lunch now?"

We dined in the sunlit café that is just beyond the European sculpture court. With its wall of windows looking out onto Central Park, the café provides a perfect view of Cleopatra's Needle, the ancient Egyptian obelisk that was placed in the park in the 1880s. Fearing the sight of it might revive thoughts of mummies unseen, I steered Lucas to the seat with its back to the window.

When our waitress finally arrived, I ordered the chicken paillard, knowing it to be a dish that is difficult to ruin. Lucas, beginning to look a little revived, ordered the same. When the waitress asked if we needed anything else, I was about to answer in the negative when I noticed Lucas shifting in his chair.

"Do we need something else, Lucas?"

"Wouldn't you like some wine with your lunch?" he asked.

Given that the morning had not gone exactly as planned, I replied, "Why not." I ordered a glass of the Chablis and, contrary to my natural sense of propriety, drank it to the bottom before the food arrived.

I wasn't sure where in the museum the Monet exhibit was being held, but it must have been nearby—because at the side of every table was one of the Metropolitan's trademarked paper bags from which poked a Monet reimagined as a calendar, an apron, or an umbrella. So, as we began to eat (and I enjoyed a second glass of the Chablis), I couldn't help but regale my nephew with a charming tale from my days at the auction house that had suddenly come to mind.

Back in the 1980s, I explained, there was an explosion of interest in Impressionist and Post-Impressionist art bordering on popular mania. This resulted in skyrocketing prices for all the leading members of the schools, but especially for the one-eared wonder known as van Gogh. At one auction after another, it seemed a new record was being set for what one of his paintings could fetch. This phenomenon culminated in 1987, when a rather dubious Australian magnate by the name of Alan Bond purchased the Dutchman's *Irises* for an eye-popping $54 million.

On the following day, images of the painting, the purchaser, and the price tag appeared in every major newspaper and broadcast around the globe. But what was not generally reported amid all the fanfare was the small matter of self-collateralization. In the years preceding the sale, you see, as prices began to rise, the venerable old firms of Sotheby's and Christie's had instituted a new policy. In essence, they would help a bidder borrow the funds necessary to make a purchase—using the painting he was *about* to buy as collateral for the loan. Since a painting is basically worth what the last person paid for it, a bidder could bid almost anything, because the bid itself would raise the intrinsic value of the collateral and thus his borrowing capacity. In scientific terms, this was an innovation akin to the inflating of zeppelins with flammable gases.

Suffice it to say, Bond's record-breaking purchase of the van Gogh was financed under such an arrangement. Though he didn't have enough money on hand to service the loan, his plan was to raise funds by producing for his fellow countrymen a traveling exhibition of the masterpieces in his collection, at the center of which would be the now world-famous *Irises*.

The only problem was that the barristers who were advising the American lenders doubted that Australian law would allow them to reclaim the painting should Mr. Bond ever tumble into bankruptcy. But if Bond couldn't bring the painting to Australia, *his* attorneys argued, then bankruptcy would be the sure result. The two parties were at an impasse. That is, until the masterminds at Sotheby's stepped forward with another innovation. At their own expense, they would have the *Irises* forged. Thus, the original could be kept in a vault in New York within the grasp of the creditors while the fake was ringing cash registers from Perth to the Great Barrier Reef.

"Will that be all?" asked our waitress, in a manner that suggested she hoped so.

"Yes, thank you. Just the check."

When she plopped down the bill, I discovered that my misguided ploy of bringing Lucas to the museum had cost me nearly a hundred dollars all told. To make matters worse, under his watchful eye I had no choice but to tip the requisite 15 percent on the meal despite the lackluster service.

The bill paid, we donned our jackets and passed through the tables with Lucas leading the way. But just as we were reentering the sculpture court, a rather commanding voice sounded from behind.

"Excuse me. Excuse me!"

Assuming I had forgotten something at the table, I turned to find an elderly woman barreling toward me with a righteous posture, a stern expression, and an outfit that Jackie Kennedy might have worn, had she been a hundred pounds heavier and hopelessly out of date.

"Are you addressing me?" I asked with some surprise.

Without answering, the woman pointed a finger at Lucas, who was now standing before Carpeaux's statue of Ugolino.

"Is that your grandson?" she asked, as if it were her business to do so.

"He is my nephew."

She now pointed a finger at the table where we had been sitting. Clearly, she was very good at pointing.

"As a grandmother, I feel it my obligation to tell you that the story you related during your lunch was utterly inappropriate for a boy your nephew's age."

"Inappropriate?"

"The portrait of human nature you painted could not have been more ugly or cynical."

I couldn't help but look around in wonder. The statue of Ugolino that Lucas was studying depicted the moment described in Dante's *In-*

ferno when the Pisan traitor, starving in a jail cell in the company of his own children, wrestles with whether or not to eat them. Beside Ugolino stood Rodin's *Burghers of Calais*, in which six statesmen in chains are being led to their execution so that their besieged city might be spared. While fifty feet beyond, Perseus was proudly holding the severed head of Medusa. And this woman was worried that the boy's sensibilities might be damaged by the tale of a forged flower?

What is one to say when confronted with such madness?

"Madam," I replied, "I regret to inform you that you are not in Kansas anymore."

The central hallway leading to the museum's exit was crowded wall to wall, as if tourists who had been laying siege to the museum had finally stormed the gates. Both to circumvent them and to provide Lucas with some consolation for missing the mummies, I suggested we take a detour through the collection of medieval armor.

Lucas indicated this diversion would be welcome, and like any boy of ten, he enjoyed seeing the artful means by which men of courage once lumbered into battle. But it was when we were on our way to the exit that something unexpected happened. As we were passing through the galleries of European Decorative Arts, Lucas pointed to a sign on the wall.

"What is a *studiolo*?"

"A *studiolo*?" I said, coming to a stop just opposite the entrance to the little room. "It's funny you should ask, Lucas. Why don't you see for yourself."

As you may know, the *studiolo* designed by Francesco di Giorgio Martini in the late fifteenth century is a rather unusual installation, even for the Met. During the Italian Renaissance, it became quite popular for gentlemen of standing to have a private room in their home into which they could retreat. In order to inspire creative meditation, these rooms were often decorated in a manner that celebrated the arts and sciences. Originally built for the Ducal Palace in Gubbio, the Met's *studiolo* is not much bigger than Sharon's pantry; but rather than being lined with cans of soup and boxes of cereal, its walls had been finished with an intricate design of inlaid woods that gave the appearance of cabinets filled with scientific devices, musical instruments, and books. In the creation of this delightful illusion, the artist had used over twenty species of trees and all the same tricks of perspective that were employed by the Renaissance painters.

As Lucas looked around the room, he didn't utter a word. But he didn't need to. I knew exactly what he was feeling—that this tiny room assembled five hundred years ago over four thousand miles away was somehow his place in the world.

Having turned around twice, Lucas exited the room in order to read the curatorial description posted outside. Then he came back and looked from wall to wall with even more care, so he wouldn't miss a detail.

"This was a room in Renaissance Italy," he said at last.

"That's right, Lucas."

"From five hundred years ago."

"Thereabouts."

"And someone took all these little pieces of wood and reassembled them here so that we can see it."

"Yes, Lucas. That's exactly what someone did."

And just like that, the preservationist is born.

Phase Two

The timing of our return to Brooklyn could not have been better. Lucas and I arrived at the very moment that Sharon was getting back from a birthday party with a drowsy Emma strapped in her stroller. Although the party had taken place at a gymnastics center oriented to toddlers, Sharon looked like the one who'd been doing the gymnastics.

"Here," I said. "Allow me."

Taking hold of the bottom of the contraption, I helped her carry Emma up the stoop.

"Do you have to lug this up and down every time you go out?"

"Rain or shine."

Once inside, Sharon let out a long breath. She asked Lucas if he would bring Emma upstairs to get her ready for her bath. She asked me if I'd like a cup of tea.

"That would be delightful," I said.

Following her into the kitchen, I sat down at the little Formica-topped table as she filled the pot. From a glance at the microwave, I could see it was only five o'clock, but as it was November, the sun had nearly set.

"I'll be right back," Sharon said after setting the pot over the flame, then she headed down the hall. When I heard the door to the bathroom close, I was out of my chair like a shot. I turned on the microwave and the dishwasher and returned to my seat. The dishwasher began swooshing as the microwave began counting down:

1:00.

0:59.

0:58.

0:57.

0:56.

0:55.

0:54.

0:53.

"Come on," I actually said to the appliance. "Come on."

Then poof. The microwave went black, the dishwasher went silent, and the room went dark.

From behind the door down the hall, I heard Sharon swear. There was a rustling, the flushing of the toilet, then her irritated approach. She paused in the doorway, illuminated only by the thin blue flame that flickered under the kettle.

"The fuse?" I asked sympathetically.

Without answering, Sharon took the flashlight from its drawer and headed toward the pantry. I stood up to follow her out of the kitchen, remembering at the last moment to switch off the dishwasher.

"Here," I said in the pantry. "Let me hold it for you."

I took the flashlight and directed the beam on the box so she could replace the fuse. The lights came back on. Sharon turned, but rather than stepping toward the door she surveyed the pantry, taking in the cans of beans, the bags of bottles, and the mop that was leaning against the wall. Other than the profanity, she hadn't said a word since the lights went out.

I switched off the flashlight and handed it to Sharon, taking the opportunity to look at her closely. What I saw was an earnest young woman doing her best under unnecessarily difficult circumstances—which made everything so much easier.

"Listen, Sharon, I don't want interfere . . ."

This preamble is usually met with an expression of impatience, and rightfully so. But worn down by her day, exasperated by the fuse, and hearing the note of sympathy in my voice, she looked up without protest.

"You clearly need to update the electrical system in your house," I said. "And you need access to your ground-floor entrance."

Sharon shook her head with a weary expression, but I pressed on.

"I gather that from Peter's point of view, you don't really need the extra space since you're just a family of four. And I understand that ousting your tenant could prove expensive, but so could a nervous breakdown."

She laughed grimly. "Do they charge for those now?"

"Top dollar. But here's the thing: Recently, I ran into an old client who is an ardent collector of Italian art; and as we were catching up, he happened to mention that the one painting he was looking for—to complete his collection—was a DiDomenico. If you and Peter were open to parting with yours, I could certainly reach out to him. . . ."

Sharon looked me in the eye, then looked away. For a moment, I thought I had struck the wrong note. But then I realized she was looking over my shoulder to make sure there was no one behind me.

She met my gaze again. "What do you think it would be worth?"

"I'm not sure. One hundred thousand? One hundred and twenty thousand? Maybe as much as one hundred and fifty thousand."

She nodded, as if she had already made a similar calculus, then said almost to herself, "We'd have to pay taxes. . . ."

"True. Although my client might be willing to pay in cash, in which case . . ."

I gestured toward the vagaries of the universe.

Sharon began switching the flashlight on and off, weighing her options, those various paths to deliverance or damnation.

"I know you're in a tough spot," I continued. "After all, the painting has come down to Peter through the family. You may not feel it's your place to even *raise* the topic of selling it. So let me do it. Get Peter to invite me for another family meal. And when the moment's right, I'll mention my old client's interest. I think if he receives some encouragement from me, and you're there to express your support, he might begin to see the time has come to place the priorities of the present ahead of those of the past."

In the kitchen the teakettle began to whistle.

"Excuse me," she said, slipping past me. I followed and sat at the table. For a moment, she stood at the stove, then she turned and took the seat across from me.

"All right, Percy. Why don't you feel out your client on what he'd be willing to pay for the painting. I'll get Peter to invite you for dinner."

I didn't bother staying for the tea.

As I descended the stoop, I couldn't help but break into a smile—because it was November twelfth, just two and a half weeks until Thanksgiving, the perfect occasion for a family gathering.

And when I happened to see an unoccupied taxi, I hailed it. Giving the driver my address, I made myself comfortable and passed the time allowing myself to anticipate my forthcoming windfall and a long-awaited return to Les Baux-de-Provence—that rocky outcrop where van Gogh once painted olive trees and where the contemporary traveler can discover quaint antiquities, breathtaking views, and one of the finest restaurants in France.

THANKSGIVING

That Thanksgiving has evolved over hundreds of years into a national holiday of eating is rather ironic given the quality of Thanksgiving food. Stuffing and roasting a twenty-pound turkey is, without a doubt, the worst possible way to enjoy a game bird. The whole notion of eating a game bird is to savor those subtleties of flavor that elude the domesticated hen. Partridge, pheasant, quail are all birds that can be prepared in various ways to delight the senses; but a corn-fed turkey that's big enough to serve a gathering of ten or more is virtually impossible to cook with finesse. The breasts will inevitably become as dry as sawdust by the time the rest of the bird has finished cooking. Stuffing only exacerbates this problem by insulating the inner meat from the effects of heat, thus prolonging the damage. The intrinsic challenge of roasting a turkey has led to all manner of culinary abominations. Cooking the bird upside down, a preparation in which the skin becomes a pale, soggy mess. Spatchcocking, in which the bird is drawn and quartered like a heretic. Deep frying! (Heaven help us.) Give me an unstuffed four-pound chicken any day. Toss a slice of lemon, a sprig of rosemary, and a clove of garlic into the empty cavity, roast it at 425° for sixty minutes or until golden brown, and you will have a perfect dinner time and again.

The limitations of choosing a twenty-pound turkey as the centerpiece of the Thanksgiving meal have only been compounded by the inexplicable tradition of having every member of the family contribute a dish. Relatives who should never be allowed to *set foot* in a kitchen are suddenly walking through your door with some sort of vegetable casserole in which the "secret ingredient" is mayonnaise. And when cousin Betsy arrives with such a mishap in hand, one can take no comfort from thoughts of the future, for once a single person politely compliments the dish, its presence at Thanksgiving will be deemed sacrosanct. Then not even the death of cousin Betsy can save you from it, because as soon as she's in the grave, her daughter will proudly pick up the baton.

Served at an inconvenient hour, prepared by such an army of chefs that half the dishes are overcooked, half are undercooked, and all are served cold, Thanksgiving is not a meal for a man who eats with discernment. So, I had quite happily excused myself from the tradition back in 1988, thereafter celebrating the Pilgrims' first winter at a Chinese restaurant on Lexington Avenue.

But in the field of fine art, one must be prepared to make sacrifices. And if helping Peter see the benefits of divestment meant eating a serving of sweet potatoes covered in marshmallows, then so be it. I awaited his call in a sanguine mood.

But after a week, the call hadn't come. In another few days, Thanksgiving would be less than a week away—a point at which the well-bred man would generally be reluctant to offer an invitation for fear it would seem like an afterthought.

Perhaps Sharon had lost her nerve.

One morning, I called the house at eleven a.m. hoping to catch her while Peter was out, but I got the machine. The next day, I called at dinnertime and got Peter.

"Peter! How is everything? Good, good. Listen, I assume that Lucas has some time off around Thanksgiving, and I'd promised him a return visit to the Met . . ."

Lucas would have *loved* that, a chipper Peter assured me. But they were going to celebrate Thanksgiving with some old college friends in Orlando, Florida. They would be leaving on Wednesday as soon as school let out and wouldn't be back until Sunday afternoon.

"Why don't we call you when we get back?" he suggested.

"Perfect," I said.

Though when I hung up, I couldn't help noting that celebrating with some old college friends in eighty-degree weather was hardly in the Thanksgiving spirit.

THE DENOUEMENT

It was the fourteenth of December, more than a month since Sharon and I had come to our understanding over the Formica. I had called the house twice during the school day, hoping that Sharon would answer. On the third attempt, I left a message on the machine suggesting we set a date for my visit with Lucas to the Met. No reply.

I had been concerned that Sharon had lost her nerve, but perhaps things were worse than that. Perhaps she had *found* her nerve. In the aftermath of another blown fuse, maybe she had confronted Peter and insisted they sell the painting only to have him declare high-mindedly that the notion was out of the question. Whatever had happened, there was no longer time to let things take their natural course. In accepting my revised terms, Sarkis had stipulated the sale had to be brokered before the end of the year. I would need to pay them a visit on my own initiative. But on what basis?

I couldn't just drop in on the pretense I happened to be in the neighborhood; no one in their right mind would believe that! I thought of bringing Peter an old photograph of his father that I had "unearthed" while going through some of my things, but having torn apart my apartment I couldn't unearth a single one—the price the universe exacts, no doubt, for failings of family sentiment. At my wit's end, I turned to the scoundrel's last resort: holiday cheer. I would take advantage of the newly fallen snow to call on them unannounced, bringing glad tidings of the season. On a Tuesday at five, I went to the corner of Sixty-Third and Third to buy a Christmas wreath from the Korean deli. I was half a block away when I turned back to get a bigger one. Though the woman behind the counter had sold me the smaller wreath but minutes before, she viewed my request to upgrade from one to the other with open suspicion. Unable to discern the nature of my scheme, she begrudgingly accepted my additional money for a wreath the size of an automotive tire, and with a red bow, no less.

Wreath number two may have been sized to impress, but it was plenty awkward to carry—especially if one was trying to keep the pine sap off of one's cashmere coat. As a result, I was cursing all the way down the subway steps and through the turnstile. So, when I sat down on the train with the damnable thing in my lap, I was a little taken aback to discover that everyone on board began to smile in my direction. One large African American fellow even began whistling a Christmas song: "We Three Kings of Orient Are," that carol dedicated to itinerant bearers of gifts. I took it as a good omen.

But as I was walking down Peter's street, I saw one of those luxury SUVs parked in front of his house. Instinctively, I slowed my pace, wondering what it was doing there among all the ten-year-old Hondas and Subarus. But I was utterly confused when, as I was about to turn up Peter's stoop, I realized the young man leaning against the passenger-side door was the wrangler from the Met—still clad from bottom to top in denim. Having climbed the stoop, I took another look back and the fellow waved. Then the door opened and there was Sharon.

"Uncle Percy!" she exclaimed with genuine affection and a complexion that could only be described as glowing.

By way of response, I held up my gift, and in that very instant, I realized, aghast, that I was offering a giant Christmas wreath to a Jewish woman!

But she smiled at the sight of it.

"What a lovely gesture. Lucas will be so pleased. He never feels we fulfill the promise of Christmas pageantry in our house." Taking my offering, she turned and called down the hall, "It's Uncle Percy with a wreath!"

The sense that I had entered some alternative universe was heightened by the fact that Emma suddenly appeared wearing a pretty little dress and barrettes in her hair.

"Come on in," Sharon said. "We're all in the kitchen." When she began walking down the hall, I hesitated, but little Emma took my hand and led me the rest of the way.

In the kitchen, I found Peter seated at the table across from a stranger who was about his age and height, and who looked vaguely familiar. They were both wearing flannel shirts and both had half-filled flutes of champagne in front of them.

"Uncle Percy!" said Peter.

"Can I take your coat?" asked Lucas.

"Thank you, Lucas."

As Lucas disappeared down the hall with my coat held high over his head, Peter introduced me to his guest, who, in a well-mannered fashion, rose from his chair. His name was Michael Reese.

Of course, I thought, as we shook hands. I remembered him now from the pages of *The New York Times*. He was the founder of some technology company based in San Francisco—one of the new breed of billionaires in baseball caps.

"It's nice to meet you," he said.

"The pleasure is mine."

Peter, Reese, and I all sat at the table as Sharon leaned against her husband's side.

Feeling a draft of cold air at my back, I wondered for a moment if Sharon had forgotten to close the front door, but I didn't bother asking. For as I looked at the beaming faces before me, I already understood the cold air I was feeling originated not from the streets of Brooklyn, but from the rocky peaks of Les Baux, where the winter wind had whistled over the ruins and rattled the empty branches of the olive trees before coming in search of me.

"So," I said, "what are we celebrating?"

"Two things!" said Peter. "But you're not going to believe the first one, Uncle Percy."

"I can't wait."

In a nutshell, here's what had unfolded: A few weeks before, while Peter and Sharon were having their usual "date night" at their favorite local haunt, Reese, who had been visiting the Brooklyn Museum, wandered into the same restaurant and happened to sit at the neighboring table. After ordering, the three got to talking, and it turned out Reese had been at Yale at the same time Peter and Sharon were at Middlebury, such that they had an acquaintance or two in common. Well, with one topic leading to another, it eventually came up that while at Yale, Reese had majored in art history and written his senior thesis on a rather obscure Renaissance painter by the name of DiDomenico.

"Can you believe it, Uncle Percy?"

"I'm astounded."

Peter turned to Reese.

"Uncle Percy is also a specialist in Renaissance art!"

"Is that so!" said Reese.

I imagine you can guess where Peter's story was headed from here. . . .

At the restaurant, Peter exclaims that he and Sharon *own* a fragment of a DiDomenico!

"Not from his Annunciation?" says Reese in shock.

Yes, in fact, from his Annunciation.

Here, Reese shakes his head in amazement. Then he explains that some years before, he began collecting fragments of DiDomenico's Annunciation, finding them in places as far-flung as Texas and Saudi Arabia. After a little luck and some hard work, as of this summer he had acquired every fragment from the original painting but one—the nine-by-nine-inch square that depicted the Mother of God.

"It's a miracle," I said.

"Right?" said Peter.

Now, obviously, the most fundamental law of dealmaking would dictate that if Reese wanted Peter's fragment, the very worst thing he could do would be to reveal that he has all the fragments but one. To do so would put Peter in the position of those little old ladies who, unwilling to leave their brownstones, end up owning the last lot on a block that is slotted for the building of a skyscraper. Nonetheless, Reese bared all, adding that he had already identified a crack team of conservationists who could reassemble the fragments and restore the painting to its original glory. So, if Peter was willing to part with his fragment, he could basically name his price.

This particular part of the conversation had taken place not in the restaurant, but in Peter and Sharon's sitting room after they had invited their new friend back to their house to see the fragment for himself. Once Reese had laid out his case and made his offer over a few bottles of beer, what did Peter and Sharon do? They called in Lucas to ask his opinion. (How that must have caught the wily Mr. Reese off guard!)

Lucas listened to an abbreviated version of the story with great interest and then said he had only one question.

"You know what the question was?" asked Peter.

"I can't imagine."

"Lucas wanted to know what Mike was going to do with the painting once he had reassembled it. Was he going to keep it? Or share it?"

Here Reese chipped in with a smile on his face.

"I laughed and laughed when that came out of Lucas's mouth. But it was the *perfect* question. What was I going to *do* with the painting? Well, in the back of my mind I had always imagined that I would leave it to the Yale Art Gallery where I had spent so many hours as a student. But what is 'the back of one's mind,' if not the place where we keep the good intentions we haven't the gumption to act upon now? So, we made it a condition of the sale. Once the DiDomenico is restored, it goes straight to the museum."

Reese suddenly looked over my shoulder and said: "Here he is!"

Lucas was coming back into the kitchen with a crystal wineglass in hand.

"I couldn't find another flute, Uncle Percy. Will this be okay?"

"Absolutely."

Lucas set the glass in front of me and poured the champagne.

"You can leave the bottle, my boy."

I raised my glass to Peter, Sharon, Reese, and the good people at Yale to congratulate them all on their mutual good fortune. "But what was the second cause for celebration?" I asked, after we set our glasses down.

Putting an arm around Sharon's waist, Peter announced: "We're pregnant."

I doubt I will ever come to accept the use of the first person plural in that particular sentence, but under the circumstances, it was somehow so perfect. You see, as the whole story unfolded, I had been a little surprised that Peter had been so ready to part with the painting. But before Reese had made his fateful appearance, Sharon had already convinced Peter the time had come to sell, and I had practically shown her the means when I had remarked that from Peter's point of view, they didn't need the extra space since they were just a family of four. . . .

"What an extraordinary turn of events," I said.

"But here's the best part," said Peter.

The best part? Better than *we're pregnant* and *name your price*?

"Lucas's provision!"

Reese smiled and then explained for my benefit. "Lucas suggested that once I restored the Annunciation, I should have painters make two duplicates of it, one that could hang in my house and one that could hang here, while the original is hanging at Yale."

Peter and Sharon smiled at their son with well-placed pride. But with the blush of the genuinely modest, Lucas set the record straight: "It was actually Uncle Percy who gave me the idea."

At which point, everyone in the room raised their glass in my direction.

C'est la Guerre

In short order, the transaction for the DiDomenico fragment (with the two codicils) was completed, the painting was shipped to a lab in San Francisco, and the restoration began.

In April, notice was given to the tenant downstairs, and in the summer, while the family was in Wellfleet, the electrical system was upgraded, a playroom and office were added to the ground floor, and a baby's room was painted upstairs. The latter was put to use in September when the family returned to Brooklyn bearing a seven-pound baby boy named Ezekiel.

Obviously, the charming and entrepreneurial Mr. Reese had had me followed by Mr. Blue Jeans in order to discover the owner of the last fragment. Then he had circumvented me by "wandering" into Peter and Sharon's favorite restaurant on their weekly night out. In so doing, Reese had cheated me out of my finder's fee; but I couldn't really hold it against him. After all, I had not been particularly forthright with Peter and Sharon, and I had also tried to rework the terms of my arrangement with the little Greek. *C'est la guerre*, as they say. So, when Reese and I parted that night on the sidewalk in front of Peter and Sharon's house, we shook hands like gentlemen, making the unspoken commitment to protect the family's idealism and each other's reputations through mutual discretion.

For my part, the year unfolded much as any other—spent on the isle of Manhattan with midday meals at La Maison and a finger of Scotch before bed. Although I did stop in at the Yale Club a little more often than I used to in order to play a round of backgammon with my cousin

Billy; and when Thanksgiving rolled around, I swapped my seat at the Chinese restaurant on Lexington for the chair at the head of Peter and Sharon's table, where I sat with Emma on my left, Lucas on my right, and Valentine Skinner's Annunciation hanging in all its glory on the wall behind my back.

LOS ANGELES

—Is this Katherine?

— . . . Mr. Ross?

—I'm sorry to bother you so late, Katherine. I just wanted to find out if by any chance . . .

There was silence on the other end of the line. I could hear twenty years of upbringing and a few hundred miles of Indiana trying to contain his emotions.

—Mr. Ross?

—I'm sorry. I should explain. Apparently Eve's relationship with this Tinker fellow has come to an end.

—Yes. I saw Eve a few days ago and she told me.

—Ah. Well. I . . . That is, Sarah and I . . . received a cable from her saying that she was coming home. But when we went to meet her train, she wasn't there. At first, we thought we had simply missed her on the platform. But we couldn't find her in the restaurant or the waiting room. So we went to the stationmaster to see if she was on the manifest. He didn't want to tell us. It's against their policy and what have you. But eventually, he confirmed that she had boarded the train in New York. So you see, it wasn't that she wasn't on the train. She just didn't get off. It took us a few days to get the conductor on the phone. By that time he was in Denver headed back east. But he remembered her—because of the scar. And he said that when the train was approaching Chicago, she had paid to extend her ticket. To Los Angeles. . . .

—From *Rules of Civility* (Chapter Seventeen)

Eve in Hollywood

PART ONE

Charlie

I N THE DINING CAR, he was seated again with the pretty young lady with the scar. She was reading that new detective story—the one with the strangled brunette on the cover. A page-turner, they called it, though you wouldn't know it from the pace she was turning them. In all likelihood, she had just picked it up in the station to fend off friendly conversation. But he could understand that. Sometimes you just wanted to be left to yourself, even when it was for three thousand miles.

He nodded as he took the seat across from her. He put his napkin in his lap and looked out the window, where the valley of the Rio Grande was giving way to the high, lonely deserts west of Exodus and east of John.

In another day, he'd be back in Los Angeles.

For the first half of the trip, he had put off thinking about what awaited him there. He had read the papers and sized up the passengers. In Kansas City, while they hitched a pair of Pullman cars from Memphis, Tennessee, he'd had a beer in the depot with a Wells Fargo man and almost missed the train.

But once they'd crossed into New Mexico, there was no more putting it off. He had to start giving it the attention it was due. In the days ahead, there'd be the selling of the house, the paying off of utilities, the closing of the account at the savings and loan. Every time he let his mind dwell on the list it grew longer. Selling his car. Packing his bags. Cleaning out that little storage space over the hallway that he hadn't visited since they'd stopped putting ornaments on the Christmas tree back in 1934. And then there was the list within the list: tending at long last to Betty's things. Her summer dresses, her aprons. Her hairbrush and brooches. Her Sunday service hats. The cookie cutters and rolling pins and pie plates that she had valued over everything else. To whom do you give a rolling pin, when every grown woman has a rolling pin of her own?

A good son, Tom had offered to travel out from Tenafly to help. And he had almost accepted his son's offer. That's how daunting it all seemed. But this was something he had to see to himself. Retired, widowed, moving back east to live with his boy, it was probably one of the last things he *would* see to himself.

On the other side of the window, the wide, cracked terrain of the Navajo reached to the horizon, ruthless and red. On his way east, he had been impressed by the buttes. Fixed against the sky, they seemed the ultimate survivors—outlasters of time and intent—as solitary and majestic as anything known to man. He had looked forward to passing back through this country, so he could study them again. But as the train rushed on, he realized they had become a blur. Without being conscious of it, he had let them recede from his field of vision so he could consider the young lady's reflection in the window instead.

He had first seen her on the platform in New York—smoking a cigarette, with a small red valise at her feet. Somewhere in her midtwenties, fine-figured, with sandy hair, elegant and self-possessed, she was hard to miss even in a crowd. Perhaps, especially in a crowd. He had taken a step to his right to get a better look, but the doors of the train had opened and she had disappeared among the others getting on.

What with finding his own compartment and securing his bag and making polite conversation with the shoe-leather salesman from Des Moines, he forgot altogether about the young lady with the red valise. Until the following morning when, as the train was nearing Chicago, he was seated at her table for breakfast.

She was gazing out the window and tapping the table with a brand-new pack of cigarettes. She didn't even look back to see who was joining her. But when the waiter offered to refill her cup, she turned just long enough to politely decline. And that's when he saw how her beauty had been marred.

He was surprised that he had missed it before. Because the scar had to be nearly three inches long—running from the top of her cheekbone to the top of her chin. He had seen hundreds of them, of course. Star-shaped scars from a bludgeon to the brow; crescent-shaped scars from a knife on Encino; wide, white scars from fat-fingered stitch-ups in make-shift surgeries in the backs of garages. But those scars had all been on men, and they had been earned. Hunted. Almost longed for. With an inward shake of the head he turned to the menu and tried not to study the young lady too closely, knowing he would get a good look at her as she got up from the table.

But when the conductor passed down the aisle announcing the approach of Union Station, something interesting happened: Turning her gaze from the window, she called the conductor back and asked how much it would cost to extend her trip from Chicago to Los Angeles. Then, having paid the supplemental fare, she signaled the waiter for that refill, after all—as if she had just bought a ticket to the end of the line so she could savor one more cup of coffee.

He had wondered a lot about that. It was one of those things he had wondered about in his berth at night while avoiding thoughts of what awaited him. Why would a young lady with a single valise who had boarded a train alone in New York suddenly extend her ticket from Chicago to L.A.? It's not as if she had received an urgent communication. Nor had she seemed particularly anxious when the conductor had called the next stop. But one thing was for certain: the decision had pleased her. Once her cup had been refilled, she leaned back with a sparkle in her eye that would have been the envy of any blonde in Brentwood.

On this morning, as he was cutting into his ham and eggs across from the young lady with the scar, two women in their thirties took the empty seats at the table. Both were wearing those pillbox hats with the little black veils that are too small to veil anything. Their clothes were nicely made, but they were made for women in their fifties. The one in the blue hat sat on the other side of the table with a Presbyterian posture, while the one in the red hat sat at his side with her purse clasped tightly in her lap. They were from somewhere east of the Mississippi, he suspected, though not too far east. Maybe Cleveland.

—Good morning, they said.

—Good morning, he replied.

The young lady with the scar read on.

—Good morning, the woman in the blue hat repeated with a polite insistence that placed her a little closer to St. Louis.

—*Guten tag*, the young lady replied without looking up from her book.

The woman in the blue hat raised her eyebrows for the benefit of her companion.

After the waiter had taken their order, the woman in the blue hat produced a small diary and began reviewing their itinerary: where they'd be staying, what they'd be seeing, a restaurant near the hotel that, according to a reliable friend, was clean and reasonably priced.

There were also some recommendations as to where one shouldn't go and what one shouldn't do. He could tell it was a conversation they had had before. They were going to have it every day until they were home.

When the food came, the woman in the blue hat again raised her eyebrows for the benefit of her companion, this time to signify the rather rough delivery of the plates by the waiter.

As they ate, the woman in the blue hat was reminded of something she had recently heard, and the conversation turned to the business of neighbors. The woman with the red hat listened with an air of having heard it all before and yet not wanting to miss a word. *It just shows to go you,* she would say, whenever a turn of events ratified her worst suspicions. Like when the colored boy who cared for the Adelsons' cars took their Cadillac for a night on the town. Or when young Miss Hollister followed that fast-talking schoolteacher all the way to Chicago, only to return Miss Hollister and child. And Leonora Cunningham . . . ? After she bought that big house in Clayton, and told everyone who would listen about these curtains versus those curtains and this couch versus that couch, the bank examiners paid a visit to her husband's office and emerged with seven years of ledgers in a cardboard box!

Well. It just shows to go you.

He crossed his knife and fork on his plate and turned to the window, feeling a certain pang. It was the sort of pang that would strike him every now and then in the moments before some memory of Betty would surface. But no memory of his wife surfaced now. It was Caroline he found himself thinking on.

When his son had first courted Caroline, he and Betty had been right proud. It wasn't because she was a college girl and the daughter of a New York attorney. Or, it wasn't only because of those things. It was because she had been so blue-eyed and bright. Sitting on their porch, she had been breathless with talk of travel and music and books and all manner of open-endedness. But just six years later, she couldn't hide a hint of impatience. Like when Tom spoke of how much he enjoyed his position at his firm; or when he showed satisfaction in some little aspect of their house. And when she described a visit to an old friend in Greenwich, she twice told Tom that he wouldn't believe the trees in her backyard—as if the trees in Greenwich had been planted by a grander divinity than the trees in Tenafly.

He had received his own serving of it too. On his first evening there, when he had told some old story from his days on the job, she had cut him short. It wasn't proper conversation for the dinner table, she had said. It wasn't proper conversation in front of the child. And the next day, when he had come downstairs for breakfast in his old gray suit, she had cast him a glance suggesting that somehow his old gray suit wasn't proper either.

Caroline had itineraries and recommendations of her own, he thought to himself a little sadly. But it wasn't a trip to California she was planning—it was her life.

And yet, even as this thought was taking shape, he chastised himself for having it. He chastised himself as Betty would have.

After all, hadn't Caroline every right to plan her life? To imagine it? Hadn't he and Betty done just the same in their time? Hadn't they spent sweet evenings in that little place on Finley Avenue picturing themselves in one of the houses on Amesbury Road? Hadn't they spent some of the best years of their lives imagining a future for their boy, even before he could imagine a future for himself?

It was the American way.

Maybe it was the way all over the world.

In the reflection of the window, he tried to size himself up. He tried to size himself up the way Caroline had—when he had sat down to breakfast in his old gray suit. In truth, he must have lost twenty pounds since Betty died. The weight had come right off his chest and arms. So now his old gray friend hung loosely on his frame, as if he had bought it secondhand. And what was he still wearing it for anyway? Where was he all suited up to go?

Well he knew that in this country, in this life, we fashion ourselves. We pick our spot and our companions and how we'll earn our keep, and that's how we go about the fashioning. Through the where of it, and the who, and the how. But if that is how we fashion ourselves, then surely it follows that with the loss of each of these elements comes the winnowing away. The burying of one's spouse, the retirement from the job, the moving from one's home where one has lived for twenty-two years—this is the undoing, the unmaking. It is through this process that time and intent reclaim the solitary soul for its grander purpose.

A humbling reminder, outside the window a telegraph wire supported by lean gray poles ran through the desert bearing news of weddings and wars.

That first night back east—when Caroline had cut him off in the middle of one of his old stories—even as his prideful self felt slighted, he knew she was perfectly right. She was perfectly right to cut him off. Not because his stories were improper for the table or improper for the child. But because they were an old man's stories. They were sorry and tired and overtold.

The vanity of vanities.

For there is no remembrance of former things. And neither shall there be any remembrance of things that are to come with those that shall come after.

———◦◦◦———

—Is it any good?

As the two women from St. Louis were paying the waiter, the young lady with the scar had looked up from her book to ask for her check, and the woman in the blue hat had made use of the opening.

—The book you're reading, she said. Is it any good?

From her tone, you could tell she didn't expect it to be.

The young lady studied her for a moment. Then she put out her cigarette, smiled like a Southern belle, and replied with the accent to match.

—Oh, it's all right, I reckon. . . . It's got all manner of nouns and verbs. And adjectives too! But it's just not true to life. Why, when the hero is slipped a Mickey in chapter twenty-two, he topples over in sixty seconds flat. But in chapter fourteen, when he gets shot in the belly, he makes it halfway across town on foot. And as for ess ee ex: Suffice it to say, there's barely a mention.

She shook her head in a manner that presumed mutual disbelief.

—Now, I'm all in favor of poetic license; but a peck on the cheek in this day and age simply tries one's reason.

—Oh! said the women in their hats.

And as they bristled down the aisle, the young lady with the scar licked her finger and turned the page.

For a few minutes, she read idly on; but then something in the book seemed to give her pause. She looked out the window. Then, after searching through a small purse, she asked if she could borrow a pen or pencil. He took the pencil from his jacket pocket and handed it to her. She flipped to the back of the book and jotted a few things down. Then she returned the pencil, looking satisfied with her efforts.

The dining car was nearly empty now. A few tables away, a mother scolded her freckle-faced boy for playing soldiers with the salts and peppers. At the table in the corner, a studious young man invested himself in a stack of books. While outside, the telegraph wire ran on and on.

—You're right about a Mickey, he found himself saying. On a man of average weight even a five-star Mickey Finn would need ten minutes to do its damage.

The young lady lowered her book in order to eye him over the pages.

—But a bullet, he said, that's another thing altogether.

She put her book on the table.

—In 1924, I worked with a man in Ventura who was shot in the eye.

The bullet glanced off his skull and went out his ear. He drove himself fifteen miles to the county hospital and lived to tell the tale. But Eddie O'Donnell? He got shot by a young lady not much older than you with a .22 caliber pistol.

He held his fingers apart to show her how small the pistol had been.

—She'd been harboring someone; I don't remember who. We were just going to ask a few questions, when suddenly she was holding the gun. She was shaking like a leaf. We told her not to do anything she'd regret; but she just closed her eyes and pulled the trigger, shooting Eddie in the leg. He couldn't believe it. *Would you get a load of that?* he said to me. But the bullet had split his femoral artery. And Eddie bled to death right there on the entryway floor.

He looked out the window for a moment, the thoughts of Eddie O'Donnell getting the better of him—getting the better of him, after all these years.

—There's just no telling with bullets, he said.

When he looked back, she was taking him in. She nodded a few times as if to show consideration for his old partner. Then she stretched her hand across the table.

—I'm Evelyn Ross.

She had a fine grip.

—Charlie Granger.

She took a new cigarette from the pack and lit it.

—So, what's your story, Charlie?

Then she pushed the pack across the table.

It was the first time a woman had offered him a cigarette in over fifteen years.

So, what's your story? she had asked, and that's what Charlie told her.

He told her how he and Betty had come to Los Angeles with their baby boy back in 1905, after they'd seen the advert in the Chicago papers looking for experienced officers willing to relocate. And how, when they got off the train, the whole town looked like an outpost for the Pony Express.

He told her what she already knew—about the rise of the studios and the matinee idols, the mansions and grand hotels. But he told her about the other Los Angeles too. The one that had emerged from the dust right alongside the glamorous one and had grown just as fast, if not faster. The Los Angeles of the gangsters and grifters and ladies of the night. That city within the city that had its own diners and cable cars, its own chapels and banks—that had its own fashioning of failure and folly, and of grace and integrity too.

When he realized he'd probably gone on too long, he apologized, but she just pushed her cigarettes back across the table. She asked him to tell her about his life on the force, and she listened as closely when he told her about the small-time felons as when he told her about the ones who landed on the front page. And when he told her about the Doheny Drowning, she just lit up with laughter.

She laughed like young ladies should laugh in kitchens and castles, in Hollywood and Tenafly, and everywhere else in the world.

When the dining car was finally empty—after the studious young man had lugged his labors back to his berth and the freckle-faced kid had deftly swept the change his mother had left for the waiter into the pocket of his blazer—Evelyn said she owed Charlie an apology.

—When you sat down, she said, you looked like a salesman who's traveled his route ten times too many, and I had every intention of ignoring you. But once you got started, Mr. Granger, I could've listened all the way to Timbuktu.

She patted the table once and stood.

—I guess it just shows to go you.

But as she began to walk away, he stayed her progress by reaching for her arm. She looked back and tilted her head in inquiry.

—May I ask you a personal question, Miss Ross?

—Of course.

—Why did you extend your ticket from Chicago to Los Angeles?

She showed a hint of surprise, then smiled.

—I'm not sure myself. I guess it just seemed like a good time for a change of scenery.

And he could see it again: that sparkle of having made the decision. A decision that was all the better for having no cause or impetus or sub-jugation to a grander scheme. And suddenly, Charlie knew that he wasn't going back to his son's.

The young lady didn't continue on immediately. She lingered for a moment, mulling over some quandary of her own as the east grew ever eastward.

—May I ask you a personal question, Mr. Granger? she said at last.

—Of course.

—How *does* one make a five-star Mickey Finn?

Prentice

O N THE SIXTEENTH OF September, at the northeast corner of the swimming terrace of the Beverly Hills Hotel, Prentice Symmons stopped to catch his breath between two chaise longues. He stopped as had Kutuzov on the fields of Borodino; as had Washington on the western banks of the Hudson having slipped through the grasp of Howe. Here on the swimming terrace, the sun paused in its course and the snap of the canopies subsided as Prentice leaned upon his cane.

In the limpid pool, a starlet swam alone. Her auburn hair was neatly tucked beneath a light blue cap, and her delicate arms parted the water's dappled surface without a sound. She was this fair city's newest nightingale. At the four corners of the pool stood cabana boys, each hoping that when she concluded her fiftieth lap she would climb from the water in his proximity so that he would have the honor of bestowing upon her a towel. Five years before, when this damsel (or rather, her predecessor) had finished her calisthenics, it would have been toward Prentice that she swam. Calling out some coy remark, she would have splashed him playfully from the pool's edge before backstroking into fame's embrace.

Alas, there is no fixing of man's position in the system of the heavens, anymore than one can fix the position of a skiff at sea. Alas, yes, alas; but also, avanti!

—Afternoon, Mr. Symmons, said the boy at north northwest. It was James, the arch one. *Afternoon*, he said without a modifier, while betraying the slightest smile, as if winking at some shared acknowledgment of Prentice's professional standing. It was a harbinger, no doubt, of the young man's inevitable success as a talent agent, or felon.

—*Good* afternoon, Prentice corrected as he passed.

At the edge of the terrace awaited the twenty-six steps to the main floor. The steps knew as well as he that not a hundred feet away an elevator had lately been installed. But he had no intention of giving them the satisfaction of using it. He brandished his cane once and launched his ascent. Five, ten, fifteen, twenty. It is a good afternoon, he remarked to himself as he crested the top. His daily exercise had been completed, the insolence of the cabana boy parried, the twenty-six steps bested, and it was only half past three.

Back inside the hotel proper, he smiled when he passed the elegantly scripted sign that pointed the way to the lobby. To refer to that space as a *lobby* was to commit a crime of nomenclature. In such a room did Kubla Khan hold court. It was a geographic pinpoint through which within the hour the world would come and go. Misguided financiers newly arrived from Manhattan with a single change of clothes would soon be signing the registry. Delivery boys would be appearing with elaborate flower arrangements commissioned to express admiration or regret. And the town's young Turks on their way to the bar would pass the late-lunching titans they aspired to supplant.

But as Prentice rounded the corner and passed between the potted palms, the Fates once again laid claim to their supremacy, to their dominion over mortal men. For there, under the painted ceiling, a delicate beauty sat blithely in his chair—turning indifferently through the pages of *Gander*, the latest periodical dedicated to the rise and fall of the latest. One could hardly blame her for choosing his chair. It was an inviting chair, plush and well positioned. And she had no reason to know better.

He stole a glance around the room, looking for the desk captain or concierge, both of whom were otherwise engaged. So, letting his eyebrows droop and leaning on his cane a tad more than necessary, he approached.

—Ahem.

Looking up from her periodical, the young woman who had seemed such a delicate beauty from afar revealed a scar on her face that could have marked the nemesis of Zorro! Her eyebrows rose with a poised curiosity. In the instant, he could see there would be no appealing to sympathies. He resumed his upright posture.

—Pardon me for the intrusion, he ventured. But would it inconvenience you terribly to move to this other chair?

He pointed his cane lightly at the empty seat four feet to her left.

—My girth, you see, demands unusual quarter.

She tilted her head and smiled.

—But they are the same size. . . .

He cleared his throat.

—Yes. So they are, so they are. And as such, I daresay I could presumably fit in this empty chair. But you see, I am afraid . . . How does one put it . . . ? It is not *my* chair.

She laid her magazine in her lap and sat back, as if to say that she was ready to hear his case with unwavering attention. God bless her!

He adopted the bearing of Cicero.

—Young lady, he began, though I have stayed in this hotel without interruption for more than one thousand nights, that should not give me claim to special privileges in the lobby. Were you to spend but a single night in the hotel, you would have every right to expect access to all of its amenities. So, I will not appeal to your sense of propriety. What I must appeal to instead is your sense of *forbearance*. For I am quite simply an aging, overweight oncewas who no longer lays claim to his city's storied indulgences—other, that is, than to invest the four o'clock hour observing the Turn of the Wheel from this my Elba . . . my fence post . . . my perch.

The young woman smiled delightfully and shifted to the adjoining chair.

—You are a woman of great courtesy, Prentice said with a bow.

—Hardly, she replied. But I've got a soft spot for oncewases.

Exemplifying the grace of the well bred, the young woman accepted Prentice's offer to share a pot of tea and a plate of currant scones with clotted cream and jam.

—What brings you to Beverly Hills, my dear? Prentice asked as he filled her cup.

—I suppose I was in the mood for a bit of adventure.

—Well, you have come to the right place. Teddy Roosevelt and Ernest Hemingway traveled all the way to Africa to see the creatures of the wild, to join in the hunt and put themselves in mortal danger. I tell you, they need only have come to this lobby.

The young woman laughed.

It was a marvelous laugh.

—Mortal danger . . . ? she queried.

—I do not exaggerate. In the coming minutes, you will see predators dressed in coats of fur as thick as an ocelot's. In the high grass around the watering hole, you will see conniving dogs lying in wait for the approach of young, unguarded gazelles. And every day at five, there is a stampede.

She laughed again, and he smiled to hear it.

There was nothing jaded or ugly about her laughter. On the contrary, it was the laugh of one who knows well the foibles of others without begrudging them. It was a tribute to the human comedy—the sort of laugh he had not heard in years, or maybe eons. The sort of laugh that should not be interrupted! (A waiter approaching with a plate of tea sandwiches is discreetly waved off.)

And what a refined sense of curiosity she exhibited in her questions. It was a curiosity one might have imagined in the young Galileo or Isaac Newton. Without a slavish adherence to the faddish certainties of yesteryear (in fact, with an instinctive suspicion of them), she had an interest in the *world*—and those invisible, immutable laws that actually spin it on its axis and keep us all from flinging into space.

So, leaving a history of Spanish missionaries and the great migration spawned by Sutter's Mill to other professors, he told her instead of the founding of Beverly Hills. A desert within a desert, Beverly Hills had lain fallow for a thousand years until Pioneer Oil arrived and drilled deep into the ground in search of petrol, only to discover . . . water— that tasteless, shapeless, colorless substance without which, nothing.

(Prentice gestured to the periphery, indicating by general reference the orange blossoms and jasmine that abounded just outside the lobby's walls.)

Then he described for her how in 1912 the Andersons secured these ten acres with a million dollars and a dream—a dream to build amidst gardens and bowers a temporary residence par excellence. And vision had led to vision. For within the hotel's walls had been imagined Caribbean battles between privateers and His Majesty's fleet; the coldhearted dalliances of latter-day Cleopatras; and the all-encompassing charity of a bowler-hatted tramp.

—Why, not a hundred feet from here Chaplin, Fairbanks, Pickford, and Griffith struck the anvil of artistic independence to forge United Artists!

Etc., etc.

Unexpectedly, the young woman repaid him in kind with one of the most fantastic tales of Hollywood that he had ever heard—one she had learned in the dining car of the Golden State Limited from a homicide detective, no less. And when she stood to go, he roused himself from his chair without his cane in order to take her hand and thank her for a delightful afternoon.

Prentice's original plan that day had been to dwell for the hour after tea in the pages of Charles and Mary Lamb's *Tales from Shakespeare*. But having completed his daily exercise, waved off sandwiches, and conversed at length with a lovely young woman, when he finally rose to leave the lobby, he felt a sense of élan.

Why rush back to one's quarters? he thought. Mr. & Mrs. Lamb were as genteel and sympathetic as any companions known to man. They would be the first to understand the cause of his delay. And with that, he headed out the lobby doors into the aromatic air.

Edgar, the bell captain, was patting the roof of a taxicab, having helped a guest into the back seat. When he turned to find Prentice before him, he snapped to attention.

—Mr. Symmons!

—Hello, Edgar. How are things?

—I'd say it's shaping up to be a beautiful evening.

—I think you're right. In fact, it seems a perfect night for an early supper at Maison Robert. Could you see if William is free?

—Yes, sir, Edgar said with verve before jogging off to the lower lot.

Maison Robert . . . , thought Prentice with the smile of anticipation (as he crossed the drive to the large Tuscan pots where the gardenia bushes bloomed). How excited they would be to see him. Without mention of the years that had passed, and without a glance at the reservation book, Robert himself would lead Prentice to his old banquette. After cold asparagus soup, Prentice would have the porterhouse steak, potatoes dauphinoise, and a soufflé. Or better yet . . . When the waiter came for his order, Prentice would say: *It is up to Bernard!* And when the last morsel had been picked from his plate, he would step once again through the kitchen's swinging doors to proclaim the only word that applied: *Magnifique.*

But as he was bending down to savor the smell of the blossoms, he heard the turn of an ignition. Looking back, he saw the black sedan, which had been parked at the end of the drive, start slowly rolling forward; and behind the wheel, a familiar silhouette.

His heartbeat quickened.

He was a hundred feet from the lobby door, and no one was about. The sedan continued to advance at its ominous pace. Then, in the very moment its engines began to race, a man and woman appeared from the other direction on foot. It was the Sandersons—the fine young couple from Houston who were celebrating their fifth anniversary. They must have just taken a stroll among the roses in Municipal Park before returning to dress for dinner.

As they approached, they gave Prentice a warm Texas greeting and the sedan's engine idled—its grim intentions for the moment foiled.

—Wait! Prentice called to the Sandersons. I was just headed inside myself. Allow me to accompany you.

On the following afternoon, when Prentice arrived in the lobby for tea, he was delighted to find the young woman with the scar awaiting him. Her name was Evelyn Ross, lately of Manhattan. When he formally introduced himself, she sat back with a look of self-recrimination, then simply said:

—Of course.

Now, having lived in Hollywood for nearly half his life, Prentice Symmons was well acquainted with the feigning of recognition. He was neither insulted by it nor did he take it too closely to heart. Rather, he completed the charade by smiling and nodding in the fatuous manner of faded celebrity with the full expectation that conversation would quickly shift to politics or other forms of weather.

But Miss Ross commenced to recall six different films in which he had appeared. By her own admission, she had been sneaking into movie houses since the age of thirteen! And to her lasting credit, she recalled his career as one who plays a game of memory, rather than one who has been presented the opportunity to fawn. With the occasional tap of a finger to her lip, she reconstructed scenes that he had stolen; she rehashed outrageous twists of plot; she rekindled romances that never had any business being doused. So complete was her inventory, they both fell silent once she was done.

Did he miss it? she asked at last. Did he miss the silver screen?

—Pah, he said with a wave of the hand.

What he missed was *the stage*!

—For the viewer, Evelyn—whether salesgirl or senator, rogue or Rothschild—the cinema is the ultimate entertainment. It is an over-flowing font of romance and danger. But for the performer, the romance and danger reside on the stage. When shooting a close-up, the movie camera must have you to itself. Thus, when you perform the most charged of cinematic scenes, you are likely to deliver your lines alone. *Lady, by yonder blessed moon I swear. . . .* Or so you proclaim to the cold, black eye of the camera before being excused to your dressing room, so that Juliet can implore in your absence *Swear not by the moon, th' inconstant moon. . . .* Wherefore art thou Romeo, indeed!

Prentice paused briefly to serve the tea before it oversteeped.

—But onstage, my dear, onstage it is in the very interstice between the full-blooded physical forms of the actors that the spark is struck. It is in that space between two gazes that search each other out, between two fingertips that nearly touch. . . . And danger? For the actor, every dram of it is in the theater. Not because of crocodiles and sabers, you understand, but because the edge of the stage is a precipice! For there are no takes in the theater, Evelyn; no second chances. One false move, and the actor plummets through the pitch toward the craggy bottom of his own self-indictments.

Her appreciation for his argument almost instinctual, Evelyn's cheeks betrayed a rosy flush.

—Then why, she asked almost breathlessly, why did you stop acting?

—You're sweet, my dear.

But in her perplexity, she seemed genuine. Genuine!

—My rotundity, he explained.

And before she could express her shock (or God forbid, her sympathy), he raised a stalling hand.

—Don't pity me for it. Are there elements of stardom that I miss? Why, there are elements of boarding school that I miss. There are elements of my most catastrophic romances that I miss. So let us agree that missing is not at the heart of the matter.

At one in the morning, the lobby of the Beverly Hills Hotel had been empty for almost an hour. There were no more guests checking in; no gilded affairs dispersing. Through the doors of the bar drifted the tinkling of piano keys at the hands of some weary straggler who finally fell asleep, having made the G major 7 with his head. While behind the desk, the night clerk, Michael, stood alone.

Under the circumstances, it was quite natural for him to welcome a chance to chat.

So, after marveling at the business of the season and remarking on a handful of recent arrivals, Prentice and Michael agreed that Miss Ross was a delightful young woman. But from where and when and how did she arrive? Well, it seems she arrived by taxicab from the railway station with a single red valise. And was she here to see old friends? It was hard to say, for she had placed no phone calls and received no visitors. On her first night, she did entrust two items of jewelry to the hotel safe: a sizable engagement ring and a diamond earring without its pair; although (as Michael noted *sotto voce*), on the very next morning, she had taken the earring from the safe and returned in the late afternoon with a selection of dresses and two pairs of shoes.

An excellent use of a young woman's wherewithal, the two gentlemen agreed.

Prentice wondered out loud if she was the same Miss Ross, friend of a friend, who lived on Gramercy Park . . . ?

No, replied Michael, turning the registration card so that Prentice could read.

—Ah, Prentice said. Well. Good night, my fine fellow.

Then he ambled down the hall with a smile on his lips. For Miss Evelyn Ross, lately of Manhattan, had apparently resided at Eighty-

Seven East Forty-Second Street. Or, as it is more commonly known: Grand Central Terminal.

At room 108 Prentice put his key in the door, eager to cast off his shoes and recline with a square of chocolate in the company of Mr. & Mrs. Lamb. But as his door closed behind him, his heart skipped a beat. Across the sitting room, a curtain billowed before the open terrace door. For a minute he stood stock-still under the grip of his accelerating pulse. He considered backing into the hallway and dialing the house phone for security. But Devlin was on duty tonight, and Prentice had called him not two weeks before, only to suffer the humiliation of having empty closets opened one by one.

Prentice attempted to steel himself to the task.

—Who's there? he called out.

With beads of sweat crawling down his back, he peeked into the bedroom, then eased open the door to the bath with his cane. After circling once and finding nothing out of place, he locked the terrace door and sat relieved on the edge of his bed. And that is when he saw it: There, between the pillows and the turned-down sheet, sat Mr. & Mrs. Lamb with an unfamiliar bookmark. With a tremble of the hand he opened the pages and felt a wave of nausea.

It had been a year since he had purged his room of memorabilia: The gaudy posters with their imperial fonts and faraway gazes; the playbills; the overtly staged studio stills; even the candids—like the shot of him and Garbo addled at Antonio's. Into boxes they had all been thrown and sent to the hotel's cellar.

Yet here, marking the first page of *Hamlet*, was a ticket to the premiere of his acclaimed run as the Danish Prince at the Old Vic in 1917.

Prentice Symmons slid from his bed to the floor and wept.

———※———

Prentice spent much of the following day in his room. When he woke, he neither showered nor shaved. When his regular breakfast was served, he left half the potatoes uneaten beside the remnants of egg and did not ring for the service to be cleared. He sat on the couch in his robe as the room filled with the odor of the unfinished breakfast and as the minutes dismantled the hours. In the early afternoon, he heard one of the chambermaids pushing her linen-laden trolley down the hallway, knocking on doors. When she knocked on his, he fully intended to send her on her way. But when he realized it was Bridie, from force of habit he invited her in.

A professional young Irish woman and mother of six, Bridie did not display the slightest condescension upon finding Prentice still in his robe. But within the instant she had whisked his plates into the hall, drawn open the curtains, and cracked the terrace door to admit fresh air. When she went into the bedroom, he watched her through the open door. He watched as she returned his shoes and jacket to their closet. He watched as she made the bed with efficiency and care, snapping the fresh sheets and tucking them tightly in place. He watched as she laid a fresh towel on the freshly made bed and then his razor and shaving brush on the towel. When she had finished, he roused himself from the couch and thanked her as one who thanks a chance apostle for the telling of a timely parable. For she was perfectly right: If one is to maintain the slightest hint of pride, his curtains must be drawn, his breakfast cleared, and his chin closely shaved.

By the time Prentice finished bathing, it was nearly four o'clock and he was famished. Having dressed in a three-piece suit and tucked his well-wound watch in the vest pocket, he set out for tea. Evelyn did not appear, but she had been kind enough to leave a note of regret on his chair and a promise to see him anon. This unnecessary gesture (coming in concert with the rare treat of cranberry scones) completed the revival of his spirits. And it was this revival, no doubt, that led him to play the part of a fool.

For when his tea had been cleared, Prentice happened to notice that lingering by the front desk was a certain actor-of-the-moment—an actor who as a younger man had played a supporting role in one of Prentice's films. And rather than keeping his counsel, Prentice strolled across the lobby with his cane in hand, calling out the actor's name.

Exhibiting a touch of surprise, the actor remarked how pleasant it was to see Prentice. Then he made a polite inquiry into Prentice's welfare (an inquiry that is best met with a generous affirmation and the word *adieu*). But in his elevated spirits, Prentice leaned upon his cane and began to harken back; at which point, this actor-of-the-moment played the part of someone who suddenly remembered an engagement somewhere else, stranding Prentice in the lobby with his days of yore.

At the front desk, it was evident from the attention Simone and Christopher paid to the shuffling of papers that they had heard every word of this embarrassing exchange—as had the young socialite who was standing by the elevator with her dog.

Prentice felt his face grow flush.

—I am expecting a telegram, he heard himself proclaiming to Simone, in the manner of one for whom telegrams urgently arrive. When it appears, send it to the pool!

As Prentice passed the elegantly scripted sign that pointed the way to the pool, he unleashed a spate of acrimony—not toward his old supporting cast member, but toward himself. For what had he expected? To be embraced and invited for supper? So that they could speak of times gone by—when their positions were reversed? At the peak of his fame, had not Prentice been strolled upon and cornered in lobbies by fading acquaintances? And had he not performed stage-left exits of his own?

Having descended the twenty-six steps to the pool at too quick a pace, Prentice found he needed to catch his breath, so he headed toward a chair at the pool's edge. Gratefully, the terrace was empty. An unseasonably cool afternoon had driven the starlets and cabana boys into their respective retreats.

But just as Prentice was about to reach his chosen resting spot, from the corner of his eye he glimpsed a figure slip behind a cabana. Feeling his heart rate leap, Prentice bypassed the chair and made for the rear gate. But the shadow, having deftly crossed the terrace, now ducked behind a closer cabana. In a state of panic, Prentice looked about for a fellow guest or attendant, and failed to see the tea table directly in his path. Thus he tripped and fell to his knees, the force of impact tearing the fabric of his pants. Prentice began to heave, knowing that above all else, he must regain his footing. With a flash of single-mindedness, he stood to his full height, but the terrace wheeled around him. And when upon the breeze he heard the whispering of his name, Prentice Symmons acknowledged the unacknowledgeable—that it was time.

On this day, on this terrace, at this Trafalgar, they would meet. Without the exchange of a word, a single hand would extend into space and topple Prentice into the pool of the Beverly Hills Hotel where, hapless, he would thrash for a sliver of eternity, before sinking at last to the depths.

Oh, fateful day.

Oh, ignominious—

—Prentice?

A gentle hand took hold of his elbow.

—Evelyn, he gasped.

—Jesus, Prentice. You're white as a ghost. Are you all right?

—Ohhh, he moaned from the bottom of his soul; and then began to sob.

She led him to a chaise, sat at his side, and took his hands in her own to still them from trembling.

—What is it, Prentice? What's happened?

—Evelyn. He was almost upon me.

—Who was almost upon you?

—Like a minion of the devil, he has haunted me. Hunted me. Waiting for the perfect moment to bring me to my end.

—Who, Prentice?

—A shadow.

—What shadow?

Silence fell around them. A silence as limitless as time. The silence from which all things spring, all things good and evil. With a great effort, Prentice raised his gaze and looked her in the eyes.

—The shadow of my former self.

It was a pitiful admission. A *comic* one. It had been written in the pages of Prentice's personal history to elicit guffaws. But young Evelyn, so prone to beautiful laughter, remained sober. Sympathetic. Unflinching.

—In 1936, Prentice confessed, on a crowded avenue, he shoved me in front of a tram. And last New Year's Eve, he nearly succeeded in throwing me from my own balcony to the flagstones below. That's why I moved to the first floor!

—But why, Prentice? What are you talking about?

Casting his gaze downward again, he saw that she was still holding his hands. And he could feel how her innermost temperature was transferring itself through his skin and coursing through his veins, bringing warmth to his core in the manner of a potent drink. And in this state of intoxication, the words spilled forth: How it all began when he was visiting his grandmother's as a boy; the lemon squares with a shortbread crust and a bright yellow curd; the bacon sandwiches, so fatty and savory and divine; then beef bourguignon with potatoes au gratin; and later, the ingenuity of the profiterole!

Ah, the very shame of it.

He told her too how he had learned to hold his appetite in check as he climbed the ladder of his career—first as a lord-officer-soldier-attendant without a single line; then, as an understudy in the wings, mouthing monologues word for word; and finally, as the dashing hero with a rapier in his left hand and a pistol in his right. But with every step toward success, he had advanced as well toward a darker humor. He became surly. Impatient. Abrupt.

—Do you know what I was doing, Evelyn, at the height of my stardom? Can you even imagine? I was starving! Over the years, I convinced myself I had built worthy defenses—a fortress against my weakness. But in the spring of 1935, left alone in a lavish hall where the press had yet to arrive, my fortitude failed me. On that day, I gorged. I gorged on honey-baked ham and Linzer torte and strawberries dipped in cream. It was my crossing of the Rubicon, Evelyn. In the days that followed, I tumbled down the vertiginous trail of my desires. Head over heels I fell; and as I passed the trees jutting from the jagged hills, not once did I reach for a branch.

In hearing this, Evelyn's eyes grew brighter with every word. She did not look disgusted or shocked. She looked defiant!

—I want you to listen to me, Prentice, she said in the manner of one who has slayed a dragon of her own. I want you to listen very carefully. Are you listening?

—Yes, Evelyn. I am listening.

—Since that day, since that day with the ham and the torte, have you been surly, impatient, or abrupt?

Prentice raised his head.

—Not for a minute.

She patted him on the back of the hand.

—Exactly.

Her expression relaxed. They sat holding hands. And as the sky began to turn indigo, an early moon rose over the hotel, giving the entire setting the look of the desert oasis it was.

—Evelyn . . .

—Yes, Prentice.

—I must admit to something else.

He shifted on the seat so he could face her.

—I have lied to you.

She did not look offended or surprised.

—In what way?

—About the lobby.

She offered a bemused smile.

—No. I am serious. Deadly serious. I have encouraged you to take up residence beside me in the lobby, calling it the world. But it isn't the world. It isn't a continent, or a country, or a town. It isn't even a room! It is a prison cell. It is my Bastille.

For the first time in years, Prentice felt the force of his own convictions.

—Providence has brought you to Los Angeles, Evelyn. And you must visit with It. Young William, one of the hotel's drivers, has been put at my disposal; I put him at yours. You must go out into the scent of the orange blossoms, out into the temperate nights of Hollywood, where all of its most elusive delicacies hide in plain sight. Go tonight. Start by dining on the Sunset Strip at Antonio's on osso buco with risotto Milanese!

—We can go together.

(So suggested Evelyn, sweet Evelyn.)

—No, said Prentice, rising to his feet. You must go without me, *mon amie*. For tonight upon the platform, before the crow of the cock, I have an appointment with an apparition.

Olivia

WHEN OLIVIA HAD ALMOST run out of questions about track and field, she excused herself politely from the table for two.

Given the choice, she would have preferred to be on the little bedroom terrace that she hardly ever used. Bounded by white stucco, climbing with ivy, bordered by love-in-idleness, it seemed the perfect grotto for the weary in waiting. But as she passed a neighboring table, she paused to accept and return the compliment from the comedian; and at the booth a few steps beyond, she told the director with the Slavic accent that she would very much enjoy having the opportunity to work with him as well. She tucked a curl behind an ear, offered a delicate smile, and continued toward the powder room, hoping to find it empty.

But of course, it wasn't.

They hardly ever were.

Leaning against the wall by the sinks was the rather rough-looking blonde whom Olivia had noticed dining alone at the bar. She was smoking a cigarette and listening to the attendant, who was describing a night on the town as she aimlessly wiped the countertop. Miguel, the girl was saying, had borrowed his uncle's car and dressed in a three-piece suit. He had taken her dancing at a club on Shepherd Avenue. A club that had the finest band en Los Ángeles . . . en California . . . en todo el—

The girl stopped short when she saw Olivia's reflection in the mirror. With an apologetic bow, she retreated to the back of the room, where she began refolding hand towels. Olivia approached a sink and turned on the faucets. The blonde didn't move. She closed her eyes and rested her head against the wall, as if she could hear the rumbas of the girl's reminiscence.

From across the restaurant, Olivia had imagined the blonde was in that league of callous women who began their workday at 5:00 p.m. at the bars of Hollywood's restaurants and hotels. But from up close, Olivia could see how terribly off the mark she had been. In the mirror's reflection, the blonde's unscarred profile suggested an almost aristocratic beauty with no hint of an ugly enterprise's toll. And she had the effortless poise of a woman raised in privilege. With her arm hanging gracefully at her side, her fingers slender and unadorned, she held her cigarette at an upward angle so that the smoke could spiral toward the ceiling with an enviable lack of purpose.

—Would you like one?

Olivia looked up to find the blonde had caught her staring.

—Why yes, thank you, she replied, though she hadn't smoked in over a year.

The blonde slid the pack across the vanity.

Olivia took one of the cigarettes and lit it. She leaned against the wall facing the blonde, assuming the blonde would make conversation, but she didn't.

When Olivia inhaled, the taste of the smoke brought back memories of hiding with her sister in the garden shed with pilfered cigarettes and a pack of cinnamon gum. They were memories from another world—a world where the two of them had shared clothes and secrets and sly remarks.

—So, is he as boring as he seems?

—I'm sorry? asked Olivia.

—Your date, said the blonde. Isn't he the one who wears the big white hats?

Olivia laughed.

—Wilmot's not really a date. It's more of a work dinner. But yes, I suppose he is the one who wears the big white hats.

—Well, every time he squints at the horizon, I fall asleep.

Olivia laughed again.

—I think they call it the strong and silent type.

—They can call it whatever they like. But from where I was sitting, he looked more like the go-on-and-on-and-on type. Do you ever get a word in edgewise?

Olivia extended her arm in an ironic flourish.

—*Give every man thine ear, but few thy voice. . . .*

The blonde raised a questioning eyebrow.

—Shakespeare, Olivia confessed. Courtesy of my mother.

—What else did your mother teach you?

Olivia considered.

—A lady never finishes a cigarette, a drink, or a meal.

The blonde nodded her head in a show of familiarity.

—My mother told me it was more important to be interested than interesting.

—Have you heeded her advice?

—Only as a last resort.

Olivia and the blonde were both silent—reflecting for the moment on motherly advice and other monoliths. Then Olivia held up her cigarette to show it had only been half smoked and, with a smile of resignation, dutifully tamped it out.

As the waiter cleared Olivia's unfinished entrée, Wilmot was explaining the insignificance of the marathon when compared to the fifty-yard dash.

—A marathon is really a contest of endurance, he was saying, not of athleticism. You'll often see a topflight sprinter excel at a variety of sports, but a great marathoner will only excel at one. And there are whole miles in a marathon that have no bearing on victory. But I think we can safely say that in the fifty-yard dash, every footfall counts.

As Wilmot spoke, he kept brushing the tablecloth with the flat of a hand as if it needed smoothing. And Olivia realized he didn't want to be there either. He too was fulfilling an obligation—playing his part in this orchestrated pairing of Maid Marian and Wyatt Earp.

But that didn't mean he was about to ask for the check. When the waiter returned to inquire about dessert, Wyatt (with his white hat securely on his head) would note how famous Antonio's was for its baked Alaska; and Marian would smile politely and say a baked Alaska sounded delicious. And they would spend another hour talking of the shot put and the high jump and God knows what else before heading their separate ways.

The blonde from the powder room wouldn't stay for dessert, Olivia found herself thinking. But then, she probably wouldn't have put herself in this position in the first place. Having dined alone at the bar, she could now pay her check and go home to her own ivied terrace. Or more likely, head off in search of the finest band in Los Ángeles. En California. En todo el mundo.

—Cousin Livvy! Is that you?

Wyatt and Marian both looked up in surprise.

It was the blonde, but she looked bright-eyed and boisterous. And she had a Southern accent. . . .

—It's me, Evvie! she said, placing her fingers on her chest. All the way from Baton Rouge!

Olivia had to restrain a laugh.

—Evvie . . . I didn't know you were in town.

—I'm here with Aunt Edith. She's waiting at the hotel, so I only have a minute. But they'd just paddle me back home, if we didn't catch up.

—Please join us, said Wilmot.

Coming to his feet, he brought a chair from the neighboring table and placed it between his and Olivia's.

—Oh no, chided Evvie. Boy girl, boy girl.

Picking up Wilmot's cocktail with both hands, she placed it gently in front of the empty chair. Then she claimed his spot as the waiter arrived with her martini.

—Bottoms up, said Evvie, emptying her glass.

—Bottoms up, repeated Wilmot a little uncertainly, as he emptied his.

—So . . . , said Olivia, what's the news from Baton Rouge?

—You wouldn't believe me if I told you, said Evvie. You remember that colored boy who worked for Aunt Ethel? Well, last Septembah he up and drove off in Aunt Ethel's Cadillac—with Aunt Ethel in it! And when the police finally pulled them over in Kansas City, it was the colored boy who was in the passengah seat and Aunt Ethel behind the wheel.

—I do declayah, said Olivia.

Evvie turned to Wilmot confidentially.

—Aunt Ethel always had a fondness for oldah husbands and youngah men. . . .

Wilmot, who was smoothing the linens again, attempted to change the subject.

—Have you been in Los Angeles long, Evvie?

—Just the batting of an eye, she sighed. But it's been divine. Why, we've seen Charlie Chaplin's house and Lon Chaney's garage. We've been to the Tar Pits in La Brea and the fights at the American Legion . . .

Wilmot blinked repeatedly, as if he were having trouble keeping up.

—Some dessert? asked the waiter, who was leaning over the table with his pad and pen.

Wilmot looked up at the waiter as if he didn't understand the question.

—I know just the thing, said Evvie. Let's have dessert in Santa

Monica. I have it on good authority that the finest churros in all of California are cooked on the pier. We can dangle our toes in the water and watch the casinos drift out to sea!

—What's a churro? asked Olivia.

—I'm not sure myself, admitted Evvie. But I gather it's like a donut from Mexico.

—It's been awhile since I've had a donut from *anywhere*, said Olivia.

—Then that settles it!

The girls turned to Wilmot.

—I'm actually feeling a little under the weather, he confessed, mopping his brow with his napkin.

—You are looking a little ashen, said Evvie. Would you like me to order you a pick-me-up?

—No, no. I'll be fine. I'm just going to sit here for a minute. Why don't you two go on without me.

When Evvie and Olivia put their napkins on the table, Wilmot looked almost relieved.

—Lovely to meet you, Evvie said.

Then she took Olivia by the hand, pulled her past a screenwriter, a leading man, and the maître d'—any one of whom might normally have waylaid her.

Outside, the fronds of the palm trees were rattling overhead and the dust was rising off the sidewalk.

—I hope that Wilmot will be all right, said Olivia.

—Oh, he'll be fine, said Evvie. He just disagreed with something he drank.

Evvie slipped past the valets in order to survey the street. Halfway up the block, a young man in a chauffeur's uniform waved. He was standing in front of a forest green Packard.

—Is that yours? Olivia asked.

—A friend of a friend's. Come on!

And the two cousins made the fifty-yard dash for the car.

———

Once they were in the back of the Packard driving along Sunset Boulevard, the blonde stuck out her hand and formally introduced herself. Then she instructed her driver to head for the Santa Monica Pier.

—You were serious? asked Olivia.

—Absolutely. The churros are the seventh item on the list. Isn't that right, Billy?

—Yes, ma'am!

—So, you've really been to those other places?

—Not to Lon Chaney's garage. But we've been to the Tar Pits and the fights. We've been to the Wishing Chair at Forest Lawn Cemetery and the parade on Santa Claus Lane. Billy helped me make the list. Didn't you, Billy?

—What is this list?

With one hand on the steering wheel and one eye on the road, Billy leaned to his right, took something from the glove compartment, and handed it into the back seat. It was a notepad from the Beverly Hills Hotel. At the top of the first page had been written: *THINGS TO DO BEFORE I SKEDADDLE*. Below was a list of twenty destinations, nine of which had been checked off in dark green ink, as if the pen had come with the car.

Leaning over Olivia's shoulder, Eve pointed to item number seven: *Churros on the Santa Monica Pier.*

—How long have you been in Los Angeles? Olivia asked in disbelief.

—About two months.

—I've been here four years and haven't done half these things.

—You've been busy.

Olivia took another look at the list.

—Skating?!

—The Pan Pacific Rink is one in a million, Billy enthused from the front seat. The real McCoy. Not only is it the largest skating rink in the world, every Saturday they have an orchestra that plays polkas and on Sundays they serve hot toddies!

Eve winked at Olivia.

—Speaking of hot toddies, Billy: What have we got in the glove?

Billy leaned to his right again and handed back a flask.

Eve took a generous swig.

—Gin, she said, like the pleasantly surprised.

But when she held out the flask, she could see that Olivia hesitated.

—Even a church bell's gotta swing, if it's gonna chime.

Olivia laughed and took the flask. She wasn't used to drinking gin with a mixer, never mind straight. The first swallow seared the back of her throat. But the second went down more smoothly. Within minutes she could feel the liquor tingling in her extremities.

When Eve rolled down her window, Olivia followed suit, taking in the brightly lit marquees of the movie houses.

It was true what Eve had said: Olivia had been busy. How many roles had she played since she had come to Hollywood? Fourteen? Fifteen? She had lost count. First, there was Dolly Stevens; then the guileless Lucille and innocent Hermia. Arabella, Angela, Elsa, and Cath. Maria, Germain, and Serena. Each one as virginal as the last.

—So, of all the men in Los Angeles, why dine with the Big White Hat?

Olivia looked back from the window to find Eve holding out the flask. Olivia took another drink.

—It was arranged.

—*Arranged!* What are you, Amish?

Olivia laughed.

—Arranged by the studio.

—Do they normally tell you who to dine with?

—Oh, they tell me who to dine with, all right. They pick the restaurant and the table. They practically pick my entrée.

Eve looked surprised.

—I'm on contract, Olivia explained. When you're on contract the studio doesn't just decide what roles you take; it weighs in on whatever might affect your image: what you wear, how you spend your weekends, who you spend them with . . .

Eve whistled, then shook her head.

—You should have the world on a string, sister.

—It's the other way around, I'm afraid.

A perfect example sprang to mind, and Olivia almost launched into its petty details. But she regretted having allowed herself to go on at such length already. What a prima donna she must sound like, complaining about the life of a Hollywood star. So she shook her head and said nothing.

But Eve had been watching.

—Speak now, she warned, or forever hold your peace.

Olivia met her gaze.

—All right, she said after a moment. Have you read *Gone with the Wind?*

—I'm not much of a reader.

—It was a bestseller two years ago, and George Cukor is making it into a movie over at Selznick. It's likely to be one of the biggest movies of the year, if not the decade, and Cukor thinks I'm perfect to play one of the main characters—a young woman who's sweet and upright, but also resilient and decisive.

—Sounds great.

—Yes. But in accordance with my contract at Warner Brothers, I'm not even allowed to *talk* with Cukor about the part. He's gone so far as to suggest I read for it covertly. He wants me to put on a scarf and tinted glasses and come up the back drive of his house on a Sunday afternoon— like a thief, or a spy.

—Even better, said Eve.

Olivia laughed, but shook her head.

—Jack Warner would *never* let me be in that film. He's said as much already. I think he's furious he's not making the movie himself. But I hardly have cause for complaint. And it's not like I'll be sitting on my hands. They have me slotted for two other pictures this spring.

As Olivia spoke, she could tell that Eve felt a sense of disappointment. Perhaps to mask it, Eve took a drink from the flask, then turned to the window where the marquees had given way to the cypress trees at the edge of the Brentwood cul-de-sacs. When Eve turned back she said:

—Don't be your own worst enemy, Livvy.

Olivia met Eve's gaze, then looked out her own window.

—It's been a long time since someone called me Livvy, she said.

Stretching a hundred yards into the sea, the Santa Monica Pier was crowded with all manner of amusements. There were tin rifle ranges where brand-new recruits in freshly pressed uniforms tested their aim, and rainbow-colored wheels of fortune surrounded by older women crossing themselves at every spin. Ditching their shoes in the sand, Eve and Olivia wandered into the carnival, beckoned by the calls of barkers and the rumble of roller coasters and the shouts of children out past their bedtimes.

It didn't take long for them to find the fabled purveyor of churros, a heavyset man with a white mustache standing proudly under a red-and-white-striped canopy. After Eve paid for their order, Olivia watched as the man took two of the sticklike donuts from a fryer and tossed them in a pan of cinnamon sugar—and she was suddenly struck by how hungry she was. It was the hunger of a lifetime of half-finished dinners and drinks and cigarettes. When Eve held out one of the churros, Olivia practically snatched it and took a wolfish bite.

—That, said Eve with a laugh, is the first real smile I've seen on you all night!

As the two of them continued down the pier, the wind seemed to be gaining force. Grabbing Eve's elbow, Olivia pointed as a fine yellow hat blew off the head of a Black girl. Her boyfriend gave honorable chase; but when the hat lofted out to sea, he took his own hat from his head and spun it like a discus into the dark.

—This wind, said Eve, appreciatively.

—The Santa Ana, said Olivia. It comes every autumn.

—From *where*?

—From all the talk.

Eve laughed.

—You mean from the gossip?

—And the auditions and directions and negotiations . . .

From the heart-crossed promises, thought Olivia, and the heartfelt excuses. All those voices in Burbank and Beverly Hills rising like a tide until they washed over the levees and flooded toward the sea, threatening to tear up all the palm trees and personas.

Now it was Eve who reached for Olivia's elbow.

A few steps away was a machine that looked like a cross between a fire engine and a calliope fitted with the pistons of a locomotive, the dials of a furnace, and the horn of a gramophone.

Standing before it was a little man with a pointed beard and pince-nez.

Eve popped the last bit of her churro in her mouth and wiped the sugar from her hands.

—What's this all about?

—This? the man repeated. Why, this is the Astrologicon.

The three of them surveyed it together.

—You will note, the little man continued, that I said *the* instead of *an*. For it is the only one of its kind in the world.

He said this somewhat sadly, as if he were speaking of the last living example of some exotic species.

—But what does it do?

—Ah . . . , he said. What does it do.

With two fingers and a thumb, he sharpened the point of his beard.

—Once in possession of a few essential attributes of your person, the Astrologicon will consult the laws of chemistry and the arrangement of the stars in order to provide you with an unassailable, incontrovertible, and indismissible instruction. For one dollar.

—Let's to it, said Eve.

The proprietor accepted Eve's payment and placed it with ceremony in a small tin box. Then he proceeded to collect her essential attributes and calibrate his contraption. He punched the letters of Eve's name into a panel of dislodged typewriter keys. He adjusted three adjacent dials to the year, month, and date of her birth, then two other dials to her height and weight. He turned an arrow embedded in a spectrum of colors to the precise pigmentation of her eyes. Finally, he handed Eve the end of a stethoscope, which was cabled back into the inner workings of the machine.

—If you would be so kind, he said, pointing shyly toward her sternum.

Eve slid the stethoscope under the neckline of her dress and you could suddenly hear the beating of her heart broadcast through the gramophone's horn.

The proprietor nodded in appreciation. After reclaiming the stethoscope, he reached into his watch pocket and produced a brass token.

—I caution you, young lady, that the Astrologicon is not to be taken lightly. I suspect the path of your life appears clearly before you—a path that in all probability is popular, convenient, and profitable. But the Astrologicon cares nothing for popularity, convenience, or profit. Rather, like the Oracle at Delphi, it will advise you to do what you should regardless of opinion, difficulty, or cost.

He handed the token to Eve and gestured to a slot in the machine marked by four converging arrows. Then he put his hands together and bowed.

Without a moment's hesitation, Eve dropped the token in the slot.

There was a buzz followed by a whir. The needles on the temperature gauges began to climb, and after a blast of steam the gears of the engine set in motion the pistons and pinwheels. The proprietor led Eve and Olivia down the length of the machine, pointing to each kinetic phase—to the interpolator and the centrifuge and the epistemolog—until with the ring of a desk-clerk's bell, an envelope fell into a sterling-silver toast caddy. The envelope was addressed to *Evelyn Ross—November 16, 1938.*

Eve thanked the proprietor. Then she led Olivia to an uncrowded spot under a lamppost and placed the envelope in her hand.

—Whatever this says, Livvy, you should follow it to the letter.

Olivia didn't smile at the suggestion. She only nodded and closed her fingers around the envelope.

Then the two continued their progress past the roller coaster toward the very end of the pier, where they could see the oceangoing casinos bobbing outside the city limits. And it felt to Olivia as if the continent was being tilted and all of California was going to slip into the sea. And though she couldn't remember the exact reference, and whether it was from mythology or the Bible, she knew instinctively as they approached the pier's limit that no matter what happened she mustn't look back.

Litsky

T HE GIRLS ON THE dance floor at El Rey's came in all his favorite colors. There were girls from across the Rio Grande with tequila-colored skin who liked to wag their fingers and shake their heads in coy dissuasion. There were girls from Alabama and New Orleans who had skin the color of bourbon and dispositions twice as sweet. And the girls from the islands came as dark as a glass of blackstrap molasses. Ocher, tawny, bronze, beaver, russet, pistol, pitch: Litsky had a taste for them all. So what did he care if he was the only cracker on Shepherd Avenue. What would he care if he was the only cracker in all of L.A.

Back in the Avenue's holy-rolling heyday, the limousines from Bel Air would idle at the curb from Friday night until the Sunday morning ser-mons. It was a colored neighborhood to be sure, but one with painted porches and barbershop poles. Back in 1927, Bernie the Wisenheimer (who had a nose for making money off those who couldn't make it off themselves) bought a roadhouse on an empty block and christened it the Rum Tum Club. He slapped tuxedos on the boys in the band and dropped some red-leather booths around the four-tops. Then he ran a rope down the middle of the dance floor, so the ises and ain'ts would know where to do their dancing.

But after the crash, Bernie went bust right along with the neighborhood. The porch paint peeled, the barber poles stopped spinning, and the highfalutins headed for higher ground. By the summer of '36, when a Harlemite by way of Havana reopened the club as El Rey's, he didn't need a rope to split up the dance floor anymore, but he left it lying there just the same. And as the bands played a jazz as half-bred as he was, the local girls would sweat through their dresses and shimmy over that rope with relish.

That's why Litsky couldn't believe his eyes when on the first Saturday in February, the front door opened at 11:00 p.m. and in walked Miss Olivia de Havilland in a strappy red dress. She was on the arm of that damaged blonde he'd heard about, the one who'd come out of nowhere. And if his eyes did not deceive him, neither one of them was wearing a brassiere. With the blonde leading the way, the girls took one of the tables near the band and ordered tequila with lime as if they'd been raised in Tijuana.

The year before, Litsky had followed Dehavvy around like everybody else—but what a waste of shoe leather. The boys at the studio had her on a short leash, and it showed. She was all seltzer at six, supper at seven, then home for a glass of milk before they tightly tucked her in. But then, you really couldn't blame them. They knew exactly what they were sitting on: the seventy-ninth element.

Because on every Saturday night when Ma and Pa went to the picture shows, what they wanted to see for their hard-earned nickels was a fanciful story with a happy ending starring the girl next door. And Dehavvy was just the ticket, as unblemished in person as she was on the screen.

Knowing everything there was to know about getting his money's worth, Jack Warner had been working Dehavvy like a horse—strapping her to a new picture every three or four months. At least, that is, until he lent her out to Selznick International for a part in *Gone with the Wind*.

Letting one of his stars work for another studio went against every bone in Jack's body. But word on the street was that after Dehavvy had cozied up to Mrs. Warner over tea at the Brown Derby, Mrs. Warner had twisted Jack's arm until he'd said uncle.

So this blonde from nowhere must have had the boys at the studios tearing their hair out. Even from across the room you could see that no one had a leash on her. With the narrowed eyes of a killer, she was sussing out the place, and she liked what she saw. She liked the band, the tempo, the tequila—the whole shebang. If Dehavvy was bandying about with the likes of this one, you wouldn't have long to wait for the wrong place and the wrong time to have their tearful reunion.

Variety may be the spice of life, but no one ever told the band at El Rey's. Because they began playing their trumpety little number for the third time. Some sort of cross between a ranchera and a rumba, this song would skip along for twenty measures, then all the boys in the band would stop on a beat and shout *La Casa!* before picking up where they'd left off. When they played the number for the second time, Litsky rolled his eyes, thinking: *Amateurs.* But when they struck it up again, the crowd broke into a head-shaking grin. Maybe the gauchos were a little more soused, or maybe they were itching to showcase the steps they'd practiced in take two, because before you knew it, they had dragged their dates back on the floor and grabbed them by the hips.

Dehavvy would have been blushing, if she weren't so busy blinking. All of twenty-two, weighing in at a hundred and one pounds with shoulder blades poking through her skin, she looked better than she had in '37—but she was still a year's worth of second helpings away from looking like a woman.

—Hey, shutterbug.

Litsky looked back from the dance floor. It was the lazy baritone behind the bar. He was drying his hands with a dirty rag.

—You gonna have a drink? Or you gonna sit there all night?

—What's your hurry?

—That perch is for the parched.

—Yeah, yeah . . .

Litsky took a bill from his pocket and tossed it on the bar.

—Gimme a rye on the rocks. And this time, pour it from a bottle instead of a jar.

Ol' Man River shuffled off and came back with the drink and the change. Litsky left a nickel on the counter to show his heartfelt appreciation for the five-star service. Then he turned on his stool, leaned his back against the bar, and stirred his ice cubes with a finger.

At the table by the band, the blonde was nodding her head to the beat of the claves with a that's-more-like-it sort of smile. She took a drag from a cigarette and shot a column of smoke at the ceiling.

McNulty, that knucklehead over at *Picture Play*, had it on good authority that she was a moll on the run from Chicago. Besides the fact that molls on the run don't hide out in Hollywood, the caption didn't jive with the candid. There was definitely a streak of the upper classes in this one. Becker, the two-bit stringer, claimed she was another Berliner fleeing the Führer. But that didn't figure either. This blonde had a *joie de vivre* that couldn't get a visa to the Rhineland.

She was leaning forward now to say something to Dehavvy. She pointed at the percussionist with a discerning cigarette. Dehavvy listened and nodded with the rapt attention of the newly under-wing.

Who the hell is she? Litsky found himself thinking, for once.

And he would have let his mind dwell on that conundrum, if down the bar two Latinos hadn't begun disturbing the peace. The first one was saying something about the second one's manhood. When the second one came to his feet, knocking over his stool, Ol' Man River put his meat hooks on the bar and told them to take it outside. The first one spat on the floor and headed for the exit with his posse in tow. The second one counted to five. Then he signaled three amigos, who were picking their teeth at a table nearby, and they all filed out in cool pursuit.

—Chicanos, said Litsky with a shake of the head. There's no one they'd rather fight than themselves.

But having turned his attention to Dehavvy, who was sipping her tequila like a schoolgirl, Litsky looked back at the three amigos who were swaggering out the door. Then he took his nickel off the bar, went to the phone near the washrooms, and dialed the closest division of the LAPD.

—I'd like to report a knife fight, he said into the mouthpiece—Yeah, that's right, a knife fight—In the parking lot of El Rey's—On Shepherd off Central—When'd it happen? Any minute now.

Litsky hung up.

This is going to be interesting, he thought to himself, like a philosopher. But when he returned to his stool, Dehavvy and the blonde were gone.

Litsky studied the path from their table to the little girls' room, but they weren't anywhere along it. So he scanned the club from end to end, and lo and behold, there they were: elbow-to-elbow on the dance floor.

The band was playing a Mexicali "Begin the Beguine." Either by order of the band leader or through some collective instinct, all the boys had gotten on one side of the rope and the girls had gotten on the other. The band's take on the number had some advanced mathematics, and the local girls were making the most of it. They were doing long division with their hips and shaking their cans to the thirteenth power. Dehavvy and the blonde couldn't keep up. They didn't have the bodies for it, or the backgrounds. But they were indisputably in the mix.

Maybe you had to give the blonde credit for taking Dehavvy to El Rey's, after all. Because if anyone on the dance floor knew who she was, they weren't showing it. By the time the locals got to El Rey's, they'd had their fill of deference for the day. (Yes, ma'am. No, ma'am. Thank you, ma'am.) And with their eyes half closed, they were swaying in a rapture serene.

At least, that's what Litsky was thinking when the band broke into "Mi Casa" for the fourth time. Within a beat, every seat in the house was empty. The blonde and Dehavvy had taken places on opposite sides of the rope and were matching each other step for step—shaking their heads in tandem and waiting for the twentieth measure, when they could stand on their toes and shout *Mi Casa!* with the rest of them.

Despite the uptick in the volume of the music, Litsky could hear the sweet, unmistakable sound of sirens in the distance. He looked back toward the club's entrance in time to see a kid in a chauffeur's getup come scrambling through the door. He took off his hat like he was entering a church. When his eyes lit on the blonde, he made a beeline for the dance floor.

Litsky got off his stool.

The kid beckoned her to the edge of the floor and whispered in her ear. From across the room, Litsky could see her eyes narrow; then she rattled off instructions like a drill sergeant. As the kid headed back to his car, she grabbed Dehavvy by the hand. She led her through the crowd, behind the bandstand, and toward the kitchen door.

Litsky snatched his bag from under his stool. He hoisted himself onto the bar and swung his legs over it, toppling a bottle of beer.

—Hey! shouted Ol' Man River.

Litsky scurried out the loading door into the night. Rounding the back of the club, he could see the lights of the kitchen shining through the screen door just as a dark green Packard appeared from the other direction. Litsky was barely ready when the door swung open and out came the blonde, dragging Dehavvy behind her. Litsky steadied himself and whistled. When they both looked up, he pulled the trigger. With a great pop the flash went off. Sparks fell to the ground, filling the air with the smell of brimstone. The blonde wouldn't let go of Dehavvy until she had her safely in the car; then with her teeth bared, she turned toward Litsky—but he was gone.

He was already cutting a wide circle through the underbrush headed toward Central Ave., where he'd had the good sense to leave his car. He slipped under the wheel, set her in gear, and turned onto Shepherd. In the parking lot of El Rey's he could see the cops conferring in tight circumference with the Latin combatants. He saluted them all as he passed, then switched on the radio.

It was another heart-warmer from that huckster Bing Crosby.

Litsky hated Bing Crosby.

But he left the dial where it was and found himself singing along in a happy-go-lucky mood. For in the instant the flash had gone off, as the girls looked up in surprise, Litsky could see that Dehavvy must have caught her dress on something while scampering out the door. Because one of her shoulder straps had snapped, the silky fabric had dropped, and staring back at him was the delightful sort of exposure that makes the cash registers ring.

As Litsky drove along Sunset, he watched the buildings slinking past his windshield. It was like turning the pages of *The Oxford History of Class Acts*: At the corner of Fairfax Avenue was the hotel where Clark Gable had tried to lower himself from a third-story window by a bedsheet; a block beyond La Cienega was Café Trocadero, where Gloria Swanson had almost plucked out the eyes of the Blue Angel; and a few doors down from there was Antonio's, where Louis Mayer had begun dining on lettuce because he could no longer cross his fat little fingers behind his back when making a promise.

On the sixth floor of the Fulwider building, the lights were out in the corner office, which figured. Humpty-Dumpty must have waddled home to catch up on the sleep he hadn't got behind his desk.

Litsky turned onto Cory and pulled into O'Malley's. As usual, the place was empty. O'Malley himself was standing on a pantry stool taking down the colored lights that were still hanging over the bar.

—Hey, Santy Claus.

O'Malley looked back with a grimace. He stepped off the stool, leaving the lights swinging from a hook.

—A round on me for everyone in the house, said Litsky.

—Hardy har, said O'Malley.

He grabbed a bottle by the neck like it was a duck he was about to strangle. Once he'd poured the whiskey, he finally took in Litsky's expression.

—You look like the canary in the coal mine.

—It's *the cat who caught the canary*, you flummox. But you're on the right track.

—Cats, coal mines, said O'Malley with a shrug. What's the difference?

Litsky waggled his empty glass and put it on the bar.

—Just keep these coming. Then maybe I'll teach you a thing or two about this town.

O'Malley reached for the bottle, and Litsky headed for the phone booth in back. After shutting himself in, he took off his hat and pulled a scrap of paper from the inside band. Ragged and stained, it listed five numbers, none too easy to come by. Litsky dialed the fifth, the home number of one Marcus Benton, David O. Selznick's personal attorney. Even from the sleepy style in which he drawled *Hello*, you could tell that Benton was an educated man. A measured man. A man who knew the difference between the penny-wise and pound-foolish.

—This is Jeremiah Litsky, Litsky said into the receiver—That's right, that Litsky—Yeah, I know what time it is—Never mind how I got your number. You'll be glad I've got it—That's it, counselor. I've a certain something you'll want to get your hands on—How big? You're going to need a ladder to see over it—You know the coffee shop on Little Santa

Monica?—Maybe you should come see me there sometime. Like tomorrow at eight. And bring your wallet.

Litsky rang off.

Because here's the thing: Ma and Pa loved to see the girl next door, all right, sitting on top of the silver screen. But the only thing they loved more was seeing her tumble back to earth. That didn't mean Ma and Pa were bad people. There wasn't a mean-spirited bone in their bodies. They just couldn't help themselves. The Krauts call it schadenfreude. Litsky called it human nature—which is just a fancy term for the God-given flaws we have no intention of giving back.

Litsky put the scrap back in his hat and his hat back on his head. Then he put another nickel in the phone. He didn't need to look up this number. He knew every crummy digit by heart. After sixteen rings, Humpty-Dumpty got around to answering.

—It's me, Litsky—Yeah, I know what time it is. Everybody knows what time it is—What's so important? I quit, that's what—Wait a second. Can you say that slower? So I can write it down? It's one for the history books—Yeah. Same to you.

Litsky hung up and exited the booth. When he got back to his stool, his drink was waiting for him.

And so was the damaged blonde.

She was sitting alone at the opposite end of the bar.

He couldn't believe it. She must have seen him driving past the club and ordered the kid to follow. Now here she was, giving him the nod of a fellow citizen who's just happened to happen into a bar.

When she ordered a Scotch and soda, Litsky told O'Malley to put it on his tab. She gave a neighborly smile of thanks, then walked her drink down the bar.

—Hi, she said. I'm Evelyn Ross.

—Jeremiah Litsky.

She gestured to a table for two in the middle of the room.

—Would you like to join me, Mr. Litsky?

—Sure, said Mr. Litsky.

As he was reaching for his bag, she picked up his drink and carried it to the table on his behalf. It was only when they'd both taken their seats that he could see what a knockout she had been. All blond and blue-eyed with a spunky little hourglass figure to boot. She wasn't Litsky's type, but without the scar and the limp she would have been everybody else's.

Tough break, he thought to himself, feeling a tremor of something that might have been mistaken for sympathy.

She raised her glass, and they drank without taking their eyes off each other.

Or maybe he had it all wrong. . . .

Maybe in this town the scar was just the ticket. In Hollywood, when a good looker gets off the bus, every dame for twenty miles sharpens her claws. And when the boys in the business meet a pretty face, they've got good reason to be wary—because they'll never really know what she's after until after. But with that scar, there weren't going to be any screen tests for the likes of Evelyn Ross.

Which made you sort of wonder what she was doing here in the first place.

As Litsky was thinking this through, she was sitting with her legs crossed, sipping her drink, and flipping her shoe off her heel—letting it hang on the tip of her toe for a beat before flipping it back on.

—So what do you do, Mr. Litsky?

He stirred his ice cubes with a finger.

—I'm a member of the fourth estate.

—A journalist? she said, taking out a cigarette. Well, that must be fascinating in a town like this. Tell me all about it.

She sat there with the unlit cigarette between her fingers waiting for Litsky to strike a match. He took a sip of his drink instead.

—You can cut the sugar, Blondie. I know exactly who you are.

—And who, pray tell, is that?

—You're the one who comes in through the lobby and goes out through the kitchen door.

Pleased by his own poetry, Litsky smiled for the first time in a year.

—Ooh, she replied. What big teeth you have, Grandma.

Litsky raised his glass in the affirmative and emptied it in her honor.

—You want to know what this town is like? he said. I'll tell you what it's like. It's like a waiting room. It's the largest waiting room in the world. We're all sitting on wooden benches reading yesterday's papers, eating yesterday's lunch. But every now and then, the door to the platform opens and the conductor lets one of us through for a ride on the Payday Express. Sometimes, it's some scribbler in a mailroom whose story's found its way to a big oak desk. Sometimes, it's a dainty damsel—like your friend—who gets plucked off the farm. But sometimes, it's for an average Joe like me.

He patted the bag that was sitting on the table.

—And when that door opens . . . , he added.

—You'd better go through it, because it may never open again.

—Bingo, Blondie.

She put her chin on her hand and looked at him all dreamy.

—That's a nice little mustache you've got there, Mr. Litsky. How do you do that? How do you leave just that little bit behind?

—I've got a light touch.

—I'll bet you have. Now I've got a story for you, she said, finally taking the time to light her own cigarette, shaking the flame from the match and tossing it over her shoulder.

The story was about a fat, little Italian who happened to make good. This guy designed scenery for the opera houses in Milan and New York before making his way out West. Once he'd poked his finger through a Hollywood set, he sent for all the boys back home—you know, the carpenters and painters and masons who'd built the Sistine Chapel, but who were fresh off the boat and willing to ply their trades for a nickel a day. Pretty soon, all the studios wanted to hire this guy. He's building

Dodge Cities, and castles, and rooms in Versailles, making half a million bucks a year. So, naturally enough, he tears down his little shack on Doheny and has his boys build him a mansion with all the fixings. He moves back in on August first, 1935, and the following morning, they find him floating in his pool.

Litsky well remembered the heat wave of '35. In fact, as he was sitting in O'Malley's listening to the blonde spin her yarn, he could practically feel the swelter; he could practically hear the water lapping at the edge of the pool as the police cruisers pulled into the drive.

Quick as a wink, the cops could see that this was no ordinary accident. There was no bump on the victim's head, no booze in his blood. So they start wondering: Did one of those vendettas get carried over from the old country? Did one of the *paesan* finally get tired of working for nickels? Or, was the competition getting antsy?

Blondie leaned back and shot some smoke at the ceiling.

—In the end, Mr. Litsky, do you know what it was that killed him?

—No, said Litsky, wiping the sweat from his brow. What?

—The metric system.

Litsky shook his head.

—The metric system . . . ?

—You see, our little entrepreneur didn't know how to swim. So when the pool was being built, he told his mason to make it a yard and a half deep—that way, he could jump in and still have his head above water. But the mason, having just arrived in America, didn't know what a yard was. And when he asked, one of his countrymen told him it was just like a meter. But as I'm sure you know, Mr. Litsky, a meter is a little longer than a yard. So that's what this man's ticket on the Payday Express bought him: five extra inches of water.

Litsky stood to go. But the room moved a little to the left.

—That's a helluva story, Blondie.

He reached for his bag. He knew there was something important in it. Something like his future. Or maybe it was his past. He couldn't remember. Either way, it was heavy as hell.

—Here, said a motherly voice. Let me help you with that.

Freed of its burden, Litsky's body floated a meter and a half off the ground, hovered for a second, then settled back in its chair.

On the shelf behind the bar, a tiny orchestra was playing that trumpety little number for the fifteenth time. Litsky put a hand on the table and tried to stand, but couldn't budge. He shook the inner workings of his head, and for a moment he could clearly see the features of this blonde who'd come out of nowhere. She was studying him the way she had studied the band—with her narrowed eyes and her that's-more-like-it sort of smile.

She leaned over him so closely, he could smell her perfume.

—Where did you come from? he heard himself asking.

—From a hurricane, she said.

Then the warm circumference of her beauty began to recede, diffuse, and finally disappear.

On the periphery of his awareness, someone a lot like Litsky knocked over a chair. Its clatter sounded through the hallowed halls of Hollywood and echoed off the tin ceiling overhead. A door closed, an orchestra abandoned its search for the twentieth measure, and a string of gently swinging Christmas lights went out one by one, leaving Litsky in the ebon embrace of the eternities.

Marcus

O N WEDNESDAY, THE FIFTEENTH of March, Marcus Benton parted
the louvers of his window shade with two fingers and looked out
onto the lot, thinking he still wasn't used to the weather. Without a
bleak winter hour, February hadn't felt like February any more than
July would feel like July. In Southern California, it was as if a glimpse of
spring were repeated week after week, month after month, year after
year.

Someone must have been listening to his thoughts, because a barefooted young man wearing a floppy straw hat suddenly appeared from
around Building Three with a makeshift fishing rod on his shoulder.

As a boy, Marcus could have assembled a better one with his eyes
closed. He could have stripped a sapling, bent and threaded a needle,
tied a double hinge. Having slipped out the back of the schoolhouse, he
could have skirted the town hall to avoid the feed store, then circled
back to Keeper's Hollow where Whistling Bobby McGuire would have
already dropped his line. But here in Culver City, the boy with the
floppy hat was stopped by a young blonde in a bright blue blouse. She
asked him a question and he pointed toward Marcus's office.

Marcus let the louvers fall.

He resumed his place behind his desk and took up the small green dossier. A glance at the photograph inside confirmed the blonde in blue was the one he was waiting for. He leafed through the file, reacquainting himself with what little they knew: that she had been raised in New York, attended a finishing school in Europe, worked for a year at a literary press, and six months ago had fled the gossip mill of Manhattan when her engagement to a blue-blooded banker had been abruptly called off.

He wished, of course, he knew more (one always did). But what he had in hand would suffice. For it was a simple matter, really—a matter of making the young woman feel part of a larger endeavor.

Marcus had learned this in his early days as a litigator in Arkansas. In the jury box of the Pulaski County Courthouse (in any jury box in the country, for that matter), one could expect to find a sample of the human condition: a patchwork of intellects and experiences, personalities and prejudices. To convince these twelve disparate souls of an argument's merit, an attorney could not rely on logic, or science, or even justice. After all, Socrates couldn't convince the elders of Athens of his innocence, any more than Galileo could convince the pope, or Jesus Christ the people of Jerusalem. To convince the members of a jury, one must instead draw them into the course of events.

One must show that they have not been called to the courthouse simply to fulfill some civic obligation. Rather, they have been called to participate. Each juror is a principal who must play his part in the trial as one plays his part at a family gathering, or at the supper table of a friend, or in the pew of a church—those places where consciously or unconsciously we know the frailties and strengths of our neighbors to be inseparable from our own.

That is how Marcus extricated David from that lawsuit back in Arkansas. Thanks to the papers, weeks before the trial the good people of Little Rock already knew that David Selznick was a Hollywood mogul. They knew he was a millionaire, a city slicker, a Jew. And that was the unstated essence of opposing counsel's case: that given who he was, Selznick deserved a little comeuppance. Thus, acknowledging that all of this was true, Marcus (his suit a little rumpled, his hair a little unkempt) took the jury back to the beginning. Calling David to the stand, Marcus inquired about his youth in a blue-collar corner of Pittsburgh; he inquired how David at the age of twenty-one had helped his family make ends meet when his father fell on hard times; overcoming objections of relevancy, Marcus inquired how David had fallen in love with the cinema while watching Buster Keaton at the age of thirteen.

Six months later, Marcus found himself pursuing a similar line of questioning in a Los Angeles County court.

When David had called asking for help, Marcus had turned him down. But David had been characteristically persuasive: It would only take a few weeks, he said; he would make it worth Marcus's while; and there was no one else in the whole country he could trust to do the job. As an added enticement, David sent a plane. With Marcus seated by himself in the passenger cabin (a glass of his favorite bourbon in hand), the plane inscribed its dotted line from Little Rock across the dust bowl, over the Grand Canyon and Death Valley, to the airstrip in Santa Monica where David waited at the side of his Rolls-Royce. And when they arrived at Selznick International and walked into Building Two, David opened an oaken door with an elaborate flourish to reveal . . . Marcus's office in Little Rock.

With a bit of help from the property department, the Selznick International set designers had engineered a facsimile—right down to the louvered shades, the antiquated map of eastern Arkansas, and the Roman bust on the bookshelf (albeit a papier-mâché Caesar standing in for a marble Cicero).

That was four years ago.

Marcus surveyed the top of his desk. Neatly arranged along its edge were seven stacks of paper, one of which stood ten inches tall. *These* weren't from the prop department. They were an essential component of the industriousness of his client—a man for whom no slight was too offhand, no promise too in passing, no penny too thin to wage a battle on its behalf. Selznick versus a Studio. Selznick versus a Star. Selznick v. Temperature, Time, and Tide.

—Mr. Benton, sounded an electronic voice. A Miss Evelyn Ross here to see you.

Marcus put the dossier in a drawer and pushed the button on the intercom.

—Please, show her in.

As was his habit, Marcus came around the desk ready to greet his guest and make her feel at ease; but he was taken aback when through the door came the blonde in blue with the barefooted boy's fishing rod on her shoulder and his floppy straw hat on her head.

She barely gave him a chance to introduce himself.

—Did you know that a few hundred yards from here is a stretch of the Mississippi River? And not only does it have a rickety dock and a riverboat, it's teeming with actual fish!

Marcus laughed.

—We do strive for verisimilitude, Miss Ross.

—I'll remember that.

She gestured with the rod toward the bookcase.

—May I?

—Of course.

She leaned the rod upright and placed the hat on the shelf next to Caesar's head. Then she took a seat, crossed her legs, and lightly bounced her foot.

Inwardly, Marcus smiled. Because in the course of sixty seconds, he had learned more about Evelyn Ross than the studio's investigators had learned in three weeks. The young lady sitting before him was no native of New York. The ease of manner, the disarming smile, the glimmer in the eye were all characteristic of midwestern beauties. Over the course of a hundred and fifty years, these farm-bred charms had evolved to provide the rest of us some consolation when losing the upper hand in horse-trading, card play, and courtship.

If an engagement had been broken back in New York, Marcus thought to himself, then Evelyn Ross was the one who had done the breaking.

She pointed to the seven stacks of paper.

—Do you buy that stuff by the pound?

—You jest, Miss Ross. But my father ran a feed store in Arkansas. I spent my summers selling all manner of things by the pound, not to mention by the bushel and the peck.

—That must have made you quite hardy.

—It made me very good at estimating weights.

—Really, she said with a playful squint. Then how heavy am I?

—That's not the sort of question a gentleman should answer.

—I'm not the type to take offense.

He tilted his head.

—One hundred and ten pounds . . . ?

—Not bad! You're only off by two.

—Was I heavy or light?

—Now, *that's* going a step too far.

Oh, Marcus could see why a young banker in Manhattan might have made a rushed proposal; and he could see why it wouldn't stick. He even felt a touch of pity for the poor bastard. But it did make one wonder: If the young man was the jilted party, why had Miss Ross left New York?

She swung her foot up and down, waiting for him to speak.

—I appreciate your coming on such short notice, he began. I hope it wasn't too much of an inconvenience.

—Not at all.

—I'm glad to hear it. The reason we asked you to stop by is very straightforward. In essence, we want to thank you. We know that you and Miss de Havilland have become good friends; but it has also been brought to our attention that last month you helped her out of something of a fix. . . .

—What are friends for, she said.

—Precisely, Miss Ross. What are friends for. Miss de Havilland is a wonderful young woman with a bright future. But as you've seen first-hand, there are those who would seek to profit from her slightest misstep. So, we would deem it a terrific favor if you would continue to watch out for her.

—Who is this *we* you keep mentioning, Mr. Benton? Is there someone hiding back there behind all those stacks of paper?

—No, Marcus said with a smile. By *we*, I generally refer to the studio. But more specifically, I'm referring to Mr. Selznick, our chief; and Jack Warner over at Warner Brothers, where Miss de Havilland is still under contract. They both have a keen interest in Miss de Havilland's welfare.

—I'm sure they do. But what sorts of missteps are they imagining? Surely they're not afraid of another broken shoulder strap?

—Of course not, said Marcus with a light laugh (followed by a thoughtful pause). Through no fault of her own, a young woman in Miss de Havilland's position is exposed to a variety of hazards. Over the course of time, there are bound to be . . . unfortunate encounters . . . awkward entanglements . . . ill-advised alliances. . . .

Miss Ross exhibited an expression of mild surprise.

—Encounters, entanglements, and alliances! Mr. Benton, watching out for all of those doesn't sound like a favor. It sounds like a job.

Having let their minds wander in the heat of the afternoon, the disparate souls of the Pulaski County jury looked up in unison. For whether they had spent their years of toil on the floor of a mill or behind a plow, a day's wages for a day's work was a principle they well understood.

Marcus opened his mouth.

Miss Ross raised her eyebrows.

But it was an impatient voice in the waiting room that broke the silence.

They both looked back at the replicated door, which flew open to admit a man in his late thirties with slicked-back hair, rolled-up sleeves, and wire-rimmed glasses.

—Is this her?

—David . . .

He turned to look at Miss Ross.

—What does she say?

—We were just finishing up. I'll come find you on the set as soon as we're done.

Ignoring Marcus, David pushed back the stacks of paper and sat on the edge of the desk.

—Miss Ross, isn't? I'm David O. Selznick, head of the studio.

David paused to make sure the full measure of this declaration could be taken. When Miss Ross acted suitably impressed, he continued:

—At this moment, we are in the middle of making what could well be the greatest motion picture of all time. And I have left the set for one reason: to tell you the most closely guarded secret of Hollywood.

Miss Ross cast a glance at Marcus, then sat up with an expression of scholastic enthusiasm. While for his part, David barreled ahead, speaking with his trademark urgency, attention to detail, and utter disregard for whether what he was saying was furthering or confounding his purpose.

—Without a doubt, there are titanic personalities at the helm of Hollywood. And to those who read the papers, it must seem that we alone deserve the credit or condemnation for what reaches the screen. But making a movie is a *contingent* art, Miss Ross. Yes, a great producer starts with a vision and personally assembles its elements. After an extensive search, he chooses the Mona Lisa as his model. He selects a dress that will drape across her shoulders just so. He arranges her hair. He locates the perfect landscape as a backdrop. He makes her comfortable, unselfconscious. Then patiently, he waits for her to express her innermost humanity through a smile, so that he can capture it on canvas. But at that very moment, the studio doors fling open to admit an onslaught of actors and extras, stuntmen and cameramen, Foley artists, fitters, gaffers, best boys—every one of whom brandishes a brush.

David spoke of his employees with a slight grimace, as if their arrival signaled civilization's second descent into the Dark Ages.

—What I am telling you, Miss Ross, is that every single one of the two hundred men and women whom I have enlisted to help make my picture can *ruin it.*

He began ticking off potential setbacks:

—A poorly scripted line of dialogue. A hapless delivery. A garish gown. Unflattering lighting. Maudlin music. Any one of these bumbled details can turn a carefully crafted romance into claptrap, or a heart-wrenching tragedy into a vaudeville farce. And to this list of pitfalls, I add the public reputations of my stars.

David stood and rolled his sleeves a little tighter, his standard cue that he was about to sum up.

—A movie is not a fancy, Miss Ross. It is not an entertainment or a midsummer night's dream. It is something more tenuous, essential, and rare. And it is my job to ensure that it reaches its audience in an utterly uncompromised condition.

He thrust his hand forward and Miss Ross took it.

—We're glad to have you on board, he said.

Then he strode out of the office, yanking the door so soundly behind him that Marcus's suit coat swung on its hanger.

Miss Ross rose from her chair. She didn't rise like David to signal she'd be summing up. She rose to put Marcus's piles of paper in their proper spots, taking the time to delicately true the edges of each stack with the palms of her hands.

How did it come to this? Marcus found himself wondering. As a young attorney, he spent a day in court for every day behind his desk. From season to season, in the upper gallery the fans would be waved or the sneezes stifled as he rose deliberately from his chair and approached the jury box to face the twelve of his fellow men who had been summoned to sit in judgment—each one fashioned in the Lord's image, yet no two alike. It was for that very moment that he had become a lawyer: the moment when the citizenry, intent on meting out the full measure of its vengeance or mercy, was still prepared to listen.

And yet, Marcus had not entered a courtroom in more than three years.

In fact, half the very documents stacked on his desk had been drafted to *avert* an appearance in court: stays; requests for summary judgment; terms of settlement. On top of the stack that Miss Ross was now straightening was a motion to dismiss—which had presumably begun its journey as a tree. Solitary and majestic, that tree had provided shade to some little patch of America. In a churchyard, perhaps, or a pasture, or along a bend in the river where Whistling Bobby McGuire had already cast his line. And then, after half a century of providing relief from the sun so reliably, this tree had been unceremoniously felled—so that a middle-aged man without a wife or children sitting in an office a thousand miles away could string his carefully qualified arguments together end to end.

Through words and clauses, paragraphs and pages.

Through quires and reams and bales.

In just three years, Marcus must have caused the clearing of ten thousand acres of virgin growth—single-handedly stripping the likes of the Ozarks as bare as might five generations of shipbuilders.

How it would have confounded his father to see it—his father, who for over forty years served four hundred families six days a week, providing all manner of seed and feedstock by the pound and the bushel and the peck, and who left behind an unlocked iron box with a marriage license, two birth certificates, a canceled mortgage, and a handwritten last will and testament for a grand total of five pieces of paper.

A ray of sunlight graced the paper-laden desk. Marcus followed its diagonal trajectory back through the louvered shades into the open air above the fartherest reaches of the lot, back over Death Valley and the Grand Canyon, back to the idylls of eastern Arkansas, where the tributaries of the Mississippi River flowed on without effort or interruption.

Miss Ross politely cleared her throat.

She had resumed her place in her chair and was smiling. It wasn't a smug smile or a cruel one. It was almost sympathetic.

—Now, where were we . . . ? Marcus ventured, a little halfheartedly.

—I believe we were talking about the difference between a favor and a job.

—So we were, Miss Ross. So we were. What exactly did you have in mind?

—I didn't have anything in mind. The fact is, I only expect to be in Los Angeles for another few weeks.

Marcus nodded in a manner that expressed his disappointment.

—If you don't mind my asking, Miss Ross, why are you leaving Los Angeles?

—It's a big world out there, Mr. Benton.

—It's a big world right here.

—Is it?

Marcus smiled in spite of himself. He couldn't help but feel a little admiration for Miss Ross, and a little envy too. But when you were employed by David O. Selznick, it wasn't to accept no for an answer.

Marcus shifted a little in his seat.

—I'm going to lay my cards on the table, Miss Ross.

She raised her eyebrows again.

—When I invited you here it was, in fact, to recruit you into the service of the studio under the guise of a favor. When you pointed out, quite appropriately, that what I was asking you to do was really more of a job, my next goal would have been to hire you for the smallest possible consideration. But in his inimitable way, David has made it quite clear that he views your services as invaluable.

Marcus paused as he would have in a courtroom.

—You say your goal is to see the world, Miss Ross. Imagine how much more of it you could see after a year of being invaluable—to an organization that measures its profits in the millions.

But even as Marcus was saying this last phrase, he regretted it. *An organization that measures its profits in the millions.* It was one unpleasant word hitched to another. And he could see from the change in Miss Ross's expression that she felt the same.

Sensing he was about to hear the word *no*, Marcus held up his hands.

—Please, don't answer now, Miss Ross. Do me the courtesy of thinking about it for a day or two.

After nodding twice, she stood and offered her hand.

—It was a pleasure meeting you, she said in a manner that struck Marcus as unusually sincere.

She walked to the bookcase to collect her things. But as she was reaching for her hat, she paused to study the papier-mâché head of Caesar. Picking it up, she tossed it lightly in one hand. Then she looked back at Marcus with the same sympathetic smile. She didn't say anything, but she didn't need to. For the question was implicit: How much does *this* weigh, Mr. Benton?

She returned the bust to its place with unnecessary care and picked up the rod and hat.

—Mr. Selznick on the line for you, said the electronic voice.

Miss Ross joined Marcus in looking at the intercom. Rather than heading for the door, she came back toward him. She leaned the rod against his desk and dropped the hat on top of his motion to dismiss.

—I think you need these more than I do, she said.

Eve

B Y EVERY INDICATION, the fifteenth of March had lined up to be a perfect day. At nine o'clock, while Eve was having breakfast on the little balcony off her living room, it was seventy degrees, sunny, and the jasmine was in bloom. At ten o'clock, Prentice called, inviting her to afternoon tea. At eleven, Livvy called, saying she had received some good news and booked a table for two at Chasen's to celebrate. Then just after Livvy had hung up, Eve had gotten a call from a Marcus Benton at Selznick International Pictures, asking if she could stop by at two o'clock to discuss something of mutual interest. That's how he described it: something of mutual interest. Most people would probably have asked Mr. Benton what he meant by that exactly. But Eve hadn't asked Prentice what he wanted to talk about over tea. And she hadn't asked Livvy what she wanted to celebrate at Chasen's. So, she saw no reason to ask Mr. Benton what he wanted to discuss at Selznick International. Why spoil the surprise? But then to top it all off, when Eve climbed into the back of the hotel's Packard and told Billy whom she was going to see, he pointed out that Chester's was on the way.

—You mean the coffee shop? asked Eve.

—The one and only.

—Why don't you hand me the list.

After pulling up to the hotel's exit, Billy leaned to his right, took the notepad from the glove compartment, and handed it back to Eve.

And there it was. Number twenty. The only destination on the list that had yet to be checked off.

—Do we have time? Eve asked.

—The Packard's got a V-eight engine, Miss Ross. Time is something we can make!

—Then let's make it, Billy.

Eve couldn't pinpoint when her dislike of lists began, but it must have been around the time she was twelve. It was in the basement of St. Mary's, where she and the rest of the sixth graders were charged with memorizing the Ten Commandments. *Thou shalt not this. Thou shalt not that. And thou shalt not the other thing.* Then there was the list painted on a sign at the country club pool to remind the children there would be *No Running. No Diving. No Splashing.* But most important was her mother's ever-expanding list of what a young lady should not do. Like put her elbows on the table, or speak with her mouth full, or slug her little sister, even when she deserved it.

Yep. In Indiana, a young girl had good reason to suspect that lists were the foot soldiers of tyranny—crafted for the sole purpose of bridling the unbridled. A quashing, squashing, squelching of the human spirit by means of itemization.

But if Eve couldn't identify when her dislike of lists began, she could remember exactly when it ended. It was while she was sitting in the dining car of the Golden State Limited, reading a detective novel.

The Crimson Gown, it was called.

Living up to the promise of its cover, the story began brightly with the strangling of a starlet. In the pages that followed, the ugly particulars of the victim's rise to fame were slowly revealed. Piece by piece the lonely detective put the sordid puzzle together. But only in chapter 19 did it finally dawn on him that the hands around the starlet's throat in chapter 1 had been those of the Oriental chanteuse whom he'd fallen for in chapter 5.

In chapter 22, when the detective finally makes his way to the chanteuse's apartment, she opens the door dressed in the prefigured gown. With a bow, she offers him a chair and pours him a whiskey. He consumes it in one gulp. Then with grim determination, he lays out the elements of the case against her—the primitive means, the engineered opportunity, the convoluted motive. *It's time to go downtown*, he concludes ominously, while rising to his feet—only to waken four hours later on the floor of the empty apartment.

And the chanteuse? She was already on a freight boat headed back to the Forbidden City.

The Forbidden City . . ., thought Eve. Now, that sounds like a place worth going.

—Excuse me, she said to the kindly looking stranger across the table. Would you happen to have a pen or pencil handy?

Armed with the gentleman's pencil, Eve flipped to the blank page that's always hiding at the back of a book like the unprepared kid at the back of the class. Across the top of it in large capital letters she wrote *PLACES TO GO*, then commenced to itemize:

1) The Forbidden City
2) The Taj Mahal

After the Taj Mahal she paused. She bit the pencil's eraser, at a loss for a third locale.

At a loss for a third locale?! she chided herself. The world is big. It's bigger than a bread box!

Eve closed her eyes and tried to remember the map of the world that had hung on the wall of her ninth-grade classroom. (She had certainly stared at it enough.) And there in the south of Spain a destination presented itself. Then one in the heart of Russia. And another on the banks of the Nile. In fact, so quickly did the destinations come to mind, the kindly stranger's pencil could barely keep up.

    3) *The Alhambra*
    4) *The Hermitage*
    5) *The Pyramids!*

Lists aren't so bad, Eve realized. They didn't have to be a catalogue of ladylike constraints. They could just as easily testify to plans and aspirations. A celebration of the not yet done. Of what *Thou shalt!* It really just depended on which side of the pencil you were on.

By the time Eve arrived in Los Angeles, she had a list of eight places she intended to visit around the globe. And, as far as she was concerned, the sooner she set sail, the better. But then shortly after arriving at the Beverly Hills Hotel, fellow resident Prentice Symmons had expounded on some of the sights that Eve should see while still in Los Angeles. Borrowing a notepad from the concierge, Eve had dutifully written them down under the heading: *THINGS TO DO BEFORE I SKEDADDLE*. That list, originally containing twelve items, was expanded to twenty with Billy's help—the very last of which was a cup of coffee at Chester's.

Plunked down on a small paved lot on a corner near the freeway, Chester's was a coffee shop in the shape of a giant coffeepot—complete with a ribbon of steam that twisted from its spout twenty-four hours a day. Other than a single bench bolted to the ground by the curb, there were no places to sit, and there was nothing for sale other than a twelve-ounce cup of coffee with cream. As the sign over the cash register made clear, the three ways you could get your coffee at Chester's were sweetened, unsweetened, and somewhere else.

Billy had heard from an old stuntman that Chester had come to California as a prospector in the 1880s. This was malarkey, of course, but Eve liked to believe there was some truth to the tale. She could just picture the cantankerous old goat sitting by his campfire on the banks of a stream tinkering with the roasting of his beans, the granularity of his grind, and the rapidity of his boil until his coffee was brewed to perfection. Then, when he finally struck it rich, rather than recline in a claw-footed tub, he bought this corner, built this pot, and set about doing the only thing the Good Lord had ever intended him to do. And what the Good Lord intended for others was their own damn business.

Sure, at first glance Chester's style of commerce seemed a little crackers—Eve would give you that. But all you had to do was spend a few bucks in an Automat to see that he was onto something. Because when all was said and done, no slinger of hash was going to master the subtleties of a lemon meringue pie *and* a chicken salad sandwich. But on this corner by the freeway? There was no hint of the half-assed. Not in Chester's paper cup. With a caramel color and smoky aroma, his coffee was incontestably good. Indisputably good. Unassailably, incontrovertibly, indismissibly good.

Come to think of it, you could make a similar claim about the donuts at that donut shop in the shape of a donut over on La Cienega. And hadn't Billy mentioned that some of the best Mexican food in the county was at a little place where they sold tamales out of a building in the shape of a sombrero? If the mayor of Los Angeles had any sense, he'd immediately establish a new ordinance requiring that every purveyor within the city limits sell no more than one item and that he sell it from a shop in the shape of his merchandise. Like orange juice from a giant orange, or whiskey from a whiskey bottle as tall as a windmill. With that one reform in place, thousands of Chesters from across the country would hear the call. They'd pull up stakes, load their wagons, and head west to this city, which not only approved of but applauded their cranky, intolerant artistry.

—One please, said Eve to the girl in the window. Unsweetened.

—That'll be five cents.

—Keep the change.

With coffee in hand, Eve crossed the lot to take up residence on the solitary bench by the curb.

At first glance, the bench had reminded Eve of one of those you'd see out on the Hoosier highways, covered in dust and dreaming of Greyhound buses. But the minute she sat down, she could understand the bench's unusual appeal: it was a privileged position from which to witness the motley splendor of the commonwealth. For as narrow as the menu was at Chester's, the clientele was just as broad.

Why, at that very moment, a pair of sleeveless Oklahomans fresh off an oil rig were sipping their coffees beside a banker in a pin-striped suit. And a matinee-idol-in-the-making was chatting up the girl at the window, while a storefront preacher waited with the patience of Job. Denizens and drifters. The fabulous and the fallen. It simply livened the spirits to see so many different kinds of people gathered in one spot for a shared devotion that cost a nickel.

Even as Eve was having this thought, a dusty black Ford with suitcases strapped to the roof pulled into a parking space ten feet away. Eve watched with interest as the doors flung open and a roly-poly pair of pensioners emerged. Before he could even stretch his back, the husband put his hands on his hips and took in the giant coffeepot from its wide blue base to its ribbon of steam.

—Now I've seen everything, he said.

Eve took a sip of her coffee and smiled at sudden thoughts of her great-aunt Polly. Clad in black from head to toe, her needlepoint never far from reach, proper Aunt Polly from Bloomington, Indiana, also liked to let people know when she had seen everything.

What was it about that phrase, mused Eve, that made it so popular with those who had no business using it?

It was in the middle of August that Aunt Polly and Uncle Jake chose to pay their annual visit. And while they stayed, no matter how hellacious the heat, afternoon tea would be served in the sitting room without fail. For Aunt Polly loved afternoon tea as much as she loved Jesus—and it was through constancy that she intended to prove her fealty to both. So, the day before Aunt Polly arrived, Eve's mother would take the fine china from the pantry so that Maisy could sweep the dead flies from the cups. And every afternoon at three, the ladies would convene around the teapot as Eve and her sister were sent outside.

At least until 1928, the year that Eve turned fifteen.

That fateful summer, Aunt Polly announced that henceforth the privilege of tea would be Evelyn's. Naturally, this privilege came with a floral dress, barrettes, and the manners befitting a lady. Since Alice was only twelve, she was allowed to wear pigtails and overalls and stick out her tongue on her way out the door. While Evelyn, hands in her lap, was left to stare at the grandfather clock.

Aunt Polly recognized the infallibility of her deity in all respects but one: He had made summer days too long. So to complete the perfection of His plan, she was intent upon fending off their influence.

How does one fend off the influence of a summer day? You start by serving tea at three in the afternoon. Then, having thanked the Lord for His bounty and passed the biscuits, you talk about relatives long since dead. You dredge up some story you've dredged up before. And when the conversation flags, rather than adjourn into the waning wonder of the vernal afternoon, you pick up a magazine.

For Aunt Polly, this was preferably a *Saturday Evening Post* she had already read before. Turning through the pages, she would occasionally stop at a photograph—say, of a short-haired Amelia Earhart preparing to fly across the Atlantic alone—in order to remark with a mix of indignation, wisdom, and finality:

—Now I've seen everything.

———————

For Uncle Jake, a harmless old broker of crop insurance who once shook the hand of Herbert Hoover, the headshaking phrase of choice was *If I had a nickel fer.* As in, *If I had nickel fer every time the papers called for rain.*

So enamored with this phrase was Uncle Jake that an *If I had a nickel fer* might well be the only sentence he uttered over the course of a family meal. Which was all the more striking when you considered that his solitary statement would linger forever unfinished.

For, whatever the recurring circumstance that resulted in this unprecedented rain of nickels upon Uncle Jake's head, he just couldn't seem to pin down *how* he'd put his windfall to use: Invest in a new pair of suspenders? Spring for a night on the town? Fly an airplane across the Atlantic, or as far from Aunt Polly as earthly geography would allow? Who could say?

Maybe Herbert Hoover, but not Uncle Jake.

One Sunday supper after a particularly interminable tea, when Uncle Jake happened to observe: *If I had a nickel fer every time I heard Roozyvelt on the radio,* Eve simply couldn't take it anymore. She couldn't abide it. Not in good Christian conscience.

—What, Uncle Jake? she implored (after dropping her knife and fork on her plate). What is it exactly that you would do, once you had all those goddamn nickels?

Alice's eyes opened wide.

Evelyn's mother turned as red as her ham.

And Evelyn's father? He simply looked forlorn.

So, in order to spare him the discomfort of administering a reprimand, Evelyn pushed back her chair and sent herself to her room. But as she climbed the stairs, she smiled to hear Aunt Polly exclaim:

—Well, I never!

Now *that*, thought Evelyn, was an expression that Aunt Polly had every reason to make use of.

———————

Once Evelyn was back in the Packard and they were on their way to the studio, Billy glanced in the rearview mirror.

—What'd you think? he asked.

—About Chester's? Why, it was one in a million, Billy. The real McCoy.

Billy smiled to hear his own phrases quoted back at him.

—Could you hand me back a pen, said Eve.

Without taking his eyes off the road, Billy handed back a pen, which Eve used to put a check mark next to Chester's.

—Well, she said, in the parlance of the town, I guess that's a wrap.

As she set the notepad and pen aside, Billy glanced again in the rearview mirror.

—Now that you've finished your list, Miss Ross, are you headed back to New York?

—Oh, I'm not much for heading back, Billy.

—Then where'll you go?

—I was thinking about heading to the Far East.

Billy whistled.

—How about you? Eve asked. Any plans of going back to Texas?

—I guess I'm not much for goin' back either, Miss Ross.

—Then how are things at the Corral?

Billy pulled himself up by the wheel.

—Pretty darn good, if I do say so myself. You know that niche I was tellin' you about?

—I remember.

—Well, I think I found it.

Having grown up on his uncle's ranch in the Panhandle, Billy had come to L.A. at the age of sixteen with a small-time rodeo and stumbled into pictures when demand was on the rise for men who could fall off horses. He was just getting his start, as he was the first to tell you, but he had already been shot twice with a rifle and once with an arrow while riding with the cavalry, a posse, and a gang of rustlers.

Like many aspiring stuntmen, Billy spent his free hours at a place they called the Corral. An old-timer there named Skilly Skillman had taken Billy under his wing. He's the one who'd advised Billy he needed a niche. Something that would set him apart and put him in the crosshairs of the camera. Skillman's route to the close-up had been through the saloon window. Sure, he could tumble down the stairs or get knocked on the head with the rest of them. But when it came to being thrown through a window, no one was his equal. He was the undisputed king of defenestrations.

Eve could hardly wait to hear what Billy's route was going to be.

—For me, he said, it's gonna be the heel-hooker.

—The heel-hooker?

Billy nodded with enthusiasm as he veered around a cab.

—That's when you're ridin' at full gallop, see, and you get an arrow in the chest, and instead of fallin' clear of your horse, the heel of your boot gets hooked in the stirrup and you get dragged through the dust. . . .

Billy passed a hand slowly in front of the windshield, as if he could see his own body being pulled across the desert into the sunset.

Heck. Eve could practically see it too.

—You can't beat a man who's found his niche, said Eve.

—No, ma'am, agreed Billy as he turned into the studio. I suspect you can't.

Once Billy had parked, he scooted around the car to open Eve's door.

—How long you think you'll be, Miss Ross?

—I have no idea, Billy. Can you wait?

—You betcha.

Eve followed a path from the executive parking area to a clearing in which a small herd of one-story buildings grazed. Since there were no signs and the buildings looked identical, Eve figured she'd have to pick one of the doors and knock. But just as she was about to eeny-meenyminy-moe, from behind one of the buildings came a barefooted boy in a floppy straw hat with a fishing pole propped on his shoulder.

—Excuse me, she said.

Yes, by every indication the fifteenth of March had been lining up to be a perfect day: a sunny breakfast on the balcony; plans for tea with Prentice and dinner with Livvy; and the unexpected tête-à-tête with the disarming Mr. Benton.

Eve had even been amused by David O. Selznick and his zingy description of moviemaking. At least, at first . . .

But on the way back to the hotel, the more Eve thought about Selznick's little speech, the more irritated she became. Sure, it had been full of fifty-dollar phrases and colorful analogies, but it wasn't hard to grasp the underlying message—that his irreplaceable genius was under constant threat from the essential fallibility of those in his employ. And this egomaniac, this latter-day Napoleon with his two-cornered hat firmly on his head, was the man who was supposed to provide Livvy with some relief from the likes of Jack Warner? The memory of the encounter began to sour Eve's mood a little. But it was only once she had returned to the hotel that the day's ill intentions revealed themselves in full.

For when she walked inside and saw Prentice in his usual chair, rather than offering his usual wave with his usual smile, he directed Eve's attention to the far side of the lobby—where Livvy was pacing in apparent distress.

Bypassing Prentice, Eve approached her.

—Livvy . . . ?

—There you are! she exclaimed, her face flush.

Eve was about to ask what was wrong, but noting the two men who were checking in at the front desk, she took Livvy by the elbow.

—Come on.

She led her out the side door and through the flower-lined paths to Bungalow 8, where Livvy had been living since December. When Livvy produced her key, Eve could see that her hand was trembling.

—Let me, she said.

Taking the key, Eve let them inside. As soon as she closed the door, her friend was in tears.

—For heaven's sake, Livvy. What has happened?

By way of answer, Livvy pointed to the coffee table on which there was a manila envelope.

Eve crossed the room and picked it up. As she began to slide out the contents, she was conscious of Livvy turning away, despite the fact she was still on the other side of the room. The envelope contained two photographs and a handwritten note. The photographs were glossy black-and-white prints of Olivia naked. In each picture she was staring directly at the camera. Behind her was a mural of a jungle scene with the figure of a leopard, which somehow added a suggestion of salaciousness to the image. But there was nothing salacious in Livvy's expression; nothing provocative or coy. To the contrary, she appeared to be captured in a moment of private reflection.

Reading the note—which was a demand for money and a promise of contact by phone—Eve could feel her own face beginning to grow flush, her own hand beginning to tremble. But she wasn't about to break into tears. She felt like every tear in her body had dried up. They had dried up from an old and relentless anger. An anger stoked by that long parade of preachers and teachers and Prince Charmings, wannabe puppeteers all. At every stage of her life, Eve had met them. But nowhere had she encountered as many puppeteers as in Hollywood. Every agent and manager, every director, producer, and studio chief had his arms out and his fingers extended, looking to grab a woman by the strings.

Eve put the pictures back in the envelope, set the envelope back on the table, and looked to her friend, who remained on the other side of the room turned toward the wall, now with her hands over her face. Eve and Olivia were both petite women. But from across the room, Olivia suddenly looked smaller. The envelope's contents had made her smaller.

Eve knew that what the moment called for was comfort. She should cross the room, take Livvy in her arms, say *there there there*, and let her cry it out. But the anger within her had overwhelmed the willingness to comfort.

Crossing the room, she turned Olivia by the shoulders and drew her hands away from her face.

—Livvy, she said in as level a manner as she could, who took them? Who took the pictures?

Olivia shook her head as the tears continued to fall down her cheeks.

—I don't know.

—When were they taken?

—I don't know!

—Are you sure?

Livvy finally met Eve's gaze.

—Sure? I didn't . . . I haven't . . . I would never!

Eve, who was still holding Livvy's wrists, gave them a squeeze.

—Of course you wouldn't.

Eve led Livvy out onto the terrace, where the two could sit out of sight of the envelope. Having collected herself, Livvy looked at Eve and almost moaned.

—What am I going to do?

—Nothing, said Eve.

Eve waved a hand in the general direction of the coffee table.

—I'm going to take care of it, Livvy. All of it. What I want you to do is put it out of your mind. Just forget it.

Those last words were sour in Eve's mouth. To ask her friend to forget something like this felt like a betrayal. But at the same time, Eve knew it was the right thing to do. For as women, this was their lot. They had to learn to live with acts of violation. Of course, Livvy would never fully forget this day. It would always be there. But by burying it for a time, she might be able to move on. Move on in some semblance of her prior self.

Eve waited for Livvy's tears to stop and her breathing to ease.

—Have you mentioned the photographs to anyone else? she asked.

—No.

—Let's keep it that way. But there is one person I want to show them to.

Livvy began to shake her head, unsettled by the notion of the pictures being shown to anyone.

—No, she said.

Eve took her wrists again, almost forcefully.

—Do you trust me, Livvy?

Olivia stopped shaking her head. She looked Eve in the eye.

—Like no one I've ever known, she said.

—All right then.

Eve gave Olivia's wrists a final squeeze and let go. Neither of them were trembling now.

—We started this day with a plan to celebrate, said Eve.

Livvy nodded.

—I learned this morning that I'll be shooting a new movie with Errol in the fall.

—Terrific, said Eve. Here's what we're going to do. We're going to Chasen's just like we planned. We'll order a round of drinks and you'll tell me all about this new picture. Okay?

—Okay.

—It's almost five. Why don't you take a moment to freshen up and then get dressed.

—You're not leaving? asked Livvy.

—I'll be right here. Once you're ready, you can come with me while I'm getting dressed.

Eve watched Olivia retreat into her bathroom. When she heard the water running for a bath, she stuck the envelope in a desk drawer so Livvy wouldn't have to see it again. Then she picked up the phone, gave the operator a number, and waited for the call to be put through.

—Mr. Benton? she said. This is Evelyn Ross—Yes, I understood that. But I won't be needing another day to think about it. I'll be taking that job we discussed.

PART TWO

Charlie

WHEN EVELYN ROSS called on a Thursday morning in March, Charlie was surprised. He was surprised to hear the telephone ring; surprised to find it was her; surprised she had remembered his name. He was surprised by all of it. Pleasantly surprised.

—What can I do for you, Miss Ross?

—I was wondering if you could come see me at the Beverly Hills Hotel. There's something I'd like to talk to you about. In person.

—Everything's all right, I hope.

She said everything was all right—with her—and Charlie was relieved to hear it.

—But I have a friend who's in some trouble. I think she could use your help.

From Miss Ross's tone, Charlie could tell the trouble her friend was in was serious. And there was a time when he could have been of help, could have been of help even in the direst of circumstances. But that time had come and gone. He was sixty-six years old and had been in retirement for almost four years now. Whatever the problem, Miss Ross would be better served by a younger man who was still in the thick of it.

—I can be there in an hour, he said.

———————

Charlie hadn't seen Miss Ross since the day they had parted on the platform at Union Station, six months before. At the time, she had said she didn't expect to stay in Los Angeles for very long, but when she answered the door, he could see the city must have agreed with her. Her face was tan and she had put on four or five pounds, all to her advantage. Wearing tan pants and a white blouse, she received him in the living room of a suite with a couch and two chairs arranged around a coffee table. It wasn't the nicest suite at the Beverly Hills Hotel, by any means, but it must have cost a pretty penny. Where did the money come from, he wondered, though only for a moment. It was an ugly sort of question, after all.

Miss Ross sat on the couch and offered Charlie one of the chairs. Charlie took the seat, holding his hat in his hand.

—You look well, he said.

—I feel well.

—I'm glad to hear it.

When Charlie had been on the force, he had sat in many living rooms like this one, facing a person on a couch with his hat in his hand. But as a homicide detective, when you sat across from someone in their living room, it was usually because the worst had already happened. It felt strange, but satisfying too to be in the same sort of seat preparing to ask the same sort of questions while there was still a chance to alter the course of events.

—What seems to be the trouble, Miss Ross?

—I think we've graduated to a first-name basis. Don't you, Charlie? Charlie smiled.

—All right. What seems to be the trouble, Evelyn?

—A friend of mine is an actress, or more accurately, a star. Yesterday afternoon, she received these.

Evelyn picked up a manila envelope, removed two photographs, and slid them across the table.

Charlie wasn't much of a moviegoer, but he recognized the subject of the photographs as Olivia de Havilland. Shown from the knees up, she was standing naked in front of a wall decorated with tropical foliage. In one photograph she had a hand on her breast as if she was touching herself lightly. In the other, the hand had moved to her abdomen. In both she was staring straight at the camera in a manner more shy than provocative. Paper-clipped to the top of one of the photographs was a handwritten note: *We'll call Sunday at noon. If you want the rest of the pictures, have a bag with $5,000 in ten-dollar bills handy.*

In his years as a homicide detective, Charlie had studied hundreds of photographs of victims—men or women who had been shot, beaten, or stabbed, the condition of their bodies testifying to the nature of their final abuse. When he had looked at those pictures there had always been a sense of indignation, a sense of indignation that was essential to the job. Over the course of an investigation there would be long days spent knocking on doors, and nights spent in one's car staring out a windshield. It was the indignation that provided you with focus and moral urgency, which in turn helped you to be dogged and relentless in pursuit of your quarry.

But he couldn't remember being this indignant in a long time.

Maybe in the years of retirement he had grown less used to villainy. Maybe when one shifted from the life of doing to the life of remembering, one became more sentimental, more susceptible to the influence of one's emotions. Or maybe it was because the young woman in the photographs seemed so fragile. Whatever her celebrity, she couldn't have been much more than twenty years old, much more than a hundred pounds.

Looking up, Charlie could see that Evelyn shared his indignation. She had been cool and collected when she had called him, cool and collected when she had greeted him at the door and when she had slid the photographs across the table, but when she looked at him now, the complexion of her face had grown darker with an anger that brought the white line of her scar into sharper relief.

The telephone rang.

—Do you need to get that? he asked.

She shook her head.

It rang five more times before falling silent.

He pointed to the envelope.

—That's what they came in?

—Yes.

Evelyn passed the envelope to Charlie.

The end of the envelope had been cut cleanly with a letter opener or scissor blade. On the front had been written *Miss Olivia de Havilland c/o The Beverly Hills Hotel* in the same hand as the note. There was no street address, postal code, or stamp.

—It was delivered by hand?

—Apparently, a Mexican laborer brought it to the front desk.

—A Mexican laborer?

—He seemed so out of place, the desk captain summoned the hotel's head of security, a man named Sean Finnegan. He brought the envelope to Olivia.

Charlie remembered Finnegan from his days on the force. Finnegan and his partner, Jack Doherty, had been known as effective officers. They had also been known to play it a little rough, but that wasn't uncommon with the boys in vice. Shortly before Charlie retired, Finnegan had turned in his badge and switched to the private sector. Charlie hadn't realized that Finnegan had ended up here at the hotel, but he was glad of the coincidence. It would make the going a little smoother.

Charlie put the envelope on the table beside the photographs.

—You mentioned that Miss de Havilland is a friend.

—That's right.

—What did she have to say? About the pictures, I mean.

—She doesn't remember them being taken.

—Doesn't remember? Charlie asked, unable to hide his skepticism.

—That's right.

Charlie pointed at the pictures.

—Those don't look like they were taken under duress. Young actresses and models have been known to let themselves be photographed. Sometimes for love . . . Sometimes for money . . .

Evelyn's complexion darkened again.

—She doesn't remember the pictures being taken.

Charlie held up both hands.

—Okay, he said.

—Do you think she could have been drugged? Evelyn asked after a moment.

Charlie shook his head.

—From the expression on her face, I wouldn't think so. She doesn't seem intoxicated or drowsy.

Evelyn nodded, having come to the same conclusion.

—Is it her intention to pay? asked Charlie.

—It is.

—Can she get her hands on the money by Sunday?

—It's in the works.

Charlie thought for a moment then shook his head.

—I think you should go to the police, Evelyn.

—I'd like to, Charlie. But they'd want to see the pictures. And they'd probably insist upon taking at least one as evidence. Do you really think a picture like that wouldn't make its way around the station house? Even rumors about such a picture could be damaging to Livvy's career. But who's to say that someone along the line wouldn't make a copy for their own purposes.

Charlie was a loyalist. He had been loyal to his department and loyal to his oath as an officer, just as he had been loyal to his wife and his vow of marriage. But he couldn't argue with Evelyn's reasoning. Were the police to become involved, there would be too many people with access to the pictures to allow a wholesale vouching for the department's integrity. In a matter like this, the fewer people who knew of the photographs, the better.

—Will you help us? asked Evelyn.

Before Charlie could answer, from behind him came the sound of the door opening, followed by a boisterous voice.

—Ah, there she is!

Turning, Charlie saw a rotund man with a cane addressing the chambermaid who had just unlocked the door on his behalf.

—Everything seems to be fine, Bridie. Thank you, as always, for your assistance.

As the interloper moved heavily toward them, Charlie slipped the photographs back in the envelope and put the envelope on the table face-down.

The man collapsed in the empty chair with a sigh.

—Thank goodness, he said, looking from Charlie to Evelyn with the expression of one who was late to a meeting.

—Prentice . . . ? Evelyn prompted.

When he raised his eyebrows in inquiry, Evelyn raised hers in response.

—Ah, yes, he said. Well. When you failed to appear at tea, naturally I became concerned. When you failed to answer your phone, I became even more so. When I explained the situation to Bridie, she opened your door *et voilà*: Here I am.

. Prentice offered them both a smile. Charlie was a little surprised to find Evelyn smiling back.

—Charlie Granger, she said, allow me to introduce Prentice Symmons. Prentice, Charlie.

With two hands resting on the top of his cane, Prentice bowed his head.

—At your service, sir.

—Nice to meet you.

—Now, said Prentice, looking from one to the other, what seems to be the trouble?

—There's no trouble, said Evelyn.

—Oh come, come. I was in the lobby when that was delivered, he said, pointing to the envelope. Not half an hour later, Olivia was pacing like an expectant father, awaiting your return. And now you've summoned this professional-looking gentleman. Something is certainly the trouble. Of that there is no doubt.

Catching Evelyn's eye, Charlie shook his head. As she herself had implied, the fewer people who knew of the photographs, the better. But Evelyn reached across the table, pulled the photographs from the envelope, and handed them to Prentice, keeping the note to herself.

Receiving them, Prentice leaned back in his chair. As he looked, he exhibited none of the indignation that Charlie and Evelyn had felt, offering only a quiet *hmm* with the consideration of each image.

—Well, he said, tossing them lightly on the table, it's blackmail, I suppose.

—Yes, said Evelyn with a slight smile.

—When were they taken?

—That's just it. Olivia doesn't remember. Charlie here is a former homocide detective. Before you came in, we were discussing whether the pictures might have been taken by a lover, or while she was drugged.

—Neither, said Prentice with a dismissive wave of the hand. I can tell you exactly what Olivia was doing when these were taken.

Charlie and Evelyn looked at each other, then at Prentice. He pointed his cane at the photographs on the table.

—Those, my friends, are pictures of an actress looking at herself when no one else is in the room. Olivia is obviously in front of a mirror.

Charlie and Evelyn each picked up one of the pictures.

—A two-way mirror, said Charlie with a touch of appreciation.

—A what? asked Evelyn.

—We use them in police stations. It's a laminated glass. If on one side of the glass the room is brightly lit and on the other the room is dark, from the well-lit side the glass acts like a mirror, while from the dark side it acts like a window.

—But where? wondered Eve.

—Here at the hotel? asked Charlie.

—Unthinkable, said Prentice, as if personally offended. But wait a moment. Let me see one of those again.

Evelyn handed Prentice one of the photographs. His eyes moved back and forth across its surface, then he tapped it twice.

—I've been here before, he said, as one on the verge of remembering. Yes. I'm quite sure of it. But it was a lion, not a leopard.

Both Charlie and Evelyn slid forward in their seats.

—Where, Prentice?

He closed his eyes for a moment then smiled, nodding to himself.

—Freddie Fairview's. That's it. By his pool there is a bathhouse with men's and women's dressing rooms. Each has its own sauna and steam room, a vanity with a large mirror, and a wall painted with an elaborate jungle scene. In the men's dressing room, it was a lion hunting among the fronds. The leopard must be in the women's dressing room. In it, I gather, there was an assortment of expensive lotions and creams—an invitation for young women to linger before the mirror, as it were.

—Who is Freddie Fairview? Charlie and Evelyn asked simultaneously.

—Freddie Fairview? Prentice responded a little surprised. Some call him a sportsman. Others call him a socialite. I call him a cad. Twice he has married to his profit. Once to a widow whom he outlived, and once to a young heiress whom he outwitted. Now he backs the occasional racehorse and produces the occasional film. But mostly, he throws parties. He's especially known for the Sunday brunches at his house in the Hollywood Hills—which he refers to, rather pretentiously, as the Hacienda.

—Do you think he sent the pictures to Olivia? asked Evelyn.

—No, said Prentice. Freddie is as unscrupulous a fellow as you are likely to meet—which, in this town, is saying quite a bit. But I can't imagine him dabbling in blackmail. He certainly doesn't need the money; and he has so much to lose were he to be caught. No, said

Prentice, these pictures are for *personal* use. And for a man like Freddie, I'd venture that having them in his possession without anyone knowing they've been taken adds to his satisfaction. I doubt he's shared them with a soul.

—He's shared them with someone, said Charlie.

Prentice bowed his head in acknowledgment.

—So it seems.

Prentice took one more look at the photograph in his hand before tossing it lightly on the table.

—It's actually quite flattering, he said.

When Evelyn scowled, he added sheepishly:

—In the aesthetic sense, of course . . .

The three were silent for a moment.

—Okay, said Charlie, looking at Evelyn. If Prentice is right, then we have two problems to solve. We have to get the images of Miss de Havilland back from the blackmailer, but also from Mr. Fairview.

—Do you think we can do it? asked Evelyn.

—In dealing with the blackmailers, we have one advantage. Blackmailers spend most of their time in the shadows. They steal private papers from empty houses or take pictures through windows in the night. Once they have compromising material, they can sit on it for as long as they want. And when they're ready to make their demands, they can do so in a variety of ways without revealing themselves. But at some point, they have to come out of the shadows—in order to collect their money.

—Okay, said Evelyn, but what about Fairview?

Charlie was silent for a moment, echoing Evelyn's question to himself: *What about Fairview . . .*

—Ahem, said Prentice.

Charlie and Evelyn turned to the rotund actor, who took a breath before speaking.

—As you have so rightly pointed out, Charles, every criminal has his milieu. Just as the bootleggers had their speakeasies and the bank robbers have their banks, the blackmailers have their shadows. And men such as yourself who are charged with capturing these criminals must know each milieu as well as the criminals know them. Just as the captains who hunted pirates on the Spanish Main had to know the prevailing currents and the location of every coral reef and shoal. Well, the milieu of Freddie Fairview is not a speakeasy or a bank. Nor is it the Spanish Main. It is Hollywood, my friends, which has its own currents, reefs, and shoals, each posing its own challenge to the uninitiated.

—What are you saying, Prentice? asked Evelyn.

—What I am saying is that if you two deal with the blackmailers, you can leave Mr. Fairview to me.

After leaving Evelyn's suite, Charlie went downstairs to the lobby. As he approached the front desk, the desk captain adopted a posture of polite accommodation, having already determined from Charlie's appearance that he wasn't a paying guest.

—May I help you? he asked.

—I'm looking for Sean Finnegan's office.

—Down that hall. Second door on your right.

Charlie walked down the hall and knocked on the unmarked door. When a voice called for him to come in, Charlie entered to find a good-looking man in his midthirties with his feet on his desk and a book in his hands.

—Hello, Sean.

Sean made a show of being mystified for a second, then broke into a smile.

—Well, I'll be damned. If it isn't Charlie Granger. Come on in, Charlie. Take a load off.

As Sean put his feet on the floor and his book in a drawer, Charlie took a seat.

—What brings you to the Bev, Charlie?

—I'm a friend of Evelyn Ross's.

—The blonde in Two-Twenty-One?

—That's right. She's asked me to look into something.

—Suits me, Charlie. As long as it's got nothing to do with the hotel.

—Actually, it's about the envelope that arrived yesterday for Olivia de Havilland. I gather you may have spoken to the messenger.

Finnegan studied Charlie for a moment.

—I thought you were retired, Charlie.

—I left the force about three months after you.

—Did you hang out a shingle?

—No. I'm just doing a favor for a friend.

Finnegan considered this, then gave a shrug.

—To be honest, this is a little outside the lines, Charlie. You being a civilian who's doing a favor for one guest while asking questions about another. But I know Miss Ross and Miss de Havilland are close, and you and I go back a ways, so we can forget about the lines for now. What is it you want to know?

—How did you end up speaking with the messenger?

—Normally, I wouldn't have. But yesterday afternoon, this old Mexican right out of Central Casting—with sandals and a sombrero—showed up at the front desk. He wasn't what you'd call exactly fluent, at least not in English, but he got it across that he had a package for Miss de Havilland, and he was supposed to deliver it by hand. Now, that was never gonna happen, which the boys at the front desk made clear. When the old man began to get insistent, they called me.

—I can imagine, said Charlie. They practically called security when they saw me coming.

Finnegan smiled.

—In fine hotels the front desk is always manned by snobs.

—I'll remember that. What happened next?

—When I showed up, the old man started getting nervous. But knowing a little Spanish myself, I put him at ease and took him back here. Eventually, he explained that he'd been standing on the corner of

Wilshire and San Vicente, you know, where the day laborers hang out waiting for the work to come find them. A guy in a blue convertible pulled up, offering him five bucks to deliver a package. He gave the old man a ride to our entrance and dropped him off, telling him he had to deliver the package in person.

—And you think the old man was being straight?

Finnegan shrugged again.

—Who knows? But while I brought the envelope to Miss de Havilland, I had one of my men follow him just in case. Sure enough, he walked to Wilshire, hopped on a bus, and rode it back to San Vicente.

—How about the driver?

—What about him?

—Did you get a description of him from the old man?

Sean shook his head.

—I didn't think to ask.

—All right. Thanks, Sean. I appreciate it.

When Charlie stood to leave, Finnegan leaned back in his chair.

—You going to tell me what was in the envelope, Charlie?

—I couldn't.

—Couldn't or wouldn't?

—Does it make a difference?

Sean smiled.

—I suppose not. But to be clear here: my job is to protect the hotel, its reputation, and the comfort of its guests, in about that order. If what you've been asked to do leads you into trouble somewhere else, mazel tov. But if you end up dragging your trouble back into my lobby, you'll wish you'd looped me in.

—I'll keep that in mind.

As Charlie walked back through the lobby, he found himself dwelling not on what he'd learned about the old Mexican, but on Finnegan's remark: *I thought you were retired, Charlie.* Charlie was no grammarian, but having been married to an elementary school teacher for over thirty years, he knew more about proper English than he cared to. And though Charlie understood it was a silly little thing, it irked him that Finnegan had used the passive voice—as if the department had retired Charlie, like a rancher putting a horse out to pasture.

—I wasn't retired by the force, Charlie said to himself as he climbed in his car. I retired from it.

And therein lay a big difference.

Didn't it?

When Charlie went to bed that Saturday night, he hoped to get a good night's rest, but when he woke at five in the morning, he knew he wouldn't fall back asleep. He was feeling the excitement of a child, the anxiety of an adolescent, the hubris of a young man, and the dread of an adult, all at once. Of the four, it was the excitement of the child he felt the most.

At a quarter to six, Charlie donned his robe, went into the kitchen, and put the kettle on the stove. He stared out the window into the darkness as he waited for the kettle to whistle. Then he poured the water over the tea bag and sat at their little kitchen table.

For over thirty years, Betty had offered him a cup of tea. On a cold winter morning or a rainy afternoon, she would make one for herself and offer to make one for him, reminding him of its merits. But Charlie was a coffee man, so he always turned her down. Then the year she died, unable to bring himself to throw her tea in the trash, he had made himself a cup and realized that what she had always said was absolutely right: *Sometimes, it just hit the spot.*

The personality of a man always poses the biggest obstacle to his own education, thought Charlie. He's either too proud, too stubborn, or too timid to submit to the process of discovery. Many of life's lessons come through trial or tribulation, and the cost of those lessons shouldn't be taken lightly. But at least half of what a man hasn't learned in his lifetime he could have learned with ease. This is one of the insights that comes with age—when one understands the nature of discovery but no longer has the time or energy to submit to its splendors. Thus, we are doomed to end our days in an ignorance largely of our own making.

As Charlie sat in the kitchen sipping his tea, his thoughts turned to the business of the day and the limitations he faced. If he'd had the time and resources, he would have done a number of things differently. He would have visited the corner of Wilshire and San Vicente and found the old Mexican in order to speak with him directly and get a description of the driver. He would have tried to track down the car. There couldn't be that many blue convertibles in Los Angeles, and maybe he would have gotten lucky—finding one registered to an acquaintance or employee of Fairview's. If Charlie were still on the force, he could have picked up Fairview, sweated him overnight, pressed him to see who else might have had access to his pictures. But Charlie didn't have the time or resources, and he wasn't on the force. If he wanted to retrieve the photographs that were in the blackmailers' possession, he was simply going to have to follow the blackmailers to them. And that was the plan he had hatched with Miss Ross.

Or rather, Evelyn.

Outside, Charlie could hear the milkman making his rounds as morning finally arrived. He heard the truck come to a stop out front and the bottle being placed on the stoop. Self-conscious of being in his robe, he waited for the milkman to drive away before he opened the door to collect the bottle.

Charlie wasn't hungry, but it was likely to be a long day and he didn't know when he would get the chance to eat again. So he scrambled three eggs with a touch of the milk, as Betty would have, and ate them with two pieces of toast. After cleaning the pan, the plate, and the cutlery, Charlie showered and shaved. As he dressed, he avoided making eye contact with the photograph of Betty that he kept on the bedside table. She wouldn't have been in favor of what he was about to do. She would have shaken her head, unwilling to say out loud what was on her mind, but confident he would know what she was thinking just the same: *You're sixty-six years old, Charlie Granger. What are you trying to prove? And to whom?*

With his back to the photograph, he went to the bureau and strapped on his shoulder holster. The night before, he had cleaned, oiled, and loaded his pistol. He had done so at the little kitchen table where he had just eaten his eggs. Now he slipped the pistol into the holster. It was the first time he'd worn his gun since he'd retired, and the shape and weight of it felt good against his side. It gave him a boost of confidence that he welcomed, even though he knew the confidence brought by carrying a gun was a confidence of which to be wary.

Fed, bathed, and dressed, Charlie was disappointed to see it wasn't even ten o'clock. On days like this, the last thing you wanted was extra time. Extra time to worry or second-guess. Or worse, to lose one's sense of urgency. Charlie sat down on the couch in the living room for a few minutes. Then he rose and walked through the house.

When Charlie had decided on the Golden State Limited that he wasn't going to move to New Jersey, he could have come home and left everything exactly as it was. But that hadn't felt right. For without Betty, the house wasn't as it was. His life wasn't as it was. And the time had come to acknowledge that, one way or another. So, even though he was committed to staying in the house, he spent two months cleaning it out. First, he got rid of some of the extra furniture, putting it on the street where it remained for less than two nights. Then he cleared out the storage area in the attic. He cleared out Betty's closets. He cleared out the kitchen, getting rid of half the table settings, half the glassware, and all the kitchen tools he wasn't likely to use (didn't exactly know how to use, if he were to be honest). He boxed them all up, loaded them in his car, and took them to a church in the barrio, where it was more likely the parishioners would have need for them. Tom said he wanted the old photo albums, even the ones that predated his arrival on earth, God knows why. So, Charlie had packed them up for shipping. At the last moment, he had put Betty's handwritten book of recipes in with the albums. Maybe Caroline would appreciate having it. Or maybe she and Tom would have a daughter one day who would want it. Wouldn't that be nice, Charlie had thought as he sealed the box.

When Charlie had finished the winnowing, the house suited him better. An old friend who stopped by said it looked less like a house that Charlie had lived in for over twenty years than a way station. That was the word for it, all right. A place where someone paused while on his way to somewhere else. One could enter one's final days laden down or light-footed, and Charlie was committed to choosing the latter.

When Charlie saw it was finally time to go, he went to the bedroom mirror to straighten his tie. Tucked into the frame of the mirror was a note he'd received from his grandson. Written in crayon on a three-by-five card it said, *We miss you!* with three *s*'s. Apparently, the boy had been sorely disappointed when Tom had told him that his grandfather wouldn't be moving to New Jersey, which touched Charlie. But well Charlie knew that if the boy had been disappointed, he was the only one. Certainly, Caroline hadn't been disappointed by Charlie's decision to stay in Los Angeles. But Tom had felt a measure of relief too. As had Charlie himself.

It is a funny aspect of life, thought Charlie, how a group of grown people can convince themselves to do something that none of them really want to do. They start by talking an idea into existence. Once the idea begins to take shape and dimension, they'll talk away their hesitations, replacing them with all the supposed benefits, one by one. They'll talk away their instincts and their second thoughts and their common sense too, until they are moving in lockstep together toward some shared intention that doesn't appeal to any one of them.

Charlie put the boy's note back in the frame of the mirror. Then as he turned to go, he found himself looking at Betty's photograph, after all.

—I'll be all right, he said.

And she seemed to appreciate the assurance.

Olivia

WHEN EVE SUGGESTED TO OLIVIA she might want to be somewhere other than the hotel on Sunday morning, Olivia knew exactly where she would go. Or not quite exactly. As she hadn't been to a service since arriving in Los Angeles, she would have to ask Peter, the concierge, for the nearest Episcopal church.

When she approached his desk, she felt a little self-conscious. As concierge, he was accustomed to making recommendations about restaurants and nightclubs and shops. What would he think when a young woman who had been living in the city for four years suddenly felt the need to visit a church?

But of course, she needn't have worried.

—All Saints on Santa Monica and Camden, he replied without a hint of surprise or curiosity. It's just a short ride from the hotel.

—Thank you, Peter.

—But if you have a little time, he added after a moment, I think you'd find that All Saints Church in Pasadena is worth the trip, Miss de Havilland. It's a little out of your way, but it's much more . . . impressive.

—Impressive? Olivia asked with a smile.

—In the architectural sense.

—Then Pasadena it is.

Come Sunday morning, as Olivia's taxi drove through West Hollywood on its way to Pasadena, her thoughts turned to the services she had attended with her family as a child.

How her sister had hated them! She hadn't liked having to sit quietly in her Sunday dress. She hadn't liked taking Communion. She hadn't liked the readings from the pulpit, bridling at the church's presumption of authority. Never mind that the pews were uncomfortable and Reverend Whitmer's sermons interminable. So, Joan had complained. She had pleaded. She had feigned headaches and fevers. Anything to avoid going.

For Olivia, it had been the opposite. For reasons she never fully understood, she had taken to church from the start. She loved the architecture with its soaring ceilings and stained-glass windows. She loved the collective silence during the moments of prayer. She loved the pageantry of the processional, with the acolyte bearing the large golden cross before Reverend Whitmer draped in his long purple stole. And the music, oh the music! To hear the organ, then the voices of the choir and congregation rising in unison. What serenity she had found there. A serenity that had eluded her at home and at school and just about everywhere else.

But Olivia had been drawn to the teachings too. Drawn to the messages of kindness and patience and humility, discovering within them a source of strength. In aspiring to those virtues, Olivia found she was better able to withstand her stepfather's petty cruelties when, for the slightest shows of independence, he would command Olivia and her sister to polish his shoes or mop the floors. She was better able to withstand her mother's compulsion to refine her and Joan through endless lessons in etiquette and posture and diction.

When as a teenager Olivia began to act, she found these virtues served her well again. For they allowed her to enter a role more effectively, as she assumed the needs and aspirations of a character in place of her own. They allowed her to strike the right note with fellow actors and, more importantly, with directors. If she had not exhibited kindness and patience and humility, she doubted that Max Reinhardt would have taken her on as an understudy's understudy when he came to California to direct *A Midsummer Night's Dream* at the Hollywood Bowl; she would never have been given the role of Hermia when both lead actresses were forced to leave the cast just weeks before the premiere; and when Jack Warner offered her a seven-year contract, she knew it was due as much to the demure impression she had made in his office as it was to the performance she had given onstage.

Yes, the virtues of kindness, patience, and humility she had embraced as a child had come to her aid time and again. Until they hadn't.

When Olivia walked into All Saints Church, she made a mental note to thank Peter, for it was exactly as he had promised. It was the sort of church one rarely saw in Los Angeles. With its gothic exterior and square bell tower it looked as if it had been built in England in the seventeenth century, then moved to California stone by stone. And it was less than half full, which suited Olivia's frame of mind.

An usher in his early sixties who led Olivia down the aisle hesitated when she indicated she would like to sit in a pew in the back quarter of the church. The gentleman's instinct was to take her closer to the front, where she would be among other parishioners. But Olivia wanted to be in this pew precisely because there was no one sitting near it.

Bowing lightly to her preference, the usher opened the little gate and let her in.

Eve had made Olivia promise she wouldn't dwell on the envelope or its contents and she would leave the whole matter in Eve's hands. But once Olivia was seated alone in her pew at the back of the church with the voluntary playing quietly on the organ, the photographs were the first things to enter her unoccupied mind.

Although, if they came to mind, it wasn't for a reason that Eve might have anticipated. Yes, the pictures had been unsettling to Olivia as a violation of her privacy in the most intimate sense. They had been un-settling because she couldn't remember where or when they'd been taken. They had been unsettling because of the sordidness they sug-gested, despite Olivia's commitment to leading a Christian life. All of this was true. But the unsettling aspect of the photographs that returned to her now was how she had *looked* in them.

The previous summer had been one of the lowest points in Olivia's life. Going from one picture to the next without a break, working long hours, she had certainly been under physical duress—losing weight and sleep. But the greater duress had been one of the spirit. For when *Robin Hood* had made stars of both her and Errol, she had imagined her life as an actress was about to change. Now, she would be given roles of com-plexity in films that explored the intricacies of human relationships and psychology. Roles like those given to Bette Davis and Elizabeth Taylor and Katharine Hepburn, in which a woman was portrayed as feminine, but also as passionate and opinionated. Instead, Olivia found herself being cast as some version of Maid Marian over and over again. There were different settings and costumes, but the role was essentially the same: a maiden in a tower waiting patiently to be saved through an act of someone else's chivalry.

What made this particularly dispiriting was Olivia's dawning reali-zation that if she was trapped in a tower, it was a tower of her own making—one constructed from those same three virtues. When Olivia looked at herself in the blackmailers' photographs what she saw was a woman who had been acquiescent for so long, she might never be pas-sionate or opinionated again.

And then came Eve.

Having exchanged no more than a few words with Olivia in a restau-rant washroom, Eve was suddenly pulling up a chair in order to save Olivia from the man in the big white hat. In a borrowed limousine, she had whisked her off to Santa Monica, where she had bought a brass token from that funny little man with the look of Toulouse-Lautrec.

And when his fantastic machine had delivered its indismissible instruction to Eve, she had led Olivia to the end of the pier and thrust it in her hand.

Olivia had understood that she wasn't meant to open the envelope right then in front of Eve, or the crowd, or anyone else. Instead, she had carried it back to the house where she was living with her mother (or rather, where her mother was living with her). Letting herself in quietly, she had gone to her room and closed the door. She had sat on her bed, taken the envelope from her purse, turned it twice in her hands, then opened it. The contraption on the pier had been so elaborate and the proprietor so verbose, Olivia had assumed the instruction would be long and poetic. But it was only three words: *Resist the Temptation.*

If Olivia had been on the pier alone that night—which, admittedly, she wouldn't have been—but if she had been alone on the pier and given the proprietor her own birthday, her own height, weight, and eye color; if she had received this brief instruction prepared exclusively for her, she probably would have interpreted it as a warning to resist the temptation presented by Errol, a man who thrilled her in so many ways, but who was crass, and inconstant, and married. Or maybe she would have interpreted it as a remonstrance that she resist the temptation to undercut her sister, with whom she had competed since childhood and who had begun to find her own success in Hollywood.

But Olivia hadn't been alone on the pier, and the instruction hadn't been written for her. It had been written for Eve, a woman who wasn't particularly patient or humble, or perhaps even kind. So even as Olivia read the note alone in her room, she understood that the temptation she must resist was to continue being the person whom others expected her to be.

In the weeks that followed, Olivia moved out of the house in which her mother was living. On New Year's Day, she made the covert journey up Cukor's back driveway in the scarf and tinted glasses in order to read for the part of Melanie. When Cukor offered her the role, she made her case to Jack Warner. And when he refused, she invited his wife, Ann, for tea at the Brown Derby and poured out her heart, holding nothing back. The next day, it was Jack Warner who acquiesced, for once.

And at long last, Olivia had been given the opportunity to show the studio what she was capable of. To show the world. To show herself.

Prentice

ON SUNDAY MORNING, Prentice had woken early, bathed, and shaved. He had forgone breakfast, just as he had often forgone meals before taking the stage to ensure he was light on his feet. He had dressed with care, opting for a white linen suit, given the unseasonably warm weather. For a moment he had considered donning a Panama hat, but resisted the impulse, having long believed in the maxim that what is best stated is understated.

When he opened his door to leave at ten, a voice in his head encouraged him to take a good long look at his rooms, as this might well be the last time he saw them. *Nonsense!* he told the voice, pulling the door shut with a bang.

In the lobby, he was not in the least surprised to find Evelyn waiting in her chair. She rose to greet him.

—Are you sure about this, Prentice?

What she really wanted to ask, of course, was whether he was up to it.

—Evelyn, he said taking her hand, on Thursday I happened to invite you to tea. When you failed to appear, I happened to meet Bridie in the hallway with her master key. And when you and Charles shared those photographs, they happened to be taken in a spot that only I could recognize. Suffice it to say that at every juncture Fate has intervened to push me further into this affair. So, am I sure about it? I am as sure as I have been about anything in my life.

In phrasing his convictions thus, to some degree Prentice was betraying his old predilection for the dramatic turn of phrase and the sweeping observation artfully put. To some degree, he was invoking Fate to cut short any attempts by Evelyn to dissuade him from entering upon this dangerous enterprise. But mostly, Prentice had described this turn of events as a matter of destiny, because that's exactly what it was: a matter of destiny. His destiny.

Patting Evelyn twice on the hand, Prentice walked out the door to where the green Packard and William awaited.

Upon seeing Prentice, William stood to attention and opened the back door.

Once Prentice was comfortably in the car, he watched as William was approached by Evelyn for a brief exchange. William nodded twice then climbed behind the wheel.

—To the Hacienda, Mr. Symmons?

—To the Hacienda, my friend.

As the Packard pulled out of the driveway—carrying Prentice from the manicured grounds of the Beverly Hills Hotel for the first time in over two years—Prentice felt a stinging in his palm. Looking down, he realized it was because he was gripping the head of his cane so tightly. Setting the cane aside, Prentice closed his eyes and concentrated on his breathing, attempting to slow the cadence of his heart even as the Packard wound upward into the Hollywood Hills, irrevocably.

—Destiny, he reminded himself.

Hearing the word, William glanced in the rearview mirror with a touch of concern. When Evelyn had pulled him aside, no doubt she had asked him to keep a watchful eye on Prentice. Under such circumstances, Prentice always found it best to put forth a positive front.

—What a lovely day to be out and about, he said.

—It is at that! agreed William with a look of relief.

To complete the show of sanguinity, Prentice took the unusual step of rolling down his window. Settling back in the warm air, he turned his thoughts to his destination.

Do you know the Hacienda? Charles had asked.

Know it? Prentice had replied. *Only like the back of my hand.*

Commissioned by William Randolph Hearst for his mistress, Marion Davies, in 1922, the Hacienda was a small mansion designed in the Mission style with white stucco walls, red-tile roofs, iron balconies, and a grove of orange trees. Prentice had been on site in 1924 (or was it '25?) when Hearst had thrown an extravagant birthday celebration for his paramour. Shortly before dusk, Hearst had summoned all the guests to the upper terrace, where a giant gift-wrapped box was on display. Remarking how much Davies enjoyed the sounds of songbirds in the morning, Hearst tore off the wrapping to reveal a golden cage filled with swallows. When he pulled a lever opening the top of the cage, the birds fluttered out, circled twice above the orange trees, then disappeared to the south, presumably in search of Capistrano.

A lesson to us all, no doubt.

When the beleaguered Mrs. Hearst finally threw up her hands and returned to New York without her husband in 1926, Davies was invited by Hearst to join him in his castle in San Simeon, and the Hacienda was put up for sale. The property traded hands three times before Freddie purchased it in 1933.

The best thing about the Hacienda, in Prentice's opinion, was that it was built into a hillside facing west, such that every evening as the sun began to set—

—We're here, said William.

—Ah yes, acknowledged Prentice. So we are.

Rather than enter the house through the front door (where he might encounter a bothersome servant with a guest list), Prentice opted for the honeysuckled path that led round to the back of the house, where the party was already under way. When Prentice reached the terrace, he paused to survey the scene.

As to be expected, the majority of Fairview's guests hailed from the top of the credits: producers and directors; actors, actresses, and screenwriters; a cinematographer or two. In addition, Prentice spied three agents, two financiers, and a gossip columnist, each of whom looked upon the assembly with ravenous eyes. And there, there at the edge of the terrace overlooking the pool, overlooking the party, overlooking it all, was Freddie, dressed in yellow pants and a pink shirt, God help us. Taking a deep breath, Prentice steeled his resolve and began making his way through the crowd toward his host.

It was a humbling journey. A gauntlet composed of every sort of slight. First there was the director of light romances who turned his body just enough to make a casual encounter with Prentice less likely. Then the actress who hadn't worked since the advent of the talkies, who waved at Prentice enthusiastically. Then the writer of droll comedies who nudged a fellow scribbler in order to make a wry remark, resulting in an audible guffaw. While scattered throughout were the starlets whose eyes barely settled on Prentice at all, recognizing instinctively from the way the others treated him that he was not a man of consequence.

Well, so be it. For that which humbles our sense of vanity prepares us to face that which insults our sense of honor!

—Excuse me, said Prentice. Yes, yes. Pardon me. *Excusez-moi.*

Once again Prentice could sense the hand of Fate when, just as he completed his journey across the terrace, Freddie happened to finish a conversation, turn from a guest, and meet Prentice face-to-face.

—A lovely gathering as always, Freddie, said Prentice with a slight bow of the head.

Freddie stared at Prentice for a moment. Then a slanted smile formed on his overly tanned face.

—Why, Prentice Symmons. Is that you?

—It is.

—In the *flesh*, as they say.

—Quite.

After smiling at his own witticism, Freddie adopted an expression of sincere interest.

—I didn't realize you'd returned from your travels. You must tell me all about them.

—My travels?

—Why, yes. Haven't you been abroad for the last few years? Circling the globe by balloon, or what have you?

Freddie waved his hand to suggest the world at large, or perhaps the flight of the balloon.

—No, no, said Prentice. I have been right here.

—Oh, said Freddie making a show of surprise. In California?

—In Beverly Hills.

—Well, you must have been keeping yourself to yourself. Immersed in some secretive endeavor, no doubt. Working on your memoirs, perhaps?

—Something to that effect.

—Then we who share a love of history have much to look forward to. Do make yourself at home, Prentice. There's plenty to eat.

When Freddie turned his back on Prentice, Prentice turned his back on Freddie—and nearly crashed into a young waitress who was holding out a tray of canapés.

—No, thank you, said Prentice, louder than he needed to.

Then he made his way back through the gauntlet, through the French doors, and into the grand Spanish living room with its overbearing furniture. Inside were several refugees from Saturday night nursing their hangovers.

Through the door on the northern side of the living room, if Prentice remembered correctly, was something of a study. But Prentice was fairly certain the photographs wouldn't be there. They would be in Freddie's bedroom, where he could peruse them at the end of the day behind a locked door in the manner of a miser counting his gold. Affronted by the very image, Prentice marched into the foyer, where the staircase curved to the second floor. At a glance, he could see it was at least fifteen steps.

—May I help you?

Turning, Prentice found a waiter on his way to the terrace with a tray of mimosas.

—I'm . . . looking for the washroom.

The waiter gestured with his head toward the hallway from which he'd come.

—Second door on the right.

—Thank you.

Making a show of heading in that direction, Prentice waited for the waiter to enter the living room, then doubled back and began his ascent, counting the steps under his breath.

— . . . Three . . . Four . . . Five . . . Six . . . Seven . . . Eight . . . Nine . . . Ten . . .

At the eleventh step, Prentice realized that down in the lobby the same waiter was returning with an empty tray. He must have been bringing the mimosas to the refugees. Freezing in place, Prentice waited for the waiter to disappear down the hall, then resumed his climb at a quicker clip.

Twelve—Thirteen—Fourteen—Fifteen—Sixteen!

On the landing, Prentice stopped to mop his brow with a handkerchief, only to feel new beads of sweat forming themselves as soon as he'd put the handkerchief away. With a quick look to his left and right, Prentice crossed the hallway and entered the master suite, closing the mahogany door behind him.

It was a large room with sunlight pouring through two balcony doors. To Prentice's right was a canopied bed fit for Marie Antoinette. Arranged on the bookshelves to his left, apparently without irony, were leather-bound collections of Dickens, Thackeray, and Balzac. There was also a three-volume set of Shakespeare's plays standing between a pair of bookends on the Louis XVI desk, as if Freddie were so accustomed to reading the words of the Bard, he needed to keep them close at hand.

Dropping into the Louis XVI chair, Prentice went through the drawers of Freddie's desk, finding nothing.

He went through the drawers of the bedside tables, also to no avail.

Looking around the room, he noted the two rather amateurish copies of Renoirs depicting women in various stages of undress: one sunning herself by a river, the other rising from a bath. Could there be a safe? Prentice wondered. Peeking behind each of the gilded frames, Prentice found only the walls.

In the adjacent dressing room were three closets, two columns of shelves, a built-in bureau. As quickly as possible, Prentice searched through them all, noting with a roll of the eyes that everything—the shirts, the socks, the luggage—bore Freddie's initials. In the bathroom, Prentice discovered that the hairbrush, towels, and bath mat were also monogrammed. But there was no sign of the photographs.

—Damn it, said Prentice, uncharacteristically.

Happening to glance in Freddie's mirror as he was leaving the bathroom, Prentice realized with a touch of dismay that large semicircles of sweat had revealed themselves under the arms of his linen jacket. Not only were the stains unbecoming, they seemed to strike a note of futility, suggesting implicitly that Prentice was teetering on the edge of failure.

With the first hints of resignation beginning to express themselves in his features, Prentice turned to the mirror, ready to see himself for who he was; for what he was; for what he had become. But as he faced his own reflection, Prentice was reminded of Olivia. Reminded of Olivia standing before a different mirror, staring shyly at her own reflection, unaware that at that very moment she was being betrayed.

With renewed resolve, Prentice went back into Freddie's bedroom. He turned over pillows. He cast aside the cushion from the seat of the high-back chair. He even got down on his knees—something he almost never did—in order to look under the bed.

—They must be here, he said when he had hefted himself back to his feet. They must be here in the bedroom because Freddie would keep the pictures close at hand.

Close at hand, repeated Prentice to himself.

Then he looked at the desk.

Crossing the room, Prentice picked up the volume of the Comedies, hesitated, then flipped through the pages. And there, pasted on top of the finest words ever written in the English language, were photographs of more than fifty women. Blondes, brunettes, and redheads. Some who were full-figured, others who were slim. Some brazen, some demure. But all betrayed. The stolen portraits were scattered throughout the volume of the Comedies and half the volume of the Histories, the pages of the Tragedies remaining uncompromised, for now.

Lifting the first two volumes, Prentice found them to be heavy and cumbersome. How was he to get them out of the house? After looking about, he went back into the dressing room and grabbed one of Freddie's overnight bags. He stuffed the volumes inside and headed out the door.

As Prentice descended the stairs, he felt a touch of dizziness and chastised himself for having skipped his breakfast. But this was no time to falter, whatever the excuse! Shifting his cane to the hand with the bag, he took hold of the iron railing that curved along the wall, counting down the steps in reverse.

When he came off the final step, he saw from the corner of his eye that someone was emerging from the kitchen. The same waiter, he presumed, only to realize a second later it was Cavendish, Freddie's prudish majordomo. Cavendish was sure to wonder what Prentice had been doing upstairs, and he might even recognize his employer's bag. Prentice began walking quickly toward the front door, but Cavendish also picked up his pace. A thinner, younger man, he was well positioned to cut off

Prentice's retreat, foiling the whole enterprise. But suddenly, the front door swung open and in walked William with his chauffeur's cap on his head.

—Sorry I'm late, Mr. Symmons! There was traffic on Wilshire. But you've still got an hour to make your flight. Allow me to take that for you.

Before anyone knew what was happening, William had whisked the monogrammed bag out of the house and into the Packard, which was parked in front of the door with the engine running.

—Alas, TWA waits for no man, said Prentice to the majordomo. Please do relay to Freddie my sincerest thanks.

Only when Prentice was in the back seat of the Packard with the door closed did he breathe a sigh of relief.

—Back home, Mr. Symmons?

—Yes, indeed, said Prentice with a smile at William's choice of words. Back home!

But as the Packard pulled forward, Prentice noted a young woman with auburn hair and dark sunglasses climbing from the back of a cab. A beautiful young woman. A familiar young woman. It took Prentice a moment to realize she was the starlet who had stayed at that hotel the previous fall and shown a predilection for swimming laps in the afternoon. Today, she was wearing a short spring dress and carrying a bag on her shoulder in which, no doubt, was her bathing suit.

—Stop the car, said Prentice.

William looked in the rearview mirror with an expression of surprise.

And not without reason. For Prentice had obtained what they had come for. And in so doing, he had survived the gauntlet of guests, countenanced Freddie's derision, bested the sixteen stairs, and narrowly escaped the majordomo—who at this very moment was probably informing Freddie of his suspicions. The most sensible thing for them to do right now, as William might say, was to make themselves scarce.

—I'll be back in a few minutes, said Prentice.

William's gaze turned to one of concern.

—Is there something I can do for you, Mr. Symmons?

—No, William. This is something I must see to myself.

Prentice climbed from the car and made his way back toward the house, back toward the party, back into the fray. As he did so, he buoyed his courage with consideration of the following paradox: Over the last few years, as he had gained in mass and dimension, he had diminished in the eyes of the town. With each additional pound, he had become a little less prominent, a little less apparent, until he was largely ignored by friends and strangers alike.

Admittedly, Prentice had initially shed some tears over this development. Once applauded by audiences, admired by peers, stopped by strangers in the street, how could he not feel some bereavement over the waning of his celebrity. But today, on the nineteenth of March 1939, on the grounds of the Hacienda, in the heart of Beverly Hills, he would *embrace* his insubstantiality. He would reenter this house of villainy and wend his way once again through the glamorous assemblage. Only this time, he would do so in the manner of an apparition.

—You are a man of no consequence, he said to himself with a smile as he reached the front door. A no one. A nobody!

Entering the house with this new mantra on his lips, Prentice walked past the mimosa drinkers unobserved. He crossed the crowded terrace unseen. Then down the steps he went to the pool. As he worked his way around its circumference, the three young women who were stretched on the chaise longues continued their conversation without casting a glance in his direction.

There would have to be a room behind the mirror, thought Prentice, with its own discreet entrance.

At the far end of the pool, Prentice walked behind the diving board, past the women's entrance to the bathhouse, to the very back of the building—which seemed, in fact, to be wider than need be. Slipping between the outer wall and a giant rhododendron, Prentice took heart from the discovery that the bush's branches had been selectively trimmed and footprints marked the ground. After three more paces, he came upon a nondescript door.

—There you are, said Prentice aloud.

Reaching for the doorknob, he found it to be locked.

Of course it was.

Taking a step back, Prentice raised his arm and prepared to crack the doorknob with the head of his cane. But as the head of his cane was made of ivory, it hardly seemed appropriate for the task. Lowering his arm, Prentice looked about until he saw what he needed under the rhododendron's branches. Sticking his cane upright in the dirt, he lowered himself to his knees for the second time that day. After digging in the soil with his fingernails, he freed a stone the size of a grapefruit. Hefting it from the ground, Prentice carried it to the door and brought it down upon the knob not once, not twice, but three times, until the knob gave way.

Tossing the stone aside, Prentice entered the chamber.

As his eyes adjusted to the dark, he became aware of a large insect-like shape standing before him. It was a camera on a tripod. After taking a step forward, Prentice could see what the camera was seeing: a large rectangular window behind which the girl with the auburn hair, now bare-chested, was applying some sort of oil to her sternum. Behind her, an Amazonian fresh from the shower was twisting the water from her long brown hair. And behind them both, poking out from the underbrush was the head of the leopard, lithe and lascivious.

Prentice felt the pressure in his jaw from the gritting of his teeth.

Turning from the window he looked about. Walking back to the door, he found the light switch and turned it on. He exited the viewing room and moved as quickly as he could around the back of the bathhouse, brushing aside the rhododendron branches. When he emerged, he opened the door to the women's dressing room, and without fully stepping inside, switched off the lights.

—What's the big idea? said a woman who must have hailed from Brooklyn.

A second later a more delicate voice cried: Is that a camera?!

As the shouts in the bathhouse increased, Prentice made his way around the pool. The three young sunbathers who had been chatting so blithely on their chaise longues had gotten up and were beginning to walk toward the bathhouse to see what all the fuss was about.

By any standard, Prentice must have presented a sorry figure. In addition to being a hundred pounds overweight and dressed in a linen jacket soaked with sweat, the knees of his pants were stained and his fingers covered in dirt. But as he passed the three young women, they noticed him not. For having feared for years the shadow of his former self, Prentice had *become* the shadow of his former self. A will-o'-the-wisp. A phantom. An invisible man roaming the Hollywood Hills in the name of justice!

As Prentice climbed the steps to the terrace (passing the gossip columnist who was hurrying in the other direction), he paused to take a few canapés from an inattentive waitress. But as he was eating the first with a smile on his lips, Prentice came to a stop. His cane! He had forgotten to retrieve it!

Upon the realization, he was about to let out a curse.

Instead, he said: *Perfecto.*

For later that day, after the commotion had settled down, after a generation of starlets had disappeared from the property like the swallows of 1924 and the gossip columnist had called in her copy from the extension in the study, Freddie Fairview, in a state of profound chagrin, would visit the scene of the disaster. And there, having noted the broken doorknob, he would turn and discover the ivory-headed cane standing in the dirt like a sentinel, and he would know exactly whom he had to thank for the turning of his world upside down.

Charlie

—IS THAT A NEW suit?

—It is, Charlie admitted with a touch of embarrassment.

—It's sharp, said Evelyn with a smile. Come on in.

Evelyn led Charlie into Olivia de Havilland's living room. The actress was staying in one of the little bungalows on the grounds of the hotel that provide an extra level of privacy for those who could afford it.

—Is Miss de Havilland here?

—No, said Evelyn. I encouraged her to find something else to do.

Charlie nodded to express his agreement with Evelyn's instinct. That Miss de Havilland wasn't here was probably for the best.

The living room in the bungalow was similar to the one in Evelyn's suite, only larger, with French doors leading onto a small enclosed terrace. On the desk Charlie could see that Evelyn had arranged for a second phone to be hooked up. On the desk was also an open briefcase that was empty.

—You moved the money to a bag? he asked.

Evelyn pointed to the coffee table, where there was a shiny black purse with gold clasps.

—A handbag?

—Why not? said Evelyn. They didn't specify.

Charlie smiled.

—I suppose they didn't. Did Prentice get off all right?

—He should be back any time now.

—And your young friend is ready?

—Billy? He can hardly wait.

Charlie nodded.

The two were silent for a moment.

—Do you think it will work? Evelyn asked.

—I don't know, Charlie replied. Like any business, blackmailing has a mix of professionals and amateurs. We could be dealing with an established operation that's seasoned and careful. Or it could be men who have never blackmailed before, men who are acting out of desperation. I like to think we have a shot either way. But our chances are certainly better if we're dealing with amateurs.

—When will we know? Evelyn asked a little wryly.

—As soon as the phone call's over.

Evelyn walked behind the desk. Closing the briefcase and setting it on the floor, she sat in the desk chair and invited Charlie to take the seat on the other side. Any evidence of the anger she had exhibited on Thursday was gone. The cool and collected quality was back. This too, thought Charlie, was for the best.

Sitting across from Evelyn, Charlie couldn't help but think back to the morning they'd met, when they were seated opposite each other in the dining car. Once again, he found himself asking if he could ask her a personal question.

—Of course, she replied.

—What were you doing before? In New York, I mean.

—I was living pretty high on the hog, Charlie. With a handsome fellow in a large apartment overlooking Central Park.

—How was it?

—Mostly it wasn't.

She shook her head at the memory.

—I guess I was a kept woman, but he was a kept man. So, at least we were even.

—Do you miss it?

—The relationship?

—No, the city.

—As far as I'm concerned, the Rockies aren't high enough.

Charlie nodded with a smile. He enjoyed Evelyn's frankness. Admired it too. He was weighing whether to ask her about this relationship that mostly wasn't, but mention of the city had apparently prompted a train of thought of her own.

—New York wasn't so bad, she said. I made the first real friend of my life there, and she and I had more than our fair share of fun. But in the end, I just got worn out by all the fairy tales.

—There's no shortage of those here, Charlie pointed out.

—You're right, of course. But back east the fairy tales are a thousand years old, handed down from generation to generation. All that happily-ever-after nonsense. Out here there are fairy tales, but it feels like everyone is making them up as they go along.

—I think they call those delusions.

—Exactly, said Evelyn with a smile.

—So, you're not interested in happily ever after?

—Not in the least. Don't get me wrong. I enjoy being happy every now and then just like anybody else. It's the ever-after part that I find irksome.

Now Charlie found himself wanting to ask about this friend whom Evelyn had left behind in New York, the first real friend of her life, but the telephones rang.

With their eyes on each other, Charlie and Evelyn answered the two phones on the fourth ring, Charlie placing his hand over his mouthpiece.

As it turned out, Charlie didn't have to wait for the end of the call to know who they were dealing with. He could tell right away they were amateurs. He could tell from the way the man talked: too fast and at an elevated pitch. Charlie guessed he was a man of nervous disposition to begin with, but he was exhibiting all the signs of someone who was doing something illicit for the first time, and reluctantly. Charlie could also tell the man wasn't in charge. As he spoke to Evelyn, twice he had to correct himself—in the manner of one trying to remember exactly what he'd been instructed to say.

In short, the man told Evelyn she should bring the bag with the money to the diner on the block of Hamilton Boulevard between South Bentley and Sepulveda in Culver City at two o'clock. She should sit in the last booth on the left by the window and leave the bag under the seat. She would be watched the whole time. If she did exactly as she'd been told, the rest of the pictures would be delivered to the hotel before the end of the day.

This arrangement was to be expected. As Charlie had told Evelyn, even the most amateurish of blackmailers understood that their leverage ended as soon as the compromising materials were within reach.

Nonetheless, Charlie quickly wrote a question on a notepad and spun it for Evelyn to see.

—What guarantee do we have that you'll deliver the pictures after we pay? she read into the phone.

The man paused.

Charlie smiled as the pause confirmed his earlier suspicion. Charlie could almost see the caller looking toward his partner—the decision-maker—for guidance on how to answer. He could hear the caller covering his own mouthpiece, then the faint indication of an exchange followed by a somewhat halting response.

—Miss de Havilland's not the only one who's been photographed, he said. We want her to be a happy customer because we're going to ask her to serve as a reference. To confirm to the others that once she paid, she received the pictures as promised.

This too was a fairy tale, of course—the idea that the blackmailers would return all the compromising materials. But Charlie sensed the caller believed it. He believed it because he wanted to believe it. The decision-maker had probably promised they would give all the pictures back and be done with it—a brief foray into the world of crime before returning to the lives of honest men. But having said this to appease his partner, the decision-maker would keep an image or two. And once Miss de Havilland had served her role as a reference, he would reach out with new demands. Which confirmed for Charlie that they had no choice but to find him now.

Wendell

WENDELL DIDN'T WANT TO be here—standing in a telephone booth at two in the afternoon with the sun beating down. Standing here for God knows how long. Wendell didn't know where he wanted to be, but he didn't want to be here. How had he let Jerry talk him into it?

Taking off his glasses, Wendell wiped the lenses with his handkerchief. Then he took a sip from the flask he kept in his back pocket. Just one to settle the nerves.

He never should have told Jerry about the photographs, that was his mistake. It had been late and they'd been drinking. And what should you do when it's late and you've been drinking? Keep your big mouth shut, that's what. As Wendell should've known better than most. But there he was sitting on his stool at O'Malley's at one in the morning letting Jerry pour him another glass of whiskey, and the next thing he knew the whiskey was telling Jerry the whole story.

Putting his flask back in his back pocket, Wendell shook his head. Because he knew that wasn't true. It hadn't been the whiskey's fault. Wendell had told Jerry about the photographs because he had *wanted* to tell Jerry. He had wanted to tell Jerry because he suspected what Jerry might say—Jerry, who knew all the angles.

Sure enough, once Wendell told Jerry, Jerry had laid it out in a matter of minutes: what they could do and how they could do it. And when Wendell showed the first signs of hesitation, Jerry made the case for *why* they should do it, asking Wendell questions and answering them himself.

How long were you at MGM? Seven years.

How hard did they work you? Like a dog.

And what do you have to show for it? Nothing.

—At this point, Jerry had said while emptying the last of the bottle into Wendell's glass, you deserve a break, Wendy. And what the rest of them deserve is what they've got coming to them.

Seven years, thought Wendell. Seven long years . . .

After finishing art school in Fresno (or almost finishing it), Wendell had gotten a job working as an assistant in the still photography department at MGM. That was back in the fall of 1932, a time when no one was getting a job anywhere.

There are dues to be paid in any line of work, and Wendell had paid his. He'd swept floors and run for coffee. He'd mixed the chemicals in the darkroom until his head was spinning. Pretty soon, he was assisting Mueller, the senior photographer. Positioning the lights and arranging the furniture. Knowing his place and doing as he was told. By 1935, he was overseeing shoots of his own, and some other kid's head was spinning in the darkroom.

When you happen to meet a stranger and tell them you work in Hollywood, they perk right up, eager to hear all about it. But when you go on to explain you're a still photographer, their eyes glaze over like you've said you work in the cafeteria. Most people outside of Hollywood don't understand what it takes to shoot a good still. Most people *in* Hollywood don't understand.

The name they gave it shows you how little they understand. Because a good still is anything but. It has to have *motion*. It has to give a sense of the action that's simmering under the surface. Like the fight about to break out in a saloon or the romance about to be kindled under a streetlamp. A good still has to communicate a mood. It has to reveal the psychology of the characters. It has to intrigue and entice. And to achieve all that, the still photographer has to have the aesthetic sensibility of a set designer, the eye of a cinematographer, and the persuasive talents of a director.

In the course of his career, Wendell had shot over one hundred thousand stills for over a hundred and fifty films. One week in the spring of '37, he'd shot six hundred for *A Day at the Races* and another four hundred for *Captains Courageous*—including twenty with Spencer Tracy submerged to the chest in stormy seas. Clark Gable in *Parnell*; Cary Grant in *Topper*; Rosalind Russell in *Night Must Fall*; Laurel and Hardy in *Way Out West*. Wendell had shot them all.

And for pretty good pay. Not enough to get rich maybe, but enough to put a down payment on a two-bedroom in Brentwood Glen with a convertible in the driveway and three hundred bucks in the bank. And every now and then, when one of your stills happened to show up in newspapers across the country, they might even give you a pat on the back. But God forbid you make a mistake.

God forbid you make one lousy mistake.

The week after he had done the stills for *Captains Courageous*, Wendell had shot Clark Gable and Jean Harlow for *Saratoga*. After taking fifty pictures of the pair—Gable and Harlow in an embrace, Gable and Harlow on a chaise, Gable and Harlow whispering sweet nothings into each other's ears—the boys from publicity asked Wendell to get a few of Harlow by herself. By that point, he had already been on the set for seven hours, and he still had to go to the darkroom to develop the negatives and print the contact sheets, because in Hollywood whatever was needed was needed yesterday. So, did he take a couple of swigs from his flask while Harlow was changing into a new outfit? Sure he did. Who wouldn't've?

Usually, when you're shooting stills it's like a doctor in a doctor's office. Stick out your tongue. Turn your head and cough. Seen one, seen 'em all. But as he was shooting Harlow lying on the chaise by herself, Wendell suddenly saw what it was that had made her a star—like an inner light shining through her countenance. A glimpse of the divine, he had thought to himself. And that's how he should have left it. To himself.

But at the end of the shoot, when Harlow went off to the dressing room to change into her street clothes, Wendell waited. He waited as the boys from publicity headed for the bar and the lighting crew were shutting off the lights. Maybe he took another swig or two, just to pass the time. When she finally emerged from her dressing room, there he was waiting to tell her: *Miss Harlow, you are the most beautiful woman whom I have ever seen.*

That was it. That was all he'd said. And she had seemed to appreciate the compliment.

But when Wendell got home, the phone was ringing so loud, you could tell it had been ringing for an hour. When he answered it, he could barely understand what the man from Mr. Thalberg's office was saying because the words were coming so fast and angry.

—What in the hell were you thinking? the man shouted in conclusion before hanging up the phone.

He didn't bother to ask for Wendell's side of the story. Wendell didn't have a side of the story. And by ten the next morning, he was out on his keister without a dollar in severance or a word of thanks. Like Jerry said: Seven years and nothing to show for it.

But that wasn't the worst of it.

Studio executives are as competitive and miserly as any men alive. They tie up their actors and actresses with contracts as long as the phone book. They stockpile scenarios and scripts they may or may not ever bother to shoot. Secretive, sly, and conniving, they wouldn't share a Saltine cracker with their own mothers. But when they let you go, they'll call every studio in town to share their opinion of you. To denounce you free of charge. It doesn't matter how reliable you've been, how dedicated, how talented. Suddenly, you're a man who's unemployable.

How does that happen? How does one go from being at the top of one's game to being a man who's unemployable? Wendell knew the answer to that question. Everyone in Hollywood knew the answer: quickly. In this town that was rule number one.

Wendell spent the next twelve months coming to understand just how out of work he was. Which is to say, all the way out. Never mind Warner Brothers, Paramount, or Twentieth Century-Fox. He couldn't get a call returned from the boys who made westerns on a shoestring.

—There's work to be had in Ojai, one of them told him with a smirk. If you don't mind picking oranges for two dollars a day.

When you're down and out in Hollywood, everyone's a comedian. That was rule number two.

When Wendell was still working at MGM, he occasionally stopped in at O'Malley's at nine o'clock for a nightcap. Once he'd been out of work for a few months, sometimes he'd stop in at five or six. Sometimes he'd stop in at four and never stop out. He'd just sit on his stool at the end of the bar pouring what was left of himself into a glass, one ounce at a time. So, when Wendell received a call from Freddie Fairview asking if he could drop by, he didn't hesitate.

Wendell had never met Freddie Fairview, but he knew who he was. All you had to do was glance at the gossip columns once in a while to know that Fairview was a man-about-town, all chummy with the stars and living in a mansion in the Hollywood Hills.

Fairview greeted Wendell at the door in a robe and slippers at two in the afternoon, the rich man's prerogative. In a living room as big as Wendell's house, Fairview offered Wendell a drink. Wendell asked for whiskey and was given gin.

After shooting movie stars for seven years, Wendell knew a thing or two about faces. As he and Fairview sat down, he could see that Fairview was past his prime. He'd had too much sun and too much high living. But he still had a sparkle in the eye, a sparkle that had probably served him well with men and women alike. Where does a sparkle like that come from? Wendell found himself wondering, with a touch of envy.

Fairview began by saying that as a friend of several stars at MGM, he had seen and admired Wendell's work. He had also learned about Wendell's recent misfortunes and the doors that had been closed to him—unfairly, he might add.

—I think I may have a job for you, if you're interested.

—I'm a man who's inclined to work, Mr. Fairview.

—I sensed as much, he said with the sparkle in his eye. Here, let me show you something.

Fairview led Wendell across a terrace, down some steps, and past a pool toward a little house behind the diving board. But then, instead of going into the little house, Fairview led Wendell around it. Asking Wendell to hold back some branches, Fairview took him to a door, which he unlocked. Inside, he switched on a light. It was a plain room with dark blue walls and nothing in it but a chair and tripod. Fairview gave a little smile at Wendell's confusion, then he switched off the lights. Suddenly, through a large window built in the wall, they could see into the neighboring room—a dressing room.

Wendell felt a sense of shock when he realized what the setup was for, but he felt indignation too. Because after sniffing around the industry, Fairview had apparently come to the conclusion that of all the photographers in Hollywood—of all the photographers in Los Angeles County, for that matter—Wendell would be the one most willing to do his dirty work. As Fairview smiled, Wendell noted once again the sparkle in his eye, and he began to understand that the source of Fairview's sparkle was self-assurance and presumption, and maybe a little cruelty too.

—I'll pay you two hundred dollars, Fairview said, to spend eight summer afternoons taking portraits . . .

Two hundred dollars, thought Wendell, running a hand over his mouth.

—They'll be familiar faces to you, continued Fairview. Women whom you've photographed before. Women whom you've helped popularize, helped immortalize, and who don't even know your name.

—Four hundred dollars, said Wendell.

—Let's make it an even five, said Fairview.

And they shook on it then and there in the near darkness of that nearly empty room.

In the summer of 1938, Wendell spent eight Saturday afternoons in that ugly little box taking pictures. He spent his Sunday mornings developing the negatives. On Sunday afternoons, he would be back in the big living room where Fairview—who no longer offered Wendell even gin—would review the contact sheets with a jeweler's loupe, choosing which images he wanted developed. By the end of the summer, Wendell had printed the portraits of over eighty actresses, most of them under the age of thirty.

At the conclusion of the job, Wendell was supposed to destroy all the photographs and negatives, and he did. Except for a small cache of some duplicates that he put in a manila envelope and hid away in a drawer. In the months that followed, Wendell never looked at those pictures, not even once, finding them so distasteful he could barely abide having them in his house. But he kept them—along with a photograph of Fairview sitting by the pool with two young actresses, which Wendell had taken with a telephoto lens from the bushes behind the bathhouse. Wendell kept them in case Fairview ever tried to pull a fast one. Wendell wasn't exactly sure what the fast one would be, but he was certain that if a man like Fairview wanted to pull a fast one, he would.

The five hundred dollars Wendell earned from Fairview carried him easily through the end of 1938. It might have carried him through all of 1939, if he hadn't been convinced by Jerry to try his luck at the ponies. By the end of January, Wendell was right back where he'd started: tapped out.

Then late one night in March—on his birthday of all nights—Wendell found himself sitting with Jerry at the bar of O'Malley's at one in the morning, the two of them drunk, broke, and out of work.

—Take a look at *them*, said Jerry with a sneer, while gesturing to the mirror behind the bar. In all your life, Wendy, have you ever seen two bums more down and out?

Wendell knew that Jerry was right. That they were a sorry pair. But for some reason the observation didn't sit right with him. Maybe because he was drunk; or maybe because he didn't like Jerry lumping the two of them together; or maybe because it was his birthday. Whatever the reason, Wendell found himself responding to Jerry with an unusual tone of defiance.

—Speak for yourself, he said.

Jerry looked up in surprise.

—Well, shiver me timbers. Is that the voice of a man I hear?

—You've got no business telling another person when he's down and out, said Wendell. When I'm down and out, I won't be afraid to tell you so. But I'm a long way from being there.

—Says the fella who needs to sit on a phone book in order to reach the bar.

—I am not sitting on a phone book, said Wendell, turning red. What I *am* sitting on is worth plenty.

—Zat so.

—It's so, all right, said Wendell.

Then just like that, he found himself telling Jerry all about it. About Freddie Fairview and his pool parties and the two-way mirror. He told him about the cache of duplicates he'd kept, just in case. From Jerry's expression, Wendell could see that he'd caught Jerry off guard; surprised him; impressed him even.

—Fairview would pay a pretty penny to get those back, concluded Wendell.

—Fairview? said Jerry.

Suddenly, Jerry didn't seem so drunk anymore. He looked around the bar, confirming there was no one in earshot. Then leaning toward Wendell, he lowered his voice anyway.

—Forget about Fairview, Wendy. It's the actresses who would pay the pretty penny for those pictures. Every last one of them!

—Maybe so, said Wendell, a little begrudgingly. But like I told you: Stop calling me Wendy.

Now here he was standing in a telephone booth somewhere in Culver City in the heat of the day waiting for Jerry's call, his nerves getting the better of him.

Earlier, the woman who had answered the phone had agreed to everything they'd asked. To the time and the place and the money.

—But what if she changes her mind? Wendell had worried when she hung up. What if she calls the police? What if they're waiting for me at the diner?

—That's why I'm going ahead of you, Jerry had explained. A buddy of mine has an office on the third floor of a building across the street. From there I'll be able to see all the comings and goings. If the cops are anywhere in the vicinity, we'll call the whole thing off. But if I'm certain—if I'm absolutely certain—that she has come alone, I'll call you at the pay phone to give you the all clear. Then you go in the diner, pick up the bag, and walk out two minutes later, easy-peasy.

Even so, thought Wendell, as he stood in the telephone booth waiting, maybe this wasn't such a good idea. Didn't the banks keep records of the serial numbers on bills? Couldn't he and Jerry be caught later on when they tried to spend the money? Maybe Jerry hadn't thought of that. Maybe when Jerry called, he would—

The telephone rang.

The sound of it so startled Wendell, he fumbled the phone.

—Hello? Hello? he said once he had the receiver to his ear.

—It's all clear, said Jerry. Remember: last booth on the left.

Before Wendell could mention the issue with the serial numbers, Jerry hung up.

So, Wendell hung up.

—It's all clear, he repeated quietly to himself. In and out. Easy-peasy.

Exiting the telephone booth, he climbed in his car and started the engine, overcoming the temptation to take another swig. At least, until the temptation overcame him.

Since it was Sunday, Jerry had assured Wendell there would be parking spaces right in front of the diner, and there wouldn't be more than three or four customers. As Wendell drove down Hamilton Boulevard, he made a deal with himself: If there wasn't a parking space in front or if there were more than four customers inside, he'd call it off. He'd go home and wait for Jerry. When Jerry came, he'd tell him the coast hadn't been clear enough. Then maybe they could drop the idea, once and for all.

But when Wendell reached the diner, there were several parking spots right in front, just as Jerry had said there'd be. And just as Jerry had said, the diner was nearly empty—with an old man eating something at the counter and two teenage girls chatting in a booth by the window.

—In and out, Wendell said to himself as he walked through the door and made his way to the last booth on the left. Easy-peasy.

But when he tucked his right leg under the seat and moved it back and forth, he didn't feel a bag. Leaning over, he did his best to reach under the seat with his right arm, but still couldn't find anything.

—What'll it be?

Looking up, Wendell discovered the waitress standing there with her order pad in hand.

What was he supposed to do now? Jerry hadn't said anything about ordering. But if he didn't order something, wouldn't the waitress ask him to leave?

—A sandwich, he said.

—What kind of sandwich?

Wendell didn't know what kind of sandwich. He wasn't even hungry. The waitress tapped her foot with impatience.

—What kind do you have?

—Same as anywhere else. BLT. Chicken salad. Tuna salad.

—Tuna salad, said Wendell.

—Anything to drink?

—No, thanks.

When the waitress headed off to the kitchen, Wendell figured he had just a few minutes before she returned. Wedging his upper body under the tabletop, he took a look under his seat and confirmed there was nothing there.

Was he in the wrong booth? No. Jerry had definitely told him to go to the last one on the left. Maybe the woman had changed her mind. Or maybe someone else had discovered the bag! Feeling a mix of disappoint and relief, Wendell began to pull his body back only to bang his head on the underside of the table.

And that's when he saw it. The woman had put the bag under the *opposite* bench.

Only it wasn't a bag. It was a purse. A lady's purse.

To reach it, Wendell had to slide so far under the table his knees were almost on the floor. As soon as he had the purse in hand, he could tell it was full of something. Being careful not to hit his head a second time, Wendell snaked his way out from under the table—only to find the waitress was already back.

—I dropped something, he said while keeping the purse under the table.

—No kidding, she said, putting his sandwich down.

After watching her disappear through the kitchen doors, Wendell opened the clasp of the purse. It was the money all right. Closing the purse, he looked around the diner. The old man at the counter was still picking at his plate, and the two teenagers were still chatting away in their booth. No one was paying any attention to him. He had a clear line to the door.

But when Wendell was halfway out of the booth, he happened to glance at the sandwich. He'd forgotten to pay for it. Reaching into his pocket he found two quarters and left them on the table.

But wouldn't it look strange to the waitress if she returned to find the sandwich paid for but untouched? *He didn't even take a bite, Officer.* That's what she would say.

After sliding back into the booth, Wendell began eating the sandwich with a grimace. He didn't even like tuna fish. He had ordered it because it was the last thing the waitress had said. Wendell forced himself to eat three-quarters of it, all the while wishing he'd asked for a drink in order to wash the sandwich down.

As Wendell left the booth the second time, he felt a touch of panic over the purse. Surely everyone would notice a man carrying a purse. *It was a lady's handbag,* they would say. *And he didn't have it with him when he arrived, Officer.*

Wendell tucked the purse under his arm in order to obscure it as best he could, then walked out the door. As he was about to place the purse in the passenger seat, he hesitated, thinking what if he was stopped by the police for some reason. If the purse had been conspicuous in the diner, it would only be more so sitting in the passenger seat of a convertible being driven by a man. So, he put it in the trunk.

Once he was behind the wheel with the engine running, Wendell looked back at the diner—just as Jerry had told him—to confirm that no one had followed him out. And when he pulled away from the curb, he looked in the rearview mirror to confirm that no car had pulled out behind him. What he wanted now more than anything else was a drink from his flask, but first he had to make the turn onto Sepulveda.

As he approached the intersection, Wendell slowed, signaled, rotated the wheel, then began to reaccelerate. And that's when the young man on the bike suddenly appeared. Coming out of nowhere, he shot across the intersection right in front of Wendell's car. Wendell slammed on the breaks, but he was too late. The grille of the car smashed into the bike and the young man was thrown across Wendell's hood. With a loud crack, Wendell's windshield spiderwebbed where the rider must have hit his head. Then the young man rolled off the hood and out of sight as the car came to a stop.

Jumping from the driver's seat, Wendell ran around the front of the car, past the wreckage of the bike to where the young man was lying on the pavement. To Wendell's great relief, the young man began to sit up, appearing unbloodied.

—Here, said Wendell, helping him rise to his feet.

The young man gave his head a shake then looked at Wendell.

—What's the big idea, mister? Taking a turn without your signal!

—My signal was on, said Wendell. You came out of nowhere!

—I came out of somewhere, all right.

—When you're crossing an intersection, you . . . you shouldn't . . .

—*I* shouldn't? Are you saying this was *my* fault?

—No. What I'm saying is—

—Maybe we should call the police and see what they have to say.

Wendell found himself glancing over his shoulder, as if the police were already there.

—You're absolutely right, he assured the young man, talking a little faster than usual. It wasn't your fault. But it wasn't mine either. It was an accident. And thank goodness no one was hurt.

—Tell that to my bike, mister.

Wendell took his wallet from his pocket.

—I'll pay for the bike.

The young man looked at Wendell skeptically.

—It was practically brand new, he said. I paid twenty-five dollars for it.

Wendell opened his wallet and saw he only had three. He felt his face growing flush. What should he do now? The young man would never accept an IOU.

—Wait a second, he said.

Turning toward his trunk, Wendell saw that two cars were approaching with their signals flashing, intending to make the same turn onto Sepulveda. After waving them around his car, Wendell opened his trunk and took three $10 bills from the purse. Looking over the top of the trunk's lid he saw that the young man was eyeing him skeptically again, maybe even suspiciously. Wendell took another ten from the purse then closed the trunk.

—Here's forty dollars, he said. For the bike and your trouble.

The kid rubbed his head for a second. Then took the money.

—All right, mister. But you should drive more carefully.

The encounter finished almost as fast as it had begun. The young man carried the wreckage of his bike to the sidewalk. Wendell got back in his car and put it in gear. With a glance in the rearview mirror, he confirmed that no one was behind him, then he sped up Sepulveda with his stomach churning and his hands trembling, driving faster than he should, paying no mind to the black sedan that pulled out of the gas station when he passed it.

Charlie

CHARLIE WAS PARKED ON SOUTH Bentley about twenty feet from the intersection with Hamilton Boulevard. He had moved from the front seat to the back, where he would be less conspicuous, but where he still had a clear line of sight to the diner.

Whoever was pulling the strings might have been an amateur, thought Charlie, but he was shrewd. The diner was on a block of small office buildings housing lawyers, accountants, architects, and the like. Since it was Sunday afternoon, the offices were empty, the diner was empty, the streets were empty. From any rooftop or office window, a lookout would be able to watch for the approach of the police to make sure it was safe for the bagman on the way in; and the empty streets would make it easy for the bagman to ensure he wasn't being followed on the way out.

Looking at his watch, Charlie saw it was a quarter 'til two. Though it was probably seventy degrees outside, it must have been over eighty in the car, and he had begun to sweat. Reluctant to lower the window all the way, Charlie took off his suit coat and laid it on the seat beside him, then resumed looking through the binoculars feeling sanguine. The call with the blackmailers had gone as he had hoped, Prentice had been successful, and Charlie was in position with time to spare. All he had to do now was wait.

In Charlie's experience, most younger detectives complained about being on a stakeout. Naturally, they found it boring to be sitting in a car or in front of an apartment window for hours on end, day after day. But they also viewed it as a waste of time. With more than a hint of frustration, they would wonder out loud why we weren't searching premises, or rousting known associates, or hauling a suspect downtown for another round of questioning.

What they didn't seem to understand was that the inaction was the whole point. The searching of premises, rousting of associates, and interrogation of suspects were all forms of direct engagement. By definition, they were adversarial, putting both the innocent and the guilty on their guard. Sometimes, it was better to take a step back into the shadows, as it were, where one could simply watch and wait. The longer you were out of sight, the greater the chance a suspect would resume some old activity, reach out to a coconspirator, make a mistake. The simple fact was that a stakeout was often the best way to get the job done. Sometimes, it was the only way.

When he was working a detail with a junior detective who seemed especially antsy, Charlie liked to tell the story of the Windsor case. Peter and Candice Windsor were a wealthy, middle-aged couple with a large beautiful house in Bel Air and a son in college. In May 1926, Mr. and Mrs. Windsor had planned a weekend of golf in Palm Springs with their best friends, Burt and Polly Baker—another handsome, wealthy couple who lived in Bel Air, but with a daughter in high school. At the last moment, Mrs. Windsor came down with a migraine, so Mr. Windsor and the Bakers had gone to Palm Springs without her. They played golf all day on Saturday and spent Sunday morning by the pool. On Sunday night, when they returned to Bel Air, Windsor found his wife lying dead on the living-room floor. At some point on Saturday, she had been shot in the chest with her own gun—a .25-caliber automatic, which an officer recovered from the bottom of the pool.

Charlie and his partner at the time, Jack Bocock, were assigned to the case. At first glance, it seemed a robbery gone awry. There was no sign of forced entry, but the Windsors were in the habit of leaving their back door unlocked. An estimated forty thousand dollars in jewelry had been taken from a box on top of the bureau—the bureau where Mrs. Windsor also happened to keep her gun, hidden in a drawer among her lingerie. The working hypothesis was that a thief, expecting the house to be empty, had entered through the back door, gone to the bedroom for the jewels, heard some noises downstairs, come down to investigate, gun in hand, and shot Mrs. Windsor when she suddenly appeared in the living room.

Simple enough.

But there were a number of things that bothered Charlie and Jack. First was the fact that a ruby necklace worth almost five grand had been left behind in the jewelry box. Mr. Windsor said that nothing other than jewelry appeared to be missing from the house, suggesting the perpetrator had been a jewel thief. But a jewel thief wasn't likely to leave one of the most valuable pieces behind, even if he was in a rush.

Then there was the matter of the gun. Yes, it had been in the bureau where the jewels were. But what had led the thief to open the lingerie drawer in the first place? There were no signs of any other drawers having been searched. Confusing matters further was the discovery that the gun had been shot twice. It took them awhile to even find the second bullet, since it was almost fifty feet behind Mrs. Windsor, buried in the moldings where the wall met the ceiling. For the working hypothesis to be right, what they were looking for was a thief who was sophisticated enough to case the house and find the gun, but amateur enough to leave rubies in the jewelry box and shoot wildly when surprised.

Finally, there was the matter of Mr. Windsor's composure. When they had initially spoken with him, he didn't just exhibit shock and grief. He was clearly agitated about something, turning red when he should have turned pale, and pale when he should have turned red.

Charlie and Jack didn't have to knock on more than four doors to learn that neighbors suspected Peter Windsor and Polly Baker of having an affair. Candice Windsor apparently suffered from *lots* of migraines, Burt Baker was often away on business, and the Windsors' car had been seen coming out of the Bakers' driveway more than once with a woman in the passenger seat who looked more like Mrs. Baker than Mrs. Windsor. Windsor clearly had a motive, and he knew where his wife kept her gun. There was just one problem: his alibi.

Charlie and Jack spoke to a slew of people who confirmed Windsor was in Palm Springs from his Saturday morning tee time until the hotel bar closed at one in the morning.

They began to investigate the possibility of a contract killing. They looked into Windsor's bank transactions, telephone records, and acquaintances. But they couldn't find a connection between Windsor and a known criminal. They couldn't find an unaccounted-for transfer of money. They couldn't even find an unusual meeting or call.

Then one day, a month after the murder, Charlie and Jack returned to the station to find Marisol, the Windsors' housekeeper, waiting. Initially, she had confirmed Windsor's assessment that nothing in the house was missing other than the jewels. But having begun to help Mr. Windsor dispose of Mrs. Windsor's things, she realized there *was* something else missing: a fancy pink negligee from a boutique in Beverly Hills.

When Jack and Charlie shared this little tidbit with their lieutenant, he shook his head.

—There you go, he said.

—There we go where? asked Jack.

—That's how the perp found the gun: He was looking for the underwear.

—Looking for the underwear?

—Listen, said their lieutenant. You two have spent four weeks trying to pin this on the husband, and all you've got to show for your work is some neighborly gossip. Well, maybe you haven't found anything substantial because you've been on a wild-goose chase of your own making.

Maybe this is exactly what it looked like from the start: a botched robbery. What you've probably got here is a jewel thief with a thing for ladies' underwear, or an underwear thief with a thing for jewelry. Either way, it's time to move on from the husband.

But Jack and Charlie couldn't move on. Something was queer with Windsor and they wanted to know what it was. They decided to watch his house. They could only do it on their own time, which, practically speaking, meant from eight at night until one in the morning. It was a narrow window, but they figured it was the right window. Whoever Windsor had worked with to commit the killing would show up eventually, and most likely at night. All they needed was a lucky break.

Jack and Charlie took turns, one night on, one night off. When it was Charlie's turn, he would park across the street with his binoculars and a Thermos of coffee that Betty had prepared. Sometimes, Charlie would get out of the car and circle around back to see what Windsor was up to. Most nights, Charlie would find him sitting alone in his living room, drinking himself to sleep. Then one night a black car pulled into the driveway at 10:30. With his pulse rate up, Charlie circled the house only to discover the late-night visitor was the family chaplain. Charlie watched as the two of them knelt on the carpet and prayed, not fifteen feet from where Mrs. Windsor had been shot.

After three weeks of watching and waiting with no result, Jack and Charlie went for a drink. Neither wanted to be the first to give up, or to admit they might have been wrong. So, they acknowledged without discussion that their time was almost up.

—One more week? Jack asked.

—One more week, Charlie agreed.

Their lucky break came on Charlie's second-to-last shift, and he almost missed it. It was shortly after eleven. Charlie was pouring the last of his coffee into a cup when out of the corner of his eye he saw a metallic flash. Worn down as he was, Charlie almost let it go. But then he put his coffee on the dashboard, climbed out of the car, and quietly walked up the Windsors' driveway. And there, leaning against the house, was a bicycle. What Charlie had seen was the silver pedal reflecting light from a streetlamp. Charlie worked his way to the back of the house. Through the window of the brightly lit living room, he saw Windsor with his lover in a heated conversation followed by a fitful embrace. Only it wasn't Polly Baker. It was her teenage daughter, Lucy.

Now, it all began to make sense. Lucy was the woman in the passenger seat who had looked more like Mrs. Baker than Mrs. Windsor. She had been left behind by the Bakers when they went to Palm Springs, so she had the opportunity. And no wonder the first shot had gone two feet over Mrs. Windsor's head. The kid had probably closed her eyes when she pulled the trigger.

The next day, they asked Windsor to come downtown so they could give him an update. He could tell that something was wrong when they had him wait in an interrogation room instead of an office. But that was just as well. They wanted him to know that something was wrong. After letting him sweat for half an hour, they joined him.

At this point, they knew the why of Mrs. Windsor's killing; what they didn't know was the how. But they were confident that would come, and quickly. Because after telling Windsor they'd seen him with the girl, they would explain what would have to come next. Talking to her. Talking to her parents. Talking to Windsor's son back at Harvard. Talking to his partners at the office and his friends at the country club. Within a matter of days, everyone would know about his sordid little affair with his best friend's teenage daughter, a crime itself in the state of California. The mere thought of it would make a guy like Windsor start to unravel.

He unraveled even quicker than they thought he would. As soon as Charlie mentioned what he'd seen through the window, Windsor was weeping. Yes, Lucy had been there the night before, he admitted with his hands over his face. Yes, they'd had an affair. And yes, she had killed his wife.

Charlie and Jack gave each other a nod.

—So, said Jack, you told Lucy where to find the gun. And when your wife decided she wasn't going to Palm Springs, you called Lucy to let her know your wife would be alone in the house.

—What? asked Windsor dropping his hands, staring back in disbelief. Told her about the gun? Called to let her know? I had no idea what she was going to do!

—Are you trying to tell us a seventeen-year-old girl acted on her own?

—Look, I admit we had an affair last spring. But after two months I ended it. I told her I didn't want to see her anymore—because I loved my wife. But she wouldn't believe me. She kept talking about the life we were going to lead when we could finally be together. It never occurred to me she might shoot Candice.

—To be frank, Mr. Windsor, it's a little hard to swallow that you had no idea. Because you sure acted like you knew something, from the first time we talked to you.

He nodded his head.

—I don't doubt that, Detective. Because I did know when we talked. I knew that Lucy had killed my wife within half an hour of finding her body.

—How was that?

He took a breath.

—A few months ago, I came home one night when Candice was playing bridge at the club and found Lucy in our bedroom wearing Candice's lingerie and her ruby necklace. I couldn't believe it. I practically had to dress her myself and drag her down the stairs. As she was leaving, she said she didn't want the rubies anyway—because they clashed with her blue eyes.

Charlie and Jack both leaned back and stared at Windsor with seasoned skepticism.

—I'm telling you, Detectives, she's crazy! What can I do to make you believe me?

That evening, they took Windsor home and had him call Lucy, saying he needed to speak with her urgently. Charlie and Jack situated themselves in the den off the living room with the lights off and the door open. Twenty minutes later, she came in the back way. It didn't take much for Windsor to get her talking. She was proud of everything she had done, proud of the initiative she had shown on his behalf. On their behalf. To top it all off, when Charlie and Jack arrested her, she was wearing Mrs. Windsor's pink negligee under her dress.

Sometimes, as Charlie would tell his younger colleagues, what the whole case hinges upon is seeing a glint of metal late at night after four weeks of waiting.

At two o'clock, Charlie watched Evelyn get out of a taxi and walk into the diner with the purse. Through the window, he could see her take the booth on the far left, order a cup of coffee, and drink it. He watched her pay, leave empty-handed, and climb back into the taxi, which she had instructed to wait. Shortly after her taxi pulled away, two teenage girls entered the diner. Ten minutes later, a blue Buick convertible pulled up and a small man with glasses climbed out.

—Here we go, said Charlie to himself.

Even if Charlie hadn't been told about the blue convertible, he would have known the man with the glasses was their target. For one, he had the physique of a man with a higher-pitched voice but he also appeared uneasy. Once he was seated in the booth, he had trouble finding the purse—at one point disappearing entirely under the table, his diminutive stature proving an advantage. Having found the purse, he ate and paid for a sandwich, then returned to his car. All the while, he exhibited nervous behavior: fidgeting when he was in the booth, looking up and down the street when he exited the diner, checking his rearview mirror twice before pulling from the curb. When he made the turn at the intersection, he took one last look over his shoulder then accelerated—right into Billy.

The accident was a thing of beauty. From a block away, Charlie could hear the metal of the bike meeting the metal of the Buick's grille. He could hear the smack on the windshield when Billy was catapulted across the hood, and his grunt as he rolled to the pavement. In fact, it was so convincing, Charlie almost sprang from his car to make sure that Billy was all right. Then he saw Billy glancing up before tossing the hammerhead under the Buick. That had been Billy's idea: to have the head of a ballpeen hammer in his hand, so he could slap it against the windshield when he rolled across the hood in hopes of cracking the glass.

When the bagman ran around his car, Billy played it just right, looking shaken but not seriously injured. As they began hashing it out, Charlie put his jacket back on, switched to the front seat, and started the car. Taking the left onto Hamilton, he passed the diner and slowed as he approached the accident. When the bagman waved Charlie around his car, Charlie resisted the temptation of taking a good look at him, confident he'd meet him soon enough. Charlie drove two blocks down Sepulveda and pulled into a gas station. Backing up to the air pump, he got out and pretended to fill his tires with air, all the while watching the road.

When the Buick finally drove by, Charlie climbed in his car and followed from half a block back, the empty Sunday streets now playing to *his* advantage. In this manner, he followed the Buick for five miles on Sepulveda. Then, somewhat to Charlie's surprise, the bagman led him onto a residential street in Brentwood Glen, where well-kept houses were separated by hedges and shrubbery.

When the bagman pulled into the driveway of a small Craftsman-style house, Charlie drove past, circled the block once, then parked. Turning off the engine, he adjusted the rearview mirror so he could watch the house. He would give the bagman ten minutes before he followed him in.

Was the decision-maker there? Charlie wondered. In a way, it would be easier if he wasn't. It would be easier to put pressure on the reluctant partner. But Charlie suspected the decision-maker would be there. He wouldn't be able to resist. He would want to take the bag from his accomplice and spill the money onto the kitchen table. Then he would pour them both a glass of something special so they could congratulate each other, prematurely. Charlie allowed himself a small smile as he imagined their rude awakening.

At 2:45, Charlie figured he'd given them enough time. Getting out of his car, he began walking toward the house. As he passed a hedge, he was vaguely aware of a shadow suddenly in motion. Almost out of curiosity, he turned to look.

Litsky

AFTER TWENTY YEARS in this town, Litsky could believe almost anything. He'd seen morons get rich and geniuses go broke. He'd seen works of art get tossed in the trash heap and bits of schlock capture the hearts and minds of America. He'd seen love affairs between consenting adults that defied the imagination. Anyone who tried to make sense of it was writing their own ticket to the loony bin. But having come to believe that absolutely anything that could happen in Hollywood would happen in Hollywood, what Litsky couldn't believe was his own good luck.

Back in February, when Litsky had admitted, hat in hand, that he'd given his notice a little prematurely, a little impulsively, a little ill-advisedly, Humpty-Dumpty hadn't been interested. He'd slammed the door of his crummy little office right in Litsky's face. But that wasn't the worst of it. The worst of it was Humpty spreading word around town that Litsky had quit because he was about to sell an Academy Award–winning photo of Olivia de Havilland to the brass at Selznick. This resulted in what you might call a loss of confidence. What Tinseltown rag in its right mind would hire Litsky, if whenever he shot a front-page indiscretion, he turned around and sold it to the studios?

—Beat it, the publishers said in unison.

Litsky had been down on his luck before, but this was a new level of down. Where the water dripped from the ceiling and the mushrooms grew underfoot.

Then one night at O'Malley's of all places, when Litsky had just about reached his last nickel, he found himself sitting next to Wendell Whatshisname. Wendy was the sort of guy who sipped a whiskey at the bar, then guzzled half a pint of peppermint schnapps alone in his bedroom. The sort of guy who sighs so much, he has to break out a handkerchief every five minutes to clear the fog from his glasses. The sort of guy to whom Litsky normally wouldn't sell the time of day.

When Wendy was still working over at MGM, he liked to pull up a stool next to Litsky and act like they were comrades in arms. What a laugh. When you're taking stills for the studios you walk onto a set where the lighting has already been adjusted and the furniture already arranged. You screw your camera onto a tripod and take your time adjusting the focus. When you tell your subjects to smile, they smile. When you tell them to frown, they frown. And when you tell them to stare into each other's eyes like star-crossed lovers, they stare into each other's eyes like star-crossed lovers. The whole racket is one step above taking portraits on the boardwalk.

Real photographs aren't taken on stage sets. They're taken under fire. They're taken at night in the street when you've got three seconds to get your angle, get your shot, and get out of there. A guy like Wendy wouldn't know how to take a picture in the city of Hollywood any more than a house cat would know how to hunt a gazelle on the savanna. Yet, this sorry son of bitch, this putz who put the putz in putzery, ends up with a golden goose flopping right into his lap: photographs of twenty actresses just as God made them. And where were these photographs? Sitting in a drawer gathering dust. Litsky couldn't believe it. In fact, it so completely tested his credulity, he insisted upon seeing them with his own eyes, despite the fact that meant having to pay a visit to Wendy's apartment.

Which, as it turned out, wasn't an apartment. It was a two-bedroom cottage on a cushy street near Brentwood.

Wendy claimed to live alone, though from the look of the place you would have thought he lived with his mother. Litsky had obviously been out of line when he'd imagined that Wendy's photos were gathering dust, because somewhere close at hand was a vacuum cleaner with ten thousand miles on the odometer. And when they came through the door, Wendy insisted they take off their shoes.

—So, said Litsky in his socks. Where are these pictures I've heard so much about?

Wendy went down the hallway and disappeared into his bedroom. Two minutes later he was back with a folder, which he put on the cocktail table. When Litsky opened the folder, there was Luise Rainer gazing up at him with a pubic triangle that would have brought a smile to the face of Isosceles. Next was Bette Davis—yes, *that* Bette Davis—without a stitch of clothing. It made your head spin. You could have seen ten of her movies and never once imagined her in the nude. But that was the beauty of it. The fact that a naked picture of Davis was virtually unthinkable is what made it so valuable. Fanning the pictures out, Litsky shook his head in wonder. Before him were women whose reputations were as white as their skin. Which is to say as white as snow. White as ivory. White as a pitcher of cream. It was a cash-register-ringing symphony in that color without hue.

And if that wasn't enough, when Litsky reached the final picture, who was staring back at him but the whitest of them all, Miss Olivia de Havilland. The only word for it was justice.

Looking up from the pictures with every intention of grinning from ear to ear, Litsky was startled to find Wendy in dismay. From Wendy's expression, Litsky could tell he was wrestling with feelings of regret, maybe even self-disgust for the part he had played in this ingenious little enterprise.

Litsky felt a touch of panic. Panic that Wendy might do something crazy like destroy the pictures before they could be put to good use—and on moral grounds, no less. So, instead of the grin, Litsky adopted the most appreciative expression he knew how to adopt.

—Oh, these are fine, he said. They're genuine works of art, Wendell.

Wendy looked at Litsky with a touch of surprise.

—You think so?

—Think so!

Litsky pulled out the picture of Bette Davis and set it on top of the pile.

—Look at this one. I mean, you really caught Miss Davis here. Her imperiousness. Her intelligence. Her dry sense of wit. I think it's a better portrait of her than I've ever seen, and I've seen plenty. Because it's not relying on all those props and costumes to tell you what you're looking at. It's just Bette Davis, and indisputably so. Why, you can almost hear her about to sum up the evening in a phrase.

—I hadn't thought of it that way. . . .

—You wouldn't have. Because you're too modest. And look at the framing! The way you've got her a little off center. It adds to the feeling that we've caught her in a moment of artistic reflection.

—Given the circumstances, there wasn't a lot of flexibility. I had to make do.

—And make do you did, Wendell. Make do you did.

As it turned out, Litsky didn't have to worry about Wendy destroying the pictures. Convincing him to capitalize on his own handiwork took all of five minutes.

Wendy had probably spent his whole life doing what he was told. And not just by his mother. He'd been doing what he was told by teachers and bosses, by bus drivers and usherettes. He had dutifully followed the instructions of street signs and owner's manuals and the religious pamphlets that were slipped under his door. If someone with the slightest hint of authority had told Wendy what to do, he had done it without a moment's hesitation or a word of complaint. But maybe, at long last, he'd had it. Since being fired from MGM, he'd been standing at the edge of his future hoping someone would come along and give him a shove. So Litsky shoved him.

The plan was simple. They would contact each of the subjects and offer to return the photos in exchange for a small consideration, a sort of finder's fee. And they'd start with Dehavvy.

Later that night, when Litsky was climbing the crooked stairs to his crooked little room, the door on the second floor opened and his land-lady poked out her head. She was a Polack through and through. If you couldn't tell by her accent, you could tell by the smell of her cooking, which after twenty years had worked its way into every mattress in the building. Her tenants may have come to Los Angeles from around the world, but once they were asleep they *all* dreamt of kielbasa.

—Thanks for waiting up, said Litsky.

She replied with a frown.

—The rent, Mr. Litsky.

—I know, he said walking past her.

—You are two weeks late.

—I already gave you my camera as security. What do you want now? My hat?

—I do not want your hat. I did not want your camera. This is not a pawnshop. It is an apartment building. With good people.

—The best people, said Litsky, as he turned out of view.

Given that back in the old country her progenitors had paid rent for twenty generations, you might have thought she'd be a little sympa-thetic. And you'd've thought wrong. She was as heartless as a Rockefel-ler. It was like she was trying to even the score on her family's behalf by squeezing the pennies out of every poor bastard who washed up on her doorstep.

Litsky let himself into his room and took a good look around: cracked plaster, busted bedsprings, a leaky faucet. He should be charging her to live in it.

Litsky hung his hat on the nail that doubled as a hook on the back of the door. He kicked off his shoes and dropped on his bed with his hands behind his head. Then he finally let himself smile.

Twenty actresses at five thousand dollars a pop. That made his cut fifty grand. If they collected from one actress a week, they would have raked all of it in by Thanksgiving. And come Christmas? He'd have put this crummy town behind him, once and for good. He'd get a new car and head straight for the border. Maybe he'd spend a week or two in Mexico City in a real hotel with clean sheets and room service. But then he'd head south to Puerto Vallarta or Acapulco. Or maybe one of the smaller towns a little farther down the coast where the gringos rarely ventured and a sawbuck can run a marathon. He'd buy a little place on the beach with a hammock strung between two palm trees. He'd put two senoritas on the payroll so they could take turns cooking his meals and rubbing his feet. Maybe he'd take up fishing or reading or some other stupid pastime to fill the long, lazy afternoons. Either way, he'd be doing nothing for nobody. Nothing for nobody nohow.

<hr />

When Sunday finally rolled around, at a quarter to twelve Litsky was in Wendy's house sitting on the couch with his new partner. To be honest, there had been a moment that first night when Litsky had considered picking up Wendy's pictures and walking out the door. After all, what was Wendy going to do about it? Put up his dukes? Call the cops? Not a chance. Then the whole kit and caboodle would be his.

But hold on a second, Litsky had said to Litsky. *Maybe it's better to have Wendy in the mix. Maybe it's much better. . . .*

So, when they prepared the package of photographs for Dehavvy, Litsky had Wendy write the note. When Litsky went to drop off the package, he'd borrowed Wendy's car. In another few minutes, it would be Wendy who made the call to the hotel. And at two that afternoon, it would be Wendy who went in the diner to pick up the cash. That way, on the off chance things went sour, all roads would lead to Wendy. The note, the car, the call. And should the cops find their way to Litsky, he wouldn't have the slightest idea what they were talking about.

Litsky could see his partner was a little nervous. So, despite the early hour, he poured him a glass of whiskey. Then he poured one for himself just to be polite.

—It's time, said Litsky, after they'd emptied their glasses.

Wendy looked at the phone with a pout.

—Why does it have to be me?

—It's like I told you: Dehavvy and I have met once or twice. If I call, she could recognize my voice.

Wendy nodded, looking only halfway convinced. But after throwing back another ounce, he dialed the number and asked for Miss de Havilland.

Litsky leaned toward Wendy so he could hear the other end of the line. After four rings, the phone was answered by a woman. As soon as she said hello, Litsky felt a surge of electricity run through him. It started in his ears, ran down his spine, spread to his fingertips, then circled back—making every hair on his head stand to attention and every nerve ending tingle. Because the voice on the other end of the line wasn't Dehavvy's. It was the blonde's! The one with the scar who came in the lobby and went out the kitchen door: Miss Evelyn Ross.

How many nights in the last month had Litsky found himself staring at the ceiling unable to fall asleep because she was whispering in his ear? *What big teeth you have, Mr. Litsky. What a nice little mustache you have, Mr. Litsky. Here, let me help you with that, Mr. Litsky.* If she was the one taking the call for Dehavvy, it's because she was the one who would be bringing the money.

Oh, it was justice all right. Divine justice. Litsky was so overcome with a sense of euphoria he didn't hear Wendy's question.

—What's that?

—They want to know how they can be sure we'll deliver the

photographs after they drop off the money, Wendy repeated with his hand over the mouthpiece. What do I tell her?

The answer came to Litsky in a flash.

—Tell her we're going to use her as a reference.

It was too perfect. They would have the blonde vouch for them, confirming to each of the other actresses that they'd been as good as their word. And in so doing, they would get the blonde's hands a little dirty while forcing her to relive the feeling of having been bested over and over again.

Wendy hung up the phone looking relieved the call was done, but nervous about something else.

What now, wondered Litsky.

—What if she changes her mind? What if she calls the police? What if they're waiting for me at the diner?

—Don't you worry about that, said Litsky in a soothing voice.

Litsky explained how he'd be in an office building across the street, and he'd give Wendy a call at a pay phone a mile from the diner as soon as the coast was clear. To boost Wendy's spirits, Litsky had shaken his hand. And while putting on his shoes, he'd reminded Wendy not to worry.

—I'll be in the building right across the street.

But shortly after two, when Litsky dialed the pay phone to give Wendy the all clear, he wasn't in the building across the street. He was in Wendy's living room.

Litsky didn't think for a minute the blonde would call the cops. She wouldn't chance it. Not if she had Dehavvy's interests at heart. But if, for some crazy reason, she did chance it, and the cops were waiting for Wendy when he came out of the diner with the money, then it was only a matter of time before they would make their way to his house to seize the photographs. And what good would that do anyone?

So, earlier that morning, when Wendy was getting ready to make the phone call, Litsky had taken the opportunity to unlock the terrace door. When Wendy had pulled out of the driveway, Litsky was hiding in the shrubbery. And when Wendy answered the pay phone, Litsky was sitting on Wendy's couch.

As soon as he had given Wendy the all clear, Litsky went down the hallway to Wendy's bedroom. While Wendy was getting the money, Litsky would find the photographs and take them someplace safe. In a way, he'd be doing Wendy a favor. Because if the cops picked him up and couldn't find any photographs, there'd be less of a case against him. A little less of a case. And if the cops didn't come, Litsky could slip the photos back in their hiding place without Wendy being the wiser.

Entering Wendy's bedroom, Litsky shook his head in amazement. It was as mothered as the rest of the place. No dust on the windowsills. No creases in the bedspread. Not even yesterday's shirt on the floor.

On the wall behind the headboard in artful arrangement were thirty stills, no doubt some of Wendy's favorites from his illustrious career. It was either a shrine to Hollywood, or a shrine to himself. Litsky wasn't sure which would be worse.

Litsky crossed to the bureau and went through the drawers one by one, being careful to put the neatly folded clothes back in their neatly folded piles, which is harder than it sounds. When he was finished with the bureau, he went through the bedside tables. Then he looked in the closets, where in addition to eight suits there were two kimonos.

—Wouldn't you know it, said Litsky.

Glancing at his watch, Litsky saw it was almost twenty past two. The diner was only about five miles from Wendy's place. If Litsky wasn't careful, Wendy would discover him in the house. Or worse, the cops would. It was time to up the tempo.

Across from the bedroom windows was a large Chinese cabinet. Litsky opened its doors, revealing thirty or forty little drawers. In something of a panic, he began opening each and every one of them until he realized the photographs wouldn't fit in the drawers anyway. But what about the top of the chest? After looking around the room for a chair, Litsky ran down the hall to grab one from the dinette set. Back in the bedroom, he climbed up and looked on top of the chest. There was no dust there either! And no photographs.

For Christ's sake, thought Litsky. It had only taken Wendy one minute to retrieve the pictures. They had to be somewhere within reach. Figuring he only had a few minutes to spare, Litsky lifted the mattress, but there was nothing under it. When he set the mattress back down he saw he had messed up the blanket. He tried to straighten it out, but whenever he smoothed a crease in one spot, he created a crease in another.

Glancing at his watch again, Litsky saw he was out of time. Returning the chair to the dinette and slipping out the back door, he ran around the house and resumed his position in the shrubbery.

—It's going to be fine, he said to himself.

The blonde would never call the cops. It wasn't her style. Wendy would return with the money. Come Christmas, Litsky would be in Mexico. Then one lazy afternoon when he had nothing else to do, Litsky would drive into town, find some touristy joint, and buy one of those postcards that says *Buenas Dias from Sunny Mexico*. On the back he'd write: *Sometimes the door opens twice*. And he'd send it with love and affection to Miss Evelyn Ross care of the Beverly Hills Hotel.

Let her stare at the ceiling for a change.

As Litsky was congratulating himself on this idea, Wendy's car turned into the driveway at thirty miles an hour. Skidding to a stop, Wendy practically jumped from the driver seat and ran to the front door—empty-handed. Expecting the boys in blue to be hot on Wendy's tail, Litsky stepped farther back into the shrubbery, but they didn't appear. After five minutes, he went and knocked. And knocked.

Finally, he could hear footsteps approaching the door, but Wendy didn't open it.

—It's me, Litsky shouted.

The door eased upon, revealing a Wendy looking even whiter than Dehavvy—and still in his shoes. Litsky followed him into the living room.

—What happened? Did you go to the diner? Didn't she show?

Wendy looked at Litsky as if he hadn't understood the questions.

—I need to brush my teeth, he said then disappeared down the hall.

—Brush your teeth! exclaimed Litsky.

But then he noticed that a side table had been knocked over and the sliding door was open. On the bricks of the terrace was what appeared to be a pool of vomit.

When Wendy emerged from the hallway, he looked like the tooth-brushing had restored his sense of self, meager as it was. Still, he collapsed on the couch.

Litsky tried to lower his voice, as if talking to a child.

—Why don't you tell me what happened, Wendell.

—I went to the diner.

—Yeah?

—And I got the bag.

—Yeah?

—That's it, he said.

Litsky looked around the room.

—So where is it?

Wendy waved lethargically.

—In the trunk.

Litsky retrieved the handbag from the Buick and set it down on the cocktail table right in front of Wendy.

What with the shoes on Wendy's feet, the side table on the floor, and the vomit on the terrace, the whole *mise-en-scène* was decidedly out of keeping with Wendy's penchant for orderliness. But whatever evidence of disarray prevailed, it seemed to Litsky that the handbag on the table provided an effective counterbalance, organizing the room, if you will. Hell, it organized the whole goddamn town.

—Is the money in there? Litsky asked.

Wendy nodded.

—Do you want to do the honors?

Wendy shook his head.

—All right then.

After shoving the whiskey bottle and glasses aside, Litsky hesitated for a moment. Then he picked up the purse, turned it over, and spilled out the contents. The bills had been bundled in stacks of fifty so they landed on the table in a disorderly pile of green and white bricks. Bricks you could throw through the windows of every man in town who'd ever given you the high hat. Bricks you could use to build a house on the beach in a small town south of Acapulco with two maids and a hammock.

—Take a good look, Wendy, said Litsky. That's our future laying there.

—It's somebody's future, said somebody.

Litsky and Wendy turned toward the sliding door, where a tall, good-looking man was standing with a smirk on his face and a revolver in his hand.

When Litsky had been sitting in O'Malley's and heard Wendy's story about the photographs, when he'd come to the house and seen them with his own eyes, he just couldn't believe it. He couldn't believe his own good luck. But when the last photo in the pile had turned out to be Dehavvy, Litsky had thought maybe, just maybe the wheel of fortune might be turning. This morning when the blonde had answered the phone, he was almost sure of it. And when the money spilled on the table, it seemed plain as day that after twenty years of watching people cash in their lottery tickets, Litsky was finally going to get to cash in his.

He should have known better.

Finnegan

IT HAPPENED ON THE LAST night of 1934, Finnegan's fifth year on the force, when he was still the new man on vice and High Collar O'Connor was chief. Shortly before midnight, they had all gathered in the shadows across the street from Ainsley Fuller's casino in the Pacific Palisades. High Collar had just sent ten boys in uniform around back and everyone was waiting for his signal when gunfire erupted from inside the casino—the rattling report of a machine gun followed by pistol fire.

—Go! Go! Go! the chief shouted.

And go they went, with patrolmen fanning out across the gravel drive, Finnegan and the rest of the boys from vice busting through the front door with their guns in their hands, rushing headlong into who knew what.

For two months the chief had been planning the raid. Fuller had been opening and closing casinos since the first years of Prohibition, evading arrest at every turn. This time, High Collar meant to have him. New Year's Eve was the biggest night of the year for the casino, and word was that Fuller liked to be on hand to count the receipts. So High Collar had commandeered a platoon of patrolmen to surround the building. At the stroke of midnight, the vice team would storm the door when everyone was singing "Auld Lang Syne." Then High Collar would walk right up to Fuller, wish him a happy new year, and serve him with the warrant.

But it just so happened that on the very same night for some of the very same reasons, Tommy Torrino had come to rob the casino. Having been let in the back door by an inside man, Tommy's boys surprised two of Fuller's guards and led them at gunpoint down the back stairwell into the basement, where the money was being counted. While Tommy covered the guards and the bean counters, two of his crew bound their hands and feet. The other two stuffed the cash into postal bags.

Everything was going like clockwork. The whole operation had only taken twenty-five minutes. But when they were headed upstairs with the money in hand, Bruiser Allen suddenly appeared at the top of the steps holding a tray full of sandwiches. Throwing the sandwiches down on Tommy's head, Bruiser slammed the door. From halfway up the stairs, Tommy and his crew could hear Bruiser calling for reinforcements. When the door opened again, they would all be sitting ducks. They had no choice but to reverse course, heading back through the basement in search of another way out. Coming upon a second staircase, they charged up and out of it, finding themselves on the floor of the casino as the countdown was about to begin.

For a moment everyone froze. The dealers, the croupiers, the waitresses, even the band. Given the crowd, Tommy could see he had no clear path to the exit, so pointing his machine gun in the air, he strafed the ceiling. As a chandelier crashed to the floor and customers ran for cover, Fuller's muscle tipped over a craps table, drew their weapons, and began exchanging fire with Tommy's men. That's when the vice boys came through the door, adding a third vector of gunfire to the melee.

When the smoke finally cleared, all of Tommy's men were dead, as were three of Fuller's, and two uniformed officers. High Collar had the bodies laid out on the veranda and the survivors assembled on the dance floor, a motley crew of two hundred people, most of them in evening dress. The vice team had gone from room to room until they had gathered everyone up, with one exception: Ainsley Fuller, who was nowhere to be found.

Every story has a moral, Doherty used to say, *but most have more than two.* In the aftermath of the Palisades raid, Finnegan counted three.

The first, which came as something of a revelation to the young officer, was that everyone was guilty.

In Fuller's casino there were at least fifty employees. These included not only the dealers, croupiers, and cashiers, but bartenders and waitresses, cigarette girls and musicians—all guilty of knowingly participating in an illegal enterprise. And there were more than a hundred gamblers, some playing roulette, some playing craps, some winning, some losing, all of them breaking the law.

But that wasn't the half of it. Because emanating outward from the gaming tables were concentric circles of iniquity. For the gentlemen who were cashing in their chips after a winning night, there was an elegant middle-aged hostess in a long red dress providing invitations to the private rooms upstairs, where beautiful young ladies were waiting to help them celebrate. For those in the sixth hour of a winning streak who were feeling their energy flag, there were two men willing to sell them a second wind. And for the losers, there were never fewer than three men willing to lend a little capital at interest rates that would make the bankers on Wall Street blush.

Fuller's casino was an elaborate, intricate, and well-oiled machine of human failings. Everyone there understood that. They all had come to either indulge in or profit from a sin. And they all had some semblance of a smile on their face, even the losers. As Finnegan took in the scene, the one thing for certain was that old or young, homely or handsome, the men and women assembled on that dance floor were guilty. Every last one of them.

The second moral Finnegan gleaned that night was that money was like the wind.

When you read the papers, you come away with the impression that money is so substantial—like a block of granite or a hunk of steel. After all, it's what's used to build factories, high-rises, and reputations. It expunges pasts and secures futures, and forms the barriers that separate whole swaths of society for centuries at a time.

But as Finnegan looked at this sad collection of sinners, some of them cowering and craven, others indignant and impatient, what revealed itself to him was the extraordinary velocity with which money moved and the circular route on which it traveled. This fellow over here, the one in the tuxedo covered in plaster dust, probably arrived with a fistful of $20 bills. Within minutes, they had scattered in every direction like game hens beaten from the brush, some of them lost at the roulette wheel and others at baccarat. The losses were disbursed among the winners, who in turn handed the bills to the bartenders, pushers, or prostitutes in exchange for champagne, drugs, or companionship. The bartenders, pushers, and prostitutes handed a cut to their employers, set aside a little for food and rent, then presumably expended the rest on passions of their own.

According to the secretary of the treasury, the government puts money in circulation, and no truer words were ever said. For round and round it goes, passing from one hand to another until it ends up back where it began, or some semblance thereof. And when it moves, it moves quickly without a sound, a second thought, or the slightest hint of consequence. Like the wind that spins a windmill, money comes out of nowhere, sets the machinery in motion, then disappears without a trace.

And the third moral? That one revealed itself to Finnegan a little more slowly.

―――――

As the assembled crowd grew weary on the dance floor, High Collar paced before them in a state of righteous fury. It was bad enough that after two months of planning Fuller had slipped through his fingers. What was worse was the likelihood that Fuller had been tipped off. And if Fuller had been tipped off, then he had been tipped off by someone under High Collar's command.

Fuller had been the prize. Without him in custody, what High Collar saw when he looked at the dance floor was a mountain of paperwork and a month's supply of headaches. Take all the well-dressed citizens. Hailing from Beverly Hills and Bel Air, they'd all prove to be members of the Rotary Club, deacons of the church, friends of the mayor. Were he to haul them downtown and charge them with gambling, the phone would start ringing ten minutes later and it wouldn't stop ringing till Easter. Most of Fuller's employees were small fry. Yes, the bartenders, waitresses, and cigarette girls were willing participants in an illegal enterprise, but in the eyes of most juries, they were just average Joes doing their jobs. And as to those who were no strangers to the police station— like the muscle and the girls from upstairs—they would get booked, printed, and released the following morning, as usual. Which meant that High Collar was tempted to let them all go.

Not Tommy, of course. He'd be given the full measure of the law. Caught red-handed during an armed robbery where two police officers were killed, he'd probably end up swinging from a rope. And there was some comfort in that for High Collar. But it galled him too. Because by sending Tommy to the executioner, High Collar would, to some degree, be meting out justice on Fuller's behalf. The fact that High Collar's squad just happened to show up on the night of the robbery would prompt cynics and enemies alike to say the chief was in Fuller's employ. And Fuller would do nothing to dissuade people from that conclusion. In fact, he'd encourage it by insinuation, knowing full well that the mere appearance of having High Collar in his pocket would be enough to make robbers and rivals think twice, providing him a measure of protection he didn't even have to pay for.

—Get him out of here, High Collar said to Doherty.

Doherty and Finnegan each grabbed one of Tommy's elbows and led him across the veranda, past the bodies of his crew.

—How's the wife and kids? Tommy said to Doherty as they went down the steps.

—Shut up, said Doherty.

On the gravel drive, the parking valets were gone. In their place were an ambulance, two meat wagons, and six cop cars parked at every angle of the compass. Off to the side were officers Meehan and Jackson, each holding shotguns, standing watch over five postal bags of cash.

When Doherty put Tommy in the back seat of the cruiser, Tommy had a big grin on his face.

—What's so funny, Doherty demanded.

—Nothing, said Tommy.

But he kept on smiling. And when Finnegan climbed behind the wheel, Tommy leaned a little forward, lowering his voice as if to take Finnegan into his confidence.

—There were six bags, Officer. Me and the boys took *six* bags out of that basement.

Then he leaned back with the smile of a man whose expectations of human nature had been met, once again.

For in the midst of all the confusion, with gunfire coming from three different directions, women screaming, tables toppling, and chandeliers shattering, someone had picked up one of the bags of money. Some bartender or musician—or maybe a cop—had picked it up and set it aside to be retrieved later.

You might think this little anecdote was just further evidence of moral number one: that everyone was guilty. And that's exactly the conclusion Finnegan drew, at least at first. But in the weeks that followed, whenever his thoughts returned to the Palisades raid, he found himself dwelling on the confluence of unpredictable events that had suddenly placed a small fortune in someone's unexpecting reach. In the years before that night, this bartendermusiciancop had probably shown up for work and done his job without much complaint. He'd probably paid his bills on time, lived within his means, and treated others fairly, if not always kindly. Then suddenly, through a fluke of the universe, he found himself in a situation he had neither asked for nor imagined—to be standing in the middle of mayhem with a bag of money at his feet.

There, thought Finnegan, was moral number three: Windfalls come to the watchful. Maybe this maxim was true wherever you went, but it was especially true in Los Angeles. In this city, where money was blowing like a hurricane, a chance to get rich was bound to present itself to an honest man eventually. The key was to bide your time. To punch the clock and file your taxes, all the while waiting for the confluence of unpredictable events to put the bag at *your* feet.

When Finnegan heard that the Beverly Hills Hotel was looking for a new head of security, he figured it was just the sort of place where fortune might trip over your shoes. So he resigned from the force and took the job. Once at the hotel, he played his part. He let the manager treat him like a peon. He helped heiresses find their dogs. He ushered drunks out of the bar, overcoming the temptation to bang their heads as he put them in the back of a cab. And all the while, he waited. He didn't think too much about what he was waiting for because he was confident he'd know it when he saw it. And that's exactly what happened.

That Wednesday, Finnegan had been sitting in his office minding his own business when the house phone rang. It was Williams at the front desk saying that some old Mexican had shown up with a package for Olivia de Havilland, insisting he deliver it by hand. When Finnegan came out, the old man became a little less insistent and a lot more nervous. By the time Finnegan had him in his office with the door closed, the old man was ready to tell him everything. Which, admittedly, wasn't very much: A slim man with a slim mustache driving a blue convertible had offered him a few bucks to deliver the package.

After sending the old man on his way, Finnegan sat in his office weighing the envelope in his hands. He bent it back and forth. Inside were almost certainly photographs, and they weren't from the studio. Finnegan would have steamed the envelope open, if he'd had to, but the morons hadn't bothered to seal it. So, he bent back the flap, slid out the pictures, and gave a whistle.

The note that included the blackmailers' demands wasn't even typed. Someone was very confident, thought Finnegan, or very sloppy. Either way would work in Finnegan's favor.

The one thing that surprised him was the size of the demand. Surely they could have asked for more than five grand. Maybe the reason they didn't was because this was going to be the first of several demands. Or maybe, just maybe, de Havilland's photographs were part of a larger scheme.

Finnegan considered offering his services to the actress. It wouldn't be that hard. He could deliver the envelope now, then ask her later in the day if everything was all right. When she tried to downplay her distress, he could remind her that he was an ex-cop. She would confide in him, eventually. He was sure of it. Then he could work the whole thing from the inside.

But he only considered that route for a few minutes. Because once he was on the inside, it might be hard to get back out. The best way to play it was from the outside, where de Havilland wouldn't even know of his involvement. She wasn't likely to go to the cops or the studio. She'd take the call on Sunday at noon, ready and willing to hand over the money, and he'd be waiting in the wings. It meant biding his time for a few days more, but biding his time was something he'd become good at. Very good at.

Finnegan slipped the pictures back in the envelope and sealed it.

Then he wound his way to Bungalow 8 and delivered the package in person.

Later that day, Finnegan could see how flustered de Havilland had become. She was pacing the lobby and wringing her hands. She was obviously waiting for someone whom she'd chosen to confide in. That someone turned out to be Evelyn Ross.

Of course it did.

Miss Ross had intrigued Finnegan from the start. As a routine matter, he received a list of everything that had been placed by a guest in the hotel safe. The previous September, he had noted with some bemusement that having arrived alone, she had stored a large engagement ring and a diamond earring without a pair. He also noted when she had withdrawn the earring the next afternoon and returned a few hours later with some shopping bags. A husband hunter, thought Finnegan. It wasn't the first time he'd seen it. With the last of her money, she was putting herself up at a fancy hotel in the hopes of getting herself well hitched. Finnegan would keep an eye on her. If she was overly forward with the guests at the bar, he'd politely show her the door.

But in the weeks ahead, Finnegan saw her refuse the advances of more than a few eligible men, including a producer, an actor, and an oilman from Texas. She wouldn't even let them buy her a drink. If she was looking for something, it wasn't a husband.

In December, when de Havilland moved into the hotel, Finnegan learned that she'd come at Ross's encouragement; and in the weeks that followed, the two of them often went out into the night. Maybe she swings that way, thought Finnegan. But in the end, that didn't add up either. Because if one of the two women was in the habit of coming out of the other's room in the morning, Finnegan would have learned it soon enough from the chambermaids.

Fortunately, the house car log was another list that Finnegan had access to. The purpose of the log was mostly to keep the drivers honest, but it also provided Finnegan the occasional glimpse into the movements of the hotel's guests. The night the photographs were delivered, Finnegan pulled the log to see where Ross had been spending her time. It was mostly a survey of popular restaurants, nightclubs, and tourist attractions. But Finnegan was intrigued to find that on that very day—at practically the same moment that de Havilland was receiving her envelope—Ross was with Marcus Benton at Selznick Studios. What would Selznick's general counsel want with Ross, wondered Finnegan, and vice versa?

At any rate, de Havilland had turned to Ross for help. The question now was whether Ross would try to handle the blackmailers herself or turn to someone else. The answer was someone else.

How Finnegan had laughed when Charlie Granger walked through his door. What was he? Sixty-five years old and four years off the force? In his baggy old suit, he looked like a guy who was about to ask you for a dime or maybe directions, not a guy who was going to solve your problems.

Finnegan didn't hold back. He told Charlie everything he'd learned from the old Mexican. Or, almost everything. When Charlie thanked him, Finnegan took a beat, then asked if Charlie was going to tell him what was in the envelope. What a touch that was! He could practically see Charlie puffing out his chest when he demurred—Sir Galahad coming to the aid of a damsel in distress.

Don Quixote, more like it.

On Friday, another messenger arrived at the front desk asking to see Miss de Havilland in person. This one was sent straight to her bungalow, because he was a manager from Wells Fargo—with a briefcase in his hand.

On Saturday night, Finnegan took himself out for a steak and two martinis at Musso & Frank's.

Come Sunday morning, he arrived at the hotel early, keeping an eye on the lobby. Sure enough, Charlie arrived at quarter past eleven in order to be with Ross when the call came in. Shortly before noon, Finnegan climbed in his car, drove out the hotel's entrance, pulled over, and waited.

To pass the time, he turned on the radio. It was another report of Germany grabbing land without any repercussions to speak of, this time in Czechoslovakia. It made you sort of wonder what would happen if the good old USA were to grab a chunk of Canada, or maybe the whole thing. Who was going to stop us? And why, for that matter.

Around one fifteen, Charlie finally drove out of the hotel, alone. Finnegan turned off the radio and followed from two or three cars back. He could just as easily have ridden on his fender, because Charlie barely gave his rearview mirror a glance. Driving at a normal pace, Charlie went west on Santa Monica, took a left on Overland Avenue, and a right onto Hamilton. He slowed down a bit when he crossed South Bentley, then slowed even more when he passed a diner. Finnegan could see him leaning to his right to peer inside. Then Charlie circled the block and parked on South Bentley, near the intersection where he could see the diner diagonally. Finnegan drove past Charlie, took a right on Hamilton, did a U-turn, then parked so he could see Charlie and the diner.

Shortly before two o'clock, Miss Ross arrived by taxi, entered the diner with a handbag, and left ten minutes later empty-handed. Ten minutes after that, the blue convertible pulled up. This time, the driver wasn't a slim man with a slim mustache. He was a clean-shaven fellow with glasses and the look of an insurance adjuster. He went to the same booth, ordered a sandwich, then walked out with the handbag tucked under his arm. Finnegan watched as he climbed in the Buick and pulled away from the curb. Looking to his left, Finnegan was surprised to see Charlie hadn't started rolling. Finnegan looked back at the Buick just in time to see it make a right onto Sepulveda—and smash into a kid on a bike.

What the hell? thought Finnegan.

But when the kid stood up, Finnegan broke into a smile. It was Billy, the wannabe stuntman who did some driving for the hotel.

—Not bad, Charlie. Not bad at all.

As the adjuster and Billy worked out their differences, Charlie turned onto Hamilton and passed the diner. He drove nice and slow around the scene of the accident, and Finnegan drove nice and slow right behind him. When Charlie pulled into a gas station on Sepulveda, Finnegan parked in front of a laundromat where he could watch as Charlie put enough air in his tires to fill a zeppelin. When the Buick finally drove by, Charlie pulled out behind the Buick, and Finnegan pulled out behind Charlie, one big happy family.

Their little caravan drove about four miles north then turned into the neighborhood of Brentwood Glen. When the Buick and Charlie took a right onto one of the narrow residential streets, Finnegan idled at the corner. From there, he could see the Buick turn into a driveway and Charlie continue past. Once again, Charlie would circle the block, which would give Finnegan a few minutes to get situated. Pulling over, he slipped on a pair of leather gloves, pocketed his blackjack, and jogged down the street until he was across from the driveway with the Buick.

Looking around, Finnegan was pleasantly surprised. It wasn't Bel Air, but all the houses were on half-acre lots with hedges to screen the traffic. From a break in the hedgerow, Finnegan watched Charlie drive past and park a hundred feet up the road. Charlie didn't immediately get out of his car. He seemed to be sitting tight for a moment, which gave Finnegan a chance to move a little closer to Charlie's car.

As Finnegan waited with his blackjack in hand, he wondered how hard he should hit Charlie. Back when they were on the force, vice and homicide didn't exactly get along, but Charlie had never given Finnegan cause for aggravation. And he was an old man, which suggested a certain amount of restraint. But Charlie had put himself in this position. And, above all else, he was a plodder. If Finnegan gave him a tap and he came to fifteen minutes later, he wouldn't turn tail. He'd plod ahead, pursuing the same ends with the same tiresome resolve. So, when

Charlie walked past, Finnegan stepped out from behind the hedgerow and hit him almost as hard as he could.

Charlie collapsed like a woman fainting at news of a scandal. Out of reflex, Finnegan found himself reaching out to catch him. With his arms under Charlie's, Finnegan dragged him back to his car and laid him on the pavement. Taking the keys from Charlie's pocket, he opened the trunk. On the floor of the trunk was a crowbar. Figuring it might come in handy, Finnegan took the crowbar, then he hoisted Charlie off the ground and dropped him in.

Before closing the lid, Finnegan patted Charlie down. He found a revolver in Charlie's shoulder holster that, like Charlie, was an antique. Slipping the revolver under his belt, Finnegan was about to close the lid when he thought to check Charlie's ankles for a backup. But of course, he didn't have one. Charlie would have found carrying a backup to be too unsportsmanlike.

—Sweet dreams, Don Quixote, said Finnegan.

Then he closed the trunk and locked it, leaving the key in the lock.

One nice thing about neighborhoods like this, thought Finnegan, is they're quiet. That's what the locals were paying for: quiet streets and quiet bedrooms to complement their quiet consciences. Walking along the quiet sidewalk past the quiet neighbors, Finnegan entered the quiet driveway where the Buick was parked. With the crowbar in hand he made his way around back in search of a rear entrance. He came upon a terrace with a sliding glass door that was partially open. Finnegan was totally exposed, but the two men inside had their backs to the window. After gently putting the crowbar on the patio table, Finnegan reached for his gun. On second thought, he reached for Charlie's. Then he quietly stepped inside.

The adjuster and his accomplice didn't notice Finnegan enter. They were too engrossed in the money that was piled on the table.

—Take a good look, the accomplice was saying to the adjuster. That's our future laying there.

—It's somebody's future, said Finnegan.

When they turned, Finnegan almost laughed aloud. It was like a bit out of Laurel and Hardy—the two of them both looking surprised but in entirely different ways. The adjuster had the open-mouthed look of a child stunned into silence. Unable to make sense of what he was seeing, a series of questions raced through his mind: *Who is this man? Where did he come from? And why is he holding a gun?* The accomplice, who had the slim mustache and who looked a little familiar, exhibited the surprise of a sage. Which is to say, his face expressed disbelief for all of three seconds. Then his eyes closed as the initially unbelievable was recognized as the inevitable. However they registered their surprise, the two looked as guilty as any two men that Finnegan had ever seen.

—Litsky! remembered Finnegan with a grin. Jeremiah Litsky.

The adjuster turned to Litsky, his mouth still open.

—Do you know each other?

—Shut up, said Litsky, while taking a step to his left in a hapless attempt to obscure the money from view. Detective Finnegan, isn't it? What seems to be the trouble, Officer?

—Would that I were still a member of the force, Jerry. That would make things so much easier for you and your friend. But these days, I'm more of what you might call an independent operator.

Litsky closed his eyes again as another wave of wisdom broke over his head. When he opened them, he stepped back to his right and gestured at the table.

—If you're looking for the money, it's right here. You can take it.

—You're nice to mention the money, Jerry. I think I will take it. After all, it's not really yours. Is it, gentlemen?

It was a rhetorical question, of course, but the adjuster shook his head in order to confirm that the money wasn't theirs as Litsky gave him a frown.

Using the barrel of the revolver as a pointer, Finnegan instructed the two men to take a seat on the couch. Once they were comfortable, he began moving slowly about the room.

This was a technique he had learned from Doherty. When they would enter the interrogation room, Jack would move unusually slow. He would slowly take off his coat and hang it on his chair. He would slowly take off his watch and set it on the table, then slowly roll up his sleeves. It would set almost anyone on edge, even the hardened sorts. Because they could tell exactly what was coming. And the slower Doherty moved, the more anxious they'd become.

Keeping the revolver trained on the two sinners, Finnegan backed up to the sliding door and slowly closed it. After slowly drawing the curtains, he slowly went about the room turning on lights. He could see the effect it was having on both of them. Litsky's right knee was bouncing up and down like a piston, and the adjuster was beginning to wheeze.

—Now, said Finnegan, where might I find the photographs?

—The photographs? asked Litsky.

Shifting his aim by a few degrees, Finnegan shot one of the urns on the bookshelf.

The adjuster let out a groan.

—Didn't your mother tell you it was impolite to mislead a man with a gun? asked Finnegan.

—You're not going to shoot anybody, said Litsky, and with such confidence.

So Finnegan shot him.

Grabbing for his foot, Litsky let out a howl. Then he began to whimper.

—Oh, please, said Finnegan.

Litsky should have been thankful Finnegan hadn't shot him in the knee!

The adjuster's chest was heaving now. He was having such a hard time catching his breath, he could barely say what he so desperately wanted to say: that the photographs were in the Chinese cabinet in the bedroom—in a secret drawer with a dragon painted on it.

—Stay right where you are, gentlemen.

Finnegan went down the hall into the bedroom and opened the doors to the cabinet. An orange dragon was painted on a piece of lateral scrolling that separated the upper and lower drawers; but it turned out to be a drawer itself. Sliding it open, Finnegan removed the folder and flipped it open.

—You bide your time, he said to himself.

When Finnegan returned to the living room, all was not as he had left it. The adjuster, for one, was leaning back on the couch looking very inanimate, while Litsky was crawling toward the front door. When Litsky looked up and saw Finnegan, he let out another whimper, then collapsed with his face on the carpet.

Keeping his gun trained on Litsky, Finnegan went over and felt for the adjuster's pulse. Bringing this comedy to its natural conclusion, the adjuster had died of a heart attack. Finnegan went back around the couch.

—The irony of this situation, Jerry, is that when I came here today, I had no intention of killing anyone. But your friend here seems to have dropped dead of his own accord. And rightly or wrongly, in the eyes of the law I will be deemed culpable for his demise. So, I'm afraid that leaves me little choice.

Before Litsky could respond, Finnegan shot him three times in the back. Then he went around the couch and shot the adjuster once in the chest for good measure. In the quiet that followed, he looked down at the empty handbag sitting beside the pile of money.

That won't do, he thought.

In a closet in the kitchen, he found paper grocery bags that had been neatly folded and stowed for future use. Taking one back to the living room, he put the money in the bag.

For a moment he wondered if he should take the handbag with him and dispose of it somewhere else. But then a thought occurred to him and a smile formed on his face. After putting the handbag on the couch,

Finnegan got down on his haunches, undid the adjuster's belt, and pulled his pants down around his ankles.

—Wait until the boys from homicide see this, Finnegan said with a grin. They won't know what to think.

Then he slipped out the back and headed for Charlie's car.

Once Finnegan was back in his own car, he drove straight to the hotel. He spent the next hour walking the grounds, talking to everyone he met, saying things like *I've been looking for you all day*. When he went into the restaurant, he said he had just come from the garage. When he went into the garage, he said he'd just come from the pool. There was little chance that the sordid situation soon to be discovered in Brentwood Glen would find its way back to him. But it couldn't hurt to reinforce the collective impression that he'd been busy on the property that day. At six o'clock, he finally bid everyone good night and headed home.

In Finnegan's last year on the force, he and Doherty had busted a young architect who was trying to subsidize his failing architecture firm through the sale of various narcotics. When they went to make the arrest, they found him in the hills off Mulholland Drive living in a house of his own design—a white box of a building with a small bedroom and a large open space including a kitchenette, living area, desk, and floor-to-ceiling windows overlooking the San Fernando Valley. The home of the future, he called it.

—The home of the future, my eye, said Doherty as they led him out the door in cuffs.

But for Finnegan that's exactly what it looked like. And in all the right ways.

In Finnegan's experience, to give a typical house a thorough search for drugs or cash could take six men six hours. Never mind that there might be seven rooms, an attic, and a basement. In each room there were closets, cabinets, bureaus. There were old trunks and traveling cases. Containers for flour, sugar, coffee, and tea. Shoeboxes, toolboxes, and books that might have been hollowed out. And everywhere you looked there was stuff. Clocks and vases that had been handed down. Trophies that had been won. Family photographs. Knickknacks and mementoes. A vast collection of a thousand objects representing memories and aspirations that were equally out of date. Most houses, Finnegan had come to believe, were an attempt at suicide in slow motion. When you finished the search, you wanted to take a shower. Not just to wash off the dust, but the greasy residue of human desperation.

But when the time came to search the architect's house, it took Finnegan and Doherty less than an hour. Because there was practically nowhere to hide anything! There was just one closet in the bedroom, four cabinets in the kitchen, and three drawers in the desk. There wasn't even a carpet to look under. And there were no photographs, knickknacks, or mementoes. It was like his life was in a constant state of just beginning.

While the architect was sitting in his cell awaiting trial, Finnegan would occasionally drive up to Mulholland, let himself into the house, and walk around. He'd sit on the couch and watch the lights coming on down in Sherman Oaks. A few nights, he even slept there.

From a pal in real estate, Finnegan found out that the architect's place was worth less than he'd spent to build it. As his pal said: It was a house in which no one wanted to live in a neighborhood to which no one wanted to drive. When the architect was convicted and the bank foreclosed, Finnegan was right there waiting. He bought it with everything in it for a song.

Finnegan wasn't much of an accumulator, but when he moved into the architect's house, he took the opportunity to toss what little he'd kept from his past. After all, the past wasn't a place he had any intention of returning to. It was the future that held his interest.

As Finnegan drove homeward up Benedict Canyon, the part of the future he was thinking about was his next step. Would he send a note to de Havilland tomorrow with a new set of demands? Or would he wait a week and let her stew over it? Why not let her stew, he thought as he pulled into his driveway.

Getting out of his car, Finnegan removed the grocery bag from the trunk and let himself into the house. The first thing he was going to do was pour himself a drink. But before he'd taken three steps, he came to a stop. Because sitting on his couch looking out at the view was Miss Evelyn Ross.

Charlie

WHEN CHARLIE CAME to consciousness, it was dark and hot and every part of his body ached. It took a moment for him to realize he was in the trunk of a car, a car that wasn't moving. His own car, if he was lucky, someone else's, if he wasn't. Slipping a hand under his jacket he confirmed with relief that his pistol was still in its holster, making it more likely he was in his own car.

Most of his body hurt for mundane reasons: because he was awkwardly positioned in a cramped space; because there was something lodged under his hip; because he was at a time in life when even the simplest effort could initiate a groan. The pain in his head, however, was not mundane. He had been hit with a blackjack, and not by an amateur. Gently probing the back of his head, Charlie was relieved to find no matting of his hair as there would have been from blood. But he had a first-class bump and it was tender. It would remain tender for a week or more, a reminder of just how cavalier he'd been, how pleased with himself, and how out of practice.

When Charlie had been waiting in the car, he had done his own version of spilling the money on the table, his own version of raising a glass and congratulating himself on a job well done, prematurely.

That's what happens when you're out of the game. Without the disciplines of daily work and the habits they instill, you start to lose the instincts that make you a professional. When he had sensed the shadow moving from behind the hedge, he hadn't even raised an arm to defend himself. He had just turned to see what was coming. But brooding over his mistakes was just another sign of how out of practice he was.

Charlie turned his attention to getting out. If this was the trunk of his own car, there would be a tire iron and a flashlight. The flashlight was easy to find because it was the object that had been lodged under his hip, adding to his discomfort; but for the life of him, he couldn't find the tire iron. In his pocket all he had was a penknife. Switching on the flashlight, Charlie aimed the beam awkwardly toward the latch of the trunk and pried at it, futilely. The latch held so fast, the trunk must have been locked.

Charlie lay back.

Had he ever been in a more humiliating position? Ambushed on his own ambush and locked in the trunk of his own car. Was he actually going to start calling for help? It was tempting to lie there, baking in the afternoon sun until he slipped into unconsciousness, eventually expiring from heatstroke or dehydration. At least then he wouldn't have to witness his humiliation come to its natural conclusion: being saved by some old woman walking her Pekingese.

But what about his grandson in New Jersey? And what about the promise he had made to Evelyn? And what, finally, of revenge? Was he so past his prime that he'd lost that old desire to give back what one had received, only ten times over?

—Hello! he shouted, resigned to seeking help but unwilling to say the word. Hello! Hello!

Given his prone position, the shouting took more out of Charlie than he expected. He wouldn't be able to do it for long. Instead, he began pounding on the inner lid of the trunk with the butt of the flashlight like a prisoner banging on a pipe. But after he had been pounding for ten minutes straight, Charlie felt himself being overtaken by a wave of dizziness and nausea brought about by some combination of the heat and the darkness and his injury. Charlie couldn't afford to pass out. So, he stopped pounding and breathed slowly. Once he had regained his physical composure, he resumed the hammering, but intermittently, hitting the inner lid of the trunk fifteen times every five minutes.

The gaps between hammerings gave Charlie time to think, time to think about what he should have been thinking about from the very start: Who had hit him? Somewhere in the back of his mind, he had assumed it was the decision-maker. But if it was the decision-maker, where had he come from? Charlie had been watching in the rearview mirror the entire time. He would have seen if someone had left the house and crossed the street. It had to be someone else.

Charlie closed his eyes, only half aware of how weary he'd become, his thoughts beginning to drift from one notion to the next. As his mind wandered, he sensed he was forgetting to do something, something he was supposed to do every five minutes. Worried he was late, he turned to look at the clock on the bedside table. But sitting there instead of the clock was a toy he had sent to his grandson for Christmas. Made of brightly colored tin, it was two young boxers in a ring who would shift their feet and throw little punches when you wound them up. What was it doing here? Charlie wondered. Had Caroline sent it back, deeming it inappropriate for the child? Charlie reached out and turned the key. As he did so, he could hear the light metallic sound of the key's teeth engaging the springs.

Then the lid of the trunk opened.

—Holy cow! You all right, Mr. Granger?

Emerging from his disorientation, Charlie shaded his eyes.

—Billy, he said in relief.

—Here. Let me help.

Without thoughts of embarrassment, Charlie took hold of Billy's arm and relied on the young man's strength to lift him up and out of the trunk. Once his feet were on the ground, he hovered for a moment, then carefully sat on the curb.

—What happened, Mr. Granger?

Charlie winced at the question. But he was too tired to fashion a version of events that spared his pride.

—I followed the subject here, he said. When I got out of my car I was sandbagged.

—Jeezo! exclaimed Billy, with more excitement than concern.

Refreshed by the cool air, Charlie felt his mind clearing.

—Billy, how the hell did you find me?

Billy nodded, as if he'd anticipated the question.

—After I took the tumble on that guy's hood, I told him how much my bike cost, just like you said I should. When he went to his trunk to get the money, I took the opportunity to grab his registration from the glove box. When he drove off, I waited a bit, then I threw my bike in the back of Mr. Skillman's truck and headed here in case you needed some backup. When I saw your car, I figured everything was copacetic. But after half an hour, with no one comin' or goin', I got a little worried. I snuck over to your car, and that's when I saw your keys in the trunk. I hope I done all right, Mr. Granger.

Charlie smiled.

—You did more than all right, Billy. Do you have the registration on you?

—You betcha.

Billy handed it to Charlie along with the keys to Charlie's car. The registration said the Buick was owned by a man named Wendell Winter.

—What are we gonna do now? Billy asked.

Charlie looked up the street. The fact that he hadn't seen his assailant coming, that he'd been blackjacked so professionally, and that Winter's car was still in the driveway all combined to give Charlie a bad feeling.

—I want you to go home, Billy.

Billy looked at Charlie with disappointment.

—You sure, Mr. Granger?

—I'm sure.

To make the point, Charlie stood up and stuck out his hand.

—Thanks for your help.

—Anytime, Mr. Granger.

Charlie watched Billy walk up the street, climb into a pickup truck, and drive off. Then he went to his trunk and removed the gallon of water he kept in case his radiator gave him trouble. He unscrewed the cap, poured some into his palm, and splashed his face. Then he took a long drink. The water was hot and tasted of metal, but it satisfied nonetheless. Charlie put the water away, closed the trunk, and began making his way toward Winter's house.

When he reached the driveway, Charlie removed the gun from his holster and proceeded around to the back, where two chairs and a cast iron table were on a small brick terrace. On the ground was what appeared to be vomit. On top of the table was Charlie's tire iron. The sliding door that led into the house was closed, the curtains drawn.

As Charlie reached for the handle, he could see it had no signs of being jimmied, but he could feel the old certainty. The certainty that something ugly and irreversible had already happened. With his pistol leveled, Charlie slid back the door, brushed aside the curtains, and stepped inside.

He found himself in a living room that was small but well appointed. None of the furniture was shabby or misused. The three framed oriental prints on the wall to his left were hung at the exact same height. To Charlie's right was a gas fireplace with ceramic logs. Despite the fact it was gas operated, next to it was a set of brass fire implements to complete the aesthetic. On the shelves on either side of the fireplace were oriental urns, one of which had been shattered.

Everything in the room was in its place except for the broken urn, a toppled side table, and the two dead men. Winter was seated on a couch with his pants around his ankles and his head tilted to the side at one of the unnatural angles favored by death. Though he had a bullet hole in his chest, there was surprisingly little blood. The second body, which was fully clothed, was facedown in a crawling position just five feet from the front door. This one had bled plenty. There was a pool of it around his upper body and a trail of it leading back toward the couch.

Charlie listened for a moment, not expecting to hear anything, knowing that the perpetrator had come and gone—had come and gone while Charlie lay unconscious in the trunk of his own car. Charlie stepped around the blood to get a closer look at the second body, the decision-maker. He had three bullet holes in his back, but it looked like the trail of blood on the carpet originated from a wound in his foot. The man's face in profile struck Charlie as familiar. Getting down on his haunches, he studied the dead man's features more closely. Charlie knew him, all right. Everyone on the force knew him.

With a deepening sense of resignation, Charlie rose and made his way down the hall. Presumably, the man who'd ambushed Charlie and who'd killed Winter and Litsky had come for the photographs too. The photographs had probably been hidden somewhere, but the tidiness of the living room indicated there had been no need for the killer to toss it. One of the two blackmailers had told him where the photographs were.

Through the first door on his left Charlie found a guest room. It too was well appointed, its bed neatly made, everything in its place. So much so, one got the sense it had never been used, adding a rather mournful note to its thoughtfully prepared décor.

Opposite the guest bedroom was a guest bath that had been turned into a makeshift darkroom.

At the end of the hall was the master suite. Passing through the bedroom, Charlie entered the master bath first, just to confirm no one was in the house. Then he reholstered his gun and went back into the bedroom.

On the wall over the bed was an arrangement of framed movie stills, including an array of Hollywood's biggest stars, presumably taken by Winter. With a shake of the head, Charlie remembered how Prentice had admired the aesthetics of the de Havilland photographs, bringing a rebuke from Evelyn. At the time, Charlie had also found the remark inappropriate. But that was just another sign of how out of practice he was. For if Charlie had latched onto Prentice's remark, it might have led him in the direction of professional photographers in general and studio photographers in particular. He might have found Winter before the drop-off at the diner, before the journey to Brentwood Glen, before any of this.

Along one wall was a large oriental cabinet, its doors open. Inside were more than forty little drawers, each with its own pull, all of them closed. But in the middle of the drawers was an artistic scrolling that separated the cabinet's upper and lower half. This was a hidden drawer that had been pulled out, and that was empty.

Charlie considered going through Winter's closets, but there was no point in doing so. Instead, he returned to the living room. On the side table that was still upright was a telephone and a small black book. Using his handkerchief, Charlie picked up the book and flipped through it, confirming that none of the pages had been ripped out. Whoever had killed Winter must not have known him, because he was too professional to have left his name behind. This increased the likelihood of a grim possibility that had been gnawing at the back of Charlie's mind: the possibility that the assailant had followed Charlie here. Charlie put the address book back.

Surveying the scene for a second time, Charlie noticed Evelyn's purse on the couch beside Winter. Looking inside, he confirmed it was empty. He knew he should leave the purse where it was, but Evelyn's fingerprints were probably on it, so he picked it up. Charlie also knew he should call the police, at least anonymously. But he couldn't yet. He needed some time to consider his next steps, especially now that murder was involved.

Charlie went out the way he had come, using his handkerchief to close the sliding door. Picking up his tire iron, he rounded the house and made sure the street was empty before he crossed to his car.

On Wilshire Boulevard, Charlie pulled into a gas station with a telephone booth so he could make the call he'd been dreading.

—It's bad news, he said when Evelyn answered.

—What's happened?

Charlie rehashed how he had followed the bagman and been ambushed outside the bagman's house by an unknown third party who was now in possession of the photographs and the money. He didn't mention where the house was, or Winter's and Litsky's names, or that they had been killed. For now, the less Evelyn knew, the more insulated she would remain and the more freely he would be able to act.

—A third party? Evelyn asked.

—Someone who followed me, I suspect. I'm sorry, Evelyn.

—You have nothing to be sorry about, Charlie. How's your head?

—I'm all right.

—Good. Why don't you come back to the hotel and we'll figure out what to do next.

Charlie looked at his watch and saw it was nearly five.

—I'll be there at six.

Charlie had given himself an hour because he needed to go home. He needed to go home because he stank. He stank of sweat and gasoline from his hour in the trunk. But he also stank of failure and frustration, a bit of fear too.

There was no question about it. Someone had learned of their intention to buy back the photographs and had followed Charlie from the diner to the blackmailers. This put them back at square one. Only now, they would be dealing with someone who was less amateurish than Winter and Litsky, and decidedly more dangerous.

When Charlie got home, he went to his bedroom and shed his

clothes. As he laid his suit on the bed, he noted with cold irony the black smudges on the brand-new fabric from his time in the trunk.

After he'd taken a long shower, he dressed in one of his old suits, poured himself an ounce of bourbon, then called the Corral. He was relieved to find Billy there because he wanted to stress to Billy that he shouldn't mention to anyone where he had been that day.

—It'll be between us, Mr. Granger.

—Not even between us, Billy.

Charlie got back in his car and drove to the hotel. When he arrived, he intended to go straight to Evelyn's suite, but he was hailed by Prentice Symmons in the lobby.

—Ah, said the old actor lifting himself from his chair. There you are!

Charlie approached Symmons and took his hand.

—Congratulations, he said.

—Pfoof, said Symmons. It was nothing.

Thankfully, Symmons did not ask Charlie how things had gone on his end. Instead, he had something to relay.

—Evelyn asked me to meet you in her absence.

—In her absence?

—Yes, she went out.

—Went out where?

—I assumed you would know, said Symmons with a touch of surprise. Because she said she was going to reclaim the rest of the pictures.

Finnegan

Miss Ross had made herself comfortable. She was sitting with an arm draped over the back of the couch and her right leg draped over the left, naked to the knee. On the cocktail table in front of her was a bottle of whiskey and two glasses, one of which was empty. From where he was standing, Finnegan could see it was his best bottle of whiskey, and that she had poured herself a double, neat, facts that almost impressed him.

When he had walked into the house, she hadn't immediately turned. She had waited a moment then looked over her shoulder, languidly— her version, no doubt, of Doherty's slow movements, executed with a similar intent. Finnegan almost smiled to see it.

—Good evening, Mr. Finnegan, she said.

—Good evening, Miss Ross.

—Won't you join me?

Finnegan gestured to the grocery bag in his hand.

—I'll just put these things away.

Stepping into the kitchenette, Finnegan opened the refrigerator door and unloaded the money and the photographs onto an empty shelf while blocking her view with his back. When he closed the door, he folded the bag and set it on the counter. Then he came into the living area and sat at his desk rather than in one of the chairs by the couch.

Ross's right leg was bouncing lightly in the air, as if she had all the time in the world.

—If you don't mind my asking, Miss Ross, how did you get in my house?

—I broke a window.

—That's not very ladylike.

—I'm not very ladylike.

Finnegan smiled, then gestured at the whiskey.

—I'm glad to see you've helped yourself.

—Yes, thank you. It's delicious. May I?

She leaned forward and picked up the bottle, offering to pour him a glass.

—No, thanks, he said. I usually save that one for special occasions.

—But this is a special occasion.

—In what way?

—It's the beginning of a promising relationship.

Finnegan waved a hand dismissively.

—I wouldn't be interested.

She raised her eyebrows.

—Are you suggesting you're more interested in men, Mr. Finnegan?

—I'm suggesting I'm more interested in myself.

—That's a trait we share, she said with a narrow smile.

And he didn't doubt it. Not for a second. She was out for herself, all right. And it intrigued him. Yes, he had to admit, he felt a curiosity about Miss Ross that he didn't normally feel about women. Or people, for that matter.

—When I suggested we might be at the beginning of a promising relationship, she said, I didn't mean it in the romantic sense. I meant it in the professional sense.

—Oh?

—Concerning some photographs of Olivia de Havilland.

—Photographs of Olivia de Havilland?

She looked at him with a touch of disappointment.

—You don't strike me as the sort of man who beats around the bush, Mr. Finnegan.

—I'm not, I assure you.

—Then why don't we dispense with the bush-beating.

He gestured for her to talk as much as she wanted.

—You'll recall, no doubt, that an envelope was dropped off for Miss de Havilland a few days ago. It turns out that two men had obtained some compromising photographs of her. We agreed to buy the photographs back and delivered some money accordingly. But before these men could complete their end of the bargain, a third party stepped in, taking the money and the photographs. I happen to think that person was you.

—Miss Ross, I'm afraid I don't have the slightest—

—I know, I know. You don't have the slightest idea what I'm talking about. But you haven't let me get to the interesting part.

Putting her right foot back on the floor, she leaned forward with her forearms on her knees, almost like a man. And as she spoke her whole demeanor brightened.

Every year, she went on to explain, the studios spend millions of dollars on publicity. Millions to spotlight, amplify, and promote the movies they've produced and the stars they have under contract. But they also have funds that are earmarked for the opposite purpose—funds set aside for the burying of stories and the silencing of rumors. And it was in this business that Miss Ross suddenly found herself. Currently, she happened to be on the payroll of both Warner Brothers and Selznick International with a mandate to protect the reputation of the studios and their stars from what she referred to as unfortunate encounters, awkward entanglements, and ill-advised alliances. And yes, from compromising photographs too.

—I believe, Mr. Finnegan, that you are on the verge of an illicit enterprise. What I have come to say is that you can do the exact same thing you're intending to do for the exact same rewards, *legitimately*. I am given a budget for acquiring problematic stories and photographs. And these payments are not made at night in some back alley. They're made in the light of day, accounted for fully and included on the studio's financial statements—as an offset to taxes!

Finnegan leaned back in his chair. He had underestimated Miss Ross in every possible way. She wasn't a husband hunter or hanger-on. She was a kindred spirit. And, of course, she was absolutely right.

For anything that was done in Los Angeles illegally could be done in Los Angeles with the full backing of the law, as long as it was set up in the right way. Because the law, like everyone else in this city, was on the payroll. It punched its own clock, made its own concessions, and swallowed its own measure of bile in order to be a cog in the great golden machinery.

If you wanted to make a questionable dollar less questionably, all you needed was someone who could feed the money through the studios so that it came out with a pay stub. For in the United States of America there was nothing more exalted or sacrosanct than a wage.

—I don't know anything about these pictures of Miss de Havilland, said Finnegan. But if I understand what you're saying, if someone were to come into possession of such a photograph, the studios would be willing to pay a recovery fee on the actress's behalf.

—That's right. With me acting as agent.

—And, naturally, as agent, you would receive a commission.

—Would you trust me under any other terms, Mr. Finnegan?

Oh, he'd underestimated her all right. But he'd make up for that. In the days ahead, he'd learn everything there was to learn about Evelyn Ross. Not just where she was from and where she'd been. He'd learn about her little private passions too, whatever they were. Once he knew what he needed to know, he would tell her that he had stumbled on a compromising photograph. Only, he wouldn't start with de Havilland. He'd hold those photos back because *Gone with the Wind* was slated for release in the fall and the value of her pictures would only increase the closer they came to the premiere. One by one, he'd dole the pictures out and collect his finder's fees, ready to turn the tables on her when the time came.

—Well, you've certainly given me something to think about, Miss Ross.

—There, she said with a smile. What'd I tell you?

Leaning forward, she poured a double into the empty glass. Then she picked up the two drinks and brought them over to his desk. When she handed him his glass, she raised her own.

—To promising relationships.

Then she emptied her glass at a throw.

—To promising relationships, he agreed and emptied his.

As Miss Ross resumed her seat on the couch, Finnegan considered asking her out for dinner. Why not? He had never been a sucker for a pretty face, but gathering dirt on someone was always a lot easier once you'd heard the official story. The official story was designed to obscure what someone wanted to keep private. So, if you turned it inside out, it became a road map for all their shortcomings, regrets, and sins. Maybe he'd take her to Musso & Frank's for a steak and martinis, just to get her talking.

—Are you hungry, Miss Ross? he asked.

—I'm always hungry, she said.

But before he could make his suggestion, there was a loud cracking sound. As splinters of wood scattered on the floor, the front door flew open and there was Charlie Granger with his crowbar in one hand and his museum piece in the other. A Keystone Kop, right to the end.

Charlie

As CHARLIE DROVE UP Benedict Canyon, he was furious with himself. How could he not have seen it? He had even told Evelyn that someone had followed him to Winter's house. But no one could have possibly known that Charlie was at the diner. For someone to have followed him to Winter's house, they must have been on his tail all the way from the hotel. That meant they must have known exactly when Evelyn expected to receive the call from the blackmailers. And there was only person who could have known that: Finnegan. He must have opened the envelope before delivering it to de Havilland and read the blackmailers' note.

It was bad enough that Evelyn had pieced this together before Charlie had. What made it worse was that there were at least three things that should have raised Charlie's suspicions. First was the fact that when Charlie had mentioned Evelyn, Finnegan not only knew who she was, he knew the number of her suite. When Finnegan had said it, Charlie had been impressed with Finnegan's command of detail. But there were over two hundred rooms at the Beverly Hills Hotel, which meant over ten thousand guests coming and going over the course of a year. If Finnegan knew Evelyn's suite number, it was because he had looked it up, and recently.

Second was the fact that Finnegan hadn't asked for a description of the driver of the blue convertible. Of course he had asked for a description! Any rookie patrolman would have. It was one of the first things they taught you at the academy—to get a description of the suspect from a witness as quickly as possible, before his first impressions began to fade. Finnegan had asked the old Mexican for a description of the driver, all right, and had kept it to himself.

And then there was that crack about Charlie being retired. Yes, it was a little ridiculous for Charlie to have been so insulted by Finnegan's grammar. But embedded in Finnegan's choice of words had been evidence of a certain smugness. A smugness not simply of the young toward the old, but of a man with a piece of knowledge enjoying the spectacle of another man in the dark.

Charlie passed Finnegan's driveway and parked at the side of the road. In the interest of time, he would have liked to pull right up to the house, but he needed to assess the situation before making his presence known.

Getting out of the car, he confirmed his gun was in his holster and moved quickly toward the house. As there were no windows facing the road, Charlie worked his way around back and found himself on the top of an embankment with the house on his right and the hills dropping away to his left. Almost the entire rear wall of the house was a sheet of glass. With the onset of dusk, those inside wouldn't be able to see much of what was happening outside, while those outside had a clear view of everything happening within. In this respect, the wall of glass was not unlike the two-way mirror in Fairfield's bathhouse, or the ones at the LAPD.

From where Charlie was standing, it looked like the entire house was a single room. Finnegan was sitting at a desk with his back to the window, and Evelyn was sitting on a couch, facing him.

Charlie's first feeling was a surge of relief that Evelyn was unharmed. But his second feeling was one of unease. For the two were acting in the manner of old friends. Evelyn was smiling as she talked, and though

Charlie couldn't see Finnegan's face, he could see that he was nodding in agreement. Then Evelyn poured Finnegan a drink, carried it to his desk, and the two raised their glasses to each other.

With a feeling akin to vertigo, Charlie wondered if they were in it together.

No.

Charlie had been sloppy from the first. He had ignored certain indications. He had allowed himself to be followed from the diner and sandbagged in Brentwood Glen. But he wasn't so old and sentimental that he could have misjudged Evelyn to such a degree. He had witnessed her indignation over the photographs, and he was sure it had been genuine. If she was smiling now in Finnegan's company, it was to charm or persuade him, but without a full understanding of the danger he posed to her.

Charlie worked his way back around the house to the front door. He tried the knob and found it locked. He considered knocking, but after the visit from Evelyn, Finnegan would already have his guard up. Charlie jogged to his car, took the tire iron from the passenger seat, and returned to the door. Quietly, he wedged the claw of the tire iron into the frame, then drawing his gun with his right hand, he pulled at the tire iron with his left and kicked the door in a single motion.

As the frame splintered and the door flew back, Charlie found himself on the other side of the tableau he'd witnessed from the embankment, with Finnegan facing forward and Evelyn's back to the door. At the sound of the crash, both looked up.

Charlie took some pleasure from seeing the surprise on Finnegan's face—that old pleasure of having done the necessary legwork and drawn the necessary connections in order to secure the upper hand. The feeling was all the sweeter for Finnegan's prevailing smugness.

But then Finnegan began to laugh, heartily.

The sound of it made Charlie grit his teeth. As a young man, he might have felt the impulse to unload a round or two into Finnegan's chest.

—Charlie? said Evelyn, expressing her surprise—and the slightest hint of irritation.

It made Charlie second-guess his decision to bust in, but only for a moment.

—Keep your hands where I can see them, Sean.

Finnegan showed Charlie both palms then laid them on the desktop, all the while maintaining his irritating smile.

—Are you all right, Evelyn? Charlie asked.

—I'm all right, Charlie.

Charlie could see now that the building wasn't just a single room. With his gun trained on Finnegan, he moved sideways to the only door. Glancing in, he saw it was a small, empty bedroom. From there, Charlie returned to the center of the room.

Finnegan shook his head with a smirk.

—Your timing couldn't have been worse, Charlie.

—There's nothing wrong with my timing, Sean.

—Surely you can tell from Miss Ross's expression that she's as annoyed by your arrival as I am. That's because we were just coming to an understanding.

—Maybe she doesn't know who she's dealing with.

Finnegan shrugged.

—She seems pretty sharp to me.

Evelyn, who was staring at Finnegan, said nothing.

—So, what's next, Charlie, taunted Finnegan. Are you going to make a citizen's arrest and take me downtown?

—Sounds good to me.

—There's just one problem with the plan.

—What's that?

—Your gun's empty.

—Is it now, said Charlie while returning Finnegan's smug expression.

But even as he did so, Charlie could feel his confidence waver. When Sean had sandbagged him back in Brentwood Glen, he would have frisked him. That was the *first* thing they taught you at the academy. And when he frisked Charlie, he would have either taken the gun or emptied it.

Charlie shifted his aim a few degrees to the left of Finnegan and pulled the trigger. What emanated from his gun was a delicate and inobtrusive snap, a snap that would barely have been noticed but for the silence in the room. And it was one of the most dispiriting sounds that Charlie had ever heard. Unable to resist the temptation, Charlie pulled the trigger two more times to the same result.

Finnegan gave his characteristic shrug. Then, as he began talking, he casually produced his Beretta.

—It must feel a little awkward to bust through a door with a gun in your hand only to discover it's unloaded. But you know what's going to feel even more awkward, Charlie? When the boys in homicide discover where your bullets are.

Six shots, thought Charlie. He had even counted them. One through the oriental urn. Three in Litsky's back. One in Litsky's foot. And one in Winter's chest.

Finnegan used his automatic to wave Charlie further into the room.

—Why don't you come in and take a load off.

He said it just as he had in his office, only now with open condescension.

Charlie came around the couch. If he was ever going to lunge for Finnegan, this would be the time. But there was a good ten feet and the desk between them. With an amateur you might hope the unexpected action would startle him enough to slow his response. But there wouldn't be any startling Finnegan. He'd be waiting for Charlie's lunge, almost hoping for it.

Charlie took a seat on the couch beside Evelyn. As he sat, he could tell she had turned her head to look at him, but he couldn't bring himself to look back.

Finnegan waved his gun idly.

—I wasn't kidding when I said your timing was terrible, Charlie. Miss Ross and I were, in fact, on the verge of coming to a professional understanding that would have proved very profitable for the both of us. But I'm afraid your untimely arrival complicates things. In fact, I think we all may have to wait until after dark and take a drive along Mulholland.

—What happens on Mulholland after dark? asked Evelyn.

—Car accidents, replied Finnegan.

As Charlie felt a wave of helplessness, Finnegan smiled at him.

—You know, Charlie, you look more rattled than she does.

—I've been in a car accident, said Evelyn offhandedly.

—Well there you go, said Finnegan.

Far below on the valley floor, Charlie could see that the lights of a thousand residences had begun to glitter. In another fifteen minutes the transition from dusk to night would be complete.

As if Finnegan were reading Charlie's thoughts, he reached across his desk and turned on the desk lamp. Then without taking his eyes off Evelyn and Charlie, he rose and slowly walked to a standing lamp and turned it on. Then he slowly walked to a second standing lamp. But as he reached for this one, he missed it. With a shake of the head, Finnegan reached out again. Only this time, he suddenly grabbed hold of the lamp with a fist, as if he needed it for support. Though Finnegan continued to keep his eyes on Charlie and Evelyn, he no longer looked so smug. Instead, he looked mildly perplexed. Then his torso began to twist away from the lamp, and his eyelids blinked, and his pistol wavered between Charlie and Evelyn. Then Finnegan came crashing down, bringing the lamp with him. As he landed, the light bulb popped and his automatic went skittering across the uncarpeted floor.

As soon as Finnegan was down, Evelyn was on her feet, working her way toward him.

Unsure of what had just happened, Charlie rose, retrieved Finnegan's Beretta, then joined Evelyn beside his unmoving body.

—*Men*, she said with disdain.

When she looked up and saw Charlie's hurt expression, she added:

—Not you, Charlie. You're a man. *He's* men.

As they both looked down, Evelyn poked Finnegan in the ribs with the tip of her shoe. He didn't respond.

—A five-star Mickey Finn? Charlie asked.

—I never leave home without one.

Charlie shook his head in admiration.

—From outside, I watched you pour his drink and I didn't see you lace it.

—It was already in the bottle.

Evelyn stepped over Finnegan and headed for the kitchen. As she walked, Charlie noticed her limp was more pronounced.

—Are you all right? he asked.

She looked back.

—What's that?

—You seem to be limping more than usual.

—Oh, she said with a smile.

Reaching down, she took off a shoe and held it up for Charlie to see.

—My heel came off when I was breaking the bathroom window.

Putting her shoe back on, Evelyn limped into the kitchen and opened the refrigerator door.

—I thought so, she said.

When she turned she was holding a folder half an inch thick and a few bundles of bills. She put them on the kitchen counter beside a folded paper bag. As she unloaded more bundles, Charlie began to fill the bag. Once she had unloaded the last of the money and closed the refrigerator door, she faced Charlie across the counter.

—He was wrong, you know.

—In what way?

—Your timing couldn't have been better.

Charlie wasn't sure he deserved the accolade, but he thanked her, nonetheless.

—What now, boss? she asked.

What now.

Charlie looked back at Finnegan. The week before, if someone had asked Charlie what he would do were he to find himself in a situation like this, Charlie wouldn't have known what to say. But suddenly, he knew exactly what to do, and the clarity gave him a measure of cold-hearted satisfaction.

That old desire to get it back tenfold, maybe he hadn't lost it, after all.

—How did you get here? he asked.

—Taxi.

—All right. Here are my keys. My car's parked just up the road. You can take it back to the hotel. I'll come for it later. But first, I want you to wipe any surface on which you may have left fingerprints. Clean the glasses and put them away. Leave everything else where it is. Then I want you to wait here until I call.

—Where are you going?

—You don't have to worry about that. I'll call as soon as I can. It shouldn't be more than fifteen minutes. But, Evelyn, if Finnegan begins to regain consciousness at any time before I call, I want you to leave immediately. Do you understand?

—I understand.

—Okay, said Charlie. But there is one more thing: I'm going to need a few of the photographs from that folder.

Evelyn looked back at him in surprise, then shook her head.

—No, Charlie.

—It's the only way, he said. We're going to need the police to find some of them.

—How many?

—Five should do it.

After hesitating, she removed the folder from the paper bag and set it on the counter.

—Be careful with fingerprints, Charlie said.

Opening the folder, Evelyn fanned out the photographs with a fingernail. She took the last picture of de Havilland from the pile, then turned away.

—You pick, she said.

Using his handkerchief, Charlie took the top five photographs, then returned the rest to the folder and the folder to the bag.

As Evelyn was washing the whiskey glasses, Charlie went through Finnegan's pockets. In addition to Finnegan's car keys, he found a pair of gloves, which he put on, and a matchbook from the Beverly Hills Hotel. In Finnegan's desk, he found a manila envelope and some masking tape. He placed four of the photographs in the envelope and taped it to the bottom of one of the desk drawers. After wiping his own gun clean, he positioned it in Finnegan's hand to transfer Finnegan's prints, then wrapped it in a dishcloth he'd found in the kitchen.

When he was ready, Charlie met Evelyn's gaze.

—Don't forget: If he comes to . . .

—I leave.

Charlie nodded. But as he was turning to go, he noted Evelyn's uneven stance.

—Where's the heel of your shoe?

Evelyn raised a finger in the air.

—In the trash can in the bathroom.

As Evelyn went to retrieve the heel, Charlie went outside.

In the driveway it was dark and quiet. From the back of Finnegan's car, Charlie could only see the lights of one house in the near distance. Charlie stashed the wrapped revolver inside the trunk. Then he climbed in the driver's seat and drove back to Brentwood Glen. When he reached Winter's house, he pulled into the driveway, after confirming there were no signs of the police.

For the second time that day, he let himself in through the sliding door. Ignoring the bodies, he went straight to the telephone and dialed Finnegan's number. Evelyn answered on the first ring.

—Everything all right? he asked.

—Everything's all right.

—Good. I want this call to appear in the telephone company's records as lasting a few minutes. So don't hang up yet.

—I won't.

They were both silent.

Over the course of his career, Charlie had encountered illicit photographs, blackmailers, corrupt officers, and killers. But as they waited on the phone, Charlie found himself thinking of the last few days from Evelyn's perspective. He tried to imagine how she must have felt when she first saw the photographs of her friend, when she brought the money to the diner, when she found herself in Finnegan's house at gunpoint.

—Are you glad you stayed in Los Angeles, he asked a little wryly.

But when she answered she was deadly serious.

—At this moment, Charlie, I wouldn't be anywhere else in the world.

When Charlie hung up, he went into Winter's bedroom and placed the fifth photograph at the back of the secret drawer, as if it had been overlooked.

In the living room, he put Finnegan's matchbook in an ashtray. He flipped through Winter's address book to the *F* section. Doing his best to mimic Winter's handwriting, he added Finnegan's name, address, and number. Then he placed the pen on that page, closed the book, and left it on the table by the phone.

In the time Charlie had been away, the pool of blood around Litsky's body had begun to dry. Charlie took the bottle of whiskey from the cocktail table and poured it over the blood, then left the bottle on the floor by Litsky's hand.

As Charlie prepared to leave, he took one more look around the room, his eye ultimately settling on the pants around Winter's ankles. It was Finnegan's doing. Charlie was sure of it. With that irritating smile on his face, Finnegan had probably ordered Winter to drop his pants before shooting him, knowing that the mere hint of homosexuality would downgrade the crime in the eyes of the homicide squad. They would draw the conclusion that a third man had surprised the first two in flagrante and killed them out of jealousy. The crime would barely merit further consideration.

But that angle wasn't going to serve Charlie's purposes. So, he knelt down before Winter and began pulling his pants back up. It was surprisingly difficult to do. He had to lift Winter's dead weight off the couch with one arm and tug the pants upward with the other, all the while trying to avoid the blood that had seeped from Winter's wound. When Charlie finally had Winter's pants back on, he tucked in the dead man's shirt and rebuckled his belt.

Once everything was ready, he went out the back, around the house, and cautiously looked up the street. His intention had been to wait for a passing car, but a few doors down he saw a man smoking a cigarette at the end of his driveway.

Even better, thought Charlie.

Stepping back into Winter's driveway, he pointed Finnegan's Beretta in the air and shot it six times with a pause after the first and third shots. Jumping into Finnegan's car, Charlie revved the engine, peeled out of the driveway in reverse, arcing backward toward the startled smoker. Then he put Finnegan's car in drive and raced down the street, veering just enough to knock over a mailbox as he passed.

It took Charlie two hours to get home.

First, he had to return Finnegan's car. Rather than leave the keys in the ignition, Charlie dropped them in a bush. This would increase the odds that Finnegan was still at home nursing his headache when the boys from homicide found their way to his door.

From Finnegan's place, Charlie walked east along Mulholland then back down Benedict Canyon Drive. Twice in the first hour he was passed by an available taxi, but Charlie wanted to get farther from Finnegan's house before hailing a cab. When he finally got in one, it was after ten. Charlie's original plan was to have the driver take him to the hotel, where he could reclaim his own car, but once he was settled in the back seat, he felt a complete depletion of energy. So he instructed the cabbie to take him home.

As they drove through Beverly Hills, Charlie knew that the investigation into the deaths of Litsky and Winter would already be under way. Having heard the shots and seen the car screeching from the driveway, the smoker would have called the police. Two uniformed officers would have found the bodies and contacted homicide. Within the hour, the detectives would have arrived, quickly finding the photograph in the oriental cabinet and the address book with the marked page. Later, they would find the other photographs at Finnegan's house and his fingerprints on the matchbook and the gun.

It wasn't a perfect frame. Charlie understood that. But there was little love lost between homicide and vice, and only a qualified loyalty to members of the force who had gone to higher-paying and easier jobs. Once Finnegan was in the crosshairs, there would be almost as much momentum against him as there would have been against the supposed homosexuals. And when the momentum was against you, exculpatory details tended to be either overlooked or swept aside.

When the cabbie pulled into Charlie's driveway, Charlie was surprised to find his car parked in its usual spot, surprised to find Evelyn in a fresh set of clothes sitting on the front steps. Seeing her revived him a little.

—Thanks for not breaking my window, he said.

—I only have so many pairs of shoes.

Charlie let Evelyn inside and led her into the kitchen, where she sat at his and Betty's little table.

—Would you like some tea? he asked.

—What I'd like is some bourbon.

Smiling once again at Evelyn's frankness, Charlie got a bottle of bourbon, poured two glasses, and sat across from her.

—It's been a long day, he said after they'd each had a swallow.

—It has at that, she agreed with a smile.

But then she grew a little more serious.

—I could tell from the exchange between you and Finnegan that you've been keeping something from me, Charlie. And it's taken you a few hours to get home tonight after taking care of whatever it was you needed to take care of.

Charlie said nothing.

—I understand what you're trying to do, she continued. Keeping me in the dark for my own good. But sometimes I feel like my whole life has been a journey from one well-intentioned silence to the next. My father kept his silence because he didn't like to make waves. My mother kept hers because she didn't like to acknowledge anything contrary to her vision of a happy Christian household. And in New York, the man I was living with—

—The kept man.

—Yes, the kept man. Well, he lived in a fortress of secrets. Secrets about his family, about his career, about his love affairs. Secrets about his apartment! But whatever the reasons they had for keeping their mouths shut, they were all just forms of lying. And I've had my fill. At this point, I want to hear *everything*. I want to hear what's happened no matter how ugly, or uncomfortable, or unnerving it might be. Because if we don't stare down the things that make us want to look away, then the world is just a mirage.

Evelyn paused to refill their glasses. Then she looked at Charlie and waited.

So he told her everything. He told her about the murders of Litsky and Winter, about the blood pooled around Litsky's torso and the pants around Winter's ankles. He told her about hiding the murder weapon in Finnegan's trunk, adding Finnegan's name to the address book, and smashing into the mailbox so that Finnegan's car would carry the marks of the getaway.

When Charlie was done, Evelyn nodded her head. She nodded not simply in understanding or in recognition of a job well done, but in the manner of one willing to take the world as it is.

—Thanks, Charlie.

For a little while, the two of them sat at the table sipping their bourbon, sharing the satisfaction of being comfortably quiet in each other's company.

But when they finished their drinks and it was time for Evelyn to go, Charlie found he had one more thing he wanted to say, or perhaps admit.

—When I was on the phone with you tonight, he said, standing in some stranger's house with a lump on my head and two dead bodies at my feet, preparing to frame a man for the crimes he committed, I knew I wouldn't want to be anywhere else either.

Marcus

IT HAD BEEN A BUSY seventy-two hours in the offices of Selznick International. It had been a busy seventy-two hours in offices all over town. Over the course of the three days, Marcus had been on the phone with each of his counterparts at Warner Brothers, Paramount, MGM, and Twentieth Century-Fox, at least five times. He had fended off more than fifty calls and two unannounced visits from journalists, initially from the trades and the *Los Angeles Times*, but eventually from leading papers in New York, Chicago, Denver, and St. Louis.

The flurry of activity began Monday morning when a prominent gossip columnist reported the discovery of a two-way mirror in the women's dressing room at the home of a certain bon vivant. By lunchtime, everyone knew that the bon vivant was Freddie Fairview and that a camera had been set up behind the mirror. One of the young actresses who was there the day of the discovery had pressed charges, so a warrant had been issued and Freddie's house had been searched. When no photographs were found, Freddie categorically denied any knowledge of the two-way mirror, suggesting it must have been set up by someone else, someone like his landscaper or the men who cleaned his pool.

But on Tuesday morning, every front page in the city ran a story describing the murder of two unemployed photographers—one of whom had worked for a studio—and the arrest of a former detective from the vice squad. Compromising photographs of actresses taken in Fairview's dressing room had been found on the premises of both the former detective and the former studio photographer. Sources within the police department suggested that only a handful of photographs had been recovered, but given the elaborate setup and the men involved, no one believed for a second that only a handful of pictures existed. So, what every studio chief, producer, director, and agent in town wanted to know was which actresses had been in that dressing room. Given the popularity of Fairview's Sunday morning parties, the list was dispiritingly long.

In film, a door slamming shut is something of a cliché indicating anger, exasperation, or the definitive end of a relationship. Much less has been made of the door that's slammed open. In those first seventy-two hours, Marcus's door had slammed open more times than he cared to count, as David burst in to express concerns, demand updates, suggest countermeasures, and threaten legal action.

Legal action against whom?

Against Fairview. The photographers. The LAPD. The whole rotten lot of them!

As events unfolded, Marcus's phone rang so often, he almost stopped answering. But when it rang on Wednesday night, he was glad he did. For the voice on the other end of the line wasn't urgent, or anxious, or frantic. It was a voice with an even tenor and a midwestern lilt. It was the one call he'd been waiting for.

—Miss Ross.

—Mr. Benton.

—Do you have the de Havilland photographs?

—I have *all* the photographs.

For the first time in three days, Marcus smiled.

—When can you come to the studio?

—How about tomorrow at noon?

—That's perfect. David has a break at noon. I'm sure he'll want to thank you in person.

—If Selznick's coming, I'm not.

Marcus nodded appreciatively.

—How about three o'clock?

—Three it is.

At a quarter to three, Marcus sent his secretary home, despite the fact she never abandoned her desk before he did. Once she was gone, he left his office door ajar. Before returning to his desk, he found himself stopping before the antiquated map of eastern Arkansas that David had duplicated on his behalf. According to the map's legend, it had been drawn in 1882. The state hadn't changed much in the interim, thought Marcus. The old charms continued to persist alongside the old injustices. Both reasons drew him.

When Miss Ross walked in, she signaled moderate surprise, as if she recognized the unconventionality of the empty outer office and the open inner door—or perhaps of Marcus standing before the old map. Once again, she was dressed in slacks and a blouse. This time she was without the fishing rod and hat, but she had a shoebox under her arm. She placed the shoebox on Marcus's desk as they both took a seat.

He gestured to the box.

—The photographs?

—The money, she said.

Marcus was accustomed to maintaining an even expression no matter what he was being told. But upon hearing Miss Ross's response, he couldn't help but exhibit his surprise. Nor could he resist the temptation to raise the lid.

But there it was: the five thousand dollars he had already expensed.

—I never thought I'd see that again, he admitted.

—It's yours, isn't it?

—Even so . . .

Miss Ross narrowed her eyes.

—I don't enjoy spending money I haven't earned, Mr. Benton.

No, thought Marcus. You wouldn't.

—Actually, she added, it's not *all* there. It's short about a hundred dollars.

—Expenses?

—I had to replace a bicycle and a pair of shoes.

She gestured to the high-heeled shoes on her feet, which were shiny and red.

Marcus smiled. Evelyn Ross had exceeded his every expectation. She had exceeded them in terms of her shrewdness, her discretion, and her readiness to act, yes, but especially in terms of her flair. There were so few people Marcus *enjoyed* working with. Which made what he had to tell her all the more bittersweet. But first things first.

—Do you have the photographs with you?

She produced a long narrow envelope and tossed it on his desk.

Marcus was a little surprised by the dimensions of the envelope. His contact at the police department had said the retrieved photographs were in a typical publicity-still size. He looked at Evelyn a little quizzically, but she returned his gaze with a cool expression. Tentatively, Marcus opened the envelope and withdrew the contents.

Inside was a stack of about twenty-five images, each two inches high and eight inches wide. Each was the face of an actress staring at the camera. Each had clearly been cut from a larger photograph, such that it spanned from the top of the actress's head to the top of her collarbones. Included among the images were the faces of leading actresses from every major studio. It was an unnerving anthology.

Bravo, thought Marcus, after he recovered from the initial shock.

For he had no doubt that Miss Ross had wielded the scissors herself and then destroyed the more revealing remnants. If a man had retrieved the photographs, he wouldn't have done so. He would have delivered them in their entirety. But to what end? For there weren't more than a handful of men in the entire business—at any level—who could be trusted to take possession of these images innocently.

When Marcus looked up, Evelyn was no longer looking at him. She had shifted her gaze to the shelf where the straw hat was back beside the bust of Caesar, its equal in every way. Marcus reclaimed her attention by placing the pictures on the desk.

—I can't overstate how appreciative both David and Jack will be when they learn of your successful retrieval of these photographs, he said. But as you know, most of these women are not under contract at Selznick or Warner Brothers. With your permission, I'd like to inform the other studios of the exposure they faced and your role in protecting their interests. I suspect that several of my counterparts will want to express their gratitude to you, financially.

Miss Ross granted Marcus her permission. But she suggested there was a better way the studios could express their gratitude. Three people had helped her recover the photographs, one of whom was an aging actor and one of whom was an aspiring stuntman.

—I'd appreciate it if the studios would keep them in mind for any upcoming roles.

—I'll see to it.

—Thank you.

—But I think it behooves me to let you know that when you're next at Selznick, I may not be here.

Miss Ross responded with a look of concern.

—Of my own volition, Marcus clarified. I've been in Los Angeles for four years now. I think it's time I returned home.

Marcus doubted returning home was something that resonated with Miss Ross as a motivation, but she nodded to express her understanding; or perhaps her sympathies. Then she rose and stuck out her hand.

—I'll miss you, Mr. Benton.

—It will be nice to be missed, he said.

This too was a sentiment that probably didn't resonate with Miss Ross, but as they shook hands she nodded once again.

As Miss Ross turned to go, Marcus understood that nothing more need be said. A difficult situation had been satisfactorily resolved. She was in good standing with the studios, he was headed home, and they had wished each other well. To this list Marcus could have added his remaining duty to the studios and the expectation of discretion intrinsic to his profession, both of which recommended his silence. Nevertheless . . .

—Miss Ross.

She turned back.

—I gather that when *Gone with the Wind* is finished shooting, Miss de Havilland is returning to Warner Brothers for another film with Errol Flynn.

—That's right. Their fifth together. A historical romance called *The Private Lives of Elizabeth and Essex.*

Marcus nodded.

—I think you should know that Jack Warner's intention is to cast Bette Davis as the female lead opposite Mr. Flynn.

Marcus could see the expression on Miss Ross's face harden.

—If Davis is to play Queen Elizabeth, she asked, then what role would Olivia play?

—A lady-in-waiting.

Marcus had rarely been impressed by anger. Over the course of his time in Hollywood, he had witnessed it in all its various forms. He had witnessed the railing of producers against unexpected expenses or the inexplicable preferences of the public. He'd seen directors throw scripts at cameramen and writers storm off sets. He'd seen actresses refuse to leave their dressing rooms for hours on end. He'd dealt with preachers and politicians who were outraged by the evidence of moral turpitude displayed in the studio's latest films. In each of these expressions of anger, there was something essentially childish. But when Marcus said the words *a lady-in-waiting*, across Miss Ross's face flashed an anger so sudden, so sharp, and so contained, he could not help but be impressed.

—Just to be vindictive, she observed, having restored the coolness of her affect.

—There is that, Marcus conceded. But I suspect he is also reminding Miss de Havilland that however well received her performance in *Gone with the Wind*, she remains under contract to him.

—*Under* is the right word, Mr. Benton.

—I suppose it is, said Marcus.

Then as she turned toward the door, Marcus found himself adding:

—If you're ever in need of legal counsel, Miss Ross, I hope you won't hesitate to call.

Eve

Moguls, thought Eve, as she stormed out of Building Two. Rajahs and pashas. Tsars and sultans. Kings, khans, and kahunas. All the different variations from languages around the world had been dragged into English for common use—as if any one of them was different from the other.

As Eve made her way toward the parking area, she came to a stop. It was only four o'clock, which meant that Olivia was still somewhere on the lot. Should Eve tell her now? Or wait until later?

Olivia had been so excited when she'd learned her next film would be *Elizabeth and Essex*. She was excited to be working once again with Curtiz, who had directed *Robin Hood*. Excited to be working with Flynn (God help her). But mostly, she was excited by the role. From what little she knew of the script, the movie was going to give her the chance to play a very different sort of woman. Instead of some damsel in distress, she would be a queen and commander who, in a time of war, has no choice but to condemn her own lover to death as a traitor. The ultimate expression of principle over passion.

But as it turned out, it was Bette Davis who would be queen, and Olivia holding her train.

Eve didn't enjoy the prospect of delivering the news. But she didn't want to give Warner the satisfaction of delivering it himself. So she turned and headed to the back forty, where the O'Hara plantation had been built.

The last time Eve had been inside Tara was during the second week of production. On that day, they were to shoot the scene in which Scarlett and her sisters—in bright, colorful dresses—descend the staircase to greet their mother, while talking excitedly about the ball that's to be held on the following night. The entrance hall had been designed to suggest the wealth and elegance of the O'Haras before the war. Above the blue-painted wainscoting was wallpaper adorned with blooming roses on a background of white. Against one wall was a couch upholstered in the European style. Against the other was a sideboard lined with candles, the light of which glinted off the polished brass fittings on the doors.

But when Eve entered the hall today, it was not as it had been. It was undergoing a transformation in anticipation of Scarlett and Melanie's return to Tara in the aftermath of Sherman's march.

To reflect the pillaging that had taken place, the entrance hall had been stripped of its furniture and candlesticks. Even the brass fittings had been removed from the doors. Directly in front of Eve, an older man on his hands and knees was scuffing the wooden floorboards with a pumice stone. On the stairway, a younger man was lightly denting the banister with a ball-peen hammer. To Eve's left, a lanky technician with an elaborate apparatus on his back—like that of an exterminator—was spraying a tainted liquid onto the wallpaper to give the impression of water stains due to a leaking roof. While at the back of the entrance hall, a man wearing goggles was using a jeweler's hammer to knock shards of glass from windowpanes, selectively.

—Excuse me, said a man with a tool belt, who having stepped around Eve proceeded to loosen the hinges of the front door so it would creak when opened.

Wandering into the next room, which had also been stripped bare,

Eve found two women hard at work: one who was painting the suggestion of cracks in the plaster and one who was brushing sepia around a taped-off square to form the ghostly shadow of where a portrait once had hung.

It was all so breathtaking.

On the day before she arrived in Los Angeles, Eve had made a list of places to visit around the world like the Forbidden City and the Taj Mahal and the Alhambra. When she had accepted the job from Marcus Benton, she had folded the list and stowed it away with a touch of disappointment. But as she stood in the transformed Tara, when that list suddenly came to mind what Eve found herself thinking was *good riddance.* After all, weren't they all just palaces?

In high school, Eve once had to read a poem about a traveler who comes upon the crumbling statue of a king in the middle of an empty desert. Engraved on the statue's pedestal was an invocation from the king to the mighty that they look upon his works and despair. Eve had liked the poem. It was short and it rhymed and it had been written brightly in the spirit of comeuppance. But, of course, it was just wishful thinking. One couldn't count on sand to bury the works of the imperious. No sands had blown in from the desert to bury the Forbidden City or the Taj Mahal, any more than they would come to bury the Empire State Building or Hollywood. Contrary to the poet's romantic assertion, history suggested that the monuments of the overreaching could last a very long time.

True, the men who had built these monuments (or rather, caused them to be built) were gone. But one generation after the next, new versions of the moguls had appeared, ready to assume the thrones and pursue their whims with the same presumption of preordainment.

No, thought Eve, one can't count on the sands of the desert or the winds of the Santa Ana to undo the works of the single-minded. For the world to have any sense of justice, a team of artisans had to come forward with their hammers and paintbrushes and pumice stones in order to patiently unmake the palaces of the proud.